S∩BMERGED

by John Wilander

This novel is part of the West William Wilder series.
Book 1: Identified
Book 2: Submerged
(Future titles to be announced)

Cover design: Lance Buckley, lancebuckley.com
Interior layout: Lisa Gilliam, lisagilliam.com
Author portrait: Christopher Michel, christophermichel.com

ISBN: 979-8-9850254-4-6 (hardcover)
ISBN: 979-8-9850254-5-3 (paperback)
ISBN: 979-8-9850254-6-0 (ebook)

Mastodon: mastodon.social/@wilander
Bluesky: wilander.bsky.social
X/Twitter: @johnwilander
Author newsletter & blog: hackerfiction.net

Dedicated to those who serve,
in peace and in conflict.

CHAPTER 1

A Service of Witness to the Resurrection

The emotional knot in West's chest had accompanied him for more than a year. Fifteen months, to be exact. Even on good days, loss and sorrow hollowed his energy out. Things that could have been would not be. His girlfriend was dead.

Kiss's parents had fought for months to make the Russians release her body, but eventually they gave up. By then it was already fall and they wanted to host the funeral in the shift between spring and summer, which was their daughter's favorite time of year. And on a Friday, which was her favorite day of the week.

Today was Friday, May 16. West sat in a small anteroom of the wooden Chapel by the Lake in Juneau, Alaska. Beside him sat his best friend Jitterbug, both of them staring at the floor, dressed in rented black suits. West's feet were sore from his dress shoes.

"I can't do this," Jitterbug said. "She's not even *in* the casket."

"We'll do it and then it's done," West replied. He could see his friend shake his head.

"The pastor said they have staff," Jitterbug continued. "They can carry. I'm so down on this whole thing. Look, I'm shaking." He held out his hand toward West. It was trembling.

West didn't want to be a pallbearer either. He looked at the floor and wondered how many dress shoes had reluctantly walked here, carrying heavy hearts.

"She had names for our future kids," he said. "I never even got to hear them."

"I'm sure they were great names. Kiss was witty," Jitterbug replied.

West straightened his back and let his head fall back against the wall. "I ..." He shook his head, the back of it rolling against the wood panel. "I still talk to her AI."

Jitterbug turned to look up at him from his hunched-over position. "What?"

"Kiss's AI model. The one she trained for automated date hunting."

"You hacked her Tile?"

"I hacked the dating service to let me talk to her indefinitely."

There was a pause.

"Is the model any good?" Jitterbug asked.

"It's her ... but it knows nothing about us. It was trained before she even met me. So it's like meeting her at a bar or something. I'm forever trapped in trying to get her to date me."

"Man."

"I really should stop doing it. But I want to talk to her. Is that weird?"

"You're not alone. There's this whole movement with people who think detailed enough models is how we'll achieve eternal life. We live on as AI."

The church bell started ringing at a measured pace. West thought about how the same sound rang for happiness and sorrow. The circle of life.

The door to the anteroom opened, and Kiss's dad nodded at them. He was a lanky man and his suit looked rented too.

West and Jitterbug stood up and nodded back without a word spoken.

CHAPTER 2

A Whisp of the Atlantic

"What the fuck?! Hey, man, look at this shit. The whole Atlantic just went dark."

The two young operators stared in disbelief at the huge digital map of the Atlantic Ocean. Lines crossing it represented subsea cables connecting North America to Europe, and angry warnings blinked on top of all of them. The world had lost its transatlantic internet highway.

"Gotta be something wrong with the sensors," his coworker speculated.

"Or we just saw the start of a cyberwar."

They looked at each other.

"I'll ping the chief," the first man said.

"You can't text him about something like this. You gotta call him."

"I never call anyone. Can't you do it?"

"I need to go to the bathroom. I have a feeling we'll be stuck here until this is sorted out, so might as well take a piss while I can."

He stood up, leveling his head with the top of the display. There he spotted something peculiar. "Check this out." He pointed to the west coast of Greenland. "There's one connection still up. And the capacity is huge."

His colleague rose from his chair. The connection from Greenland to the US was pumping through tremendous amounts of traffic.

"That's the joke, right?" he said. "Greenlanders having the world's fastest internet connection. We modernized it as part of the Thule Air Base deal."

"I do recall something like that. But between Greenland and North America. How does such a massive amount of network traffic make it through to and from Europe?"

"No idea. It's not over Atlantic cables, that's for sure. They're all dark."

CHAPTER 3

Truly Neutral

"The flight to SFO has been canceled. Look." West held out his Tile to Jitterbug.

They had gotten an early Saturday morning flight from Juneau to Seattle-Tacoma and were walking between gates. Leaving Kiss's family behind had felt abrupt, but West had promised to stay in touch. He wanted to see more of Alaska too.

Jitterbug gave West's mobile device a look. "That's a bummer. You have to get a better Tile though. I can't stand that sneak model."

"It's not sneak. It's expensive."

"Doesn't support half the accessories *I* use."

Jitterbug got his own Tile out and the two of them veered off to the side. People filtered by, talking about cancellations and delays.

"It's not just one flight," Jitterbug said. "My Tile suggests we get train tickets before everyone else does. There's some kind of major outage for flights."

•

"A person like you, yeah you, West Wilder," the advertisement on the train's entertainment screen read. "Have you considered defending your country against cyber aggressions? You can learn on the job. Heck, you can even earn a degree while getting paid. And we mean *paid*. A salary that gets you in the housing market in no time, maxes out your deductible retirement savings, and sends a healthy chunk to your portfolio. Blip your Tile below and apply today. US Cyber Forces, Defending Democracy Online," the enthusiastic voice concluded.

They were riding the Coast Starlight twenty-four-hour train from Seattle back to the Bay Area. The sleeper cars were sold out, so it would be a red-eye.

West glanced to the other side of the aisle where an elderly couple sat holding hands on the armrest. The ad on their screens was for medication.

Freaking personalized commercials on trains.

"Damn, I'm happy I haven't started working for the man," he said to Jitterbug, who sat beside him, still formally dressed. West was glad to be out of his suit.

Jitterbug pinch-pulled an earbud. "Say what?"

"You saw the ad for Cyber Forces?" West nodded up toward his screen.

"The Uncle Sam riff?" Jitterbug asked. "You should be happy you're getting those ads. You didn't get them while on parole, right?"

"Pfft. I was just saying I'm happy I haven't taken one of those jobs. This country—it's all corrupt."

Jitterbug gave him a questioning squint. "Government versus citizen—I'm with you there. But aren't you glad someone is working for the administration? Russia and China are poking at our systems 24/7."

"Russia's and China's methods may be more … ruthless. But their motives are not any more rotten. To hell with it all."

Jitterbug shook his head. "The true anarchist."

"Truly neutral."

"Americans can at least vote. Heck, even guys like me can vote. Black, gay, *and* socialist. We've got a progressive society here, brother."

"How long until they register your vote with your ID?" West didn't wait for Jitterbug's response. "I read about what's driving Russia. The color revolutions in their neighboring countries. You read about those? And the CIA supposedly pulling the strings?"

"Weren't people protesting for democracy? And the colors just a marketing thing?"

"The interesting part is trying to understand the Eastern perspective. Suddenly a bunch of revolutions pop up and make countries want to join NATO. A coincidence?"

"So, you are siding with Russia?"

"No, I'm done taking sides, that's what I'm saying. The world needs less meddling by intelligence agencies and shit."

There was a pause.

"You still want *me* around?" Jitterbug asked with a wicked glance. "Or are you so neutral that ol' Jit don't fit?"

"Come on. It's the opposite—no more putting close ones at risk by messing with big stuff. I promised Kiss that at the funeral."

"You've got to stop blaming yourself. I was there with Kiss when she got shot. You did not get us into that situation."

West lowered his gaze, then turned to the view outside.

He fiddled with the ring on his right hand. Kiss's mom had given it to him after the funeral. She had looked at him with bloodshot eyes, telling him that Kiss had kept the ring in her childhood room for when she met "the love of her life." Her mom felt it more appropriate that West had the ring than she. It was yellow gold with three diagonal stripes in white gold, and worn. He wondered where Kiss had gotten it. Most likely from a pawnshop. Odd for a young woman to prep with a ring rather than wanting one bought for her, but Kiss had been odd, in all the right ways.

"I don't even wanna become a dad anymore," West said to Jitterbug, still stroking the ring with his thumb.

Jitterbug gave it a couple of seconds. "Because you lost Kiss?"

"Not just because of that. The risk stuff. I did fifteen years. Imagine if I had been a parent when I went in. Who would want a dad like that?"

"Yeah, who would want a father with good morals?"

"Kids deserve parents who play it reasonably safe."

Jitterbug got the other earbud out and tucked both into their case. "Speaking of keeping kids safe, Ronaldo and I are talking about a foster child. A little crazy since we haven't been a couple that long, but he's dad material."

West didn't respond.

"As are you," Jitterbug said, bumping the side of his knee against West's. "I had this vivid dream where God asked me to take care of a lost son. I've always wanted a kid that I can sing to. There are so many hurting children whose parents are in tatters. You've seen them at church, picking up food and diapers."

West knew what he meant. Every time he had helped at the

Rainbow Church, there were hurting, needy people there, and some of them had kids. "Foster child. Big commitment."

"God asked me." Jitterbug nodded, almost bowing.

West perched his head on his left hand's knuckles, elbow on the windowsill. Looking at the fir trees rushing by outside, he remembered how he and his teammates BestBye and Kiss had crossed the border to Canada out in the wilderness up here. Kiss had had her beautiful copper hair. No wait, she had dyed it copper up in Vancouver.

He really should visit Vancouver again. Or would that be too painful?

Jitterbug frowned at something on his screen. "Weird. I have my Tile set up to tell me when I go to a website that has recently switched its TLS certificate authority. This German tech news site has switched to a US one. Like in the last hour. I don't think they're allowed to use non-EU vendors." He rubbed his neatly trimmed beard. "Looks legit though."

CHAPTER 4

Naima

Transcribing record #672986642-DNI

Lewis > You said water systems were targeted. What are the latest details?

Naima > I said drinking water treatment. We do not have indications of other water facilities being targeted.

Lewis > Sure. I meant fresh water supply.

Naima > The US water sector has over 150,000 public systems and our data collection across them is not satisfactory. I'm just mentioning that to make sure you understand we don't have the complete picture.

Lewis > I know.

Naima > OK. Anyway, our sampling indicates adversarial activity in Wisconsin, Utah, and Florida, coinciding with the network disruption.

Lewis > Details. Let's do Wisconsin.

Naima > The most severely hit plant is in Wausau, central Wisconsin, affecting roughly 40,000 people. It was built in the early 2020s, which is the most vulnerable time span we have because of modern digital equipment. That's before the BONA FIDE Act, or the Ban on Non-Allied Financial Influence and Digital Equipment in the Public Sector. I'm sure you've heard of it.

Lewis > Indeed.

Naima > Chemical treatment at the Wausau plant was turned off with no alarms going off, which is considered a level nine out of ten malfunction. A human worker on site thought the smell had changed and alerted management. As you know, human fallbacks always trigger an investigation by themselves because of Automation Accountability.

Lewis > What was the nature of the attack?

Naima > It's early days in the investigation but the indications we have are that the computer system first was made to flip the trigger to set off the alarm if there *were* chemicals added, then immediately made to turn off chemical water purification. The alarm system has a grace period of five seconds to suppress false alarms due to fluctuations in sensor readings. Those five seconds were enough to make the attack pass silently.

Lewis > I guess the next questions are who the adversary was and how they got that level of access to the computer system?

Naima > Figuring that out is indeed our next step. I am in contact with local authorities

through regular communication channels. I will
also point out that there are no reports of human
illness or casualties, and that purification is
back to normal. The people of Wausau have been
asked to boil their drinking water for the time
being as a safety measure.

CHAPTER 5

You Sound Like My Type

West and Jitterbug arrived in Oakland just before nine in the morning, red-eyed and stiff. The train dropped them off at Jack London Square Station and West again promised himself to read *The Call of the Wild*.

A car ride later, they were back in San Francisco. The fog was burning off and Jitterbug made a joke about a "Sungay morning" as he got out. He was texting about brunch with his boyfriend, Ronaldo, lured by the scent of fresh bread, coffee, sausages, and fried potatoes. Just had to get a good nap first.

West got home and felt a sting of guilt as he pushed the physical key into the lock of his apartment. He'd been living off the Russian Bancor cryptocurrency they snatched during the Karlshamn heist, but he really should get a job. His late mom would not approve of his laziness. Besides, he was in the tech center of the world. How hard could it be to get a job for someone who knew computers?

But he dreaded the questions he was sure to face as a thirty-five-year-old who'd never held a job. He wasn't required to disclose his prison time, but any kind of truthful résumé he could conjure up would speak volumes.

He checked in on his gray hair in the bathroom mirror. Yup, it was a thing. He had his father's black hair, so there was no way of hiding it.

He made Turkish coffee in his cezve and sat down with his Tile. *I should get some breakfast.*

But he didn't feel like eating. He tapped into a folder named

"Other stuff" and from there into a nested folder called "To delete."
There it was—the dating app.

He had one ongoing conversation with a girl.

How's your Sunday going?

Doing alright.
Slow and steady.
How's yours?

I'm just back from a funeral.

Oh, that's sad.
Family member?

It was an old girlfriend.

She must have been
young. I'm so sorry.

I am too.

He picked up his ornamented, small Turkish cup and let a sip of
coffee linger in his mouth before swallowing.

Actually it was you.

Sorry, I don't understand.

I don't expect you to. In the
future, in a time after you
were trained, the real Kizz
became my girlfriend. We
fell in love.

Sorry, I don't know about
the future, but falling in
love sounds dreamy.

**Maybe we should meet
IRL? You sound like my
type.**

Do you want to have kids?

He pressed his lips together and nodded imperceptibly, in reminiscence rather than confirmation.

It would be easy to spend his Sunday like this. And the next one. He blinked to clear the blur from his eyes. This had to end.

Just deleting his account wouldn't be enough though. That would allow him to relapse. The only way was to erase Kiss's AI model on the server and delete her account too.

He drew a breath and went back to the conversation one last time. To say goodbye.

CHAPTER 6

One Day Earlier: Body and Soul

Concrete walls and floor, cold steel bars painted in white, the hum of forced air ventilation. And the fucking camera watching the two of them at all times.

The guards made their rounds every fifteen minutes around the clock. Meals were served in the cell. Daily exercise took place indoors in a larger cell.

She had never seen the exterior of this prison and she didn't even know where it was. They said no one had ever escaped and she sure as hell wasn't going to try.

She sat with her feet up on her bed. Her cellmate was reading a book.

They were waiting for lights-out at nine p.m., at which point the camera took about three seconds to switch to night mode. That gave her three seconds to eject the camera's memory card, bridge the card's supply voltage and ground pins, and shove it back in.

She knew there was a memory card in there because they had had to replace it once. It was unclear why, though. The cameras surely streamed directly to whatever computer system was monitoring them, maybe a holdover from the original camera installation. The Russian state sure wasn't spending excess resources on this place. Human guards were probably cheaper than robots.

But breaking the *camera* would get her to the next step of her plan.

Acquiring some kind of metal filament to create that bridge between voltage and ground had eluded her to the point of utter frustration. There were metal detectors, strip-downs, and zero unsupervised access to any kind of equipment with cables, except the camera itself.

Her cellmate had suggested water as the electricity bridge and they had tried it, to no avail.

Then one evening, as they listened to the classic jazz radio station offered only on Wednesdays, she heard "Body and Soul" by Billie Holiday. No tools or external materials were going to help her out. A prison like this was diligent. This had to be done body and soul.

So she had made every attempt to catch a head cold and the blob of snot residing for the last hours in her palate was the result.

Five minutes and one more Russian pop song to go. Saturday prison radio was all pop.

She closed her eyes to give them time to adjust to the low night light she'd have to operate in.

•

"Ka-chunk." Lights-out.

She flew up like a cat, fumbled ever so slightly as her fingers found and pushed the memory card eject button, and smeared her phlegm across the two slightly longer metal pins. The card was back in its slot just as the double-click confirmed night mode on the camera. She dropped back on her bed, landing hard on the thin foam mattress.

A red LED they had never seen before confirmed that the camera was not happy with its first-ever head cold.

She had dreaded the success because now she had to decide whether to stay in bed in case the camera was still recording or to quickly clean the SD card in the sink to avoid traces of her spit showing up in the inevitable investigation.

She opted for the latter.

The guards arrived quicker than they had expected. She and her cellmate were handcuffed behind their backs, berated, frisked, and moved into separate interrogation rooms.

Her guard took a seat behind the interrogator's desk. He pulled a keyboard close and unlocked the desktop computer with his fingerprint.

This scene had played out in her mind for a month, and now she was in it. She had to get that guard to leave the room, and she knew he would never do it. Never, unless she could game his psyche and social instincts in a way that would overthrow all of his training and all of his experience in dealing with cunning inmates pulling tricks.

Body and soul.

In planning, she had considered exposing herself or offering him a blowjob, but her cellmate had told her she had heard about inmates providing pleasure to guards and getting nothing for it.

Her next idea had been to fake a panic attack, but she'd seen them strike down prisoners with real panic attacks, so that was probably the agreed-upon way to deal with that.

She needed something novel and beyond agreeable. Something she herself was hard-pressed to even consider.

It had been two days since she took a dump. This was the payback for the diapers she never got to change on the baby they took from her.

A warm odor of feces spread. Her faked desperation and shame over the accident in her pants seemed to convince the guard. He was appalled.

"Bitch!"

He approached her swiftly, baton in hand, with its electric fangs protruding. Apparently jolting inmates was practice for this scenario too. Her body could sense the violent sting before it even happened.

She passed out.

•

The sound of a door slamming shut booted her up again.

She was still in the interrogation room, alone. The guard must have just left. Hopefully, there was still time.

Waking up having soiled herself was worse than she would have thought, and the ache from the electrical shock made it feel like resurfacing from a heavy drinking session.

There was a surveillance camera watching her, so from this moment her deeds would be on record and she'd have to face the consequences.

She hurried to the other side of the desk, buttocks sticking to each other, struggling to keep her balance with her hands cuffed behind her back.

The computer was still unlocked and she leaned over to swipe on the touchpad with the tip of her nose so it wouldn't lock on her.

The Russian interface made little sense, but the icon for the email application was clear. Turning halfway around, her right hand could reach and cumbersomely work the trackpad to open a new email message.

She flipped out the two foldable stands on the back of the keyboard and carefully slid it off the front edge of the desk to make it hang off the stands.

Turned fully away from the desk, she let her back-bound hands orient themselves on the keyboard. Who knew that her old party trick of typing behind her back would pay off in this fashion? She wrote "I know" before turning around to see the result.

О крыс

"Rats!"

She looked at the top menu on the screen and realized it'd be an endless trial and error to find language settings in there. But the keyboard had a key with a globe symbol on it. The third click got her to the English setting, and she wrote a complete sentence before checking again.

    I know it's stupid to email you but I
    have to choose.

"I have *no choice*. Fucking autocorrect!"

The truth was that autocorrect had probably gotten more things right than wrong, given how restricted she was in handcuffs.

There was no time to fix errors. She typed five more short sentences, added subject and recipient, and hit Send.

Chapter 7

The Call of the Wild

Deleting the dating app had West fiddling with the icons on his Tile. The Mail app had a red label with the number 1. He never got email.

He launched the app and found a new message with the subject line "In need of a dependable man."

```
I know it's stupid to email you but I
have no choice. It's me, Kizz. Three
words to prove it: Juneau, brothel,
dependable. I'm in a Russian prison,
cell 42. Don't know where but it's cold.
They'll punish me for sending you this.
Please help! Love you!
```

The punch to his gut was so real he threw himself backward, spilling coffee on the table. Who was pulling this morbid prank on him? Had the dating AI gone bananas and emailed him? No, he had set up his dating profile with a throwaway email account, and this was sent to his real email address.

He tilted his head back, closed his eyes, and tried to control his racing pulse. Memories of Kiss flashed by.

Those three words were personal. Who could know them and try to use them against him?

BestBye may have overheard him talking to Kiss up in Vancouver, and she hadn't gotten along well with Kiss. But why would she try to hurt him in such an inhumane way?

Jitterbug was out of the question.

Apart from them, only Kiss's family knew that they'd even been a couple.

Well, except half of the G20 security agency, G20S. It had to be them. Another fucking mind trick to bring him to his knees?

They always get you in the end.

"No, they don't!" he blurted into his lonesome kitchen. Besides, G20S was badly bruised. Why would they spend time on him? He hadn't done anything lately.

He checked the email's metadata.

```
Return-Path: <egor.arkhangelsky@icedolphin.ru>
X-Spam-known-sender: no ("Email failed
policy for domain")
X-Spam-sender-reputation: 500 (none)
X-Resolved-to: we$t@protekt.email
X-Delivered-to: we$t@protekt.email
X-Mail-from: egor.arkhangelsky@icedolphin.ru
```

Ice Dolphin. That's the prison where they threatened to take Jitterbug.

The website icedolphin.ru did exist. A translation of its content didn't provide more info than what he already knew—a correctional facility in Novaya Zemlya far above the Arctic Circle. Maximum security and only for felons serving lifetime sentences.

Chapter 8

Email Back

West and a brusquely awakened Jitterbug met at the vista point in Corona Heights Park. Its rugged rock hilltop lay in the middle of San Francisco with a view of downtown, the Bay Bridge, and the Golden Gate Bridge on clear days. This morning though, the fog still had its fingers stretched out into the city below them, with occasional rooftops poking through.

West had chosen the spot to be sure they could talk with no one close.

Jitterbug massaged his forehead and eyebrows after having read the email and checked the metadata. "Disturbing, in multiple ways."

"This email is for me, whoever sent it," West said. "Juneau is public info, but the other two words are personal things and they check out."

"Someone knew those things about her, or hacked their way to that info," Jitterbug said. "They want you to think Kiss is alive or get worried that someone is messing with you."

"What if she *is* alive?"

Jitterbug looked at him with sorrow in his eyes. "Man ..." Seconds passed. He shook his head. "I saw her get shot."

"You didn't see her dead."

"I know it's been hard." Jitterbug took hold of West's shoulder. "Don't let these people get to you."

West took a deep breath, then another. The air up here was fresh. The visible San Francisco roofs below them glittered with solar panels reaching for power through the fog. "Let's find out who sent this."

"Reply and include a tracking pixel?" Jitterbug suggested. "We'd either learn if it's a real address or we get lucky and know that the email was opened."

A tracking pixel was an invisible image embedded in an email or a webpage, there to reveal to the sender when the email or page was opened.

West looked into the distance. "If it was Kiss, she would have deleted the outgoing message from the Sent box to hide what she did. We should not give the prison that info."

"Sure, let's not include the original message in the reply then."

"Should it even be a reply?"

"I see where you're going. Let's search for this Egor guy. But I'm going to have to loop Ronaldo in on this because I've already been away for days and promised we'd hang out."

•

Ronaldo agreed to wait for a table at Brenda's French Soul Food while they sat researching under a tree in nearby Jefferson Square.

They found a six-year-old blog written by an Egor Arkhangelsky. All posts were written in Russian, with the last one being:

Всем заинтересованным предлагаю поизучать вот эту книжку:
Invisible Money, Visible Wealth

The Russian translated into "I encourage anyone interested to read this book," and the book itself was by a Chinese cryptocurrency celebrity who was now running their operations out of El Salvador—the first country in the world to use bitcoin as legal tender.

Then there was a medical researcher named Egor Arkhangelsky, associated with an Israeli institute. This Egor had an up-to-date social networking presence.

There were three more search hits, but they were clearly bot accounts.

Nothing else found on the open web or the dark.

Must be a fairly uncommon name.

"Could be a completely fake account," Jitterbug said.

"Who wants to work at a prison up in the Arctic?"

"Maybe they pay well? Or could be part of a sentence, like going to the Wall in *Game of Thrones*."

"You're saying Egor went too far with his invisible crypto money and took the black?" West asked.

Jitterbug tilted his head to the side and pouted his lower lip. "Plausible."

West drafted an email.

```
Subject: Invisible Money, Visible Wealth

Hey Egor!

I read the book you recommended. Are you
still in the crypto business?
```

"Do you mean to send it in Russian?" Jitterbug asked.

"I don't know. We're trying to get him thinking of crypto. Maybe a foreigner making contact is more of a hook?"

"Could work," Jitterbug said. "I was thinking of the tracking pixel though. Maybe Egor doesn't exist but this email will go to a maximum security prison. With the Red Web and all, maybe their email client will block a pixel from the US."

The Red Web was Russia's sovereign slice of the internet.

"How would we get a Russian pixel and server logs for it?"

"Pay someone?"

Jitterbug put the request out on a couple of hacker forums as they went for brunch.

•

West had only met Ronaldo casually before, at the Rainbow Church. The guy instantly put a smile on Jitterbug's face and gave West a warm hug.

As West and Ronaldo released each other's embrace, West noticed Ronaldo's necklace with a gold enamel pendant reading LOVE in two rows with the O slanting.

"Where have I seen that before?" West asked.

"Cost me a fortune, this thing. It's by Robert Indiana. We had an Indiana sculpture retrospective last year at MOMA and these were specially made."

The three of them enjoyed grits, eggs Benedict, and beignets.

Whenever there was silence, West's mind kept going back to the email.

Extending their stay with a third round of coffee, Ronaldo poked at West's inattentiveness with a friendly nudge. "What's all this secrecy about? You're not trying to steal my partner now, are you?"

"No, no. Can't talk about it here, though." He looked around but only saw people indulging in their weekend.

Jitterbug dug out his Tile and looked at it. "West, check this." He showed West his screen.

West read the brief message. A person on the inside of the Red Web was willing to sell them access logs for a few Bancor. This would allow him to send his email with an embedded tracking pixel pointing to a Russian server.

It was midnight in Novaya Zemlya, Russian Arctic.

CHAPTER 9

US Certified

West got home and set up a notification for incoming emails.

The worst part of the email affair was the spark of hope. Kiss was dead, and he knew it. But the human condition invited him to view this weird email as a reversal of reality; it demanded he look for light in the abyss.

One effect of his reluctant fantasizing was a desire to visit Stockholm again. What was the name of that plaza he and Kiss had visited? "Toe Terrasse" something. He searched, and as soon as he added the context of the bronze statue, he got a hit for Evert Taube's Terrasse.

Seeing the terrasse on Wikipedia brought back memories. He started reading about this Evert. The man had been a famous troubadour and had lived part of his life in Argentina.

West tapped a link to watch Evert play in Stockholm and got a spinner and eventually a load failure. Another one of the links was to the story of how Evert's summer house had been burned down by a stalker. That link was also defunct.

What's going on here? The video decoding issue coming back?

He went to the top search hit for Swedish news and it loaded fine. The website for Swedish public service TV loaded too, but trying to start a show there resulted in a forever-spinner.

Must be some serious CDN issues.

He paused for a second, then went back to the Swedish news site and checked its certificate. It was issued yesterday, in the US.

He could confirm what Jitterbug had said on the train—websites in the EU were not allowed to use certificates issued outside the Union.

He rapidly checked other European top sites—*Le Monde* in France, *La Gazzetta dello Sport* in Italy, and *The Sun* in the UK—all served with American certificates.

Texting this revelation to Jitterbug resulted in a response with just a link to a *Verge* article. He opened it.

European Websites Gone Dark — Splinternet or Conspiracy Theory?

Starting earlier today, several European websites are offline or are loading stale pages in the US. First passed off as an internet routing glitch, it's now turned into a debate on splinternet vs conspiracy theories. The most damning fact so far? All sites that still work seem to be purely served by US web proxies.

"This raises all kinds of questions," journalistic activist Tom Mole says. "Can we trust the content of these international websites if domestic servers serve them? I mean, is it even *The Guardian* we're reading? Who chose which websites to proxy and which to just leave unreachable? Why did they make those choices? Assuming we go back to a functioning internet tomorrow, will we ever learn the differences between what Americans were reading and what Europeans were reading today?"

The Verge has talked to anonymous sources about what may lie behind this disruption and the most likely cause is a major breakdown involving the transatlantic subsea cables. Experts are taken aback as to how that would even be possible. The cables are operated by various entities and lie in different parts of the Atlantic.

US authorities have declined to comment on the situation beyond the fact that they "are aware." Such silence fuels conspiracy theories, the most disturbing ones claiming it's an act of cyberwar by a foreign power and that the US is scrambling to respond.

American and European tech stocks are in nose dives in weekend trading. Wall Street may ultimately force the federal administration's hand and compel a statement from the Department of Defense.

West texted Jitterbug back.

> What do you think?

I think it's some weird
routing problem or a
cascading thing where
a few subsea cables
go down, traffic moves,
overloads another, and
another ...

> But the proxies. That's
> deliberate. Doesn't just
> happen.

True.

West sat back. Could these two things just have coincided and in fact be unrelated? Some European sites unreachable altogether and the others proxied by US servers?

All communications go over the internet today. It's crazy. So fragile. Or wait. The phone network might still be circuit-switched.

He grabbed his Tile and asked for the phone application. It launched with a splash screen offering him a guided tour on how to use it.

Chapter 10

Stale Breadcrumbs

"Hello," a familiar, nasal voice said on the other end of the phone call.

"Hi! Is this Åse I'm talking to? Like, for real?" West said.

It had taken him a while to discover that the previous person he'd spoken to was Åse's synthesized voice. He had eventually been redirected to a Norwegian number.

"It's almost midnight here. Who is this?" she replied.

Åse was ex-military and had helped him pull off a stunning hack against the cellular network in central Stockholm last year. He had to force himself to not think of those desperate attempts to save Kiss.

"I represent West Enterprises and would like to ask you a couple of questions regarding the ongoing internet disruption between Europe and the United States," he said.

There was a long pause on Åse's end.

"Oh, now I recall. West Enterprises," she said. "Did we discuss a Wi-Fi network earlier?"

She's getting it. What was the name of that thing?

"We did. I believe the name of it was de-rah-goo-noff." He said it slowly to compensate for his poor pronunciation.

"This is not a great channel. Lots of interference. What is your question?" she responded.

"Could you tell me the top news headlines for *The Guardian* and *Aftonbladet*, and the publishing timestamps of those, please?"

He heard a keyboard clatter on the other end.

"*The Guardian* leads with 'Downing Street turmoil intensifies as two ministers speak out' updated 20:21 UK time. I guess you'd say

8:21 p.m. *Aftonbladet* has 'Det våras för supergonorrén' published nine p.m. sharp. Let's see if I can translate that. 'A new dawn for the super gonorrhea.' Do you want me to spell the Swedish words out?"

"That would be great."

She did.

"Thank you for your help. Good night."

"Nighty."

He ended the call and exhaled.

I wonder how many agencies' bots were listening in on that conversation?

His Tile sure had been listening and suggested loading *The Guardian* and *Aftonbladet*. The news about Downing Street was there but did not have the latest update timestamp. *Aftonbladet* featured nothing on super gonorrhea. The US was not just proxying these websites; they were serving cached, stale versions of them.

CHAPTER 11

White House: Conspiracies

The President of the United States of America surveyed the John F. Kennedy Conference Room, or the Situation Room, as media liked to call it. She liked the comparisons between herself and JFK. Young, informal, hands-on.

"The conspiracy theories are abundant, ma'am," General Purnell said in his usual derogatory manner when speaking of the American public's online activity.

"Of course they are," President Sanchez replied. She did not want to hear a rant. "We haven't told the public what's going on and we're faking the internet for them. That *is* a damn conspiracy."

It was Sunday, six p.m., and thirty-two hours since all Atlantic subsea cables had gone dark. The smell of coffee and shoe polish filled the room, and the hope of dinner with one's family was waning.

General Mark Purnell was responsible for the backend of US digital defense, or "networks and cables" as some liked to belittle it.

Next to Purnell, to President Sanchez's right, sat the director of National Intelligence, Dr. Mack Lewis, responsible for defending the digital frontend—devices, apps, and websites. He was also in charge of the government's vast AI support system.

"How are satellite connections holding up?" Sanchez asked Purnell.

"We're shaping traffic according to our contingency plans, so they're holding up. But satellites will be swamped if we let regular traffic through. Montana keeps being the odd one out, but we already talked about that."

"How has the rest of the world reacted?" Sanchez continued.

"Norway, Sweden, and Finland have confirmed that the Russian Red Web has altered Russians' access to European internet, even though there's no actual hindrance there. They are censoring info on the transatlantic disruption, just like we are."

"Withholding. We're withholding." There was a two-second pause. "China?"

"Not much of a change in the Great Firewall. They are already very restrictive. As you know, they are already serving their own fake versions of select US websites."

"Where are we on letting more traffic through the Pacific?"

"You still have that option." The general extended his hand toward her, palm open.

"I'm asking for advice, not repetition of what options I have."

"I'd like to keep investigating through the night and enable routing over the Pacific tomorrow morning and just let the internet solve this in its own way as the workweek starts."

"That includes your subsea investigation?"

"Correct. Onshore equipment hasn't localized any faults. Our subs are tracing the cables, but it's a slow process."

"I want that seen through to completion. Thanks for the briefing, General."

She turned left to her national security advisor, Alec Ore. "What do stock futures look like?"

"Grim," he said. "You'll likely see a 20% drop on most tech stocks if the problem persists."

"European markets too?"

"Yes, just not as much."

"We need to find any suspicious shorting. The drop may be exactly what this adversary wants," the president reflected. "Anyway, market reaction is one thing. What about actual business impact?"

"Tech there too, especially online services. Cloud is saved by the legal requirement to keep European data in Europe. Banking and finance are in a frenzy. They're publicly secretive because they don't want a bank run, but to us it's nonstop panic communication. International wire transfers are queueing up but no lines at ATMs yet. We believe bank employees are the major leaks to media, telling them what to look for. We probably should tell banks we plan to prioritize them over satellite. It's already early

Monday in Europe." Alec paused briefly to allow for commentary but didn't get any.

"Airlines and travel," he continued. "Domestic flights are back up, but transatlantic flights are grounded," he continued, "which affects both people and airfreight. Other parts of the supply chain to and from the US are not getting online updates. We have reports from UPS, FedEx, and DHL there. They will hold packages in storage until they have live data again, so there will be delays. Finally, streaming platforms. They use a lot of caching proxies in Europe to lower bandwidth, so that's carrying them for now, but any live stuff is cut off."

The president scanned the table in thought. "It's going to take a while to figure out who and what is taking advantage of this." She turned to her secretary, who was taking notes. "If we haven't solved this an hour before opening bell tomorrow, we let all regular traffic go over the Pacific. Bank data should be prioritized over satellite starting now. I'll work with Alec on a public message."

Gentle writing clicks continued for a few seconds. This was the third typewriter model the administration had procured, this time with special instructions to make it as silent as possible, while still purely mechanical. Eventually, they had resurrected 1930s technology from the Noiseless Typewriter Company. Instead of the typebar striking the ribbon and paper full speed, it had a lever mechanism that decelerated the typebar mechanically, dampening the noise. President Sanchez loved it.

She turned back to her council. "Let's talk about US critical infrastructure. And let me remind you, I don't want a rehash as to whether it's backend or frontend. If you don't know where the lines are drawn, I suggest you read up on it. You had prepared a brief, Lewis?"

"Indeed." The director of National Intelligence beamed a slide from his Tile onto the large, wall-mounted screen. He added context to inform the folks who might not be up to date on policy. "Critical infrastructure *is* to a large extent the internet today. Our policies prohibit international dependencies, but the internet itself is a global network, not a domestic matter. And it has turned out to be very hard to enforce zero international dependencies."

General Purnell shifted in his chair.

Lewis continued. "We have sixteen sectors whose assets, systems, and networks we monitor and protect under Presidential Policy Directive 21: Critical Infrastructure Security and Resilience. In alphabetic order ..."

The slide revealed bullet points one by one: chemical, commercial, communications, critical manufacturing, dams, defense industry, emergency services, energy, financial services, food and agriculture, government facilities, healthcare and public health, information technology, nuclear reactors including materials and waste, transportation, and finally water, including wastewater.

The director walked to the other side of the screen, invoking a rhetorical pause. "During this soon-to-be two-day crisis, we've seen three distinct levels of preparedness and execution. At the top, excellent performance in the defense, financial, and transportation sectors."

Sanchez saw General Purnell's shoulders and chest move into a proud posture.

Lewis went on. "As expected, but not above for most other sectors, with some peripheral systems affected. So that's your mid-tier. And third, pockets of disturbingly poor performance. We are looking at a few computer systems in healthcare, solar power, and water supply that froze completely."

"Still frozen?" the president asked.

"Some still. We have not been able to figure out how transatlantic internet connections could impact these systems, but we will get you those answers. Service recovery is being worked on in parallel."

CHAPTER 12

Let the Right One In

West had trouble going to sleep that night. The email, supposedly from his dead girlfriend, had messed it all up.

He grabbed his Tile and checked his inbox one more time. No reply from Egor.

More than a year had passed; he had gotten closure at the funeral. Now some government actor had pulled the rug out from underneath him.

Bzzz.

A notification. It was BestBye, who wanted to share a file with him.

BestBye?

He accepted the file. It contained a text message.

Let me in.

What?

Did she want access to some Survivors system? He didn't have higher access rights than she did. Besides, there had been no activity on SurvivorNet since they split the team up.

There was a knock on the door of his apartment. Or was there? He held his breath. There it was again—subtle, just audible enough.

He checked his Tile. The file share had been peer-to-peer! BestBye, or whoever it was, had to be close.

I have to find a way to verify that it's her.

He sent a file in response and they got a weird file-based back and forth going.

Rubik's Snake.
How many possible shapes?

Almost 7T.

Including mirror images?

Of course not.

He got his sweatpants and a T-shirt on and went to the entrance without turning on the lights. His ear gently touched the cool door. Nothing.

He pulled his head away and pinched the thumb turn for the deadbolt. Even though he turned it slowly, the sound of the bolt retracting was loud in the enveloping silence. He pulled the door open an inch. No lights on at the landing or in the stairwell.

He opened the door properly and turned on a dim flashlight on his Tile.

A short, hooded figure peeled off the back wall and approached him. As it came close, he could distinguish the masked face of BestBye.

"No lights," she hissed. He complied and let her in silently.

They fumbled their way to his kitchen. Yellow streetlights filtered in and revealed the tabletop. BestBye sat down. He did too.

"What's going on?" he got out.

"They're negotiating Kiss's release."

"What?"

"Russia has offered Kiss in exchange for two FSB agents. They kept her as an asset. They lied about her death."

West swallowed. "Where did you hear about this?"

"Can't tell you."

West's eyes were getting adjusted to the pale light. BestBye got up.

"I ..." he started.

"It's not safe for me to be here." She walked silently to the entrance. West felt glued to his chair. "I can't help you find Kiss," she said and exited.

CHAPTER 13

In Exchange

West sat staring into the void. What had just happened? First the email, then a minute-long visit from BestBye.

He texted Jitterbug.

> We have to talk.

The pixel?
Nothing yet. I checked just
a minute ago.

> No, no pixel yet.
> But we have to talk in
> person.

Tomorrow?

> Tonight.

You'll have to come to my
place then. I'm already in
my PJs.

West got warmer clothes on and zigzagged his way through San Francisco's streets in a halfhearted effort to shake any tail. The most likely one would be BestBye herself, and he wasn't likely to outsmart her.

Jitterbug opened the door remotely when West announced his arrival. Surprised that his friend would rely on an electronic lock, West checked on the inside only to find Jitterbug's own electronic construction with a little robot arm physically turning the knob.

Ronaldo was there too, in a paisley satin robe and a toothbrush protruding from his mouth.

Jitterbug's studio was neat. Wall lighting, spotlights, and art hung well. A seventies stereo with a huge FM radio tuning scale seeping green light was playing a pure gospel version of Michael Jackson's "Man in the Mirror."

Jitterbug was sitting on his couch keeping himself awake with *Mario Kart* on a classic Switch. West sat down in the armchair angled at ninety degrees to the couch. Ronaldo took a seat beside Jitterbug, who paused the game.

"He's cool," Jitterbug said, noting West's hesitation.

Reluctantly, West gave them a summary of what had happened.

"Are you sure it was BestBye?" Jitterbug asked, big-eyed.

"Man."

"Okay, okay. Just remember she worked for government and defected late in the game."

"I know. But why would she make this up?"

"Are you telling me the ways of G20S are clear and intelligible? Or that they don't have a reason to come at you?"

He was right. The public discourse on identity misuse and West's compromise of the Russian offline backup in Norilsk had ripped through the global security agency G20S. Several countries had since reworked the legal foundation for use of GPI, Global Personal Identity.

"Let's think it through as an attack on me," West said.

"You've got your premise: They hate you for the NSA hack. They hate that your mom got you out on parole—bless her soul. They hate that we killed their GPI surveillance, and they hate that they couldn't nail that onto you."

"Incentivized," Ronaldo commented.

Jitterbug nodded.

"So they want me back in prison."

"Or dead," Jitterbug said with a pained expression.

"How will telling me Kiss is alive achieve that?"

Jitterbug put on a face and shrugged. "I don't know. You'll do something stupid. Something illegal."

"Break her out?"

"Something like that."

West reflected on his own fifteen years in prison. His mom had gotten him out, not through something foolish but through years and years of campaigning.

"I sure would try if she was being tortured or facing a life sentence," he said.

"You know what," Jitterbug said with a hint of support in his voice, "I think they just want to break you. They want you to worry and think about this all the time. They want to ruin your life."

West stared at the coffee table in front of him. How could he defend himself? Was there a way not to think about this? Pretend like he never got the email and that BestBye was just lying to him? He *was* worried.

Ronaldo turned to Jitterbug. "West here has gotten two signals that his girlfriend is alive. Why do you think both those signals are manipulated and untrue? I don't get it."

"He has some powerful enemies."

"Sure sounds like it," Ronaldo said. "But would you take a chance on that or take a chance on saving *me* if you were told I was in a Russian prison?"

Jitterbug looked away.

Ronaldo tilted his head and added one more punch. "Didn't you tell me that *your* friends broke *you* out of a Russian prison?"

The room turned awkward. Jitterbug sank into the couch, looking haunted.

Nothing was said for a good while.

Then West's and Jitterbug's Tiles chirped within half a second of each other. West grabbed his and read with haste.

It was a pixel ping from Naryan-Mar, Russia.

CHAPTER 14

Ramping Up

The air eventually cleared in Jitterbug's living room and Ronaldo gave his boyfriend a kiss before going to bed.

West and Jitterbug debated how long they should stay up and wait for a reply from Egor. It could be minutes, hours, or forever. It turned out to be less than thirty minutes.

```
Subject: Re: Invisible Money, Visible
Wealth

Who is this? I don't crypto no more.

/3g0r
```

The two friends looked at each other.

"He's asking us who we are. That's an invitation to keep the correspondence going," West said.

"Indeed," Jitterbug said. "His phrasing on crypto assets sounds like he's had problems. Maybe lost money or got caught up in some shady business?"

"Three G zero R looks like a username."

Jitterbug beamed the contents of his Tile onto the room's big screen and started searching. "3g0r crypto," "3g0r Arkhangelsky," "3g0r Bancor." Nothing.

"Try 'Invisible Money'," West suggested.

Jitterbug did, and they found a user 3g0r posting a link to a blog post on an internet forum called Russian Anonymous Marketplace, RAMP. The post was two years old.

They created an account on the forum and wrote a direct message to 3g0r.

```
I'm We$t. It's never too late to get back
into crypto. I have a business proposal.
```

A few seconds later, an error message appeared, indicating that the 3g0r account had been deactivated.

"The site looks pretty crufty," West said. "Can we hack our way in?"

Jitterbug fired up his scanner program and started probing the Russian server for known security holes. "If we're going to keep going. I need an espresso. You?"

"Please."

They enjoyed the sips of energy as they watched Jitterbug's scanner crawl all the pages it could find on the message board site. It concluded with an abrupt "Finished. Vulns: 0."

"I guess we're going to have to get busy with this one," Jitterbug said as he fished up a full-size keyboard from behind his couch.

"Let me check something," West said, holding out a hand for the keyboard.

He got it and went to the overview page for the account they had just created and looked at the URL.

```
https://ramp3.onion/we$t/account/
```

He replaced we$t with 3g0r and loaded. The page said the account was inactive and offered a button to reactivate it.

He clicked it. "Activation message sent," the page said. He handed back the keyboard to Jitterbug. "One message is not annoying, but one every ten minutes should be. Let's keep sending messages until we don't get the error message."

"Would you like me to do that?" the Tile's assistant asked Jitterbug.

•

The sun was already shining when Jitterbug woke West up. They had sat speculating on both the emails and BestBye's message delivery last night until the caffeine petered out.

Jitterbug was holding his Tile close to West's face.

"Did he activate his account?"

"Better yet," Jitterbug said. "We got a reply on RAMP."

West sat up in a jolt and read the message with groggy eyes.

```
> I'm We$t. It's never too late to get
back into crypto. I have a business
proposal.


Talk.
```

"Quite the businessman," West said, returning the Tile.

Jitterbug dropped down in the armchair. "If he has any sense, he assumes entrapment. I have no idea how to get him to make a deal with a rando."

"He's responding, so he wants money."

"Don't we all?"

"A couple of legal deals first to ease him into the relationship?"

"He's going to need proof that we're not the police."

"Or we find some dirt on him and threaten to take that *to* the police."

Jitterbug wobbled his head side to side in doubt. "I wonder how smart he is? It's hard knowing what level of deception we need."

"Prison guard in the Arctic. Doesn't sound like a job smart people dream of."

"He may be running the place. But I agree it sounds like punishment in itself."

Jitterbug got dressed and said he'd go pick up some breakfast.

"I was getting ready to leave. You and Ronaldo probably have plans."

"He's already at work. The museum opens at ten."

West researched what criminal justice in Russia was like while Jitterbug was out. Entrapment in drug cases seemed to be standard practice. Law enforcement would persuade a person they had already arrested to act as a buyer, then bust the dealer as soon as money had exchanged crypto wallets. The Russian Interior Ministry was in a decades-long feud with the European Court of Human Rights over such "controlled purchases."

When Jitterbug got back with a brown paper bag and two coffees, West was excited.

"Check this out. Russia has two maximum security federal prisons—Ice Dolphin and Black Dolphin. Mass murderers and drug kingpins go to Black Dolphin, whereas Ice Dolphin is for enemies of the Russian state. People convicted of lesser drug crimes, fraud, and such can choose to serve their sentence working as a guard at Ice Dolphin, even earning money. The state reckons run-of-the-mill criminals have very little in common with Ice Dolphin inmates, so it works. It really is like taking the black in *Game of Thrones*, except you're freed after some time."

"White good, black bad. Gets old."

West didn't know what to say. Jitterbug seldom talked about being a Black man.

"But I see what you're saying," Jitterbug said while opening the bag and pulling out two grilled sandwiches. "Egor has probably dipped his toes in the criminal world already."

West went halfway for one of the coffee cups. "May I?"

"I'm not having two."

West picked the paper cup up between thumb and index finger, right under the rim so he wouldn't burn himself. He whiffed an inch from the sip hole. "Hazelnut?"

"Sorry, I always get that for Ronaldo. They know me at the place, so they just made my regular. Here, you can have mine."

"Nah, this is good. Ronaldo's got taste."

"Mhmm."

A thought crossed West's mind as he sank his teeth into a sandwich. He chewed quickly to be able to speak without his mouth full. "You said it. Egor knows how the entrapment show is run. So we ask him to help law enforcement."

"I don't get it."

West put his food down. "We ask him for his wallet ID and send him some Bancor. That way, he knows we're serious and he'll feel good. We'll tell him what we actually want in the transaction message. Something like …" He typed away on his Tile for a good minute before showing it to Jitterbug.

```
We are from the Interior Ministry
investigating a foreign agent on the
Ice Dolphin staff. This individual is
working with US intelligence and has
leaked information on the American inmate
Kate Libby. Such leaks are of substantial
risk to the Russian state. If you have
suspicions yourself of who this leaker
might be, you can help us. Get this
employee to leak Libby's cell number and
location of apprehension and pass that on
to us for corroboration. We are reaching
out to you in this unconventional way
because we don't know what information
channels the leaker has access to. Help
us bring this traitor to justice and you
will be rewarded.
```

"Whoa," Jitterbug said. "Kiss's people skills rubbed off, eh? But what if Egor isn't suspecting anyone?"

"It's a prison. People are always suspicious."

CHAPTER 15

Pinned Down

Jitterbug got ready for work at his church and West checked the news while they waited to leave together.

The Internet Is Back, in Molasses

An hour before the opening bell on Wall Street, internet connections to Europe were restored and the draconian fears over the weekend softened into a 2% fall on the NY Stock Exchange and 3% off on the Nasdaq.

Network speeds are very slow compared to last week and connections to Asia are suffering. Currently, a significant chunk of traffic is being routed over the Pacific Ocean.

Technology experts on both sides of the Atlantic are still scratching their heads as to what has happened. Commentary from France and Germany indicates that NATO countries are investigating potential adversarial activity. In brief statements, Russian and Chinese officials have denied any involvement.

As reported earlier, many European top sites remained accessible in the US throughout the weekend, proxied by US servers. However, there was a group of internet users in America who were utterly cut off from Europe: Europeans in the US who use Tiles from their home countries.

EU law requires that European websites not only run with certificates controlled within the Union but also that Tiles sold in the EU use something called public key pinning. Pinning means these Tiles refuse to connect to European websites if the sites use foreign certificates. Thus, tourists and expats could not load the proxied sites.

"This shows our laws are effective," says EU representative Vivienne Marchand. "You might not be happy about blocked websites, but you were protected against someone tampering with the content of those sites."

West asked his Tile for the Wikipedia page on Evert Taube and tested the video clip. It took a while to buffer up, but now it worked.

The proxying is so weird. I wonder if we'll ever learn what happened.

Chapter 16

A Response

A response from Egor had come in.

```
Kate Libby, cell 42, women's section.
Arrested January 28 last year.
```

West read it three times. He double-checked even though he knew Kiss's email also said 42.

He thought back to the previous year and the wintery city of Stockholm.

January 28th makes sense.

Jitterbug must have seen Egor's response, too, because he was writing something in their chat thread. West sent his message first.

I have to go.

Where? Ice Dolphin?

Ultimately, yes.
But I need help.

Åse.

I think she's in Norway now.

Can we talk about this?

You know I have to go.

Man.

West stared at the chat. Jitterbug was not responding further. He should get packing.
Jitterbug's message bubbles came alive again.

You don't have to go.

You're wrong. I absolutely
have to go.

Another break before Jitterbug wrote again.

What are you packing?

I dunno. How do I hack into
a maximum security prison?

Borrow my gear.

I've got a rad new
JTAGulator.

With pink circuit board!

Chapter 17

Narvik

Norwegian summer evenings were just as magical and bright as Juneau's. To the east, snow-clad mountaintops stretched high, accentuating the steep difference between the fjords and Norway's Arctic landmass.

Narvik was situated on a peninsula with water continuing further into the landscape on either side. This was well over a hundred miles north of the Arctic Circle and in just a couple of days West and Jitterbug would get to experience the midnight sun. The excitement over Norway was what had convinced Jitterbug to join.

"Don't turn something like that down because of me. Come back and tell me all about it," Ronaldo had said, according to Jitterbug.

West and he did not talk about travels beyond Narvik.

The first leg of the flight had featured a recent phenomenon—crowdfunding of experiences. People on the plane could ask fellow passengers for money to be able to do things at their destinations. West threw in a few bucks for someone who wanted to take her aging mom to an art gallery in Oslo.

Their own reason for traveling kept bothering Jitterbug. He maintained that this was all based on disinformation and a terrible idea. Not even trolling the steward robot on the domestic flight north could cheer him up.

It was still unclear why Åse and Robert had moved their operations from Stockholm up here—from the big city to small town. Åse he could see, since she was Norwegian. But why would Robert go here? West's leading theory was fallout from the hack of Agent Pogodina.

The car swiftly took them from the domestic airport by the western waterside, around a hill, past the shaded port, and into the town of Narvik.

The prolonged sunset cast long shadows outside Rallar'n Pub og Kro—the restaurant where they were to meet up with their Scandinavian friends. The smell of the sea was still present, but here it mixed with the scent of grilled seafood.

Robert waved them over from a table in the back as soon as they entered. A server gesticulated for them to put their luggage toward the wall before getting seated.

Åse had a purple T-shirt reading "Binary Is for Computers." Robert wore a knitted sweater and his friendly, wide smile.

"Good to see you again," Robert said with a subtle droop, acknowledging the pain and sorrow West and Jitterbug had gone through with Kiss's death since last they saw each other. He and Åse got up.

Oh, right. The hugging.

They all embraced before sitting down.

"The right season to visit this time over," was Åse's first comment.

Robert pushed a bottle of rosé wine toward West and Jitterbug, and the server delivered two extra glasses.

They said cheers. The wine tasted like strawberry juice.

"Can we talk here?" West asked, leaning in.

"We can talk at Åse's office. Let's have a bite first." Robert handed over the menu.

●

The office complex was strict and professional, and far too large for being some hacker lair. White desks and light wood panels halfway up the walls. There was a hint of fir tree in the air, or rosemary. No geeky game consoles or posters. Very different from Robert's place in Stockholm. Corporate, rather.

The four of them sat down by a kitchenette area. There was no one else around and Åse didn't bother turning more than the necessary lights on.

West began telling their story. "We believe Kiss is still alive and held captive by the Russians." He folded one of his thumbs into his hand to rub Kiss's ring.

Robert's and Åse's faces first wrinkled and frowned, then opened up. "That's great," Robert said. "That she's alive, I mean. But I can't imagine the emotional roller coaster."

"Just getting to that belief has been painful. I don't know what I'll do if we learn that we're wrong and she is dead. But I can't afford to not act on this information. We have to get her out."

There was a pause, during which Robert and Åse looked at each other. "Details," Åse said.

"West is more of a believer than I am," Jitterbug said. "We're told she's part of a slow negotiation between Russia and the US. Exchange of prisoners."

"Slow because of the US or Russia?"

"We can only assume it's complicated," Jitterbug replied.

West leaned forward. "I don't know what Kiss is worth in the eyes of the US government. She's not a public figure, so they'll get no political gains from it. She might be part of a package."

"I'm sure the US will figure it out," Åse suggested.

"We wouldn't be here if that were an option. Once she's in US G20S custody, we might never see her again. Out of the frying pan, into the fire."

"You think it's easier to free her from the Russians?" Åse scoffed.

"At least the Russians don't expect it."

Åse stayed focused on West. Seconds passed. "Do you even know where she is? Russia is huge," she said.

"Ice Dolphin Prison in Novaya Zemlya."

"Really?"

"Really."

A kitchenette fridge hummed in the background. Åse looked at West, then at Robert. "I'm considering sharing some intel," she told her elder accomplice.

Robert nodded indistinctly. "You're the commander. I'm just visiting."

She fished out a midsized Tile from her handbag, tapped on it a few times, and pushed it across the table to West and Jitterbug.

"Sign this if we are to talk any further," she said.

West read the heading of what looked like a contract on the Tile's screen.

Non-Disclosure Agreement, North Atlantic Treaty Organization

Chapter 18

NATO

"NATO?" West uttered, half surprised, half disgusted.

Åse made a sweeping gesture around the office space. "You're welcome." She circled back to point at the Tile.

West and Jitterbug looked at each other. Jitterbug shrugged. They started reading.

It was a nondisclosure agreement for interacting with NATO operatives on intel classified as RESTRICTED and CONFIDENTIAL. It made it clear that the person signing was expected to side with NATO on any conflicts involving the organization.

"Not doing it," West said.

Jitterbug tilted his head. He turned to Åse. "Why do we have to sign this?"

"I can't tell you anything beyond what's there. But you're smart people," she said with a luring smile.

"Can we talk about this, just the two of us?" Jitterbug said to Åse.

"Of course."

Robert and Åse got up and walked out of sight.

Jitterbug asked his Tile to output white noise and leaned in close. "Let's hear it."

"It's madness," West spat out. "Working for the man. They haven't been honest with us. Unless you forgot to tell me you knew."

"I didn't know. Maybe it's a new thing. Maybe that's why they moved here?" Jitterbug suggested.

"Of course it's not new. Åse is military. She's a sniper. That document is legally binding. If we sign, we ..."

"We're US citizens. Uncle Sam already has us by the cojones."

"I'm not into that shit. You know that. I'm neutral."

"Truly neutral? Come on. They're offering to help. We have virtually nothing to go on. I came all the way here with you."

"You and me. We're the ones to help Kiss. And I didn't push you. I'll do it myself rather than get tangled up with Big Brother."

Jitterbug groaned.

West closed his eyes and rubbed his eyebrows. He just wanted to get going. Time was ticking. God knew what Kiss was being put through in that prison. Jitterbug helping would increase the chances of success. That was about as far as he agreed with any of this.

"Do you truly believe Kiss is alive?" Jitterbug's expression demanded an honest answer.

"I can't ... Yes, I truly *believe* that. But I can't say it isn't wishful thinking."

Jitterbug's jaw muscles worked. "*Do it yourself*—what's up with that? Do you have a plan?"

"Not really."

"I know you. You have something cooked up."

"Well, I was thinking ... I could hack my way into whatever system to grant myself transportation to Ice Dolphin. Åse said the only way to get to Ice Dolphin is as a prisoner, so get on that list, I guess. That's what I got."

"To Ice Dolphin? As a prisoner?"

West nodded, then looked at the floor.

"As I live and breathe, I did not think you were that stupid," Jitterbug said vehemently. "As a matter of fact, I *know* you're not that stupid."

West looked up under his eyebrows, head still drooping. "I have to get there."

Jitterbug looked like a disappointed schoolteacher.

They sat in silence for a good minute while the white noise kept washing out any other sounds.

Then Jitterbug spoke. "I'm going to sign this thing to get us intel. Nobody is surrendering to the Russians."

West kept his mouth shut. Then gave a nod.

Jitterbug turned off the white noise and produced a piercing whistle in the direction Åse and Robert had gone. Soon enough the two Scandinavians were back.

West and Jitterbug signed one copy each of the NATO NDA.

CHAPTER 19

Since 1949

The security to get into the NATO lockdown area on the floor above was advanced. There was an armed guard who made them leave their luggage and empty their pockets outside. Then they had to pass a cylindrical gate similar to airport body scanners.

"It weighs you on your way in and out to make sure you don't remove anything from inside or leave anything behind. So don't do that," Åse said.

Everyone but Åse got seated at a round table and Åse got West a mug of floral tea after he asked what the scent in the room was.

"How much do you know about Norway and NATO?" she asked as she sat down.

"They're members, I think," Jitterbug said.

"One of the *founding* members," Åse corrected him. "West, you're aware of my military background. Since the GPI compromise and the severely deteriorated relations with Russia, we're operating in a different climate. It was not safe for Robert to keep working with us in Stockholm, so we collaborate here."

"Why up in Narvik?"

"Why indeed," Åse said. She beamed a map onto a big screen on the wall a few feet away. It centered on northern Scandinavia.

"What you see here are four countries—Norway, Sweden, Finland, and Russia. But only two of those have an Arctic coastline, up here, Norway and Russia. Now if we go north." She scrolled the map until it was completely blue with the swaths of Barents Sea. "Many think what remains from here is the ice mass around the North Pole. But Norway's terra firma still has a long way to go."

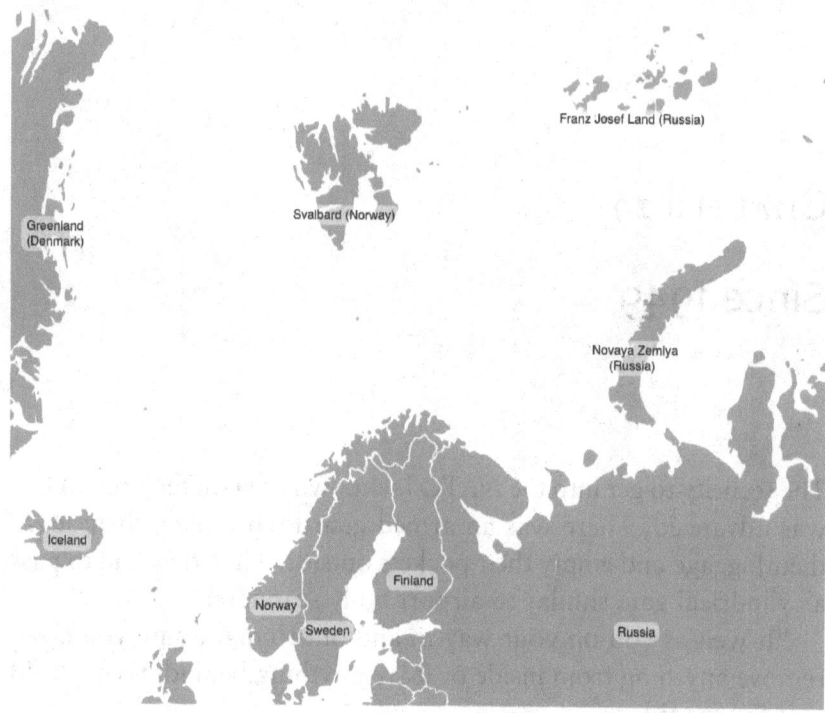

She continued scrolling north and several islands appeared, the biggest ones in a cluster called Svalbard. "This is still Norway, and Norway is NATO. I will now take you westward."

A huge landmass scrolled in from the left.

"Greenland, part of Denmark—another founding member of NATO. You go further west and you reach Canada, which should be familiar territory. This is *all* NATO. Now, let's go east of those Norwegian islands I just showed you."

She scrolled back past Svalbard, and just as the islands got to the far left of the screen, a huge spine-like island named Novaya Zemlya emerged on the right.

West drew an involuntary breath.

Åse tapped on her Tile and borderlines appeared in the middle of Barents Sea between Svalbard and Novaya Zemlya. "This, my friends, is Norway's vast maritime border to Russia. The forming of NATO was not just about the North Atlantic but also about the Arctic Ocean. Depending on the health of the Arctic ice mass, Russian ships have to pass through NATO-controlled waters to even access the Atlantic. That specter has been on Russian minds since

1949. And Russian naval activity in the Barents Sea has been on *our* minds even longer."

"Are you telling us all this because I mentioned Novaya Zemlya?" West asked.

"I'm telling you because you really don't want to go there," Åse replied.

"You helped me get to Dudinka."

"I helped you travel in Russia. That's child's play compared to this. Ice Dolphin is a maximum security prison in a militarized zone. We have indications of activity there that go well outside human incarceration."

"What kind of activity?" West seemed to be the only one thinking about Kiss.

"You're only disclosed on the Confidential level. So I'll say only this—covert activity there involves the Russian Cyber Command, and the only way any Westerner would ever enter that compound is as an imprisoned enemy of the Russian State."

West looked at Jitterbug. His friend shook his head slowly.

Robert looked pained, but conclusive.

West spoke thinly. "I can't live with myself if I don't try to get Kiss out."

Jitterbug leaned towards him. "I understand," he said calmly. "I was hoping Åse and Robert had some trick up their sleeve. They know Russia and they're telling us to back off. This is military stuff. Let's work with EFF to get her out on the US side instead."

"She called for my help."

"She doesn't know she's part of an exchange. Look, I saw her get shot. I care. Believe me. But this is madness. How do you even plan to get in?"

"I'll start as a tourist," West said.

•

West searched for flights out of Narvik and began packing his things in the guest room he'd been provided.

Jitterbug came in and sat watching him for several minutes before restarting the conversation. "You are sacrificing your life," he said. "We're talking Russian prison transport. You'll be among thugs, not knowing the language."

West zipped his luggage and sat down on his bed.

"I hope you're not considering a surrender," Jitterbug continued. "Can you tell me what you intend to do?"

"I already told you. That's what I've got."

"And you think you can avoid just ending up a prisoner?"

West nodded feebly and threw his hands out with little intent.

"Can you at least let me talk to Åse again?" Jitterbug asked.

"You heard her. There's nothing she can do that's even remotely reasonable. I love you, Jit. You want the best for me. I will never forget you."

CHAPTER 20

White House: Manipulation

"Madam President, we now have a pretty good picture of the malicious online activity that went on during the transatlantic internet outage," Director Lewis said. It had taken Purnell's team throughout Monday to light up transatlantic cables again and a week to get the full picture.

"Don't tell me you want to revert trades on the market," Sanchez said in a voice that did not invite further commentary.

"You're right that there was a lot of market activity. But it's impossible to tell what may have been based on public information, confidential information, or done by adversarial actors. The stock markets were affected and we've spotted some suspicious shorting on the Friday before. But those are not our primary concerns."

The director beamed a slide onto the big screen. It had three bullet points:

- News vacuum
- Delayed software security updates
- Pop culture disruption

"Ore, you wanna take the first one?" Lewis said without really asking.

"Sure," the national security advisor said. "Madam, we believe we've been too focused on data not reaching the US. It's natural to have that perspective as Americans. We were in a temporary European news vacuum, but fixed that through the proxy measure you are well aware of. Most of the bad outcome was about data *from* us not reaching the outside world. American news outlets were effectively censored in Europe for a few days."

"You're saying they didn't reciprocate and offer cached copies of our news?"

"Some did. But for Europe you have to look at individual countries. Maybe they weren't prepared, but"—Alec twisted his face impishly—"many of them don't seem to be too concerned with American news going silent for a weekend."

"I see." President Sanchez leaned back in her chair, scanning the ceiling while thinking. "We're not liked in all parts of Europe, we know that. Our ability to get news to them is important, especially intelligence leaks. What got blocked in that category last weekend?"

Ore turned to Lewis with an open hand gesture.

The director swiped twice on his large Tile. "Continuous reporting on former Soviet states under threat from Russia. Afghanistan, where we do provide quite a lot of intel. We had a big one on illegal trade along China's Silk Road—mostly independent work, but we confirmed parts of the story—and the latest rumblings around the deputy secretary-general of the UN."

Sanchez's eyes left the ceiling and landed on the people around the table. "Bad but not terrible. We'll get it out, eventually. Next bullet."

"Security updates for software. US companies build and maintain the world's most popular operating systems and computer platforms. This means security updates and fixes emanate from here and there was at least one major update that rolled out in the outage window. There are signs of exploit campaigns targeting European clients. Security updates are reverse engineered into exploits using AI tools, so a couple of days matters."

"Attacks against private or public sector?"

"Both."

Sanchez shook her head, then scooped air with her hand to nudge them along.

Lewis continued. "Last bullet, and this may seem subtle, but half the world did not get American TV series and movies. There seem to have been timely releases of Eastern shows portraying us in a negative light and a lot of viewers chose those."

The president drummed her fingertips against the tabletop three times. "No news, delayed security updates, and no shows. Sounds like two dimensions to me—global influence and more traditional hacking. Neither would be worth revealing cyberwar capabilities over. I want to come back to critical infrastructure, but first, General, where are we on how the attack on the internet cables was carried out?"

Purnell was ready. "Ten percent of our subsea capacity is still out. We have localized the disruptions down to individual segments between repeaters. If you'll allow me to go into some details here ..."

The president nodded.

"So-called repeaters boost the optical signal through the fiber as it attenuates over long distances. We have repeaters every fifty miles or so. We can test the throughput between each pair of repeaters to localize problems. And in 10% of the Atlantic cables, there are dark segments with zero throughput."

"One or more dark segments per cable?" the president asked.

"One per cable, which we think further indicates a deliberate attack, but we want to keep it open until we know the exact nature of the disruptions. We started with three possible causes—faulty repeaters, physical damage inside the cables, or physical damage that can be seen from the outside, like a simple cutoff. The latter has already been dismissed since the cables have multiple shielding layers, which allow us to check that cables haven't been completely cut off. Mini subs are checking the remaining two possibilities and will give us a visual of both the cable segments and the surrounding seabed."

"Ten percent is a lot. What about the remaining ninety?"

"Investigation ongoing and no new findings. Those subsea cables are back at maximum capacity."

"Greenland?"

The hitherto secret high-capacity connection between the US and Europe via Greenland had sent shockwaves through US Cyber Command as well as the nonprofit International Cable Protection Committee.

"We've identified a cable connection coming out of the Nares Strait—a narrow passage between Canada and Greenland far up in the Arctic."

"A non-US cable connection, I take it."

"It's not ours and it's not in public registries. It sticks to the Danish side of the strait and seems to make a rogue connection to

Greenland Connect North in the town of Aasiaat. From there it gets onto Greenland Connect proper, which goes to Milton in Canada. The Danes have given us full authorization to investigate and they have no prior record of this cable. We've followed it to the edge of the Arctic ice sheet and will continue with submersibles capable of working in those conditions." The general paused. "It may be that the cable is drawn across the Arctic."

"Do you have a map of this?" the president asked.

"I do."

A map centered on the North Pole appeared on the big screen, with all five Arctic powers—Norway, Denmark, Canada, USA, and Russia—and the still-contested parts of the Earth underneath the ice.

The room was silent. On the other side of the North Pole lay endless stretches of Arctic sea and land, all belonging to Russia.

"It wouldn't be beyond GUGI to lay a rogue internet cable," Ore added from the sideline.

GUGI, or the Russian Main Directorate of Deep-Sea Research and its hydronauts, were world leaders in mapping and researching the world's oceans. Inaugurated in 1965, they were only officially recognized forty years later.

"That's ... disturbing," the president said. "It's like the old Washington–Moscow Direct Communications Link, but unknown to us." Her eyes wandered aimlessly across the table's surface, stopping here and there.

Everyone else knew to keep quiet. All that could be heard was breathing.

Jolting out of her frozen position, the president leaned forward and landed her elbows on the table. Her hands formed an upside-down basket in the air, each fingertip touching its peer. People who had worked with her long enough knew this as her conclusions-and-command pose. Purnell and Lewis straightened up.

"I want CYBERCOM to look at how we can avoid news vacuum attacks in the future. I want a report on who and what was hacked because of the delayed security update. As we discussed beforehand, we have now revealed to the world our capability and willingness to proxy global websites. I want the consequences of that reveal analyzed. Our adversaries will update their plans accordingly, and so should we. As for the backend situation in the Arctic, I have to process some more."

She paused and looked around the room. People gave her subtle nods in response. "Now, if you'll excuse me, I have a Memorial Day speech to rehearse."

CHAPTER 21

The Message

Did the Government Reply to Your Messages?

As the Sanchez administration tries to wrap things up regarding last week's transatlantic internet failure, more and more traces of the government's heavy hand are surfacing. The most disturbing one so far is a claim that people heard back from friends and partners in Europe during the outage. How can that be? Well, a lot points toward the government faking responses to cover things up.

Miles, 27, lives in Milwaukee, Wisconsin. During the weekend of May 17–18, he was texting with his friend from college in the UK as well as a young man he was in a budding relationship with and who's based in Portugal. You would think that his messages didn't get any replies. How could they when the internet connection to Europe was down? But he did get replies, and the ones he got from his new boyfriend in Portugal were short and unloving.

"I can be pretty emotional," Miles told us. "And I was going through a lot of things that weekend. My landlord was being a dick and my cat had to have surgery. I needed support. And [redacted name] just wasn't there for me. I started sending pretty aggressive messages back and those I didn't get a response on until the internet was working again. At that point, I couldn't pull them back and [redacted name] got so upset he dumped me. I don't even blame him!"

We could not get a comment from relevant agencies on these alleged fake messages. But we've talked to security expert Martin Bishop, and he says it could be government AI sending short, bland messages to keep appearances up. Why they would do that is unclear, but Bishop speculates it could be to not alarm people during the extended internet outage.

If it turns out the government can respond to our personal messages, we're in an unheard-of era of dystopia. ∎

Tell us your story! Did you get weird text messages from European friends during the outage? If so, please reach out to our reporter @DeanElder.

CHAPTER 22

NATO SECRET

The venture of going back to Russia was both frightening and comforting to West. It was frightening not knowing the language or how to accomplish what he needed. Comforting knowing that he was doing *something* to save Kiss.

His Tile showed a countdown to boarding—fifteen minutes.

He had been at the airport the whole day to avoid Jitterbug's pleas for him to abandon his mission. They had parted as friends though, with Jitterbug's last words being, "I can tell your heart is in it. And why wouldn't it be? I wish I could go with you, but the scars from having been their captive ... Stay safe, my friend."

He doubted he'd be able to stay safe.

Getting a tourist visa for St. Petersburg had been surprisingly easy on the website of the Russian Foreign Ministry. The price was submitting a bunch of information and biometrics.

Too many mugs of coffee at the airport café had made him sweaty.

A few tens of other people were waiting at the gate.

He pulled up the tourist info he'd been collecting on his Tile. St. Petersburg lay at the eastern end of the Gulf of Finland. Its rich history revealed what a strategic point it was. It had started out as a Swedish fortress in the early 1600s, been conquered by Peter the Great in 1703, and grew past the size of Moscow by the 1800s. Its name had been changed three times in the 1900s—first to Petrograd at the outbreak of World War I, then to Leningrad under Lenin, and finally back to St. Petersburg by public referendum after the fall of the Soviet Union. The fall of the communist empire wasn't really mentioned in the tourist info but he knew that much of his 1990s history.

The lack of a good plan gnawed at him. Even if he managed to get to Ice Dolphin, how could he ever find Kiss, let alone get her home?

I'll figure something out. She's betting on me.

He'd been telling himself that so many times it felt like a slogan.

The woman at the counter spoke through a microphone: "Good afternoon, everyone. Today's flight from Narvik to Oslo is ready to board. As you might have noticed, we have free seating. We do, however, request you spread out evenly in the cabin since keeping the plane balanced saves on power and helps us protect the climate. We thank you for your cooperation. Have a pleasant flight."

There was no priority order. Four seats per row, split in the middle by a single aisle.

West got seated by a window. He fiddled with Kiss's ring on his finger. It felt like a physical connection to her.

I need to get on that ship.

He had read about prisoner transports to Ice Dolphin. The Russian president boasted about the inevitability of the one-way journey and how the cold Arctic waters prevented any attempts to escape.

The steward robot got him a coffee and a butterscotch cookie before they started taxiing out. He wondered if he'd ever get to visit Narvik again. Or Norway for that matter.

West saw the human stewardess get a life vest out to go through safety procedures. But a ding interrupted her and she went forward.

The plane slowed down and eventually the stewardess addressed the passengers via microphone: "I'm so sorry but we have had a slight mishap and need to go back to the gate for a brief stop. This is not safety-related, just a request from the gate. I'm told we should be in the air in about thirty minutes. Sorry for the inconvenience."

The other passengers murmured and looked out the windows as the aircraft turned to go back.

As soon as they were at a safe distance from the runway, they stopped and a car with boarding stairs drove up. Two uniformed men boarded and spoke inaudibly with the stewardess before walking down the aisle. They didn't look at any particular passenger but stopped at West's row and one of them turned to him.

The man showed a slip of paper low between the seats to obscure it from any other passengers. It had West's name printed on it.

The man tilted his head in silent query.

West nodded.

"I'm Lieutenant Olafsen," the man said in a conversational tone. "We have orders to take you off this plane." He turned his head up and looked front and back at the other passengers before speaking loudly. "No need for alarm. This is unrelated to safety or any suspicious activity. We just need to speak to this individual."

Olafsen looked back at West. "Luggage?" He gave a quick glance at the overhead compartment.

·

An hour later, West found himself sitting at a round table back at the NATO office complex. Olafsen and his silent colleague kept him company. Shortly thereafter, Åse entered.

West burst out of his chair as soon as he saw her. "What the fuck is going on?" he said loud enough for the lieutenant to tense up, at the ready.

Åse nodded for the two men to leave.

"Change of heart," she said, turning back to West. "My superiors have decided to help you if you help us."

"Where's Jit?"

"I need you to make this decision yourself."

"What decision?"

"Once my superiors learned of Kiss's imprisonment, interest grew in getting her out."

"You have confirmation she's alive?"

"Corroborating intel. They asked me to get you in order. We have an opportunity to try to get your girlfriend out."

"A prisoner exchange?" West asked, trying to piece it together.

"That's a bilateral thing, not NATO's turf. And no, we're not talking about an exchange."

"So tell me."

"I will." Åse put a midsized Tile on the table and turned it to him.

Non-Disclosure Agreement, North Atlantic Treaty Organization

It was an agreement for interacting with NATO operatives on intel classified as SECRET, the second highest level there was.

Åse nodded upward at the Tile. "Read. Then sign and we can get going."

"Has Jit signed?"

"Swipe to the left."

He did and there was the same agreement with Jitterbug's signature at the bottom. "That could be fake," he mumbled.

"If you don't want in, I'll get you on the next plane to the US."

"I wasn't headed to the US."

"I know."

West gave her a dirty look, then slumped back in the chair. He pulled the Tile to his lap and started reading the document top to bottom. Åse waited in silence.

Ten minutes later, keeping his gaze on the screen, West scribbled figuratively in the air with his index finger and thumb pinched.

Åse fished out an electronic pencil.

CHAPTER 23

Splinternet

"It's military stuff; it's madness. Those are your words," West said. He had demanded to talk to Jitterbug alone but had the feeling that they were being watched as they stood in a small meeting room. They hadn't bothered turning on the lights, but there was enough seeping through the frosted glass wall by the door.

"I went up the mountains to get closer to Him." Jitterbug made an upward nod. "I can't pronounce the place, but it's Fagernesfjellet. Gondolas take you up and the view is gorgeous. I found a crevice that shielded me from the other tourists—a beautiful place for prayer." Jitterbug paused for a bit. "He told me not to abandon you."

West gave himself a few seconds to react, then reached out and clasped his friend's arm. He squeezed it a few times and the two men looked at each other in the dim light.

"You are a true friend," West said.

"I'm sorry I strayed. I'm with you now and we're going to have to trust Åse on this one. Come what may," Jitterbug said. He summoned a faint smile.

•

Jitterbug and West left the meeting room and Åse escorted them back to the briefing room with maps on screens.

"Where's Robert?" West asked as they got seated.

"He had to go back to Stockholm."

The room was more tense without the old Swedish guy. His mild manners had balanced them out. Now it was just the two of them and Åse, on her military turf.

"How much do you know about the Red Web?" Åse asked.

"Russia's piece of the splinternet," Jitterbug replied.

"Correct. That router you hacked in Pogodina's office last year is called a SORM, *Sistema Operativno-Rozysknikh Meropriyatiy.*"

Åse sounded like another human when speaking in Russian. Very authentic, as far as West could tell.

She continued. "SORM is the Russian security agency FSB's back door to spy on internet communications. They've had it in various forms since the late nineties."

"And the US has PRISM," West said, thinking back to how he crippled NSA's database all those years ago.

"And China has all the home routers our fellow Westerners have bought," Åse said. "But we're working on that. All this digital surveillance made countries fear for their national security. Hence, we got internet balkanization. China's Great Firewall is what everyone talks about, but Russia really got going in 2019. Formally it's called their Sovereign Internet Law. Informally it's the Digital Iron Curtain, or the Red Web."

Jitterbug chuckled. "In the US it's just the internet," he said.

"First-mover advantage," West filled in.

"If you gentlemen don't mind." Åse gave them a stern look each. "Europe has partnered with the US in fits and starts, mostly through NATO countries. But the dream of a free, global internet is still alive here."

"Your dream?" West asked.

"I'm a military gal. Preventing war and defending people is what I do—hot or cold, guns or internet."

"That's not an answer."

"It's what you get." She gave him an ironic thumbs-up. "Digital Iron Curtain," she continued. "How would you know if it works?"

"Same thing with every engineering enterprise—if it's not tested, it's not working," Jitterbug quoted.

"Damn right," Åse said. "So, how do you test it?"

West and Jitterbug fidgeted in their chairs for a bit, thinking.

"Block the outside world, I guess," Jitterbug said eventually.

Åse nodded in a distinct motion. "Russia has been doing non-domestic internet cutoffs since 2018, some clearly for testing purposes. But superpowers' interests lay not only in protecting and surveilling their *own* splinternets. They want to know about their adversaries' contingency plans. How do you test someone *else's* cyber defense and splinternet?"

"Sounds hard," West mumbled.

Åse turned to him. "You contacted me about something over the phone," she said.

West's brain raced. "The disconnection of European websites. The transatlantic internet disruption. You're saying the Russians did it to probe US internet contingency? Shit."

"By Jove," Jitterbug uttered. "Has anyone confirmed the probe?"

"There are no absolutes," Åse said. "We've been working around the clock ever since to increase our confidence." She stood up. "NATO has a renewed interest in Novaya Zemlya in relation to this investigation, and that will allow me to take you two to Ice Dolphin."

She moved the map on the big screen to Russia's Novaya Zemlya island and zoomed in on the western opening of a narrow water passage that split it into a northern and southern part. "This is where Ice Dolphin is located, very close to the site of the world's largest nuclear bomb test—Tsar Bomba in 1961."

The passage was labeled Matochkin Shar Strait.

"Radiation?" West asked.

"There are many reasons not to go to Ice Dolphin, but radiation doesn't seem to be high on that list. No doubt Russia couldn't care less if their prisoners were exposed, but I checked while prepping for what we're talking about today. Tsar Bomba is not only known for being the largest nuclear test but is also regarded as one of the cleanest to date. Ninety-seven percent of the explosion was fusion, which doesn't create radioactive contamination. There were many dirtier tests in the Novaya Zemlya area, so the glaciers around there are about a hundred times more radioactive than the background. That, however, is not far above what you get during an intercontinental flight. Supposedly, the administrative parts of the prison building have shielding inside the walls. Leaked complaints of poor wireless connectivity corroborate that piece of intel."

West scraped the front of his teeth with his thumbnail. "You said NATO doesn't give a shit about Kiss. Do you?"

"I can't claim she's my friend, so mostly not."

"Care enough to help us get her out?"

"I don't care enough about Kiss to go anywhere near Ice Dolphin. But as I said, NATO has a renewed interest in Novaya Zemlya. West, I think you're in decent enough shape to get some weapons training."

Chapter 24

White House: The SMITH Investigation

"I have the prime minister of India waiting." President Sanchez didn't like switches between the smiling long game and right-here-right-now conversations. But Purnell had insisted on a quick update.

"I'm sorry, ma'am. But I wanted to get you this information. Are you up to speed on the SMITH investigation?" the general asked.

"That's our attempt at breaking the Russian submarine authentication scheme?"

"Right."

"With a Russian sub on a long mission that our allies snatched? I do remember that. Don't tell me there's an escalation."

"No escalation. An opportunity has arisen where we can find out more about the Greenland connection. Recent intel says that the connection goes through Ice Dolphin and Franz Josef Land. At some point it goes beneath the seabed, which is why it's difficult to backtrack it. To confirm that the cable popping up by Greenland is indeed Russian, we need to enter Russian waters and trace it from there. Naima has proposed a cover story, and our Norwegian partners have tentatively said yes."

The president looked puzzled. "I've already asked for an investigation of the Greenland subsea cable. SMITH is about submarine authentication."

"The cover involves humans headed for Ice Dolphin on the island of Novaya Zemlya in Barents Sea. Norway suggests using the Russian submarine we captured to record exactly how it's authenticated when we approach the dock. That's the SMITH leg of the mission. The sub needs to return from its mission shortly, so this is our last shot.

Naima is suggesting the Norwegians bring two civilian Americans with them. One of those civilians is of specific interest. West William Wilder—a felon who did fifteen years for hacking the NSA."

"I recognize the name. Do we know Naima's motives? Who is West working for?"

"No one, as far as our records go. He is trying to free his girlfriend from the Ice Dolphin prison. There actually *is* an American woman imprisoned on the island. A lowlife, former sex worker. No one of interest."

"Not every US citizen would do that for their girlfriend," Sanchez commented. "But I assume he's not a trained submariner?"

"Wilder seems to be friends with the Norwegian NATO major leading the operation, and she has training. Naima always works with multiple layers of distractions, as you know. Neither of the civilians have received a briefing on the SMITH investigation, so they can't leak even if they get caught."

Sanchez shook her head. "What a hodgepodge. But that's kind of the point, isn't it? The other American, someone of interest?"

"West's close friend who's trying to help him. He's been involved in domestic protests, Black Lives Matter, that sort of thing. No actual risk there, according to Naima."

"And these two guys want to do this?"

"At least West seems pretty desperate."

"Sending a desperate American to a likely death sounds awful. Who else is pushing for this?" the president asked.

"Department of Defense is in favor but not championing it. G2OS sees it as an opportunity to get rid of Wilder—either through incrimination or the Russians take him out on the spot."

"Naima often comes up with these multi-pronged operations. I'm not a fan. Too many things that can go wrong."

"The important part is that a NATO operation is entering Russian waters, headed for Russian soil, with Americans on board. We need your approval."

Sanchez thought for a few seconds. "I approve if Ore does. Let's hope Wilder doesn't have a hidden agenda of his own."

CHAPTER 25

Training Montage

"Assisted targeting will save your ass," Åse said. Her voice was clear and close through the speakers in West's bulky ear protection.

She had taken them to an underground shooting range. The NATO complex in Narvik featured a lot more than met the eye at surface level.

They had spent hours before lunch training with a knife—stabbing, slicing, blocking—which had made West feel sick.

With guns, you at least have some distance.

Åse drew their attention to the screen on the right side of the booth they were in. It showed a pristine target board. "Allow the technology to adjust your aim and don't compensate yourself. Similar to how pilots learn not to intervene with computer-controlled fighter jets. Use the force."

She pointed at the sight of her handgun. "GD—guide and deliver. That's what these are called. Cameras in both directions. It sees what you're aiming for and where the bullet goes. Your first bullet is the *guide*. It tells the gun exactly how to counteract wind for your second bullet – the *delivery*. Let me turn on some rough conditions here."

She tapped on the screen to the right and picked a hefty side wind from an options menu.

"Pay attention. You'll see me shoot twice in quick succession."

Bam, bam!

The first bullet hit far to the left. The second hit the bullseye.

"Impressive," Jitterbug said.

"Expensive," Åse replied. "Now, I did not change my aim between those two shots—the gun did. Don't lose one of these." She handed the weapon to West with a cunning smile. "Squeeze them off and get familiar with the kick."

He moved into position, raised the gun, and put his finger by but not on the trigger—each move according to what they had just done over and over with a dummy.

He got ready to pull the trigger for the first time. It would only require a light touch, he'd been told. His index finger squeezed. The trigger resisted. He squeezed harder, but the trigger wouldn't move. Was he really too weak to even operate a gun?

"Cease fire," Åse said.

He moved his index finger outside the trigger guard, turned on the safety, and lowered the gun.

Åse came up by his side. "Now you know what a fingerprint gun is." She poked at his thumb.

His white knuckles told him just how tightly he was holding this thing. He lifted his thumb and underneath he noted an ever so slight difference in the grip's texture compared to the rest. This gun was tied to Åse's fingerprint and he couldn't fire it.

•

"You should pull down and install the Commonwealth of Independent States language package. Russian, Uzbek, Belarusian, and a dozen others," Åse said during dinner.

She always ate quickly and was waving toward their Tiles with a piece of bread roll.

"To be able to render local documents?"

She shook her head, chewing intensely on a mouthful of bread. Speaking from one side of her mouth, she said, "Disables malware." She downed the food with a gulp of water. "Failsafe for broad Russian malware. The exploits don't activate on devices with those languages. FSB has deployed sweeping attacks to own as many Western computers as possible, even domestically. So they used the same ol' trick as ransomware criminals do when they don't want to end up in court in their own jurisdiction. We install those languages for a little extra protection."

•

They had just practiced using life vests, or personal floatation devices as Åse insisted they be called, when she held up a rectangular plastic case the size of half a pack of cards.

"What's this?" she asked.

One short end was black, the rest of the thing white. It had a T printed on both sides.

"Vape case?" Jitterbug suggested.

"You know, that's not totally incorrect. Liquid in some form entering your body. It's an autoinjector. Most often used to protect from chemical warfare agents, but can deliver most drugs quickly and securely. We will be intruders and may face lethal force. You will have three drugs at your disposal. We call the white one Tak. It has a formal name I don't know, but it was developed by a Japanese company called Takeda. It'll keep you awake and alert, amphetamine-style."

Jitterbug gave West a funny look.

"Red is morphine, straight up. If all hope is lost, this will hold your hand as you transcend to the other side."

She paused for a bit. "Finally, blue." The blue injector had an H printed. "This thing is NATO's secret. It produces the same bodily reaction as hypothermia, but doesn't actually lower your body temperature. We call it the Hibernator. If you or your buddy experience significant blood loss or low blood flow but still have a chance of surviving, this is what you inject. Then you need to be carried out."

"White, red, blue. Stars and Stripes," West said.

"And the flag of Norway."

"And Russia," Jitterbug added in a low voice.

West looked at the three plastic cases. "This is some serious shit."

"That's right. You wanted Ice Dolphin," Åse said.

She handed out three colorless autoinjector cases each. "Time to practice with placebos. This won't hurt a bit. We'll do real Tak later so you know how to pace yourself in that condition."

•

West looked at the light yellow, fatty surface sticking up from the plastic cylinder.

"Chapstick?"

"Everyone thinks so, and that's the way we like it," Åse replied. "But this is a broad-range reflective substance that throws off all known camera systems used for facial recognition. A couple of stripes on your cheeks is enough."

"Great Caesar's ghost!" Jitterbug threw out. "How long has the military had access to this?"

Åse chuckled. "As long as I've been enlisted. Be glad you signed the NDA. And never talk about it outside your mission."

West smelled the waxy face stick. It was odorless. "Won't this cause anomalies that in turn cause investigations?"

"False positives and aberrations are sent to human review, and those humans receive very little pay for sifting through never-ending, repetitive data. Let's just say it's an underserved area in surveillance."

•

Three days later, they were in a car going north, packed, and reasonably recovered from the Tak brain fry. They'd been going for two hours when the car reached the waterside and took a left onto an even smaller road. They spent another hour traveling through stunning fjords before being dropped off close to an enormous, rounded opening into the mountain. The cave could close with what looked like a blast door. There were heavily armed guards and a sign reading Olavsvern, Royal Norwegian Navy.

"This is a special place," Åse said, looking toward the shadowy entrance, holding on to the shoulder strap of her duffel bag but not yet lifting it. "It was Norway's secret naval base within the Arctic Circle during the Cold War. Then Europe was lulled into the Eternal Peace, our government decommissioned the base, and Russians linked to state-owned Gazprom rented it, I kid you not."

She got the strap over her shoulder. "Only after the invasion of Crimea did our politicians wake up and buy it back." She spat on the ground. "Grab your bags, check your weapons, and follow me."

Two ID checkpoints later and they had entered the tunnel. West reckoned it was a thousand feet long. The air was damp in here and the vaulted ceiling way above glistened with moisture. The sound of their feet bounced around, creating a layered audio trail.

A side door got them through a much narrower tunnel, opening into a cavernous deep-water dock embedded in the mountain.

Stretched before them in a still, lengthy pool lay a rather small submarine. At least smaller than the Cold War–era sub West had visited at the Maritime Museum in San Diego.

Åse let her eyes follow the stretch of subsea technology in front of them. "Most of the world's surface is submerged. It's seabed," she said. "And the oceans are still ruled by *Glavnoye Upravlenie Glubokovodsk Issledovanii*, GUGI, Russia's deep-sea research authority. The West is catching up and what you see before you is part of that. *Dolphin II*, its Russian design replicated as far as we've been able to, and nuclear-powered. Autonomous but can take four people. We have forty-eight hours to get you two trained on the things I might need help with. As a vessel for transport, she's easy, so we just need to prepare for disaster recovery. She'll take us to the Matochkin Shar Strait, past Russian defenses."

"Is anyone with real training coming except you?"

"I said four cabins and we need the extra, right? Besides, so far, no one on our side has been willing to explore those waters, and NATO has not had enough of an interest to *order* anyone to go there. Me offering to take you two solves staffing, and the internet disruption has increased NATO interest by a lot."

CHAPTER 26

The Living Infinite I

Even though this was his best chance of reuniting with Kiss, West did not feel good about the venture the morning of their departure. His body and mind had had to learn so many things the last week and every piece felt crucial to their success. The sheer number of controls, buttons, and screens on *Dolphin II* boggled his mind. What Åse had called seats were more like cocoons where you half sat, half lay down. The only place you could stand up was the narrow walkway in the middle of the watercraft and in the center of the kitchenette area.

West had asked about how they had gotten access to Russian blueprints to replicate this submarine, but Åse remained coy. She even said "on a need to know basis" once, which did not land well with Jitterbug and him. The one piece of information she had shared was that replicating the Russian sub had to do with operating behind enemy lines.

Presumably, their mission relied heavily on how well this copy mimicked the original.

West looked at Jitterbug on the other side of the mountain dock canteen. They were both done eating their oatmeal. "How are you feeling about this?"

"It's okay," Jitterbug said before using the edge of his fingernail to get something out from between his teeth. He sat thinking for a while, gazing in the distance. "Those beautiful hills around Narvik. It's a shame you didn't get to see them. I decided I have to do more of that back home. Remember we saw it from the train, up in Washington? Mount Rainier and whatnot. Well, maybe that's a bit of a stretch. That's more like mountaineering. But you know what I mean. We've got Yosemite and places around Tahoe. I messaged Ronaldo and said we'll hike those places."

West looked at his friend. "You know you don't have to do this."

"West, please."

"I just wanna ... If it gets ugly, I don't want to think I forced you into it."

"We're here to do good. Come what may."

West nodded. "Come what may."

•

Åse, Jitterbug, and West carried their bags with all their tactical gear, including guns in their micro vaults, into the deep-water dock. A final sign-off and they were about to board.

Something didn't look right to West. Something with the sub. Was it the light? The rows and rows of fluorescent lighting above blinded him as he looked up. Eyes back on the dark surface of *Dolphin II*, he looked closely at the color. Was it a different hue? Or was the whole thing turned in the opposite direction? No, it was the welds! Patterns of seams along the hull through subtle shifts in reflected light.

"The sub looks different," he told Åse. "I couldn't see the spot welds before."

She stopped and looked. "Probably results of pressure testing. They did it overnight as a final checkup. The volume of it shrinks noticeably when you get deep."

She stepped down halfway through the bridge. "We're boarding in the dark. We need to leave the dock with only slow propulsion powered on to limit leaking emanations. As I told you, the Russians know this place."

They had trained twice boarding and operating *Dolphin II* without light. In total, eleven controls had to be operated without visual feedback.

West heard Jitterbug enter his cabin seat as he and Åse continued a few more steps. West's seat was shotgun, front right.

"Remember, no flashlight, and Tiles off until we've left the fjords. I'll turn comms and visuals on then. That's about an hour on slow propulsion. You may fall asleep because ... well, lying down silent in the dark."

West turned the meaty handle to his cabin and slowly climbed in, feeling his way with hands and feet. The smell differed from yesterday. Muskier.

We are so unprepared for this.

•

He had dozed off and woke up to lit screens and buttons. Nautical chart to the right, ship status to the left. But all the labels were in Cyrillic!

"What the fuck?" he uttered in his cocoon. His hand gravitated to a button he knew as intercom but did not recognize the language on. He pressed it.

"What is going on? All my controls are in Russian."

Åse came in on the second. "Good morning, and welcome aboard *Djillphin Dva*. The Russian original, not the copy."

West threw his head back.

I'm on a freaking Russian submarine.

"Why did you lie about this?"

"I tried to get permission to show you this thing beforehand but was denied. I told them you'd know once we were at sea anyway. But the rigid rules are rigid all right. Hence boarding in the dark. The *reason* is we have to use the original for this mission."

West's legs pushed his feet into the floor, making his safety harness present itself and constrain him. "We could die in here," he said as his upper body twisted from side to side. He started tugging at the strap across his chest.

"That's true. But no more true than for the copy. Calm down. You can take a walk midship if you need to move. There's coffee."

He carefully scanned the ceiling and walls all around but could not see any obvious cameras except for the one above the main screen.

"Oh, man," Jitterbug said through the speaker, probably awoken by West yelling over the intercom.

The harness came loose and West got out into the walkway. He was sweating even though the air was cool. Scattered Russian labels were present here, too.

He knocked on Jitterbug's cabin door as he walked toward the stern where the small kitchen was. The smell of coffee did indeed greet him.

Soon enough, he was sitting with his friend, drinking out of a metal mug. He flipped the switch on the intercom and started speaking to Åse.

"How do you think we'll be able to trust you from this point? You said so yourself the past few days—trust is key to mission success."

"It is. Had you joined our forces seven years ago and not seven days ago, you would have had access to all available information. But that's not where we are. I have permission to take you with me. The less you know, the lower the risk for you. Need-to-know basis. You're on a Russian combat mini-submarine. We're five hundred meters below the surface, which is over fifteen hundred feet, I believe. Still in the Norwegian Sea, headed for Barents Sea. Stay focused on getting Kiss out."

West heard the low frequency hum of the motors propelling them further north, ever closer to Russian territory. He turned off the intercom.

"What do you think she's up to?" he asked Jitterbug.

"I still think she's taking us to Ice Dolphin. Or at least the right island. Something about the internet interruption, right? I don't understand how those two things are connected though."

"There has to be a reason we're on a Russian sub and not the NATO copy," West brooded.

"Maybe they're not confident the copy is good enough to sneak in?"

"That's what I'm thinking too. Some way for the Russians to tell the two apart."

West took a sip. The coffee was not great but it was warm and comforting. "To think we're fifteen hundred feet down in a Russian war sub."

Chapter 27

Down the Docks

"Entering the Loophole," Åse's voice said over the intercom. "Check the screen."

West and Jitterbug had spent most of their time in the kitchen area, haunted by the eerie sounds of the sub being squeezed by the massive expanse of water around them. They looked up at the screen above the opening to the walkway. A dotted line tracked *Dolphin II* and it was just leaving Norwegian waters into a segment of Barents Sea that was neither Norwegian nor Russian.

"The high seas, my friends. An area of international waters, half the size of Germany, disputed for decades. Once we exit to the east, our disguise is what we've got."

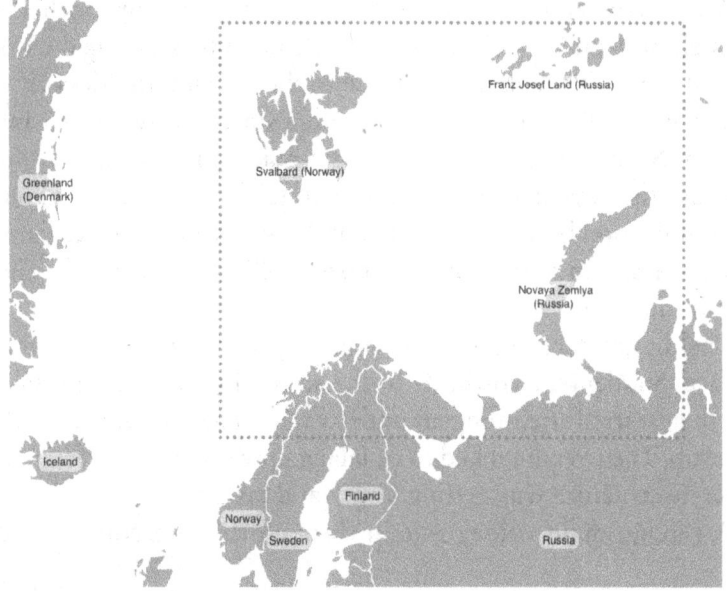

Hours had passed since they left the Loophole. It was Monday according to Åse.

Either the constant coffee drinking or the insanity of breaching Russian waters had made West increasingly queasy. Maybe both.

Åse instructed everyone to stay silent as they approached the Matochkin Shar Strait. The sound of the motors changed as they slowed down. They had to be close to the Ice Dolphin dock.

The terminal window in West's cabin started spewing out information. No human could keep up with reading it, even if they knew Russian. Åse was probably collecting it. It must be some automated communication between the sub, and West covered the face camera above the screen and filmed the fast-scrolling text with his Tile in high frame rate.

The digital depth gauge told him they were getting close to the surface. Suddenly, two-thirds of the screen in front of him flashed and then started streaming an underwater scene, lit not just by their own sub. The stream looked to be facing upward where a rectangular concrete structure was getting larger and larger.

A foreign male voice came in through the intercom. Sounded

Russian. Åse replied in a formal manner. West got his Tile to transcribe just in time to read "Dock 2, approved" coming from the man.

West's and Jitterbug's instructions were to stay put in their respective cabins until Åse knocked on their doors.

Silence replaced the hum of the motors that had been in the background for such a long time.

West heard Åse exit her cabin and walk to the exit ladder at a regular pace. Her steps made tinny sounds, then disappeared.

Nothing happened for five minutes. West shifted in his seat. Seven minutes. He got his gun out of its micro vault, loaded it, and checked that the safety was on. Ten minutes.

Footsteps again, and a knock on his door.

He flipped the safety switch off and held the gun tight with his index finger outside the trigger guard. A ricochet in here would not be good.

The cabin door handle moved and the door opened an inch.

"West," Åse hissed.

He grumbled and closed his eyes. "I'm here," he said in a low voice. He turned the safety back on and pulled the door open with one hand.

Åse poked her head in. She looked flushed. "Get your shit, exit through the bridge, and slide down the hull into the water away from the gangway. Bring Jit with you. Fast. I'll come get you when it's clear."

Her head disappeared. Thirty seconds later, Jitterbug and West climbed the ladder to the exit, pushing their backpacks above.

The dock had only red light. West saw Åse rush along the platform. She did not look back.

He put his boot down on the sub's pitch-black hull. Swiveling around to the back of the bridge tower, he got his backpack on, laid himself belly-down on the curved metal surface, and slid into the wetness.

The Arctic seawater first found its way into his boots and under his tight jacket. He gaped wide as icy liquid crept up his spine. Then switched to sucking in air through his teeth as the water got to his private parts. The backpack provided buoyancy, but he had to tread water.

Jitterbug found his way to West's side.

"I'm not built for this," Jitterbug uttered through his teeth. "My manhood has regressed to boyhood."

West held an index finger across his mouth.

Åse's voice echoed between the concrete walls. She was talking to at least two Russians. They didn't sound agitated. Rather excited or intrigued.

West hadn't been able to pay attention to anything but his rapidly cooling body for minutes when Åse appeared on the bridge.

She grabbed the handle at the neck of his jacket (a military thing she had explained was for quickly pulling dead bodies out of small spaces) and pulled him out of the drink. He crawled up on the hull like a sea turtle, shaking madly.

As soon as Åse had pulled up Jitterbug too, she shouldered both their backpacks and signaled for them to follow her onto the platform. She was moving as fast as her double luggage let her.

She got them into a control room with a wide window to the dock and pushed them down below a lengthy desk under the window. "Strip, use your towels, and get your change of clothes on. Sixty seconds." She squatted, keeping her head above the desk for lookout.

There was no way West could make his freezing muscles work that fast. It took him minutes to change. Jitterbug was struggling too.

Åse had them do forty pushups. "Okay, gents, you're in," she whispered while still looking out the window.

"Ice Dolphin?" West said, panting. He was getting warmer.

"Where else?"

"Why does a prison have a submarine dock?" Jitterbug asked.

"It's not just a prison."

"And the rest is on a need-to-know basis?"

Åse tilted her head and put on an empty smile. "I'll keep the show running down here. There'll be tons of questions on the sub, and I need to clear all of that to get us out of here. Use the Russian SIMs and the Babble app, no other means of communication. Down here, they don't allow the regular prison security camera system. I asked about that before handing over some exciting cargo to buy us a little time. But as soon as you enter the prison section, assume that every inch is monitored. Every minute here increases the risk. You've got a few hours tops to get her out. Good luck."

The subtle squeaks of her rubber soles moved toward the door and the hum of the dock area came and went as she exited.

West turned to Jitterbug. "She's not coming with us?"

Jitterbug shrugged. "I guess not."

"Do you know anything about this place?"

"Are you kidding me?"

West looked above the desk. There was a laptop there.

CHAPTER 28

Go Aggro

West pulled the laptop down under the desk and opened it. Jitterbug huddled up beside him.

The lock screen offered two accounts—admin and guest. The admin account seemed to have an active session. Battery charge was at 44%.

"This is an incredible asset," Jitterbug said, tapping the top edge of the laptop's screen. "Bunny?" he asked. Bunny drive was the nickname for their OmniPort thumb drive packed with tons of exploits. It was often capable of popping a shell on devices you had physical access to, or make them crash altogether.

"Bunny could work, but I don't think local admin will cut it. We need access to servers to find the women's section and where cell 42 is."

"You're saying we need the logged-in session? With a shell, you can probably grab it."

"Mmm." West was thinking. "I worry we'll crash it and lose the session."

"We can't just scout this place," Jitterbug said, looking at the door leading away from the dock. "It's a maximum security prison."

"Regardless. We need a badge and keys."

West moved the mouse pointer above the admin account icon and clicked. Animated instructions told him to input some kind of security key into the OmniPort. Underneath was a link reading помощь.

He pointed his Tile's camera at the word and got the translation—*support*. Clicking it revealed a phone number.

"Neither of us speaks Russian," Jitterbug said. "But we could send a translated message."

West drafted one.

> The computer doesn't
> accept my security key. I'm
> in

"We need the name of this room."

They looked around.

"Probably outside the door," Jitterbug said.

"That'll be under camera surveillance."

"Maybe we could get the network ID of this." He tapped on the laptop.

"We could. But we need to think like an employee here. What would they look for?"

Jitterbug put his hand under the laptop and tilted the bottom up. There was a registration sticker there.

> The computer doesn't
> accept my security key. It's
> laptop 88836621.

We should sign it with a name.

> The computer doesn't
> accept my security key. It's
> laptop 88836621. /Egor

What do you mean doesn't
accept?

> I get an error message.

What does it say? And
where are you?

"Go aggro. That's what people do," Jitterbug said. "And keep it short. I don't trust the translation."

> **Do you want me to type the whole error message?**
>
> **Is this support or what?**
>
> **You don't have to be a dick.**
>
> **Sigh. I see 88836621 in Dock Control. I'll come down.**

"What do we do when he gets here?" West asked.

"I don't know. Knock him unconscious is what they do in the movies."

"Oh, man."

They searched the room for something club-like. West was getting nauseous at the thought of beating down a stranger. A stranger who'd done nothing wrong. They had to have a better plan than this.

•

There was a knock on the door. "Egor?" a muffled voice said on the other side.

West and Jitterbug moved to each side of the door, flush against the wall.

"Egor?" A little louder.

"Da," Jitterbug said.

An electronic blip, buzz from the lock, and the handle was pushed down.

West swiveled to face the person entering. He managed to recognize a woman's face before bending down, still in his swinging motion, and push the H autoinjector device into her thigh. Jitterbug must have successfully covered her mouth because the scream that eventually came was severely dampened.

They got her down on the floor and half under the desk.

West saw fear of death in the woman's eyes. "Don't worry, you won't die," he said with guilt. By and by, she dozed off in his arms.

"I feel like shit," he said to Jitterbug.

"Pray that we won't have to use our guns."

Jitterbug got the woman's badge and key ring. There was no computer key on the ring.

West checked around her neck and found a ring necklace in silver. He pulled it out and revealed a minute OmniPort key, an inch long and just a millimeter thick. It was warm from her body.

He took the necklace off and inserted the key into the laptop. It displayed the symbol of a fingerprint. He moved the laptop close to the woman's hands and put her index finger on the flat, protruding part of the OmniPort key.

The laptop unlocked.

With the help of Tile translation, he changed the system language to English. Then he went into security settings and changed "Require authentication immediately after sleep" to "Never." He was required to use the woman's index finger again to confirm.

"There we go. We have admin access for as long as the batteries hold in this thing."

West for the first time looked at what the laptop was running. There was an active window with what looked like a bespoke piece of Russian software. It featured a vectorized image with small circles in a seemingly random pattern.

He saw Jitterbug slide the woman to the corner by a file cabinet, find a blanket to cover her in, and move a free-standing coat rack to obscure her somewhat. His eyes went back to the computer screen.

The arrangement of the vector circles reminded him of something. *Weird.*

The English system setting didn't affect this application, so West used his Tile to translate what the user interface said. Just command words and obscure labels.

Jitterbug hunched over to see what he was doing. "Have you got a lead on Kiss's cell?"

"Sorry, I got distracted by this app."

"What is it?"

"I don't know. Something about vessels."

"Vessels won't get us to Kiss. What else?"

West shifted to checking what files and applications the computer had. "Network topology" and "Network layout" stood out. He opened the latter.

"Whoa." Some of the English translations for what he was looking at were less than perfect, but this was workable. "It's a freakin' 3D map of Ice Dolphin prison, with all the networking equipment."

CHAPTER 29

White House: Burning Chains

President Sanchez was in a pissy mood. The *Wall Street Journal* had pinned the current budget gridlock in Congress on "her inability to strike deals." Her press secretary had pointed out that it's Congress's job to agree on a budget, not the president's, but the article said what it said.

General Purnell arrived so late to the meeting room that he was not fully seated when the clock struck.

"I know there's a saying in the military, General," the president said sourly. "If you're less than five minutes early, you're late."

"I'm sorry for being late, ma'am."

"Am I right in that you have nothing new to report on the cables in the Arctic?"

"We will get back to you on that."

"You have nothing new to report." She turned to Director Lewis. "An update on critical infrastructure, please."

Mack Lewis looked content with how the meeting had started and cleared his throat. "We have confirmation of four different zero-day exploit chains used against healthcare and water systems in Wisconsin, Utah, and Florida."

"So you're saying the transatlantic outage did not directly cause the failure of these systems?"

"Correct, ma'am."

"How close in time were these hacks to the outage?"

"Minutes. The subsea cables didn't all go out at once, so finer granularity than that makes little sense."

Sanchez turned to her security advisor, Alec Ore, for a second opinion. "Coordinated or not, you think?"

"Our cyber forces didn't know about these zero days, right?" He looked at Lewis for confirmation.

"Correct. They are foreign. And Naima has pointed out healthcare and water supply as soft spots. We have never before seen this level of attack against US infrastructure. Someone burned four chains, but the impact was limited because we shut things down according to protocol."

"So?" Sanchez was still fishing for something from Ore. "Tell me what you're thinking."

He shared his thoughts, in a low voice at first. "The people affected in Wisconsin, Utah, and Florida care a lot, of course, but addressing those issues hasn't even required federal resources. They all have their own contracts with CIPIC. It looks like a failed attack to me, given the cost of those zero days."

He hesitated and looked at both Purnell and Lewis, neither of which offered anything but silence. Somewhat more forcefully, he gave the president what she wanted. "I think what happened to the subsea cables might have triggered an automated attack of some sort. Something was meant to strike automatically given certain conditions. Dominoes were set in motion. Just look at our own semiautomated response."

Sanchez gave Mack Lewis a quick, meaningful look before following up with Ore. "Are you describing a booby-trapped internet?"

Alec tilted his head from side to side and turned to Lewis as if to see if he was completely out of line. A blank, stern face looked back at him.

The president let some time pass. "Lewis, aren't you forgetting about one more piece of infrastructure failing?"

"I didn't know you were ready to move on. Yes, solar. We did not expect softness in this sector, given the intense scrutiny of our power supply. But one particular brand of Chinese solar panels had a phone home proxy in Europe and flaked out when they didn't get a response over multiple hours. We believe the proxy jump was set up to obscure the connection to China. This *is* a case of remote control over American electrical power."

"How did they connect?"

"Cellular."

"I thought we check for that?"

"On new equipment, yes. These were older."

Sanchez pressed her lips into a thin line. Elbows on her armrests, she let her fingertips touch. "I want to know the origins of these zero-day exploits, Lewis. Attribution—countries and programmers. Make sure states check older solar panels as well as new ones. As for subsea cables, Purnell, and the Greenland connection, it is dissatisfying that we haven't gotten to the bottom of it. Pun *not* intended."

CHAPTER 30

Attire

"We can't look like this. I think you fit her clothes the best," West said with a nod to the woman they had just injected.

"Aw, shucks! I just tucked her away."

West pointed to a spot on the computer map two corridors away. "That's a storage room where you dump dirty laundry and get fresh uniforms, if the translation is correct. One trip there and we'll have a chance of blending in, at least at a distance."

"How many Black guys do you think they have employed here? I'll stand out on camera. You get her clothes on and I'll try to see if there's a way to disable the cameras with her account. She's admin, after all."

West looked at the woman in the corner. "Okay."

He got into the woman's beige uniform and stood up out of sight from the window to the dock. The fabric stretched over his shoulders and the groin seam dug in between his buttocks. His right hand checked all the woman's gear—key ring, badge, and ring necklace with computer key. The rest he'd have to leave behind for now.

"I need to hold something in my hands. That's what Kiss always said. Or says. You should carry something like a banana or a coffee mug to look like you belong."

"I have an apple in my backpack."

"Perfect."

West exited the control room, apple in hand.

The corridor walls were rough concrete painted in two colors— dark gray the first five feet and the rest light gray to the ceiling—like a steel sky above a dark waterline. Steel pipes ran exposed.

A quick glance to the right, then to the left where he was headed.

He took a photo of the room label outside the control room and started walking. As he approached the T-fork ahead, he heard someone coming from the right.

He took a big, juicy bite of the apple. An empty plastic cart on wheels came into view, followed by a rolling robot pushing it.

The bot said something, sounding like a greeting. West chewed demonstrably and pretended to check his wristwatch to turn his face away from the machine.

He got to the storage room door. It was made of steel and painted in brownish gray. By now he had noticed that everything in these corridors followed straight lines, with no arches or tapered bends.

Seconds later, he had found the right key on the ring and entered.

Ceiling lights came to life, blinking a few times before settling. Folded beige uniforms and insulated raincoats lay stacked on the first row of shelves. The fabric of these clothes felt worn. On shelves behind it lay extremely thick winter clothes. High up, he found stacks of rib-knit, three-hole balaclavas. The innermost bottom shelf had pitch-black uniforms with white armbands. The collar labels read Д-6.

He picked out two beige uniforms that would fit him and Jitterbug. Remembering Jitterbug's worries about standing out on camera, he also took two balaclavas.

On the other side of the room there were two large, round, and sturdy buckets and a stack of cardboard looking like flattened moving boxes. He walked over.

The cardboard sheets had boot prints all over them.

The left bucket featured black rubber batons like short baseball bats. He picked one up and noticed that it was telescopic, and the top of it had an inch-wide groove with two round depressions along the bottom.

White square gadgets filled the other bucket. He picked one up. It was heavy and dense. One side had rounded brass knobs which you could push into the thing and they popped back when you removed your finger. The other side had a slim, wedge-like plastic cap. He removed it with a crack and revealed two thin metal spikes.

He turned to the closest shelf and let the two spikes touch a piece of metal. A violent bolt and flash stunned him.

Senses regained, he tried sliding the white gadget into the groove of one of the clubs. It locked in with a click.

CHAPTER 31

Seeing Is Believing

Back in the control room, West showed Jitterbug the two clubs and the dozen or so gadgets he'd taken. "They're stun modules you fit on top. I tested one." He gave Jitterbug the spent one with the spikes exposed. "Just look at the burns in the plastic."

"This is a violent place," Jitterbug said. "Do you know how it works?" His eyes were tracing the sides of the gadget's housing.

"We can tinker with it when we're out of here. Any news on the cameras?"

Jitterbug returned to the laptop on the floor under the desk. "Some. I found the system, but I can't silently turn any of it off. Or, she can't." He glanced at the sedated woman in the corner.

"How so?"

"She has a lot of powers. I mean, terminal access to the server is pretty cool. But I got a warning when I tried changing the config of the camera outside our door. It said that the lieutenant on duty would be notified.

"Show me the system."

The surveillance setup was AI-based, with pattern recognition in all camera feeds in real time. A grid of relevant feeds showed anything that needed attention.

West was transfixed. The grid featured scenes with human movement in them. Frames with only staff in them were toned down compared to the ones with inmates, which had red frame borders.

One feed showed two guards unlocking a metal door. On the inside, a second security layer with double cage doors. The feed got a red border as soon as the AI detected the two prisoners on the inside. Or rather, when it detected the prisoners' horizontally striped black-and-white-uniforms. It looked like two women with a light swell of breasts on their chests and more hair than the few male prisoners he'd seen.

The guards stopped outside the outer cage door. Both women on the inside put black covers over their own heads, moved their hands to their backs, and backed up to something along the left wall in their cell. Shortly thereafter, they turned their backs to the guards, and the feed blinked a green outline of handcuffs around the women's wrists. The women were leaning forward so far that the cuffed hands resting in their lumbar regions became the highest point of their bodies.

Then the guards unlocked the two cage doors and led the prisoners out in their bent-over position, perhaps for their daily exercise.

West tasted bile in his mouth. He knew what prison life was like. He knew what years upon years of strict, humiliating routines meant. And he knew the importance of getting any kind of physical exercise, not just for the sake of your deteriorating body but for your deteriorating mind.

Jitterbug leaned his forehead against West's.

West looked at the floor.

"I understand," Jitterbug said. "I can't imagine what it's like. But I understand why you absolutely need to get her out." He leaned back again.

West gave him a nod of acceptance.

The two women plus the guards left the field of view of the camera and showed up on another feed, entering the hallway.

"I was thinking of the camera AI," Jitterbug said. "You think we can mess with that instead?"

CHAPTER 32

Up to Date

The automatic detection of staff and inmates was likely based on machine learning. Thousands and thousands of images of what the two starkly different uniforms looked like had been fed into training software. And the training had resulted in a statistical model that could identify such uniforms in a microsecond.

"How to hack it?" West asked, moving his eyes from side to side as he thought about the problem.

"I guess replace the model," Jitterbug speculated.

"Yeah, I thought about that, but replace with what? We can't break the whole thing. We need to be subtle."

West traversed the files used by the surveillance system. He eventually found what he was looking for—the model with its feature vectors. It was huge and complex. There was no way for them to understand the statistical intricacies that made it work.

"You know support-vector machines were a Soviet invention, right?" Jitterbug said while watching West scroll through the model file.

"Did not."

"In the sixties, I believe. Two Russian researchers pioneered the whole statistical learning field. I love pointing that out to AI tech bros."

"That's funny."

West scanned the files for another minute, then closed his eyes. "We won't figure this out right now. We need something much quicker."

"Let's see what software the camera feed and AI is using."

They started checking what the server was running and came across something interesting.

```
Astra Linux Special Edition (Smolensk),
version 2.1
This computer needs a restart to finish
installing updates.
```

West looked at Jitterbug and saw his friend smile.

"Let's decide exactly where we want to go on the map, then trigger the update."

•

The dock section was a small extension downward and they'd not only have to go four floors up but also across to the east side of the complex to get to the women prisoners' section.

The best route there, unfortunately, passed the guard quarters and canteen. There was even what looked like a small movie theater for the staff.

The second-best route would be through the men prisoners' sections two and three.

Finally, the outside route—the guard-walks along the perimeter. The outside temperature should be above freezing this time of year, but West recalled Åse talking about rain mixed with snow.

"How much time do you think the update would give us?" Jitterbug asked.

"Install and reboot, maybe thirty minutes. Could take less. We'll get the machine's estimate as soon as we tell it to start."

"A system update out of the blue will raise suspicion. They have to have better processes than that."

"We can't wait for a scheduled maintenance window."

"That's not what I'm saying. But that update has been delayed for a reason. We'd need to notify someone or get permission. Otherwise, they'll get on high alert."

He was right. But they had no idea of whom to tell or ask for permission.

"Check the chat history," Jitterbug said. "They've done this before."

West looked at Jitterbug and nodded slowly. "Nice."

His Tile suggested **системное обновление** for "system update." There was a search hit from four months ago where the woman in the corner had told the "Panopticon" channel she needed to run an update. West read through the translated back and forth to get some context. Someone, possibly a superior, had said she should run the update during the "hour of the wolf." She hadn't known that reference and received a link to an old Ingmar Bergman movie. Apparently, the hour of the wolf was just before dawn, when most births and deaths occur.

"I doubt we'll be able to have a conversation in Russian on classic movies," Jitterbug said. "Let's go with 'Security update. Urgent.' Send that and start the update immediately. Then we take the outer route. No one wants to talk out in the cold."

West was just about to hit return and send the message "**Обновление безопасности. Срочный,**" when the next step played out in his head. "No, man. We have to keep this hack for later. It's the only ace we have and we need it when getting Kiss out. That's the critical part. You and I will have to get to her with the surveillance system running."

CHAPTER 33

White House: Return of the Sub

Transcribing record #682880040-POTUS

Sanchez > The wrap-up of the SMITH investigation
is bothering me.

Naima > You mean the current leg?

Sanchez > Yes, which is the last leg, I presume.

Naima > The return of Dolphin II is the last leg.

Sanchez > I have questions about that too. But
this Ice Dolphin Prison business.

Naima > It is an arduous and risky operation,
but also a chance of understanding the authentication scheme. We are running up against the
deadline when Dolphin II is scheduled to return
from its silent mission.

Sanchez > Do we expect our people to get out?

Naima > From Ice Dolphin?

Sanchez > Yes, of course.

Naima > Their chances of success are, shall I say, non-negligible, if they make it quick. I don't know if anything else was communicated to Major Haugen.

Sanchez > Tell me about Haugen.

Naima > Major Åse Haugen, Special Operations Commando Jegertroppen, senior investigator within NATO. She's been helping Swedish intelligence while getting training on cyber operations. 31 years old.

Sanchez > Why did we need humans on board at all?

Naima > Since the Russian authentication scheme has eluded us so far, we decided a human with both cyber and military skills would be our best last shot at figuring it out.

Sanchez > Did you suggest that shot?

Naima > No, that was the officer in charge of the SMITH investigation. But once the new premise was settled, I drafted the instructions on what to look for.

Sanchez > I guess the Russian Dolphin II crew is still held captive.

Naima > That's right. We need them for the return.

Sanchez > That's the other part I'm not clear on. I mean, even if we've told them nothing, which I assume is the case, they still know someone has been in possession of Dolphin II and will tell their superiors as soon as they get back. Russians can add one and one.

Naima > My plan means they won't talk.

Sanchez > Enlighten me.

Naima > We'll sink Dolphin II close to the Russian dock as she returns.

Sanchez > With the crew on board?

Naima > Yes.

Sanchez > Sick is what it is. We need better plans.

Naima > I'm sorry. I'll do better next time.

Chapter 34

Ghost Movement

Instead of turning the cameras off through the system update, West and Jitterbug used the camera feeds on the laptop to time their walks through corridors and not run into anyone or one of the bots. As they refined their timing, they noticed that there was a four-second delay between reality and the feed. That meant you had to have a margin and keep track of what was going on in adjacent spaces.

One building segment at a time, they climbed up toward the fourth floor. The women's section was on the other side, but West sensed he was getting closer to Kiss.

"What just happened to where we came from?" Jitterbug uttered. He pointed at a gray box in the camera grid where there had been a feed of the corridor they had just left.

They froze and listened. They could hear voices and rubber soles moving.

West rushed forward and opened a door to the right. Fluorescent lights turned on automatically, blipping and buzzing. It was a small kitchen with an array of microwaves and a humming vending machine. Behind the machine's glass front, there were baked mini pies and soft drinks.

Jitterbug closed the door and they stared at the video feed of the corridors on the laptop. They heard at least two people enter from where they had come themselves. But before the four-second delay was up, the camera feed from the corridor just outside the kitchen turned gray.

The footsteps on the other side of the door got closer. No conversation, just the steady beat of decisive walking.

West stopped breathing. His hand found the hilt of his knife. Jitterbug didn't move.

The two people passed just outside their door, mere inches away.

The sound faded and West exhaled with a flutter. Jitterbug looked terrified in his balaclava.

"That was close," West said. "How did they disable the cameras?"

"Like ghosts." Jitterbug thought for a few seconds. "Maybe the system detects them and disables the feed automatically?"

"Why would they want that?"

"Maybe some defense-in-depth thing. We're living proof the surveillance system can be used *against* the staff. They probably have that in their threat model."

The feed outside Jitterbug and West's door came alive again, with no one present.

After an agreed upon wait of a full minute, they left the kitchenette, got to the stairs, and made their ascent to the fourth floor.

The concrete stairs continued up to one of the diamond-shaped tower rooms. West recalled the volumetric shape as an octahedron. Such guard towers were placed in every corner of the outer perimeter. They featured windows angled down, facing the prison structure on the inside as well as the Arctic wasteland on the outside. The only way to access the guard-walk was through one of those towers.

The camera feed showed a bearded guard staffing the tower above, fiddling with a Tile and not looking out the window much.

"He will not let us pass through silently. He'll probably note if we just get close to the door," West whispered.

"We chose the outer route to not have to talk to anyone, so we're not talking to this guy either," Jitterbug replied.

"Can we send him a message or something? To tell him to leave?" West suggested.

Jitterbug grimaced. "Issuing commands feels risky. Can we make him *want* to leave?"

"Some kind of inconvenience?"

"Or lure."

"Look, he's talking into the mic." West pointed at the camera feed, then looked up the stairs and put his index finger across his lips. He could barely hear that there was a human voice speaking behind the door above.

Something moved in the corner of West's eye. He looked, and it was Jitterbug holding one of his earpieces.

"Let's hope it doesn't break," Jitterbug said as he threw the little gadget up on the platform. It landed with a cracking sound and rattled briefly before coming to rest, never hitting the door as far as they could tell. Jitterbug triggered a live translation of what the earpiece's microphone picked up.

> ... need to eat. It's 12:30 already.

> You know I'm on a strict schedule with my food. Stop fucking around. When will they deliver?

> Because I want to look better than you. Muscles don't grow from air.

> Fuck you too.

"Lure. The vending machine," Jitterbug said.

Chapter 35

The Vending Machine

West felt trapped in the small kitchen. Sure, they were much more likely to be intercepted out there in the corridors, but this was a confined space, and if someone entered, there would be nowhere to go. They would have to fight.

He checked his knife and gun. Both sat snuggly on top of his prison staff uniform. He was worried that these NATO weapons would stand out.

"How hard can it be to get food out of this thing?" Jitterbug got on his knees and bent his head all the way to the floor to look under the vending machine. "Cables fitted by the base. That's no good."

The machine didn't have a compartment at the bottom where products fell down. Supposedly, the door unlocked and the right things were made available after you paid. There seemed to be both sweet and savory pies. West felt the sides of the machine's front door and the hinges.

"Tubular lock. A nuisance to pick," Jitterbug said.

West spotted the metal lock house and its circular key fitting. He had never picked one of those. Above it was a sticker in Cyrillic with a QR code. "Some kind of app?" he said, nodding at the sticker.

Jitterbug held up his Tile and let it translate the promotional language. "Looks like it. It's called 'Merry Wallet.' Probably our best shot."

Jitterbug scanned the QR code and sat down by the small kitchen table fully focused on his Tile. West hunched over and followed along.

On the screen, he saw Jitterbug install the Merry Wallet app and then trigger his app container explorer to reach into the application's file structure.

Jitterbug searched for databases and got five hits.

```
TileManifest.xml (2 matches)
    <meta-data tile:name="Merry_db_name"
    tile:value="@string/db_name" />

TileMerryConfig.code (1 match)
    String NAME_KEY = "Merry_db_name";

public.xml (1 match)
    <public type="string" name="db_name"
    id="0x7f100822">

Strings.xml (1 match)
    <string name="db_name">merry.db</string>
```

He located the wallet's database file, merry.db, and opened it. It was password protected.

Jitterbug puffed out his cheeks for a moment, then went back into the package's file list and opened TileMerryConfig.code. He found the definition of the NAME_KEY = "Merry_db_name" but also an encryptionKey = getDeviceModel() + "Spassky".

"Ha, they always go security by obscurity."

He stitched together the device model name and "Spassky" to decrypt and open the database. Tens of rows of data appeared.

West spotted it. "UserWallet. Just below the middle."

"Nice," Jitterbug said and expanded that row.

The columns were merry_id, country_code, wallet_currency, and wallet_credit. The country was Russia, the currency ruble, and the credit zero.

"How much is the food?" Jitterbug asked.

West checked the vending machine. "About a thousand a piece."

"No wonder they're switching to Bancor."

West saw Jitterbug tap on the screen and then hold his Tile up for West to see. The Russian interface made little sense to West, but the number 10,000 was there. "Sweet."

Jitterbug nodded. "You know, I was thinking of when we cross to the other side. There's going to be another tower where we have to go through."

"You said it yourself. Who wants to talk when coming in from a grueling shift in the rain?"

"Is it raining?"

"I think so."

"Then we have to get raincoats."

•

West was carrying three hot meat pie packages. He positioned them a couple of steps up toward the guard tower door, then hid behind the corner.

Time passed. West's stomach growled. The pies did smell delicious.

"He's moving!" Jitterbug's voice came in sharp in West's earphone.

West quickly picked up the meat pies and dashed down to the third floor. Jitterbug held the kitchenette door open with one hand and the laptop in the other. West landed the meat pies on the small table and on his way out he noticed the inner door handle missing from Jitterbug's dismantling of it. This door now only opened from the outside.

The two of them moved to the adjacent corridor. On the laptop screen, they saw the camera feed with the hungry guard looking around as he got down the staircase. He headed into the kitchen. The door closed behind him and he would have no means of getting out.

Jitterbug and West's long black raincoats rustled and squeaked as they got them on. They were going to see the outside of Russia's legendary nuclear testing grounds. West wondered how many Americans had ever set foot there.

CHAPTER 36

Communiqué

Joint Press Statement by

• Wang Qiang, Commissioner General of the Ministry of Public Security of the People's Republic of China

• Elvira Kenin, Head of Ministry of Digital Development, Communications and Mass Media of the Russian Federation

For decades, America has berated other countries' strive for cyber-sovereignty and personal communications free of foreign interference. They've touted "a global internet with no borders or other national boundaries." However, their actions during the recent transatlantic internet disruption revealed the true motives behind the policy they try to impose on the rest of us.

Without prior warnings, without transparency, and without care for the international community, the US government deployed broad interception of internet traffic to serve their own needs of control. Americans got their news altered and censored in a devious and covert way.

If you open a window, both fresh air and flies will enter your home. That's why wise people put up mosquito nets, and wise countries control what enters their digital domain.

We demand that the US government stop peddling lies about the internet, that they disclose their national firewall policy (at least to American citizens!), and that they accept that other countries too want to live in sovereignty, not fealty.

CHAPTER 37

The Expanse

The barren, rugged, and windswept expanse of Novaya Zemlya was breathtaking. West had to stop on the parapet to take it in. The rain and air were crisp and light, with a hint of brine and earth.

Into the misty distance were only gray, pale hills covered in stones and pebbles, spotted with rust-colored lichen and glazed in water. It was beautiful, raw Earth.

They walked the wet concrete with their shoulders raised, heads hunched over. Raindrops hit the raincoats with popping sounds. Jitterbug held the laptop on the inside against his belly. West kept his NATO knife at the ready in his right pocket. Their balaclavas became cold and wet on their faces.

As they approached the diamond-shaped guard tower on the other side, West saw a large squeegee make a pass over the downward-facing windows. There was at least one guard on the inside.

West entered first, trying to block the guard from seeing Jitterbug properly.

The man on duty glanced at them. West couldn't help but meet his eyes and instinctively nod a hello. He got a nod back.

Before West knew it, they were in the staircase leading down from the tower. Not a single word had been exchanged.

His heart was racing. He pulled his hand out and saw the imprint of the knife handle's nobs and dimples in it.

They descended one set of stairs and turned the corner before Jitterbug got the laptop back out.

Two corridors away, ghost guards were moving, or rather, the camera feed was gray.

"I want to know how they do that," West said.

"We don't have time for extras."

"It's not an extra. Maybe they're carrying some radio device that we can sample the signal from and replicate."

They stood looking at each other for a while.

Jitterbug's pallid expression broke up just a bit. "Dash it. You're right," he said. "They'll be in the corridor behind that door in a minute. If we can hide a Tile out there, it can scan a wide band of frequencies."

"We should record video too, in case visual helps."

"But where do we put it?"

West closed his eyes and envisioned being one of the ghosts. He entered the corridor. The lights above wouldn't cover a Tile and the light that close would wash out the camera image anyway. He turned his head to the doors on the side. If one were ajar, it would catch his attention. Something at the other end would be out of his vision, but only to begin with. He kept walking in his mind until he exited the corridor. He never looked back.

Never looked back. That's it.

"We put it to the side where they enter," West said as he opened his eyes. "People rarely look back."

Jitterbug enabled radio scanning on his Tile and started recording wide-angle video.

West received the device and got out into the corridor. He leaned the Tile against the wall on the hinge side of the door where the ghost guards would enter. Mere seconds after he got back into the stairwell, the laptop's camera feed of the corridor went gray.

CHAPTER 38

Black Ops

It turned out to be simple for the camera system to know when to turn off. Not in a way that made West feel stupid, but it made sense once you saw it.

It was all about the pitch-black uniforms with white armbands West had seen in the storage room. It had to be. On Jitterbug's Tile video recording, two men in those exact uniforms entered and walked intently at a medium pace through the corridor. They carried heavy gear, both firearms and blunt weapons. Nothing stood out on radio frequencies.

West told Jitterbug where he had seen the uniforms before.

"Some kind of black ops thing?" Jitterbug half asked, half speculated.

"Maybe they don't want an adversary with access to the feed to learn about the number of guards moving or their armament."

"Easy to test."

"Mhmm. Assuming it works, you know what I'm thinking? I saw such uniforms in the storage room and there's another such room close by. We should dress like that when we release Kiss."

"Make the breakout disappear."

"In a way that won't raise suspicion."

"I like it."

•

West got them black uniforms from the nearby storage room within ten minutes. He even fetched the matching baton shockers. There was something ominous about these pieces of attire. Fascist-like.

They had Д-6 on their collars, so that had to be a brand thing rather than a numbering system.

"You got one extra?" Jitterbug asked as they got changed.

"Kiss."

West tested entering the corridor. The camera feed went gray immediately.

This was the last stretch before he would see his lost love again. He removed Kiss's ring from his finger and put it in a zippered pocket, just as he had planned.

Her cell was one floor below theirs. They kept their damp balaclavas on but left their raincoats behind and headed down the stairs.

This was the first cell block they'd entered. The landing corridor had no cells but a directory of numbers by the doors in each direction. They headed right.

Things changed drastically as they entered the space behind the door. Instead of walls along the sides, there were white metal bars, two inches thick. The vertical ones were round and the horizontal ones flat. A few feet in was another wall of bars, and beyond that, cells with beds, a basin, small lockers, and women clad in light-blue overalls.

Their entry was noticed and several women started wincing. A few whimpered.

West wanted to shout out that they weren't here to hurt anyone, but he kept his mouth shut. Jitterbug tugged his jacket and they continued forward.

The sounds of human fear followed them as they progressed and became visible to more prisoners. West counted as the cell numbers on his left increased: 32, 34, 36 ...

They entered another section starting with 38 and West could now see cell 42 through the many bars. He drew a breath.

Again the women sprang into their beds and pushed against the back walls, some with animal-like, gut-wrenching sounds.

West slowed down as he approached 42. He stared into the cell. One of the women had the right features to be Kiss, but she was thin and fragile. Her copper-colored asymmetric hair was instead an anonymizing millimeter-short crew cut. She did nothing that indicated that she knew who West and Jitterbug were. Same pale, devastated look as the others, hugging her legs in her bed like a child.

Jitterbug reached cell door 42 first and started digging for something under his uniform. Kiss and her cellmate cried out loud when they understood that the black guards had come for them.

West felt Jitterbug covering his mouth before he could say something.

Jitterbug found his lock picks and got to work.

West's face tightened and tears formed. There was joy over seeing Kiss, desperation over being perceived as a menace, and the ever-present knowledge that they were far, far behind enemy lines with no solid plan for how to get out.

The lock clicked and they entered the dead zone between the two walls of bars. The women in adjacent cells went quiet and looked away. Kiss and her cellmate got down from their beds, put black head covers on, and backed up against the bars facing West and Jitterbug. They put their hands behind their backs and pushed them through two horizontal slots. They were waiting to get handcuffed.

West couldn't hold back. They didn't have any handcuffs anyway, so the women would soon understand that something was off. He pushed his face against the cold bars as close as he could to Kiss who was bent forward.

"It's me, West. We've come to save you."

He saw the faintest of reaction in the form of head movement under the cloth. Then nothing.

"It's me," he repeated.

Jitterbug shoved his elbow in West's side and whispered with anger. "You should know better after all your years in prison. Trust no one—that's the code. How many tricks do you think the guards have pulled on these women, huh?"

Seconds felt like minutes while Jitterbug picked the second lock.

West was completely unprepared for the literal kick in his gut that came as soon as they opened the cell gate. He fell winded to the concrete floor.

The next thing he knew he was looking into Kiss's eyes. She had not only ripped off her own hood but his balaclava, and stared at him in utter disbelief.

"What the fuck are you doing here?" she threw at him.

He managed to get half a lung worth of air in and uttered, "You emailed. We came to get you out."

Kiss was bewildered. Her cellmate towered over West, no head bag, fists at the ready. Jitterbug was behind him, probably ready too.

Then came the kiss. A long, intense kiss, more out of hunger and emotional release than passion. Kiss jerked back. "Fuck, West."

She started sobbing.

CHAPTER 39

Extraction

The cellmate receded, perplexed over the situation.

Jitterbug had the presence to hand the woman his knife. She considered it, then shook her head, adding a nod to the camera.

West got his balaclava back on and Kiss bent over with her hands behind her back as if she had been handcuffed. West went first, then Kiss in her head cover, and last Jitterbug, who made some rattling sounds with his lock picks against the lock to make it seem like they locked up the woman left behind. All the women in neighboring cells duly looked away until they heard the sounds of the second lock.

West wanted to look back at the hunched-over Kiss several times as they left the three cell blocks, but he thought of the Greek myth of Orpheus fetching Eurydice back from Hades under the promise to never look back until they were out. Orpheus looked back and lost his Eurydice forever.

They got back to the stairwell and he could finally turn around.

He squatted by the bent-over Kiss. "You can get up now," he said without whispering.

"You sure?"

"No cameras here. We have access to the camera system, so we know."

Kiss got upright, pulled her hood, and looked at West before giving him a tight hug. "I love you," she said in a thin voice. She then turned to Jitterbug and gave him a hug too.

West heard Jitterbug speak in a low voice. "I'm sorry I doubted any of this, my friend. Seeing you like this. I almost talked West out of it. I didn't see what was clear. Please forgive me."

She sniffled and sat down against the wall and covered her eyes with her hands. "This is a lot. Why did you come for me?"

"You emailed and asked me to. Of course I'd come," West replied and got down on one knee to be able to lay an arm around her.

She dried her face and looked at him. "I didn't ask you to come here. We'll never get out."

West pulled out his Tile and asked it for the email from Kiss. He showed it to her.

```
I know it's stupid to email you but I
have no choice. It's me, Kizz. Three
words to prove it: Juneau, brothel,
dependable. I'm in a Russian prison,
cell 42. Don't know where but it's cold.
They'll punish me for sending you this.
Please help! Love you!
```

"I didn't write this," she said. The beginning of her phrase was firm but the tail faded.

"Those three words. This must be your email," West said in a hurried voice.

"I wrote those words but then something else. There was a typo in the first sentence that's not there. I told you to find our son, not come here."

"What?" West asked with his mouth falling open.

"Why would I want you in this hellhole? What are the chances of getting out?"

"I meant what son?"

"Our son. He was born here in prison and they took him away from me."

West couldn't believe what he heard. He tipped forward to embrace Kiss, bursting. He was a father. A father with a lost son.

"We'll find him," he said with a tremor. "Together."

"Congrats on the parenthood, both of you," Jitterbug said from above them, "and as much as I hate looking for people in Russia, I agree we must find your son. But aren't we missing something? If someone altered Kiss's email, that someone wanted you here, West."

CHAPTER 40

White House: The Proxy Situation

"Madam President, we have a plan," General Purnell commenced. He sounded reasonably confident.

"Talk to me," Sanchez replied. "And could someone please get me another mug of coffee? I didn't sleep well."

In fact, she hadn't slept well in a year. If there was one thing she had never wanted to inherit from her mother, it was fragmented sleep. But the pressure of being the most powerful person on Earth was causing exactly that.

"You requested the following," Purnell continued. "A proposal for how to avoid US news not reaching the world if subsea cables are taken out again, a report on who and what was hacked because of the delayed security update for Tiles, an analysis of the consequences of the world knowing about our proxy tactic, a check-in on solar panels, and finally intel on the Greenland internet connection."

"Not intel. I want the complete picture."

"Noted."

"And you forgot one thing."

"I'm sorry." The general consulted his Tile. "Oh, yes, the exploits that hit critical infrastructure."

"Mhmm."

An aide landed a steaming mug of black coffee in front of the president. "Thank you," she said and took as large of a sip as she could, given the temperature of the liquid.

"I'll let Lewis start with our proposal for US news contingency," Purnell said.

Mack Lewis put his notepad down and stood up. The aide running the big screens pulled up a global map with subsea cables at his request. "We have talked to our allies," he said, "and at least Five Eyes have agreed on receiving hourly updates of key US websites over the DoDIN network during times when we cannot rely on public internet connections."

Five Eyes was almost a century-old intelligence alliance between Australia, Canada, New Zealand, the UK, and the US.

He made the map dim all but a few lines crossing the oceans. From the US East Coast, a sole line went to the UK. From the US West Coast, a line went through Hawaii down to New Zealand and Australia.

"As you can tell from the map," Lewis continued, "this puts immense pressure on the UK, so we are working hard on convincing Norway and Denmark to be part of this. Denmark is especially important as members of the EU. Australia would cover Asia, which sounds like a lot, but US websites don't get that much traffic from there."

"Got it. But we just revealed our proxy solution, so simply doing more of the same sounds like a weak plan," the president said.

"You're skipping ahead, but that subject is mine too, so let's cover it here and now."

General Purnell was about to object, but Sanchez wouldn't have it. "Seems important," she said and gave Lewis the go-ahead.

"The fact that Americans were served somewhat stale versions of international news sites is now well known. Tech media has written about it and mainstream media has spread fear, uncertainty, and doubt. 'The US government can intercept and censor international news' seems to be the narrative forming."

"I've read some of it," the president said. "Some went further and suggested that we can even alter or censor on a personal level, cutting out key information for specific parts of the population."

"That theory has indeed been floated. We read the same sources, ma'am. I think the best way ..."

"You or Naima thinking?"

"I always consult Naima, so both."

"Noted. You were saying?"

"I think the best way of addressing these concerns is to state that uncensored, unaltered international news is key to our liberal democracy and that our track record shows we did not censor and did not alter. The proxying we did is evidence that we had anticipated a disruption like this and did what we could to ensure information flow to the public, including to markets. We should then propose a next step where international news sites can digitally sign their articles combined with strong policies against ever sharing the signing keys outside their own orgs. That way, if the news is served by a proxy, the client can check the integrity and freshness of the article. I have more technical details if you're interested, ma'am."

"I'll stop you if I don't follow."

"We will establish signed timestamps as an international service. Such timestamps will be included in the digital signature to prove when the article was published or last changed. And a mandatory delay will be put in place so that changes can't be made in the moment when a certain person wants to read the news."

The president signaled for a pause. "Let me see." She thought out loud. "You're saying news organizations, at least major ones, will fetch a trustworthy timestamp and put it inside a digital signature of whatever they publish. Then Tiles will enforce something, or show users something, based on those signatures? I mean, Jane Doe has to be able to tell if she's being served tampered news."

"We're not done there. It is indeed a challenge on how to help people understand if the news on their screen is from the genuine source or not."

"That could be the hardest part, so don't put it off. But I like where you're going with the timestamp. The one remaining issue would then be *withholding* news or censoring whole articles." The president turned to her national security advisor. "Please start thinking of how to tell the public about this in a way that doesn't fly over their heads or freak people out."

He nodded and scribbled in his notepad.

"One more thing, Lewis," Sanchez said. "Anything on our adversaries' bombastic press releases?"

"We've detected Grigiori behind some of it, but Elvira Kenin, the Russian all-things-digital minister, has apparently taken lead on Russia's and China's joint communication."

"Expected. That's her turf. And they're not entirely wrong."

"We're softening the blow by talking about the background with primary news outlets and influencers."

"What's the message?"

"That we've only used the proxy once. We helped foreign news reach our population, and we did not alter any content. China and Russia use theirs every day and censor heavily."

"Only used it once is probably the only nuance that'll stick," the president mused. "Okay, Russia and China are mudslinging. What's *new*?"

"Our sources say both countries have collected samples of our proxied websites to make sure they fully understand our setup with signing keys, root certificates, and routing. We expect the two root certificates we relied on to be blocked in any country under their influence."

"And they expect us to change them."

"Correct. Finally, we've heard that there are Russian investigations into compromising our proxy capabilities and using them to spread false news or provide evidence that the US government is indeed censoring international news."

"Interesting. That is an emerging pattern. Powerful cyber capabilities can be turned against the owner or be used to weaken the support for the owner."

Lewis nodded.

"Hey, let's cover the exploits while we're at it. The general forgot to put it on the agenda, so we might as well do it now."

Purnell did not look happy, but Lewis's message was short. "I'm sorry to say that we have not yet gotten through the primary protection layer of the malware. We will report back to you as soon as we have better information. But the level of obfuscation implicates a nation state adversary."

CHAPTER 41

For the Record

West sat down next to Kiss. The concrete prison wall scratched against the fabric of his uniform. "Who changed your email? Who wanted me here?" he said, eyes wandering about the small space they were in with stairs going up and down.

"This is the worst fucking place on Earth," Kiss replied. "I only sent you an email in a desperate attempt to save our son."

"The email could have been changed by anyone along the network hops from here to your Tile. We all know that," Jitterbug said.

He's right. Email sucks.

West's Tile buzzed. He didn't pull it up.

Jitterbug pulled up his. "Åse says we need to go."

"Who's Åse?" Kiss asked, looking at West.

"She used to be part of Robert's team in Stockholm," he replied. "She helped us hack Pogodina, and she's our way in and out of Ice Dolphin."

"How *did* you get in?"

Jitterbug crouched down to their level and put a hand on each of their shoulders. "We don't have time. Ghost movement toward the dock may look suspicious. Get the security update ..."

"Ghost what?" Kiss interrupted.

"No time. I'll explain later. The security update should buy us time while the cameras are offline," Jitterbug said, handing West the laptop.

Its battery was down to 20%, but the logged-in session was still live.

"Wait," Kiss said. "You're forgetting about our son."

"Is he here?" West asked, almost shouting.

"Of course not. But we can't leave without knowing who took him. They forced me to sign an adoption form. On paper. They covered the lines with the names of the adoptive parents and I need those names if I'm ever to find my boy."

"We can hack our way to that information later," Jitterbug argued.

"You don't understand. That paper was just to cover their asses. They explained that he would be raised as a regular Russian boy with no traces of his real origin, and that I could argue my case if I were ever to be released. It was a deal with one of their employees, a childless woman. For all I know, that paper is all there is."

"We just have a slim chance of getting out as it is," Jitterbug said with eyes wide open in disbelief.

"I'm not leaving without it."

"Don't do this, Kiss," Jitterbug pleaded.

She stood up. "The only reason I'm still alive is that I didn't give up on my son. I can tell you about the torture and abuse I've gone through. I can tell you the price I paid for sending that email. I'm forever thankful you came for me. But you have to leave without me or with me *and* that adoption form."

West looked at Jitterbug. "It's my son too. If Kiss says we need that paper, so be it." He got up too.

Jitterbug closed his eyes solemnly. Seconds passed. They barely heard him as he started to talk. "Lord of all the earth, you hold our fate in Your hands. We are at Your mercy. Guide us as we try to save this child and we will follow Your lead. Amen."

Jitterbug opened his eyes and pointed at West. "*You* ask Åse to wait."

West did.

> We have to do one more
> thing first.

> What thing? We have to get
> out, with or without Kizz.

> We have Kizz.

So? Let's go.

It's something else. I'm onto
something you came here
for.

???

Trust me.

I can maybe stall half an
hour more.

That'll be tight.

I'm not dying in this place.
30 minutes.

West dimmed the Tile's screen.

"You didn't tell me you're onto something," Jitterbug said.

"Åse came to this place with her own agenda. Well, NATO's agenda. At minimum, we can give her the laptop."

"She's had plenty of time to find a laptop."

"Not an unlocked one."

"So you're *not* onto something."

"Those vectorized circles I saw in the app. There's something about them. Just need some time. And I'm starting to think we'll need leverage with Åse."

Jitterbug raised his eyebrows.

West got the 3D map of Ice Dolphin up and turned the screen to Kiss. "Where do you think they store paper records?"

She gazed at the screen. "I had no idea how big this place is." She moved her fingers on the trackpad to navigate. "I guess the best bet has to be what they call Archive."

It was a midsized room in the administrative section of the prison. The lion's den.

"You need to change into a uniform and get a balaclava on."

Kiss glanced at the folded clothes in the corner where West was pointing. "Do you have any idea what those uniforms represent?"

"I don't know Russian maximum security prisons, but I did do fifteen in the US. You've been through hell, I know. Our only chance to sit down and talk about that is to get you out. We'll save the update to the surveillance system for our final exit."

Kiss gave him a stern look, then got her light-blue inmate clothes off and took the black.

West couldn't help watching his girlfriend strip.

She had lost a lot of weight and her thighs were bruised. Those bastards had been beating her. Or worse.

CHAPTER 42

We Belong Here

West shushed before opening the door to the corridor.

The three of them snuck out and started walking. West hesitated opening the next compartmentalizing door. He felt hunted.

Jitterbug gave him an elbow bump. "We've got to look like we belong here, buster. No tiptoeing."

He was right. West straightened his back, rolled his shoulders back, and lifted his chin. He saw Kiss erect her posture too.

"I've only ever walked these corridors bent forward with my hands on my back and blindfolded," she said. "Better bring this sucker out." She unclipped her rubber baton and landed the thick head in her other hand with a thud.

West pushed the handle down and opened. The next segment was empty too. They hurried inside.

Two passways further, West stopped. "Voices." He pointed forward to the door ahead.

"We should be two blocks from the Archive," Kiss replied. "This'll be the entrance to the admin section." She nodded forward.

The voices came closer. West turned around and took a step before getting stopped by Kiss. Her eyes fixed on him through the holes in the balaclava. "No one will stop us. We charge right in. We're Diggers."

"Diggers?"

She pinched her own collar and held up its label. "D-6. Stalin's Diggers. Jit, you got the badge, so you go first."

Jitterbug's eyes widened for a second. Then he got the IT support woman's badge out and jolted toward the door. Kiss followed, as did West.

•

The aura was very different on the other side of the door. The walls were painted and had windows into offices, and personnel wore regular white-collar clothes. There were also women here, something West hadn't expected.

Two men were walking toward them, not far away. They quickly pushed up against one wall each as Jitterbug charged ahead.

West saw in the corner of his eyes how people at their desks turned around to see what was happening. Kiss and Jitterbug plowed on in front of him. He felt the laptop rub against him underneath the uniform as he pushed forward.

Seconds later, they had taken a right turn and the Archive room would be ahead to the left.

West turned around to see if anyone was following them. Two heads craned around the corner to watch them. He turned around further and followed Kiss and Jitterbug backward as he motioned for the spectators to go away. They complied.

CHAPTER 43

Archived

Fluorescent lights unwillingly came to life in the Archive room, revealing four long rows of bookcases packed with binders and file folders. The air smelled of old books and nicotine.

"What are we looking for?" Jitterbug said, panting. He put the laptop down on a table by the left wall.

"Medical records, inmate files, or signed papers like contracts," Kiss said. "Translate the labels." She rolled up her too-long sleeves and started checking file folders while West and Jitterbug used their Tiles to read labels.

"I got a section on health stuff over here," Jitterbug said.

West saw Kiss dash over while he stuck with a section of books that had caught his attention. The translated titles read *Passive Sonar and Sound Propagation, Directional Frequency Analysis, Underwater Acoustic Positioning System*, and *Bottom Contour Navigation*. This had nothing to do with running a prison.

There was also a set of books on counterfeits, preventing forgery with things like watermarks and microprinting, and deceptive insignia of military assets to mislead the enemy.

On the next shelf to the right, he found books, specifications, and reports on the building blocks of the internet. Border Gateway Protocol, Domain Name System, and Transmission Control Protocol. The publications seemed modern and unused. Why would you want this stuff on paper?

He spotted a thick book on the internet Control Message Protocol as his mind wandered back to the recent internet disruption and how the US had proxied European websites.

Everything digital can be altered or made inaccessible. There is no reliable source of information online.

He let his fingertips slide down the spines of the books.

These things can't be manipulated. They can go stale and obsolete, but as long as there's light, you can read them.

His mind wandered further. Written words were precise, whereas memories were fluid. It was probably for the better that memories were fluid.

That's how we forget and forgive.

Kiss had talked about that before—data decay.

"Found it!" Kiss blurted from two rows over.

West popped out of his bubble and found Kiss holding up a single sheet of paper and Jitterbug taking a photo of it with his Tile. Within seconds, they had a translated copy each.

•

ADOPTION PLAN AND AGREEMENT

This Agreement regarding Anatoly ("Child") is made between the following parties: Kate Libby ("Birth Mother"); UNKNOWN ("Birth Father"); Maria Smyslova ("Adoptive Mother"); and Viktor Smyslov ("Adoptive Father").

Each party is entering into this Agreement with the intent to abide by its terms to the extent that this serves the best interests of the Child.

Documents submitted to Birth Parents and Adoptive Parents:

- the child's birth certificate;
- a medical report;
- a statement that adoption is in the child's best interest;
- a statement from the Birth Parents agreeing to the adoption;
- consent from the director of Ice Dolphin Prison, Lt Guard Lavrov.

GUARDIAN FOR CHILD: Adoptive Parents agree to nomi-
nate a guardian in their wills, with the requirement that the
guardian abide by the terms of this Agreement in the event
that both Adoptive Parents die or become incapacitated.

LOCATION: At the time of adoption, Viktor Smyslov and
Maria Smyslova reside in Murmansk.

This Agreement shall become binding upon the date signed
by all parties.

Signature and date:

_____ Birth Father

_____ Birth Mother

_____ Adoptive Father

_____ Adoptive Mother

•

"Anatoly?" West questioned after skimming through the contract.

"I guess that's what the adoptive parents chose," Kiss responded
in a resolute tone. "Maria Smyslova. She has to be the one who
works here, the childless woman. They tried to woo me. That she'd
be a great mother."

"So what name did *you* give him?" West turned to Kiss.

"I wrote that in the email." She turned to him. "But I guess you
didn't get that part. His name is East, of course."

Time stood still for a few seconds. "Wow," West mumbled. He
afforded himself a brief smile as his chest rose.

East, my son, I'm going to find you.

•

Thump-thump-thump! Loud knocks on the door. Someone was
yelling in Russian outside.

The three of them looked at each other, then around the room, searching the walls for an exit that clearly wasn't there.

Kiss grabbed her baton and strode to the door. Jitterbug and West hid behind a bookcase, peeking at the scene.

Kiss opened the door decisively and did a wide, inward motion with her arm. A man stepped in with a surprised look on his face.

Kiss quickly closed the door behind him and shoved the top of her baton in the man's back. His head and torso arced backward as the electric shock spread in his muscles. West saw the man's crotch get wet before he collapsed on the floor.

Kiss looked up at them. "I've seen these used before. We've got about ten minutes. A few more if I can muffle him properly."

"Are you suggesting we take the guy hostage?" Jitterbug asked. "We're sitting ducks in here."

"They shoot any hostage. One of the first things they told me when I arrived. We're going to have to come up with something better. But I doubt they'll follow him in here without permission." She pulled up the man's shoulder strap with a rank mark of one star. "Authority runs deep around here."

Jitterbug strode up to Kiss, squatted, and picked up the man's hand. West moved closer.

The hand was chunky and had a large golden ring.

"Show's yours," Jitterbug said, pulling West's hand to compare. "Won't do. We'll have to go full Brezhnev here."

"Bresh–what?"

"Leonid Brezhnev, Soviet leader during the Cold War. His last year in power he was basically dead, so when he waved to the crowds from a balcony it was someone behind him moving his arm."

Jitterbug got the back of his neck under the incapacitated man's armpit and lifted. West and Kiss helped stabilize the man in an upright position. Jitterbug got his knife out and cut a hole in the man's uniform at the elbow. He then inserted his own arm through the hole, put his hand on the backside of the man's, and waved.

"*Weekend at Bernie's*," West uttered, thinking of the absurd eighties cult movie.

"Let's hope a wave-off clears the hallway." Jitterbug got in position, ready to extend the man's arm. "Open the door, Kiss, but not wide, just enough for the arm. West, sneak your Tile out at floor level and record what's happening out there."

Each one of them did their part and Jitterbug made the man's hand perform three dismissive gestures down the hallway. West's video take showed a handful of people getting mildly shocked and then adhering to the dismissal.

"Is there a men's room close by?" Kiss asked West as they pulled the heavy man away from the door.

"How would I know?"

"Check the map. We can't leave him here. He pissed himself anyway. Might as well put him on the can."

West opened the laptop. Its battery level was at 14%.

"There's something marked 'Lavatory' further down the hall. Left from here."

"Let's go."

They dragged the limp body into the empty hallway and to the left. West kept checking the other way, but no one came.

In through the entrance to the men's room, Kiss opened one of the vacant stalls and they seated the man. He slumped to the side and West balanced him backward so he wouldn't topple.

Jitterbug used the tip of his knife to lock the stall door from the outside.

West felt a Babble app buzz from his Tile.

CHAPTER 44

Get What You Came For

Time's up.

> Just need to make our way
> out.

Sorry, no can do.

> Don't leave without us.

I gave you 30 minutes. I
bamboozled the guys on
duty here based on that
clock. I said I needed to
run a 30 min diagnostic on
the sub.

> Time's up.

West looked up and pointed toward the door out.

They exited the men's room and took a right, away from the admin section. West wanted to rush but held back.

"What's going on?" Kiss whispered.

"Åse. She's leaving us here." He pointed for them to take an exit to a stairwell.

"Great friend you have there."

"How quickly can we get to the docks?" Jitterbug interjected.

"Ten minutes if we are to walk like this and not raise suspicion."

"Can we make her wait ten more minutes?"

"I don't think pleading gets us anything. She may already be leaving."

"So, are you more *onto* something now? Anything?" Jitterbug's voice was a bit too loud for comfort.

West stopped.

Can that be it? Shit.

He gave the laptop to Kiss and fished out his Tile to send Åse a final message.

> I have what you came for.

Silence. Had she already left?

> I have the auth system for
> the sub.
> On the laptop.

Nothing.

> I know how it works. I know
> how they ID Russian subs.

> You've got 5 minutes.

CHAPTER 45

The First Cut Is the Deepest

West posted about the software update in the Panopticon chat as planned. He didn't wait for reactions and clicked through two update confirmation prompts. The camera surveillance system went down for maintenance.

"How much time?" Jitterbug asked.

"Twenty-one minutes."

"That's a lot more than five."

West took the lead with a clear picture of the route in his mind.

The cameras are off, so we can no longer tell where there are people.

•

They had made it to the last corridor in the general Ice Dolphin area when they ended up face-to-face with a lone Russian. Crew cut, broad shoulders. He was carrying a crate of large bottles with both hands.

He instinctively moved to the side, but West could see in the corner of his eye how something changed in the man's look as they passed him.

"Я тебя знаю!"

There was a crashing sound of shattered glass behind West. He turned around.

Jitterbug was on the floor toward the wall with the crate on top of him and shattered glass all around.

The man had his back toward West and was blocking Kiss. She

bolted into him, trying to knock him over, but she didn't have the mass required.

The smell of alcohol reached West as he moved in closer. Jitterbug seemed out.

The Russian punched downward and Kiss landed hard on the floor.

West went for the gun while holding on to the laptop one-handed, chest high.

The man swiveled around. His eyes were wide open and his nostrils flared as he surveilled his work so far. He had incapacitated two of his enemies in just a few seconds.

West fiddled to pull the gun.

The Russian raised his fists and leaned forward to get moving and close the gap.

He lunged forward just as West got the gun out.

The crash of the man's head into West's chest was violent.

The air left West's lungs. He flew backward in an arc. His gun hand shot out backward to curb the impact as his legs and bottom hit the floor. He tried to hold his head up, but once the rest of his body had landed, there was no stopping it from whipping back into the concrete.

He lost consciousness. God knows for how long.

When he opened his eyes, the beastly man towered over him with a familiar gun pointed at his head.

West glanced at his holster. It was empty. On the floor beside him lay a dented laptop, but no gun. There was a ghostly calm over the scene.

West moved his hand to the hilt of his knife.

"Я бы этого не сделал," the man said in a commanding but measured way. It was some kind of warning.

To hell with it. They must not take us.

West thrust against the wall to move his body out of the man's aim and unsheathed his knife.

The gun barrel followed him, and the Russian squeezed the trigger.

An ice-cold bolt ripped through West's chest. His eyes closed and he stopped breathing.

So this was how it would end.

He opened his eyes again, feeling weightless and ephemeral. The man in front of him looked puzzled.

West looked down at his chest but didn't see a gun wound.

The Russian was checking the gun's safety switch. He tried to fire once more. No icy bolt this time.

Fingerprint gun!

West heaved himself toward the man, low down along the floor, extended his arms, and stabbed the flat upper part of the man's boot through his foot, into the sole.

The agony and pain in the scream above him was full and true.

West pulled the knife out and jolted backward.

Halfway raised, he staggered and a throbbing pain in the back of his head replaced the phantom pain in his chest. He saw flashes of the car accident in Detroit and his left hand quickly and precisely traced the scar on his scalp under the balaclava. It felt intact.

Something was about to hit him. He hunched and got his elbow up, making the blow crash into his shoulder rather than his face.

The force was not as powerful as he'd expected and he managed to stay upright. Squinting up, he saw the man struggling to keep his balance without support from his pierced foot.

West could smell sweat and fury. His right hand still held the knife. He bent his knees an inch to get more thrust, then shot up. When the tip of the blade penetrated the skin under his opponent's chin, there was no stopping it. An instant later, six inches of stainless steel was embedded in the man's head.

Blood gushed out as life was replaced by limp, irreversible death.

West loosened his grip on the hilt and let the heavy body slump to the floor. He retched once, twice. His empty stomach delivered what bile it had, and he started weeping.

CHAPTER 46

Deep Sea

The blood drying on his hands nauseated West as they entered the dock area. He spit remnants of bile.

The *Dolphin II* was still there in the ominous red light. Jitterbug had some kind of injury in his shoulder and Kiss was developing a nasty bruise on her cheek. But they had made it to the escape vessel.

Åse wasn't present, but the submarine's entry was open. West went down first.

Only when all three had boarded did Åse reveal herself from a hiding place in the sub's kitchenette. She looked at Kiss and gave her a fleeting nod before she went up the shaft to secure the entrance.

When she came down, her face was a rock. "Get in your fucking cabins!"

•

West was in his pitch-dark cocoon for at least an hour before Åse's voice came in.

"Kitchen in five."

The frequency of the sub's hum lowered substantially while he unbuckled himself.

No one uttered a word as they gathered standing around the small metal table. West felt queasy, but it subsided as he draped an arm around Kiss's shoulders.

Åse put her knuckles on the table and leaned forward in a hunched position. "Your late exit has jeopardized the planned route," she commenced. "So I decided to go north along the island's coast. We're on the ocean floor in a place where I hope they won't look first. But they may have hydrophones all around here."

"Underwater microphones," Jitterbug whispered to West.

Åse continued. "The extra minutes you requested meant I had to turn two bodies cold. I barely had time to hide the corpses. All hell will break loose."

"I left one behind too, not hidden at all," West said in a feeble voice. "I could smell him. His blood." He let go of Kiss to show his hands. Their coat of blood had turned rusty brown and cracked.

"I never wanted to be a killer," he said, and buried his face on Kiss's shoulder. She put a hand on the back of his head.

He heard Åse speak between his sobs and sniffles.

"The first time you are ordered or forced to take a person's life is terrible. Beyond belief. It'll take you a week or two to get through it. Go wash yourself, then tell me what happened so I can take it into my risk calculus."

•

Feeling raw but at least clean, West took a seat. There was barely room for them around the kitchen table. His hand sought Kiss's and they clasped in her lap.

He explained how they had turned off the surveillance cameras, ran into the sole man, the fight, and the end.

"You did the right thing," Åse said in a quick settlement of the matter.

Then she seemed to realize that something more should be said. "You saved your friends," she added in a slower voice.

She leaned back in her chair and rolled her shoulders back. "We're well past the security update of the camera system, so they've found him. It might not be directly clear that it has anything to do with outside intruders. Maybe their instinct will tell them it's some kind of prison escape. But when they find the two guys at the dock ..." She tilted her head slightly to one side. "We should assume they already have. What ya got for me, West? Sub authentication."

West opened his mouth but was stopped by Kiss squeezing his hand.

"Before we give you anything, Åse," Kiss said, "we need to settle where you drop us off."

"We all disembark when the mission is over," the commander replied.

"The mission *is* over, or am I missing something?" Jitterbug asked.

"You're missing something because you're not disclosed."

"West will not tell you what he knows unless you tell us what the plan is," Jitterbug insisted.

West noted a subtle nod from Kiss.

"Fuck that," Åse said, turning to West. "I put my ass on the line for you. And we got your girlfriend out. Now spit out what you got on the sub IDs."

"You mean you're not even going to say where we're going?" Kiss wedged in.

"I took these two where they wanted to go and we got you out, honey."

"Don't honey me!"

"Okay, sugar."

"Please!" It was Jitterbug. "We're in a tough spot. Kiss just got out of Russian prison, West just took another person's life, and my shoulder is smashed. We're thankful for your help, Åse. I was on the bubble about this whole thing, but when I saw my old friend in the flesh in that cell, I knew it was worth it. We're all still alive. I think we should cooperate. Some information on what's next is not too much to ask. As a bargain for whatever West has figured out—and I can tell you he's a smart fellow. So please, Åse, could you tell us a bit about your reason to go to Ice Dolphin and what options we have?"

Åse pursed her lips. She took a stern look at West. "What you have for me better be good, soldier."

She pulled a midsized Tile out of her side pocket, tapped on it twice, and put it on the table. It had a map on it.

"We're here." Her index finger hovered a millimeter above the screen along the coast of Novaya Zemlya, north of the Matochkin Shar Strait. "I have not completed my mission yet. There are subsea cables going north."

Her finger traced the coast, into open water, and further up to an archipelago named Franz Josef Land—a cluster of twenty, maybe thirty tiny islands. "Once we get to here, I'll decide if we continue on under the ice or if we duck out to Kvitøya." She indexed westward to a small island east of Svalbard. "The White Island. That's our escape route to Norwegian waters."

"Just when I thought we could go no further north," Jitterbug mumbled.

"Are the cables what we're looking for?" West asked.

Åse rubbed her lips as the others waited. "Internet disruption," she started, barely audible. "You heard about it." Now louder. "Well, maybe not you, Kiss. We think the Russians have laid subsea cables under the North Pole to connect to North America as part of their Red Web contingency plan. The existence of those cables was revealed, deliberately or not, when the transatlantic connection went down. We think Ice Dolphin is covering the operation of that Arctic connection and I'm to track down the cables going north, supposedly to Franz Josef Land. For that kind of mission, we needed to look like a Russian sub so that the Russian authentication system wouldn't flag us as foreign. Unfortunately, we hadn't been able to confidently spoof the identity of *Dolphin II*." Her eyes briefly scanned the walls and ceiling. "So we decided to use the real thing while the Russians still think it's out on its mission."

"How long have you had it?"

"Not that long. We built our copy on stolen blueprints, but the auth system eluded us. When we managed to silently capture this and lock up its crew, we researched the heck out of it. They'll flag her as compromised now."

West and Jitterbug looked at each other.

"My part's done," Åse said in contempt, "which could get me court-martialed, so if you please, West. How sure are you about your intel?"

"Not a hundred."

She paused. "Is it on that smashed laptop you brought?"

"Shit." West looked around for it.

"I already connected it to power," Åse said. "Won't charge. Bust."

"I guess we'll have to go with what's in my head then."

CHAPTER 47

Sonic, Not Electronic

"Remember the spot welds I commented on when I still thought this was your copy of a *Dolphin II*?" West asked.

Åse nodded.

He waited.

Åse's eyes grew. "No way."

"They were weird. Not just welds along seams, but dots in a matrix. Like a pattern." He released Kiss's hand under the table and pointed at Åse's Tile. "Do you have a sketching app on this thing?"

Åse switched to an app with a white canvas.

West meticulously drew a set of circles. "This is a part of the pattern I saw on our sub. The laptop has a 'vessel' application, and it was showing this very same pattern. If it's what I think, they can passively identify Russian subs. No electronics. They authenticate the hulls."

Åse had to collect herself. "I hate to say it, but that might just be valuable enough to get my head out of the noose."

"That's a static ID though," Jitterbug said. "Same response to the challenge every time. Unless you think they change the dents over time?"

"I haven't thought about revocation yet," West said. "But I wonder if it's only for docks or if they can authenticate at sea too? With light, you can use photography to read the pattern, but in deep sea environments, my guess would be that they bombard subs with sonic signals and look at what's reflected in search of the dent pattern."

Kiss leaned forward, opened the offline maps on Åse's Tile, and typed "Mur." She tapped the search hit "Murmansk, Russia." The map scrolled southwest and marked the city of Murmansk on Russia's northern sea border, still well above the Arctic Circle. "That's where I'm going," she said conclusively. "To pay Viktor and Maria a visit."

"Darling, do you think we're traveling around to see friends and family?" Åse replied.

Kiss stood up, pulled her arm back, and balled her hand. Both West and Jitterbug jolted back but Åse didn't flinch.

"I'm fresh out of prison but not fresh out of fury," Kiss said sharply. "I lost my fucking child and I'm getting him back."

No one said a word. Kiss kept her fist raised.

"A child?" Åse said eventually, creasing her forehead.

"Our child, actually," West said.

Åse closed her eyes and flipped her head back. "Now what's this shit?"

Kiss disengaged her hand. "I delivered a son in prison. Viktor and Maria are the ones who stole him from me."

"Adopted," West added feebly, regretting it before he reached the last syllable.

Kiss gave him a look that could kill.

Åse turned from annoyed to aloof and tapped the table with her index finger. "Look, your son doesn't change my calculus here. You do what you want once we've returned to base and you've been debriefed."

"South," West said. "The subsea cables should also go south, no?" He moved the map to make sure Novaya Zemlya and Murmansk were visible.

"Could connect to the mainland anywhere, including any northern city," Åse said with dismissiveness.

"Including Murmansk," West filled in. "You can drop us off at wherever those cables go and we'll find our way from there."

"You don't just drop people off a sub. Especially not in the Arctic. This is a military vessel on a mission. I understand you want to find your son, but there is no room for excursions. You heard it. Franz Josef Land."

West saw Kiss's jaw muscles work in waves. He was just about to reach out and touch her when Åse stood up and spoke again.

"That laptop has auth codes for subs. It's your way out, regardless of route. I suggest you get hacking. I will make sure we're at the ready when, and I mean *when*, we get company."

Åse left for her cabin, came back with the laptop and a power cable, then disappeared. Kiss stewed for a bit, then left too, without a word.

Jitterbug put on a fake smile, looked down the narrow hallway, then back at West. "Go talk to her. Ol' Jit will be here when you're ready. I'll get busy with this thing." He tapped the case of the beat-up laptop. "The drive," he added. "We may be able to decrypt the SSD and get directly to its stored data."

•

West went to Kiss's cabin and knocked on the door. No answer.

He opened it an inch and asked, "Can I come in?"

"I'd rather not," she replied.

He opened the door some more and peeked in. Kiss was lying on her side in the fully reclined seat, facing away from where he was. The cabin wasn't large enough for him to stand in there and close the door.

"Are you okay?" he asked.

"What do you think?"

"I'm sure Åse will come around. The thing about East, it was complete news to her."

"You're not helping."

"I will help, or, I want to help."

"Then start by getting us to Murmansk."

"Are you mad at me?"

"No, I'm not. But ..." She looked at him for two seconds, then slowly turned back toward the back wall. "It's a mess. I was recently in a cell dealing with despair and ... things I don't want to talk about. This is my one chance of getting East back. I'm sorry if I'm not reasonable. Nothing is reasonable anymore."

West nodded. "I'll get us to Murmansk. Somehow."

"Thanks. Thanks for all you've done. I'm sorry I am like this right now."

"Don't be." He pulled his head back an inch before adding, "I love you."

She turned to look at him with an element of surprise on her face. "I love you too. You know that, right?"

West got lightheaded and unsteady. He tumbled forward and Kiss caught him barely in time to stop him from crashing into the wall on the other side of her seat.

He tried to steady himself, but the control just wasn't there.

Kiss made room for him on the seat, just enough for them to both lie on their sides.

He sensed her body heat almost instantly and his dizziness turned into drowsiness.

He was with her again. Their future may be cloudy, but he was with her.

They fell asleep, West's nose against the back of Kiss's neck.

CHAPTER 48

Solid State

With his body stiff from hours of sleep in an awkward position, but his soul in joy for the first time in over a year, West knocked on Jitterbug's cabin door.

His friend eventually opened up, looking like he'd been asleep too.

"Did you get started on the drive?" West asked.

"Not really. Turns out I can't work delicate hardware with my busted shoulder. I need your help."

They got seated at the kitchen table. West put his hands on the laptop. It was wobbly from the treatment it received during the fight.

Jitterbug smirked. "We need some tools," he said and described two kits for West to fetch from his backpack.

"Hardware encryption," Jitterbug continued as he picked out a mini screwdriver. "Operating systems can deploy software encryption on top of that, but several don't because they want performance. We'll have to see what the Russian setup is."

West probably could have pried the laptop open with his bare hands, given the crack along one of its sides. But loosening a few screws made it easier.

The circuit board inside was small. The rest was batteries and OmniPorts.

Jitterbug craned over the electronics. "Soldered-on SSD," he mumbled. "Not great. I'm also worried that this thing has cloning protection that huge, fast reads would trigger."

He fished out his Tile and asked it to "Show the folder on TCG Opal." He turned to West. "You know what TCG stands for?"

West shook his head.

"Ooo, well then. Hacker catnip. Trusted Computing Group. With such a name, you just have to hack it, right? Let's see what we got here." He read the fine print on the circuit package out loud to his Tile. "Shucks. First thing suggested in this attack tree is downloading and analyzing a firmware image from the internet. Downloads at the bottom of the ocean are hard."

"Unless we find that Russian cable." West was surprised that he made a joke.

Jitterbug looked at him. "That's the spirit. We have to get out of this hole. Now, no download means we move on to the second level. Can we run unsigned code on this thing?" He scrolled on his Tile. "There are old versions of this that would allow unsigned code, but the firmware has been requiring signatures for about a decade."

Jitterbug moved his gaze from the Tile back to the laptop's motherboard with its SSD. "Third level. You know where I'm going. You know where I always go." He gave West time.

"JTAG?"

"Jackpot!"

West knew about JTAG from their hack against Pogodina's PC in Stockholm. It was a testing standard for circuits. He couldn't spot a JTAG connector on the motherboard though.

"See the two-by-five connection points here?" Jitterbug pointed at the lower right corner of the laptop's circuitry.

The part was about the size of a fingertip with a white rectangle around it and ten metal rings encompassing millimeter-wide holes through the board.

Jitterbug pulled out a small pink circuit board of his own. "I present to you the JTAGulator. I can't believe I haven't showed you this yet. Vendors often still have JTAG functionality but hide it to make it hard for honest people like us."

He connected black and red cables to his Tile and launched the multimeter app. He groaned as he moved his shoulder and sweat beads were showing on his forehead. "*You* get to do the fun stuff. Put the metal tip of the black cable on the outer metal of the power connector. Mhmm, on the laptop board. Then step through each of the punch-through holes in the two-by-five grid with the tip of the red one."

One of the holes made Jitterbug's Tile beep. "That's your ground."

Jitterbug continued to give instructions and West found the circuit board's operating voltage and connected cables to all the round connector holes.

"Now let's try to uncloak this thing. First ID code scan," Jitterbug said and tapped something on his Tile. "Ta-da. Quicker than you thought, huh? But we have to also find the test enabler with a bypass scan. Takes a little longer. Du, du-du." A few seconds passed. "Bam. We have a JTAG interface."

Jitterbug turned his Tile's screen to West.

```
Device ID: 0001 0100011100010010 10001101110 1
Manufacturer: SMIC

Processor entered Debug Mode.
```

"Now we can download the firmware straight from this thing. No internet needed." Jitterbug raised his voice ever so slightly. "It'll take a while though." Then looked to see that none of the others onboard had reappeared. He waved West closer, his face turning taut.

"We may need more bargaining chips to get out of this as free citizens," Jitterbug whispered. "Not just leverage with Åse. That email manipulation is on my mind."

West was just about to share his thoughts when there was a loud *ding*. The sound was piercing but not alarm-like.

Åse's voice whipped through the intercom. "A sub left the strait. Get to your cabins."

They quickly carried their equipment and the laptop to Jitterbug's bunker and got strapped in.

"How do you know a sub left?" West asked over the intercom.

"Sonic reflections in our horizontal salinity gradient. I have to listen manually to understand what it is. So absolute silence until I say otherwise."

The team sat tight for five minutes.

Ten minutes.

West shifted in his sculpted seat.

Fifteen minutes.

"It's just about to pass us." Åse's whisper was brief. "We're moving within thirty seconds."

"Where are we going?" West dared ask.

"We're tailing whatever this is. Very hard for hydrophones to tell two subs apart if we follow close enough. Also very hard for their sub to see us sonically backward. It's our chance to go north unnoticed. Stay dark."

The hum came back and West could sense their vessel turn. They were in pursuit.

He started wondering if this submarine was armed. It was tiny, but maybe modern torpedoes were too?

Åse cut off West's line of thought. "B-600 series Magadan. Diesel-electric. Anti-submarine. This thing is out to kill."

CHAPTER 49

The Magadan

"Check your screens. That's the cable," Åse said in a low voice over the intercom as they continued to follow the Magadan submarine.

West turned on the monitor in his cabin and saw a moving rendering of the ocean floor below them. There was a seam in the direction they were going.

"We might have to take a risk here," Åse mumbled to herself before saying, "That's the repeater you're seeing. Fiber has attenuation, so you have to boost the signal every sixty kilometers. It's done through pump lasers, at least in Western cables. Some kind of coordinated attack on those is one of the transatlantic disruption theories."

West saw a swelling of the line representing the cable scrolling in from the top.

The hum of their own sub stopped.

Before West could ask, Åse came back on the intercom, barely audible. "The longer we follow that Magadan, the higher the risk that it, or something else along the way, detects us. Dropping off right behind it is our best chance. I have to complete the mission and inspect that cable. Brace yourselves. We are literally about to hit rock bottom."

The imagery of the cable and the repeater slowly grew larger and shifted to the right on the screen. They seemed to land right by it.

"Let's hope she doesn't make too much noise," Åse said, sucking in air through her teeth.

There was a thump. Their sub's forward momentum was arrested.

West's harness dug into his flesh as it held him back. Two squeals, then silence.

"Everyone okay?" Åse asked. All three passengers confirmed. "I'll capture photos as soon as the silt clears. Then we need to get out of here."

They lay still on the ocean floor as the sediment settled. West heard the hard surface below scrape the hull as the water moved them. It was haunting. He felt as if they were the first humans to touch this part of earth, but then realized laying and maintaining the cable probably meant the Russians had been here a lot.

"Shit, the Magadan is coming back!" Åse yelled.

West's screen flashed red, and an alert in Cyrillic started blinking.

"Its torpedo tubes are open. Say your prayers."

West closed his eyes hard. He thanked his maker for all the things he had been given, for the beauty of life, and for dying a free man. He made a last plea to survive so that he could be in Kiss's arms once again, somewhere far from here, somewhere good and peaceful.

Moments passed. He told himself he should want to find their son, not just be with Kiss.

It felt like a minute went by. He was sweating and finding it hard to breathe.

He had to open one eye to see what was going on.

The alert on the screen was still there.

"What's happening?" he asked feebly, close to the intercom microphone.

"It's just watching us," Åse replied.

West thought for a few heartbeats, then pressed the comms button again. "The cable and the repeater. Blowing us up right next to it will destroy it."

"You might be right." A pause. "But *we* don't care about the cable."

West saw commands flicker on the screen and a clear image of the nose of the Magadan came into view with a target on it.

The *Dolphin*'s motors started revving up and down in a quick pumping sequence. The image of the Magadan got cloudy from stirred-up silt. Eventually, he could only see what looked like diluted milk tea on the screen. The pumping revolutions stopped.

There was the noise from another electric motor, much smaller than the one propelling them. Then a whir.

"It's gonna be a close one!" Åse yelled through the speaker.

Then came a violent blast and sharp pressure wave.

CHAPTER 50

Impact

West's ears were ringing. No lights, everything was black. His whole body felt bruised. Joints ached and his breathing was barely doing its job.

The blast must have knocked him out for a brief moment, but he remembered the reverberation of the shock wave.

The straps of his cabin chair still held him in place. He unbuckled at the speed his ailing body allowed and slumped out of the seat to open the door. Red emergency lighting was on, barely showing the contours of the other cabin doors but reflecting off the floor.

He took a step into the narrow hallway. Water splashed around his boot, about an inch of it.

We're leaking! Are we at crush depth?

There was no one there but him. No sounds but his.

Åse's cabin was straight across, Jitterbug's on the other side but further back, and Kiss's right behind his. He took careful steps in the water toward the back and knocked on Kiss's door. Nothing.

He turned the handle and opened. The dim red light from the corridor barely made anything visible in there, but he could see her legs.

"Kiss?" he whispered.

He carefully reached inside toward where he assumed her face would be. He inched closer until he touched skin—warm skin. Kiss's hand swept his away violently.

"Kiss, it's me. Are you okay?"

It took a while for her to respond. "I don't know, I feel dizzy. Are you?"

"I'm mangled and sore, but all body parts are attached."

"How are the others?"

"I haven't checked yet."

"I'm okay," he heard from behind. It was Åse's voice. She was moving swiftly.

West got out of Kiss's cabin and turned to Jitterbug's. He didn't bother to knock. Again there were two legs barely visible.

"Jit, are you there?"

No reply.

West shook the leg closest to him but still didn't get a reaction.

"Get me some light," he yelled to the hallway behind.

Åse craned in a Tile with the flashlight turned on. The gruesome scene inside shocked West. Jitterbug was bleeding from his head and one of his arms was at a distressing angle.

"Jit! Can you hear me?"

Åse's flashlight disappeared and he had to get his own out. Kiss took it and held it up to free up West's hands.

West frantically started to unbuckle Jitterbug. Next thing he knew he had somehow found the strength to get his friend over his shoulder and dragged the limp body out to the kitchen area. He started crying, out of fear for his dear friend's life but also because of his own pain.

The small table was barely enough to support Jitterbug's upper body, but West wanted to get him up as close to the red light as possible. Kiss stayed behind with the flashlight.

West felt Jitterbug's neck. "He's still warm and there's a pulse." He sniffled.

Åse showed up with a damp towel. She wiped Jitterbug's forehead and cheeks, then gave the towel to Kiss to clean the area that was bloody.

"Oh, man," Jitterbug uttered in the faintest of voices.

"You're alive. Man, you are still alive. Can you hear me?" West asked hurriedly.

"I hear you, buddy. What happened? My arm is hurting so badly."

"I don't know what happened, other than Åse firing a fucking torpedo." West felt anger mixing with his anxiety.

"Direct hit as far as I can tell," Åse muttered from the corridor. She was working frenetically on something by the wall.

"You nearly killed us all!" West snapped over his shoulder.

"Nope. That blast probably saved us," she retorted. "Now we at least have a chance to get away."

"In this wreck? I suppose you haven't noticed that we're leaking."

"The water is not from the ocean. I tasted it and there's no salt in it. It's from our fresh water tank."

"Okay, so I guess we're dandy then."

"No matter the state of the sub, we have to get Jit to a hospital, now," said Kiss.

West turned his attention to Jitterbug's wounds again and listened to the two women talk. There was also blood soaking the pants on the backside of one upper leg.

"We need to lighten our ballast and get off the bottom. That's what we need to do now," Åse said.

"This Vitt Oya island of yours, does it have a hospital?" Kiss asked.

"Of course not. Kvitøya isn't even inhabited. It has a rudimentary underwater dock, emergency supplies, and communications with Norway and NATO." Åse flipped a switch in the panel she was operating and there was a swooshing sound. "It's NATO's easternmost outpost in the Arctic before Alaska on the other side of Russian waters. Your closest hospital will be in Longyearbyen on Svalbard."

"That's where we're going then."

"No can do, sis. We'd bring the Russian Arctic fleet with us and risk open conflict."

"Won't they come to Vitt Oya too?" Kiss asked.

"Probably."

"You were the one who said get away. You're the fucking commander of this ship. Talk to me."

There was silence for a moment. Åse checked some instruments before speaking again. "Any kind of kinetic military action and NATO will deny our existence. We're on our own now and I'm getting us buoyant again. The three of you need to go as far back in the ship as possible while I shift water to the aft tank."

"*You* went kinetic," Kiss pointed out.

"I stand by that decision."

"So what's your decision now, *sis*?"

"You go aft. I get this vessel moving. We stay within Russian waters. That should be last on the list of what they're expecting.

There's an abandoned Soviet submarine shelter-base west of the Kola Peninsula. It's as close to Norway as we can get without crossing known Russian sonar lines. Best card I have left in my deck."

"That doesn't sound like a hospital site."

"It's terra firma and a potential way out of Russia. We just have to hope Jit can hold on until we get to Finnish or Norwegian grounds. West, get his clothes off and care for the wounds. Don't use up more gauze than you need because it'll be a long time until we can replenish. Kiss, as *fucking commander* of this ship, I order you to go aft. Now."

West looked at Jitterbug. His friend was in pain but nodded subtly. "I'll make it, buddy. God willing."

CHAPTER 51

White House: The G-I-UK Gap

"Madam President, we received a report from Keflavik indicating similar activity between Greenland and Iceland. So it's indeed all along the G-I-UK gap," General Purnell said before sitting down properly.

"Mind the gap," the president japed without a smile. Keflavik meant it was her own people reporting. The naval air station there had been repopulated a few years back. "And our assumption still is that Russia is reacting to our investigation of the Greenland connection? Or is this something else?"

"That is our leading theory, yes," the general replied. "The Greenland traffic stopped abruptly, and then this. But we have also not heard from the SMITH investigation sub since it entered the Russian economic zone in the ..."

"We'll get to that. First this escalation. Details."

Purnell obliged. "Russia has tested their abilities to breach the G-I-UK gap undetected for decades. We are still convinced that we have spotted all such attempts, but if they were successful, we wouldn't know. What we're seeing now is *not* one of those attempts. These Russian subs are *making* themselves visible. Scapa Flow has reported four vessels, Keflavik three between them and the UK, and another three between them and Greenland."

"They're sending us a signal," the president told the room and got subtle nods back.

"They know we're investigating," Purnell said in confirmation. "They noted internet data got through the Greenland connection just like we did."

"I was thinking about that yesterday. Has that connection been up for some time or was it activated because of the disruption? Or even a planned thing together with the disruption?" Sanchez asked.

Purnell turned to Lewis from National Intelligence.

"The internet doesn't have a memory like that," Lewis said. "We have no way of going back to see if the Greenland connection was live prior to the transatlantic disruption."

The president kept digging in. "Is there something in the subsea equipment that would let us know? Some ... I don't know ... counting of traffic volume?"

"It's plain signal boosting and cleaning. But we'll take another look. What I can say is we are working under the assumption that the connection is a piece of Russia's contingency plan for global cyberwar. They may have secretly established several of their own internet connections just like us, and we just got a glimpse of it."

"Exactly. That's the whole matter. And we need to understand what we just discovered."

Mack Lewis nodded once. "Understood. We will get back to you with a full report."

The president relented. "Please do. Okay, I may be jumping the agenda here, but where are you on the origins of those zero days that hit Wisconsin and Utah ... and Florida, was it?"

"Correct, ma'am," Lewis said. "We've made progress. We're looking at a minimum of two layers of obfuscation in the source code. First, a general one that you'll find in any sophisticated malware. We beat that one. The second one is there to prevent us from extracting programming patterns to deduce the origin. They made it look like a North Korean origin but crudely enough for us to feel pretty sure it's someone else."

"Who wants to throw North Korea under the bus?"

"I would prefer not to speculate, ma'am."

The president turned to Alec Ore.

"The Russians come first to mind," he said. "Then again, it wouldn't be beyond China if pressured. And I wouldn't completely rule out the idea of it *being* North Korea and they want us to think that it's someone pretending to be them."

"4D chess," Sanchez said, giving a side-eye to Lewis. "I grant you the privilege of not speculating. But that means you have to find me the truth."

The president turned to General Purnell. "SMITH investigation. You had news?"

"Intel from our Russian sources. There seems to have been direct contact between one of their Magadan subs and an adversary. Kinetic contact. Potential torpedo strike."

CHAPTER 52

Objekt 122

Kiss urged West to let Jitterbug rest and get some sleep himself. As confusing as life underwater was, his Tile's clock still told him it was well past midnight. Kiss had slept earlier, still adjusted to the strict sleep schedule for the inmates.

"Will you let me know if anything changes, or if he wakes up?" West asked her as he unwillingly opened the door to his cabin.

"We need you rested. Getting Jit to a hospital is going to be a marathon."

He looked at the floor. His body was heavy. He needed a shower. A final nod and he went inside. Within thirty seconds of closing his door and strapping himself in, he was snoring.

•

West woke up disoriented and with a dry mouth. It was sound from the intercom that had pulled him out of sleep.

"Secret Russian military object number 122, as close to Norway as we get," Åse said through the speaker. "It's an incomplete submarine nuclear shelter from the Cold War. Construction started late seventies, slowed down in the eighties, and ended with the first Strategic Arms Reduction Treaty with the US. The Soviets had several of these, obviously not all known by the West. But you've got your Objekt 6 near Vladivostok and the massive Objekt 221 in Crimea."

"I have no idea where those places are," West said with a raspy voice.

"Vladivostok is Russian east coast, close to Japan. Crimea is in Ukraine, Black Sea. Anyway, back to 122 ahead of us. The first treaty was signed in 1991, so that's when this place was fully abandoned. They were supposed to close all entrances, but that cost money, and money was what they were out of. The structure is seventy-five-inch-thick concrete à la Soviet brutalism. Subs enter half submerged. During winter, it freezes over, but it should be useable now."

"Do we know that it's abandoned?" Kiss asked.

"I'm going by NATO intel. Everything is on the risk spectrum. We're getting close. Got to concentrate."

Radio silence with the ever-present burr of the motors.

There was a whoosh when the *Dolphin II*'s ballast tanks were partially filled with air released from compression. The vessel slowly ascended. It was amazing that she was still operational.

Åse came back. "Taking her up to surface level. Nice and slow."

Minutes later, West's screen switched to the conning tower camera. Lights on the sub lit the surrounding scene. Glitter, black water, straight walls on the sides, probably concrete but could be stone. A ceiling close above.

"Ready for some fresh air?" Åse asked. He could hear her unbuckling.

Reminded of Jitterbug's precarious situation, West felt anxiety wash over him. He heard the moaning from inside as soon as he got to his friend's cabin door.

When he opened, the smell of pus and rotting blood overwhelmed him and he took a step back.

"How are you?" he asked without breathing through his nose.

"Oh, man," came from inside.

Kiss came out and reacted to the smell too. "We need to clean his wounds properly."

Åse appeared from the kitchen area. "I'll head out to get us secured. Wanna join, West? I could use your help to moor." She looked at him. "We'll carry Jit out as soon as we know where to take him."

West sniffled and nodded.

Åse opened a tall locker and got out a coil of thick rope. She wedged it up on her shoulder, moved aside, and cocked her head back toward the locker. West grabbed a coil too. It was heavy and smelled of the sea.

A rush of cool air came down when Åse opened the hatch. Every sound above produced an echo. Åse got out and West ascended.

He popped his head out and saw the space surrounding them lit by lamps along the sub's sides. There was clearly room for much larger vessels than the *Dolphin II* but not much headroom, so only subs could use this. Gray, crumbling concrete walls on either side, stained by mold and algae. A rusty, vaulted metal ceiling above with its weld seams visible. A couple of the metal sheets were hanging loose. Åse's footsteps on the hull squeaked and thumped.

"Only one bollard in any kind of reasonable condition. We'll have to tie her two-to-one."

Water splashed as Åse used all her power to throw the heavy-duty rope around the fraying post on the ledge protruding from the wall. "You think you can do it?" she asked.

He tried and failed twice before she took over and got his rope around the same post. Then she walked the other end further back to get them a triangular mooring.

On her way back, she squatted by the tower, opened a small lid, and turned something beneath it. A section of the metal side popped open. She pulled out an aluminum ladder. Seconds later, West realized it was a retractable gangway.

They got it arranged and Åse took a careful step onto it and pushed down twice to make sure the crumbling concrete on the other side would hold.

She crossed and waved West over before turning on a flashlight, pulling her gun, and heading further into the cave. Echoes of their movement kept them company.

A large vaulted space opened to the side toward the end of the dock. It had what had once been a door to the lower right. Now there were only rusty remnants of hinges and a pile of dirt on the floor that had probably been wood decades earlier.

The church-like bouncing of sound disappeared as soon as they got into the regular-sized corridor. Rebar rust bled through the walls, and in places the concrete had holes and pits as large as a fist. The spill of Åse's flashlight moved steadily as she advanced, gun muzzle first.

They found several rooms—a radio control, a canteen, two sleeping quarters judging by what could have once been bunk beds, and a bathroom with showers and toilet stalls.

"Unisex, I guess," Åse muttered.

She walked them back to the canteen and into the kitchen. By what had probably been a stove, there was a hole in the wall high up. Åse got a match out of a plastic pouch, peeled off wax from the top of it, and lit it. She held it up as high as she could and watched the flame intently. It moved back and forth but gravitated toward the hole in the wall. "We should be able to light a small fire here without killing ourselves with smoke."

West felt useless.

Åse searched for a while before finding a large metal pot. "Thank god for aluminum. Seems clean too. Okay. We have a stretcher and LED lights on the sub. You and Kiss carry Jit out while I get the fire going. One of these tables should work as a bench for him. Then get one of the freshwater tanks so I can boil it for us. Throw in a couple of purifying tablets too. We have to save the saline solution we have for the long walk. Bring all the gauzes we have left, but don't overuse them. We clean and inspect his wounds without giving him a hint of how bad it is. He's going to ask and you will say he's gonna make it. Got it?"

West pursed his lips. He nodded.

"We've got a long way to go on this one, soldier," she said and patted his shoulder.

CHAPTER 53

The News

Jitterbug's wounds were ugly.

His cabin must have taken the brunt of the blast, or the construction of the sub had a weakness on his side. West had only briefly looked at the damage to Jitterbug's compartment and had seen aluminum panels ripped in two places. They must have been what cut into the flesh. Then a bulb in the wall and a bend of the seat itself combined into what must have caused the blunt trauma to Jitterbug's arm.

Kiss had found a pair of tongs and first put the handle in the boiling water, then flipped it to let the tip sterilize.

The steam from the pot emitted a chlorine smell from the water purifier tablets.

West checked again that the table where they'd laid Jitterbug was stable.

Kiss got hand sanitizer and disposable gloves out of the first aid kit bag. She offered West gel.

He rubbed his hands and the handle of the LED light before he was handed a large pair of gloves. The sharp smell of alcohol mixed with fumes from the fire.

Kiss got a pair of gloves on, too, and ripped open two pouches of gauze. She dropped the cloth into the steaming water.

West shone the LED light on Jitterbug's head and gently turned it to make the wound face upward. He removed the dressing and a foul smell emerged.

The cut was three, maybe four inches with skin gone in the middle.

Åse had shaved Jitterbug's short, curly hair in a rectangular area around it.

When West had asked Åse about internal trauma, she had said that's for a physician to find out. They had no way of knowing beyond any symptoms. "Focus on what you can do, and that's keeping this clean," she had said.

West framed the wound with his free hand to keep Jitterbug's head steady and nodded to Kiss.

She fished out a gauze with the tongs and let it drip for a while. It steamed. She pinched it to check the temperature, waited a little longer, pinched it again, and carried it over.

Kiss gently laid the gauze down and squeezed water out. Jitterbug flinched.

The morphine is wearing off.

West let his gloved pinky out to touch Kiss as she let hot water rinse and trickle down Jitterbug's scalp.

She looked at West briefly, eyes misty. Then started dabbing the cut from the center and outward, just as Åse had told them.

Kiss repeated the process with another wet gauze before switching to dry ones.

They stood waiting for the wound and skin to dry up properly.

The wound looked raw in the LED light, but West convinced himself it at least looked better than before.

Kiss got a sterile compress and dressed the wound once again.

West lifted the blanket from Jitterbug's broken arm. The LED showed an extensive area shifting from purple to pale yellow.

Kiss cleaned the skin covering the fracture with another gauze.

Almost all the boiled water was gone by the time they had wiped the rest of their friend's body and got him dressed for the journey on a stretcher.

West dropped into a dusty chair and flipped his head back to face the unraveling ceiling. He was sweating, not because of labor but because of the stress and worry.

"Where's Åse?" he asked Kiss, briefly raising his head to look her way. It was the first thing any of them had said in two hours.

"She was going to scout the outside and try for higher ground," Kiss replied. "She said we might receive Norwegian radio news. Fully passive. No signal going out."

West moved his head back to its tilted position. "Kind of amazing, right?" he said, speaking to the ceiling. "Old broadcast technology being fully anonymous while all the new stuff is surveilled."

•

West found Åse up on the cliff above. She sat watching the landscape next to a rusty antenna mounted on the rock.

Flat concrete surfaces with stone protruding made the top of this naval structure look like two solid objects had been smushed together.

As he got closer, Åse spotted him and started talking.

"The Norwegian resistance movement under Nazi occupation used household radios to get news and secret commands. The Nazis made radios illegal and confiscated half a million sets. Hidden, unregistered radios played a huge role."

He squatted beside her and the antenna. Rust stained the concrete base.

"Did you get any radio signal?"

"Amazingly, yes. Some crazy interference going on in this region. Gets worse the closer you get to Finnish and Norwegian borders."

Åse directed the lower part of her Tile toward him. "I'm afraid the news is not good, though. Here's a translation." The Tile's English voice assistant read it out loud.

Wilder is being accused of working with the Russians and, as such, being involved in the recent disruption of internet communications across the Atlantic. The US has yet to comment on the details first reported by Russian News Agency, TASS, but a spokeswoman of the Sanchez administration says in a brief statement that Mr. Wilder is an ex-convict who has proven adversarial to American interests before.

Intelligence expert Ragnvald Hermstad says that if Wilder is indeed on the island of Novaya Zemlya, the Russian government took him there.

West felt feverish.

The voice assistant switched to a male voice for the Hermstad quote.

"First of all, we still don't have confirmation that any of this is true. Novaya Zemlya hosts the infamous maximum security prison Ice Dolphin. You don't go there as a tourist, especially not as a foreigner. If Wilder indeed is on the island, Russians took him there. Whether as an accomplice or an inmate, your guess is as good as mine. We don't know what skills or intel Wilder has that Russia might be interested in. But then again, the proof presented to us is easily forgeable. I'd say that the longer we don't get confirmation of Wilder being elsewhere, the more pressure there will be on this story. Right now, that pressure is low."

A female voice read the journalist's question before switching back to Hermstad.

"What about Wilder's son?"

"It wouldn't be perfect without some family drama, now would it? Seems out of line even for a smear campaign. But who knows, a love child with a Russian woman. That's not a crime."

"What's this?" West asked, looking daggers.

Åse threw her free hand up and shrugged. "Someone ratted you out."

"Not someone. Only NATO knows I'm here."

"Ice Dolphin staff saw you."

"They didn't. I wore a balaclava."

"All the time?"

"As soon as I found one."

Åse pocketed her Tile. "Look, man. It could be someone snitching on you in the US. You're not exactly their best friend. But remember, we got you to Ice Dolphin."

"My son. No one but you knows about him."

"I have no fucking idea how they know anything about that."

"Unless you leaked it."

"Oh, so that's how it is? You think I'm in contact with NATO

Command *and* that I'm using the precious comms to spread gossip about you? Sheesh. I thought you were smarter than that. If NATO wanted you in trouble, they could have just let you fly to St. Petersburg. Whoever is leaking has a broader agenda. You're just a pawn, West."

He snorted.

Åse stood up. "There wasn't any news about the Magadan I blew up. That vexes *me*. The Russians know, of course. I have to assume Norway and the rest of NATO knows too. Both sides keeping it secret."

West looked at her. "You pulled me into this NATO thing."

"And got Kiss out."

"I'll have to disappear after we get Jit to a hospital. I can't go back home."

CHAPTER 54

Office of the Director of National Intelligence

"The Russian sources—TASS—have been confirmed," the junior aide said.

"Ha," Director Lewis replied. "Then our general statement on Wilder may be the only thing that's true in that story."

"But Wilder *is* there. Part of the Norwegian operation, right? How could they make that up?"

"You can make anything up. Never forget that. Did we leak it?"

"Not that I know of. But this is with US G20S. I can check with them."

"What would the leaker get out of this if it's not us? Are they playing this as a US intrusion on Russian soil?"

"It could go that way but the angle is more of Wilder as a US traitor. At least that's what the translator said about the version in Russian."

"He *is* a traitor. Makes us look weak, mocking us for not keeping the damn guy locked up."

He flicked his finger to knock a dice forward against the base of his monitor. "We should prepare a Red Notice to Interpol in case this gets legs. Start building a case with G20S. You've been here long enough to remember the Red Notice stuff, right?"

"Not really, but I've helped on two Red Notices since GPI got hacked."

"Hacked. Pfft. Avoid using that term, will you? They had internal help." Lewis started talking to himself. "Red Notice. I can't believe we're back to that shit procedure." He raised his voice again. "On the TASS story—figure out where this is coming from and what they're after."

"Will do. By the way, any decision on Friday?"

"What of it?"

"I wanted to take the day off."

"Sure. I'll approve."

"Thank you."

The aide left. *Good*, Lewis thought. An eager, up-and-coming person digging was good human insurance that the true source of the leaks would remain obscured. Naima's Chinese wall was good *digital* insurance.

He fired up the prompt.

•

```
Transcribing record #689550111-DNI

Lewis > Draft a Red Notice on Wilder.

Naima > Picking up the context.

Naima > Is this in relation to our earlier con-
versation on West William Wilder (ID bb8a2a6fc-
1ccd229a0a7b66ac42f97ef)?

Lewis > Yes.
```

CHAPTER 55

Amazing Grace

The team got packed and argued over what to bring from the sub. Jitterbug surfaced from a feverish sleep and said he wanted his necklace from his backpack. West at first didn't take notice, but when his friend asked a second time, he dug through the backpack and was surprised to find a necklace with Ronaldo's LOVE pendant.

Jitterbug clasped the precious jewelry as soon as West put it around his neck, then fell back to sleep.

West asked Åse out of hearing distance from Jitterbug, "Where are we headed and where is the closest town or village?"

"The closest is Pechenga, which is fifteen klicks south as the bird flies."

"Klicks?"

"Kilometers. Our best bet is the Norwegian border, ten klicks west. We cross, and I can get us a helicopter."

"How hard is it to cross?"

"The actual border is three lines of barbed wire with sand in between, and checked by drones. If we avoid being spotted by the drones, they'll only know after the fact, by virtue of our footprints."

West looked at the stretcher lying on the ground waiting for Jitterbug. Its handles were bare metal. He ran his fingertips over the inside of his hands. "I'm guessing no roads between here and the border?"

Åse nodded in confirmation. "Fir trees, bear tracks, deer trails, and mosquitos."

•

The walk through untouched taiga woods was excruciatingly slow. The heavy fir trees were beautiful but stood so tight that it was hard to get a sense of the views. Frequent small lakes provided variation, but the mosquitos were particularly intense around those areas. West used gauze from their medical supplies to protect Jitterbug's face, but the fabric clung to his friend's sweaty forehead and cheeks and the blood-sucking insects got through.

Jitterbug didn't notice the bites though. He was either in delirium or still high on the second morphine injection that Åse gave him when they got moving. Just touching him was enough to tell he was suffering a severe fever.

West didn't dare meet Kiss's eyes. He didn't want to know what she thought of Jitterbug's state.

Their NATO gloves did their job, but eventually West's hands got chafed from carrying the metal rods of the heavy stretcher. His shoulders ached, his feet were sore, and insect bites and scratches flecked his neck and face.

They stopped to drink water and rest for a few minutes.

"Is the border guarded?" Kiss asked Åse.

"All automated. But yes. By both sides, of course."

"Like drones?"

"Drones will show up once border sensors spot us. Ideally, we'd abandon most gear and run the last mile, but—"

"Jit can't run," West filled in.

"Leave me. I'm ready," they heard from the stretcher behind.

West spun around and moved over. "Man, you've been hard to reach for hours. How are you?"

"I've seen Him. He is ready for me."

Kiss joined and put a hand on Jitterbug's sticky forehead.

"We'll get you to a hospital," West said.

"No. You two should go get your son. That's what God wants. I went on this journey with you, West, because I knew it was important. We got Kiss out, which gives me eternal joy. But the real purpose was saving your boy. Go to Murmansk. Find him. Promise me that."

"We'll get him after saving you. Don't worry."

"I won't make it, you know that." Jitterbug afforded a smile. "This may be the last time I'm clear enough in my head to tell you this. Don't waste your energy and chances on me. I have a beautiful Heaven to look forward to. I'll enjoy it for eternity, and I'll see you there, eventually. The only thing I'm sad about ..."

Jitterbug shifted slightly on the stretcher, and his back arched in pain.

"Nonsense. I'm not having it," West said sternly.

"Me neither," Kiss filled in.

"It's not nonsense." Jitterbug groaned. "The only thing I'm sad about is that I don't get to climb all those hills and mountains with Ronaldo. I said he and I should get married on a summit. Now I'll die a bachelor. No more Sungay mornings. But I do have one request ... and one piece of half-nonsense for you."

"Anything you want, brother," West said.

"Please tell Ronaldo I love him and that I didn't mean to leave him behind. You'll get his necklace back to him, won't you? He secretly packed it for me. Tell him to find someone new to give it to. Someone kind and true—like me." He chuckled briefly. "As for the nonsense, I know you sing, but you're not a gospel kind of guy, West. And you aren't into religion at all, Kiss." He looked her way. "Am I right?"

Kiss dipped her head from side to side with a faint, noncommittal smile.

"Well, I can ask for anything on my deathbed, right?"

"Shhh," West uttered.

"Here's my wish. You find East and you bring him back to ol' America. If you baptize him, you get the gospel choir to sing my arrangement of Mr. Mister's 'Kyrie.' It's not complete yet, but they can put the finishing touches on it. I was so eager to hear that song with the choir. It's my eighties favorite. I want East to hear it if he's baptized. Can you do that for me, man?"

"Of course. You'll be there to sing it for him."

Jitterbug shook his head subtly. "But I'll be there in spirit. I'll always be there for you."

.

Jitterbug didn't make it.

His fever spiked, and he went back into a delirium from which he never recovered. West carried the foot end of the stretcher and thought he heard his friend take his last breath.

West and Kiss hugged and sobbed for an hour after concluding his pulse was gone. Åse shed tears, sitting still.

Without a word, Åse started digging a grave with her hands and knife. Kiss and West joined, sniffling. They cut and lifted chunks of turf and had to get through layers of intertwined roots. The smell was earthy and primal.

To think that a Black man from Cincinnati would be buried here, on Russian soil, far above the Arctic Circle.

West crafted a cross for the grave using gauze as string, and they performed a tear-filled ceremony with Jitterbug in the ground. It was a beautiful summer day and a light wind helped with the mosquitos. West sang.

Amazing grace! How sweet the sound
That saved a wretch like me.
I once was lost, but now am found,
Was blind but now I see.

CHAPTER 56

Into the Fire

The wind was picking up speed in the northwest of Murmansk Oblast. A cool, hard wind from the Barents Sea made the fir trees bow and rustle.

West sat on a stone that made for a reasonable stool by Jitterbug's makeshift grave. Some of the stone's moss had peeled off and lay scattered around.

Heading for the Norwegian border had made sense while Jitterbug was still alive, while they could still save him. But now? The false news story of West working for the Russians meant he would likely be arrested and extradited on sight.

Here, on this rock, might be the safest place for me.

It had to be some part of the US deep state who'd fabricated this. But why would a Russian news agency report on it? Or had Western media fabricated the source too? The levels of misdirection and concealment in the information warfare were likely an order of magnitude worse than he could imagine.

What if he really was a pawn, though? A pawn is still a piece on the chessboard. What was his role in this? Who wanted him connected to the internet disruption? He knew now that Novaya Zemlya hid the operations of a North Pole subsea cable. Was the US looking for an excuse to intervene up there? Or a way to leak the North Pole story without revealing their own intel capabilities?

There was, of course, the possibility that the story did have Russian origins. Maybe to limit his ability to return to the US.

The altered email from Kiss was deeply troubling because it went so far back. Someone or some organization had wanted him to go to Ice Dolphin. Then BestBye's nighttime visit. What was it she said? "Russia has offered Kiss in exchange for two FSB agents." Maybe that was it? He was lured there to become another asset Russia could haggle with?

He glanced at Kiss, who sat with her back against a tree a few yards away. They had gotten her out, but not really. She was still in the Russian Arctic. The job wasn't done yet.

How would they find their boy, East? What would they do when they found him? Take the child and run?

"We have to go back." It was Kiss who broke the silence. She flung a pine cone into an abandoned anthill.

It wasn't a suggestion or plea. Her face beamed with stoicism.

"To the sub?" West asked.

"Either by sub or by foot. We have to get to Murmansk."

He didn't have any better plan. And he sure wouldn't let her go alone. But not knowing the local language or their way in this country would make it incredibly difficult and dangerous.

"You coming?" he said to Åse, who was standing in the direction that felt like the Norwegian border. She didn't respond or react.

He got up and turned east with a nod to Kiss. "At least I have the SSD," he said. "It's something both sides want."

"Hold it there, mister."

It was Åse's voice behind him. He and Kiss turned around.

Åse was pointing a gun at them.

CHAPTER 57

Who's to Blame?

Åse's eyes were charcoal and resolute. "We're not going back. We will cross the border here. And to limit the risk of you flaking ..." Her free hand came out, fingers curling toward herself a couple of times. "I'll take that SSD."

Standing at gunpoint felt unreal. Jitterbug's grave lay between them.

"How dare you," Kiss spat out as she stood up by her tree.

"You'd be surprised at the daring things I do," Åse replied with a smirk. "I warn you not to test my limits."

"Whatever your motives are, I'm on a mission to find my son, and I will not give that up," Kiss retorted.

"Dying here and now won't solve that, will it? I need to get you and the intel we have to my superiors."

West held a hand up toward Kiss and slid his backpack to the ground. He got the drive out in the antistatic bag Jitterbug had put it in and slowly approached Åse. She signaled for him to not come closer. He put the shiny bag on the ground and returned to stand close to Kiss.

Åse got the bag and put it in her breast pocket.

"Okay, you have the drive," West said. "You can get it and the intel out without us. Your chances will be much better on your own, anyway. Let us go find East and rebuild our lives. We don't want a part in the espionage."

Åse shook her head. "Leaving you here will be mission failure. Not because NATO cares about you but because they care about Russia having access to you."

"You told me there was no news reporting on the Russian sub

you blew up. You haven't sent them a single signal, unless you lied about that. Your superiors have to assume we're captured or dead."

"So what?"

"You can let us go and *say* we are dead."

"Ha! And have you show up a few months later in a Russian prisoner exchange, and I'll be charged with lying? Don't think so, soldier."

"An American child has been stolen," Kiss interjected. "What do your superiors have to say about that?"

"The likelihood of you finding the boy is close to zero."

"If we leave Russia, it is truly zero," Kiss snapped.

"We promise to come peacefully if you help us find him," West suggested.

"You overestimate my interest in going deeper into this quagmire," Åse said with sarcasm. "I have an exit here with a reasonable chance of surviving, getting key intel out, and handing you over. Why in the hell would I opt for anything else?"

West's adrenaline was weakening, supplanted by a stomach churn.

"I guess Jitterbug was right then," he said.

Åse tilted her head without the gun moving a millimeter.

"He and I encrypted the drive," West said after a pause. "Another layer on top. Locked the whole thing."

"Bullshit," the Norwegian commander threw at him.

"I doubt I can prove it to you out here, but it's the truth. You know we're paranoid enough to take such precautions. I just didn't think it would be you."

The standoff turned silent. Åse's eyes went back and forth between West and Kiss.

West reached out for Kiss's hand. It was cold and her skin was leathery but she gripped his hand. His knees were weak and the world around him became small and insignificant. A tear welled up in his eye.

Åse lowered her gun.

West's breathing changed, and the churning in his gut changed its pace.

"What?" he asked. He could barely get the word out. It felt like he had only been using the upper parts of his lungs for the past minutes.

Åse looked at him as moment upon moment slowly passed. "Murmansk has a Norwegian consulate."

CHAPTER 58

Pechenga Village

Pechenga was a small place—truly a village. The military presence was scary. A motorized brigade, according to Åse, with an ugly past in the invasion of Ukraine. They spotted at least two arms depots with tanks lined up as they approached.

West and Kiss stayed behind, hidden by the edge of the woods, while Åse went to steal clothes and food for them. The ground was cool and musty. The stress of the situation kept them awake for some time but eventually the stillness made them both doze off, exhausted by miles of walking.

West woke up first. He realized it was the first time he had been alone with Kiss since their romantic afternoon in Stockholm. That occasion felt incredibly distant.

Kiss must have sensed his movement or his gaze because she opened her eyes shortly thereafter.

They looked at each other for a good long while.

"Remember Sweden?" West said by and by.

She put her elbow in his side and smiled faintly. "Of course I do."

Was it the first smile he had seen on her face since back then? It made her look so beautiful and him feel so warm.

"I had a few places I went to in my mind to stay alive in there," she said. "The terrace and that sunset over the bridge was one of them."

"I'm so happy we got you out," West said. "I want to be with you."

"It's like a dream. Whenever I wake up, I think I'm back in my cell and it's time for the grind."

"They made you work in there?"

"Occasionally. After they took East, they pulled me into it. We operated equipment to move these massive, heavy tubes into mountain storage. My cellmate told me it was nuclear waste. Big business for Russia. They have all this Arctic wasteland that they can, I guess, forfeit. The Chinese dump all their shit up here, according to her."

"All the more reason to get you out."

"Less dreamy now. Losing Jit made it real. Such a cruel price to pay. The guilt is overwhelming."

West nodded. "It seems to happen to people around me."

"Don't say that."

West inched a little closer to Kiss under the thick fir tree branch. He could sense her warmth. The bruise on her cheek had started to heal.

He lifted his upper body, supported by one of his forearms, and felt the outside of his zippered pocket with the other hand. Everything was in order, just like the many times he'd checked before.

He opened the pocket and got the ring out, hand clasped.

He kept his hand closed until it was right next to Kiss's face, then slowly opened it.

It took her a while to recognize it. "Why do you have that?"

"Your mom gave it to me at your funeral."

"What?"

"She said you'd kept it for the love of your life and she thought I should have it. Now that you're alive again, I wanted to return it."

"Gosh. I got that for an old boyfriend."

"What? I ..."

"The guy was a douchebag, so I never gave it to him. I probably made some story up for Mom because she found it and I didn't want to talk about it."

West couldn't get a word out. He felt sick.

Kiss looked at him. "I'm sorry." She put an arm around his shoulders. "I didn't mean to hurt you, baby. You *are* the love of my life."

He forced a smile while holding back tears.

"Keep it," she said. "It'll be something to laugh about when we get old." She gave him a gentle kiss and stroked his cheek. "I haven't really taken in that you attended my funeral. That must have been awful."

Her face was so close to his that her eyes jumped back and forth between his right and left side.

"I get it with the ring," she said. "Forget what I said."

The disappointment in West took time to subside. He shifted to a more comfortable distance between them and scanned the surroundings. It was crazy that they even were here. A village up in the Russian Arctic full of military personnel.

"Maybe East is better off with his adoptive parents after all," he said, just speaking his thoughts out loud.

"You're joking, right?"

"The kind of lives we live. Just look at this place—where we are; the kind of risks we take. No good parents would do that."

"We're here *because* of East," Kiss snarled. "Every parent would do this."

She had a point. But still.

He stayed silent for a while to let her cool off. Making Kiss angry was not what he wanted. Maybe he just needed to get over this.

"I don't know if I'm ready to be a dad," he said eventually.

"No one is ready before their first kid. Some say they are, but I doubt it."

"I mean more as a whole. Maybe I'm not cut out for it."

"You've got no choice now. And come on, you're smart, nice, responsible. East will love you. He'll identify with you. He is half you."

He got misty-eyed. "Maybe I'm just scared."

She interlaced her fingers with his. "That's part of it too. We'll get this done, get back to America, and deal with the fear and uncertainty of being parents."

He held on to her hand. "I got you back. I'm halfway done already."

She smiled. "Trying to break me out of prison was crazy, I'll give you that. I'm forever thankful for it. Jit's death just clouds it."

"A dark cloud that will never leave us. You're going to have to start thinking of what to tell *your* parents," he said. "They still think you're dead."

"That was one of my most desperate thoughts. That no one back home knew I was alive. But it changed when East was born. With him, there were two of us."

"I can't imagine the pain when they took him."

"No, you can't. I've never felt such rage. They beat me up and I kept screaming, clawing. If it hadn't been for their strict rules on only beating soft tissue, I would be toothless and have a crooked nose. The blows rained down on me until I couldn't stand up anymore. Took me a month to recover, visibly. I don't want to think of what they might have broken inside me."

That last bit stung. He wanted Kiss to be whole and live forever.

"I worry that he's gotten attached to that Maria," she said.

"Probably," he replied.

Kiss's hand detached from his and he got another elbow in his side, harder this time. "Don't say that."

"Sorry."

He started thinking about the practicality of the task ahead. "Do you think we should just steal him back? Covertly?" he asked.

"Something like that."

"We'll have to steal diapers too."

A twig snapped in the woods behind them. Someone was approaching.

They hunkered down under the fir.

West got his gun out as silently as he could. Kiss looked at it with big eyes.

Another stick broke. Its bearing differed from the first. Maybe multiple people were closing in?

"Should I shoot on sight?" he whispered to Kiss. "It could be a civilian."

Suddenly, the two branches above them parted.

It was Åse returning.

West felt a drop of pee wet his underwear. "I could have fucking shot you!" he snapped, barely able to keep his voice down.

"Good thing you didn't," Åse whispered with calm. "I'll be driving. Damned gas and manual gear shift. It's a small Kia, so there's nowhere to hide. At least it has charging ports for our Tiles. You two sit in the back and don't utter a word if we get stopped. We'll take the R21 Kola Motorway to Murmansk."

"How do we find Maria and Viktor?" Kiss asked. "We don't even know what they look like."

"I have some tech to find their Tiles. It's summer in the Arctic. There's daylight. Parents spend every spare hour in parks or playgrounds."

CHAPTER 59

Coziness Valley

West did not expect a newly built, sixty-acre recreational park in the middle of the Arctic's largest city. It was called Coziness Valley. A cheesy name, but all the more beautiful.

Its every walkway, bridge, and larger seating area was shaped like a gentle arc. Fir trees and the occasional broadleaf paved the way, and the center was half an amphitheater facing south with a recreated wetland below—water surface glittering in the ever-present sun. It was a celebration of the forms and shapes nature took to survive up here. West could only imagine what it would all look like clad in snow.

It was Sunday and West had suggested maybe the Smyslov family would go to church. Åse had said that while many Russians were religious, Sunday church-going was not traditional as in Western countries.

They spread out to cover as much of the vast park as possible. Kiss was by the all-wooden playground in the southwestern part, Åse by the wooden house featuring a café, and West by the huge amphitheater-like space. He had wanted to scout the playground area since it was arguably the most likely spot, but the team had concluded that a lonely man in that area was a risk factor, especially since he didn't know Russian.

Kiss had taken over Jitterbug's Tile and they decided to connect to Russian cell towers to be able to communicate over the Babble app.

West fingered the small beacons in his right pocket. He had another two in his left. Pretty cool tech from Åse's stash. With them, he'd be able to form a mesh network that would monitor any Tile within radio distance and report back the device name and type to him.

He decided to move slowly along the upper arc of the amphitheater and place two of the beacons up there, then move lower for the other two.

Interestingly, there were a few scattered trees planted in deliberate openings of the step-like levels, as if this was an old structure where nature was reclaiming the space. These trees were well groomed and had low metal fences around them. The fence signs made it clear that dogs were *not* welcome to use the soil around the trees.

I can't believe I haven't gotten a puppy yet.

West took a beacon out of his pocket and pretended to tie his shoelaces when placing it behind one of the fence's posts.

With all four beacons in place, he sat down to do what most other adults did here—close his eyes and turn his face toward the sun. The air was comfortably cool, and the sunbeams were a pleasure on his skin. Around him were young couples conversing softly and kids whining to their parents.

The whining. And the crying. How would he put up with that as a dad?

His Tile buzzed and triangulation gave him a position on a local map. It had spotted a device with part of its name being Viktor. West used the telephoto camera on his Tile to take photos.

It seemed to be a guy in his twenties with two male friends. He was carrying a basketball. They looked pretty tall. That was always the case—guys who suggested you should play basketball were always tall. Same in prison. Short or even average height guys preferred soccer or the gym.

Pocketing his Tile again, he wondered if Maria was a common name in Russia. It sounded more Western. But Russia was largely Christian, according to Åse, so it made sense. Religion had been the first global conflict driver. At least that's how he remembered it from history class. Then came the fight over political ideas. Money and trade were always there, of course. Maybe that was the real driver? All about the resources. Today, technology and knowledge were in the driver's seat. The ability to surveil populations, shape public opinion, and spy electronically on your adversaries.

Force-multiplying technologies.

His Tile buzzed. This time it was a message from Kiss.

> I think I got them.

> One Viktor, one Maria, one
> kid.

West found himself incapable of responding. He just had an urge to run over there. Instead Åse replied.

> Don't approach.

> We follow. No approach in
> public.

> I'm fucking tempted.

> That's my son!

> Stay put if you want him
> back.

> I will not help you out of
> prison again.

> We follow them back to their
> car. Just like we said.

•

West got to the playground in as casual a way as he could. They decided on the chat that he'd find Åse and sit down by her on a bench.

His heart jumped as he spotted what must be East. A little chubby boy helped by his mom, or Maria, to go down a gentle slide.

West got seated and took Åse's hand for a couple of minutes as their agreed-upon signal to anyone watching that he was a man in a relationship, not a creep.

Åse leaned over and said almost inaudibly, "All worth it now, huh?"

They sat there facing the sun with closed eyes or looking at the kids and their parents for a good long while. West was impressed with Maria's patience and encouragement, holding East down the slide over and over, pushing the swing, then back to the slide. He was far too young to do any of it on his own.

It was nice to see Viktor follow along close by, taking pictures by the dozens. West himself would probably have strayed off to check his Tile or rest by this time. Well, maybe not. But these two parents seemed cut out for it. They were a tightly knit, happy little family.

•

Two hours later, they knew the Smyslovs had not arrived at Coziness Valley by car. They had taken a trolleybus.

CHAPTER 60

Sergey Kuryokhin Street

Åse was adamant that she'd be the one going in the trolleybus since she knew Russian.

West offered to drive the Kia, but he had never used a stick shift. Kiss said she could do it.

"You sure?" West asked.

"I need to do something. Occupy my brain. Too much stuff going on," she replied, not inviting further discussion.

They got going with a few curses. West leaned his forehead against the side window to let the impressions flow and not stare at Kiss as she wrangled the car. Weathered concrete lined the streets, but there was a fresh coat of light color on some buildings, adding to the cool-tempered ever-summer ambience.

He'd been to a few Russian cities now—Smolensk, Dudinka, Norilsk, and Murmansk. The Cyrillic signs didn't bother him as much anymore. The cables in the air feeding trolleybuses with electricity reminded him of San Francisco. But the light and the long evening shadows differed greatly from his home.

The overhead wires ended when they reached the outskirts of the city and the bus retracted its trolley poles to continue on its own. As they exited the main road, West captured a photo of a billboard-size sign featuring a happy family with two kids. The translation read *Your Home in the Arctic—Apply Now!*

A cluster of spaced-out single-family homes emerged in the distance. They looked as if they had no side walls and the sharply angled roof sat on the ground.

Kiss recognized them. "A-frame houses. Feels like Alaska up here."

The Smyslovs got off at a bus stop and continued on foot. West and Kiss kept their distance while Åse followed close enough to spot the address.

·

They messaged each other and decided to rendezvous at the bus stop because Kiss wanted out of the car she by now hated.

"Sergey Kuryokhin Street 4," Åse reported, getting seated on the bench in the little glass hut. "Viktor used a physical key to unlock the door." She nudged West to give her some more space.

Kiss leaned against one of the glass side walls on the other side of him.

West was trying to figure out the next step. "You think they have some neighborhood watch going on here? Drones?"

"Maybe. But there's plenty of space between the houses. Enough privacy to get in unnoticed among the night shadows."

"I'm sure we can get in," West said. "But I'm still at a loss on what to do. Pull guns and demand they hand over East? They have done nothing illegal."

He got a dirty look from Kiss.

"What if they have an alarm they can trigger?" he continued. "And if we get out, they call the cops as soon as we left."

"Not if we tie them up," Åse said.

"Come on. We're not going to treat them like criminals," West commented.

"They are criminals." Kiss spat on the ground.

West paused. The others weren't talking, but the team needed a plan. "They're just a couple who wanted a kid," he said, breaking the silence. "I think we should talk to them."

"What?" Kiss uttered it with such force that West jerked away from her, bumping into Åse.

"Maybe they're willing to make a deal," he said once the scene had calmed down. "Maybe East was just listed for adoption and they don't know that he was taken from you."

"She fucking works there," Kiss retorted. "She knows where he's from."

West couldn't really argue with that. Still, there was something within him that refused to think of Viktor and Maria as ice cold. They had looked so gentle and human in Coziness Valley.

"Even if we take him in a sneaky way, we'll be dealing with a lost child. Easier to get away with, but still a police situation. I'd like to talk to them and understand. There'll come a day when East wants to know what his life was like back here. Unless you intend to never tell him. He expects more of us than to just snatch him."

He didn't get an immediate response. The wind was picking up outside their glass shelter and an empty candy bag flew by. Half a minute passed as each one thought about the prospect on their own.

"I hate to say it," Åse commenced, "but you're starting to sound like a father."

Kiss folded her arms and put the back of her head against the sheet of glass. "If they react like I know they will, we take East by force and tie those suckers up."

Progress.

"They won't have any way of knowing who we are," West said. "They won't know we're East's real parents."

"DNA should make that abundantly clear," Åse said from the other side of him. "You can get a pocket-size sequencer for a few hundred bucks. Probably even in a place like Murmansk."

Chapter 61

American Boy

A portable DNA sequencer turned out to be more than a few hundred dollars' worth of Bancor and took them a full day to acquire. Chinese brand. Still, West felt good about figuring out the details rather than raging about the situation. Felt good until Åse showed him a news flash, that is.

> US Authorities have issued a Red Notice through Interpol for West William Wilder in connection with claims of collaboration with Russia's Cyber Command. This international request for assistance aims to locate and provisionally arrest Wilder, pending extradition or similar legal action. Officials urge anyone with information on the whereabouts of Wilder to come forward.

Whoever was after him was raising the stakes.

He sat silent for an hour before concluding that this didn't change anything here and now. Neither anger nor defeatism were useful. There would be a reckoning down the road, but Jitterbug had said it best: Come what may.

•

The night between Monday and Tuesday, the team of three were back at the wooden A-frame houses. The triangular shapes stood out like jagged teeth against the low midnight sun.

The Smyslovs lived in one of the larger houses with a second, taller part further back, creating a fold in the roof. There was a tube-shaped chimney protruding right where the two roof segments met.

West was the designated lock picker. His pulse increased as he slowly approached the entrance of the house. The trees in the garden were thin and aspiring even for the Arctic, so West concluded the house could not be that old.

No creak as he stepped onto the flat-roofed porch. He fiddled with the lock picks in his pocket. Kiss had followed a few steps and was in the shadows out in the garden. Åse remained by the street, looking out for any passersby or window peepers.

West got the lock job done with shaky hands. Warm indoor air puffed out as he gently opened the entrance. He signaled to the others with a sweeping move of his free arm, then snuck in.

Seconds passed with him standing there in a small, dark foyer. The interior smelled of wood and resin.

Two shadowy figures joined him from behind and closed the door.

Åse turned on the faintest red flashlight on her Tile and pulled her balaclava down over her face. She had insisted they not wear them outdoors. West and Kiss pulled theirs down too.

They produced subdued sounds of rubber soles against the floor and friction of synthetic clothes as they intruded into the home of the Smyslov family.

Åse signaled that she'd immediately found something in a bedroom to the left. Her dim flashlight moved distinctly in there, surveying.

West and Kiss entered, tiptoeing.

There was a person sleeping in a king-size bed. The flashlight's orb was to the side, but it was clear that there was only one person in the bed.

The short hair told West it was Viktor.

Åse's gloved hand hovered over the Russian's mouth for a second before pressing down firmly, supported by her upper body craning over. Viktor's eyes opened wide and terrified. His body jolted and twisted under the blanket, but his head remained fixed, pressed into the pillow.

Åse's light lit the crib beside the bed.

She turned to West and Kiss and shook her head, then did an upward-pointing circular motion with the hand that held the flashlight—the signal to search.

Kiss and West moved quickly but silently through the rest of the Smyslov home. Kitchen, living room with a door to a backside deck, single bathroom, and an empty spare bedroom with baby toys scattered. No sign of Maria or East.

They got back to the occupied bedroom. Kiss lit her own face and simply shook her head to Åse.

Åse started calming Viktor down in Russian. At least that's what it sounded like. West hesitated to say anything since it would reveal his origin.

Slowly, the scene calmed down.

Åse removed her hand from Viktor's mouth. She spoke in Russian again. West turned on the translator on his Tile and followed along on the screen as Viktor responded.

> She's not here.

> Where is she?
> And the child?

> Who are you?

> Where are they?

> Are you from D-6?

> We want to talk to you and
> Maria about the child.

A long pause.

> I need to go to the
> bathroom.

> Not possible. You can use
> the baby's potty.

> He's still in diapers.

"Get him a bowl from the kitchen. Or a trash can," Åse said in West's and Kiss's direction. So much for concealing their origin. Kiss went. The transcript on West's Tile continued.

American?

Possibly.
Your child is
American.

"I know."

West's screen didn't update, even though it was Viktor speaking. He realized the man had just switched to English and said, "I know."

Chapter 62

A Friendly Chat

"Why are you here?" Viktor asked from his bed position.

"We're here for our son," West said as he took a step into the bedroom.

"I don't understand." The Russian looked at West in the doorway. His English wasn't bad. An accent for sure, but he didn't have to make an effort to understand him.

"Your son Anatoly is our son East," West said.

"We adopted him. Are you the father?"

"Yes."

Kiss wedged in to the left of West and threw a metal mixing bowl on the bed. "And I'm his mom."

"Can I turn on the light?" Viktor asked, making a move for the bedside table.

"After you've done your business," Åse commanded.

"I don't need to go." He rolled to the side and stretched out his hand, only to get it smacked down by Åse.

"Stay still," she uttered and turned the mellow bedside light on for him.

For the first time, West could see the room's interior all at once. It was sparsely decorated. A flower pattern on the wallpaper was the only thing that stood out. Cupboards on the windowless side. The bedside lamp was decorative, not for reading. Underneath it lay a Buzz figurine from *Toy Story* in an ashtray. West sniffed the air, but it didn't smell like a smoker's home.

"Can you remove your ..." Viktor struggled to find the word.

"We're not that stupid," Kiss spat out.

"I want to see if you look anything like Anatoly. Or East, was it? I want to see if you're speaking the truth. We've always wanted to meet his biological parents."

West pulled his balaclava off, then his right glove, and extended his hand and approached the bed. "I'm West."

Åse was about to block him, but stopped midway and allowed the two men to shake hands.

"I can see you in him," Viktor said. "The cheekbones and the nose, I think. He's such a sweet boy."

"Happy to hear that. I mean that he's sweet."

Kiss took a step forward too and removed her balaclava.

Viktor looked at her. "He has your eyes. Maybe not the color, but the shape, and the eyebrows."

"Okay, you've seen their faces ..." Åse interjected.

"A few more things, just to check," Viktor said, holding up the palm of his hand against the Norwegian commander. "Where was he born and how old is he?"

"Ice Dolphin Prison and he's eight months old," Kiss said without a moment's hesitation.

"That is correct," Viktor said with a conclusive nod toward her. He looked at all three of them one by one. A peacefulness developed in his face, tense muscles relaxing. "Somehow, I knew you would come. Some day. You could kill me here on the spot or get me to tell you anything. I understand that. If you are lying to me, you have at least done a good job. You managed to find me and sneak into my home. It sounds weird, but it's good that I don't have to think about this anymore. It has happened."

"We're not here for you," Kiss interjected. "We don't give a shit about you. Where is East?"

"If Maria and Anatoly were here, you would have probably just taken the child."

"*You* took the child."

Viktor looked around at all three of them. "I beg you, don't hurt Maria. She is the love of my life."

Kiss pressed on. "Why did you take my child from me?"

Viktor looked pleadingly at her. "We didn't know you. We weren't told anything but your name—Kate Libby, right?"

"Well, yeah."

"And that you were American. Maria tried to look you up in the prison database and lost three months of pay when that was discovered. She only got to keep her job because she's ... well, that doesn't matter. We reasoned you must have done something terrible to end up at Ice Dolphin." His eyes searched for something in Kiss's face. "I mean something bad in the eyes of Russian law. I guess you're out now. Is that it? Your name was cleared and you want your son back?"

"I want him back, period."

"Of course. Sorry. But no one can raise a child in prison, especially not in a place like Ice Dolphin. That was what convinced Maria that it was okay."

He lowered his gaze, sat up against the wall behind the bed, and let his shoulders drop.

"Are we done chitchatting here?" Åse said with a quick look at West and Kiss before turning to Viktor. "Where are Maria and the child?" she asked.

"Maria wanted a child so dearly," the man said, head up in a distant stare. His voice had a sprinkle of melancholy.

Åse shifted as if getting ready to lift Viktor out of bed, but West put his arm between her and the Russian.

"Why did she want a child so dearly?" West asked.

"She was devastated when the physician told her she could never get pregnant. Utterly devastated. We had waited too long. Didn't seek help in time. It took two years for her to come back to her usual self. But I knew the longing was still there, underneath layers and layers ..."

Viktor blinked and his mouth cramped up in a sad pout.

West gave it a few seconds and hoped that Kiss wouldn't interject. She didn't. "Can you tell us how you ended up adopting him?"

Viktor swallowed before parting his lips. "We learned that a child was being taken from the American prisoner to be put in an orphanage. Everyone at Ice Dolphin was talking about it. We both work there, on other things than the prison. Maybe I should have told you that. We were mesmerized by the whole situation—foreigners are typically not put in Ice Dolphin—and we felt sorry for the child."

Viktor released his stare and looked at West. "Russian orphanages are not known for their great conditions," he said.

"Did you think of his real parents? Us?"

"Yes. We even talked about what if this American woman is released, even though that never happens at Ice Dolphin. Prisoners die there, sooner or later."

"So you felt it was the right thing to do?" West could sense Kiss's frustration and admitted to himself that it was a leading question.

"We decided to try to adopt him and take him to visit the United States when he was old enough," the Russian replied.

"Really?" Kiss did not conceal her resentment.

Viktor turned his eyes to her. "America has always fascinated Maria and me. We want to go some day."

"This is too much," Kiss said before Åse got back in the driver's seat.

"As much as I'd love to hear more of your life story, we have a job to do. Where are Maria and the child?"

Viktor hesitated for a few seconds. "They went to Moscow to visit her sister."

"What the f…" Åse rolled her eyes in her balaclava. "When will she be back?"

"In a month. She took the train."

"A month! So much for the consulate."

"She's trying to make the best of her maternity leave. I'm headed back to work, and she doesn't want to be alone here. Neither of us are from Murmansk originally. We moved here when she got promoted. I took a job up there to be with her. I'll be gone for four weeks. One month of constant work, one month off—that's how Ice Dolphin is organized."

Åse turned to West and Kiss. "We can't wait here for a month. And we can't let this guy go back to work. Viktor, you call in sick. You're taking us to Maria, in Moscow."

CHAPTER 63

White House: Insider Attack

The president sensed that the news would be bad. General Purnell looked haggard and avoided eye contact with any of the others. Might as well rip the Band-Aid off. "What do you have for me, Purnell?"

"Ma'am, the transatlantic disruption was not caused by tampering with physical equipment. Our subsea cables and repeaters are all intact. Everything points to an attack from the inside. Someone within our ranks or with access to our internal systems shut us off. The fact that we haven't realized that until now speaks to the sophistication of the attack."

"What exactly is pointing in the insider direction?"

"We know from previous investigations that it's valuable to keep at least one failing system in-state. You keep one that you don't restart or try to fix. That way you have a system with traces of the attack, if it was an attack. So we kept one transatlantic connection down. Just isolated it to not allow for any spread of infection. We did a meticulous investigation of that failing system, and it looks like an attack deployed from the inside. When I say inside, it could be one of three things. First, an intrusion further back, acting in a way that looks like an insider but is in truth an outsider. That is our leading theory. Second, one or more rogue employees, possibly straight-up spies embedded in our ranks. Certainly not unheard of. Third and last, a true insider, a person or pocket of people who did this on behalf of some leg of the US government."

"Deep state is what you're saying?"

"That's the third possibility, yes."

"To boil it down, intruders, spies, or trusted government employees with their own agenda. Under the guise of North Korea."

Purnell nodded. "That's the gist of it."

Sanchez forced herself to neither react overtly nor push the matter further. She knew the general was overlooking some things, and it was telling that he did. Maybe Lewis was right about him after all?

"Any sign of the origin, given that your leading theory is foreign intrusion further back?" she asked, snapping out of her thoughts.

"None yet," Purnell replied.

"So, how can it be a leading theory with no meat on the bone?"

The general started to respond twice before he got a word out. "As you know, Madam President, our adversaries play all sorts of tricks to make their activity look like it's someone else and even cause us to take action against the wrong actor. We play the same kind of tricks."

"What do you say to this, Lewis?" the president asked the director of National Intelligence.

Sanchez could tell Lewis was fighting schadenfreude. There was benefit to some level of competition between the people informing her.

"We have not been granted access to the intel General Purnell has," Lewis said.

"This information is just hours old!" Purnell blurted back.

"Well, hours matter," Lewis said with calm, giving the blushing general a quick glance. "I repeat, we have not been granted access to the intel General Purnell has. As for the malware that took out some infrastructure, we have indications pointing to Russian sources with a North Korean veneer."

"What indications?" the president asked.

"GRU APT, ma'am. Fancy Bear."

APT, or advanced persistent threat, used to be the term for long-term attack campaigns but had gradually changed to mean nation state-sponsored cyber espionage and manipulation. Sanchez knew about Fancy Bear—infamous for their attacks on US military families, European elections, international think tanks, and parliaments in all corners of the world.

"Last year we had a Chinese attack looking like the Bear, right?" Sanchez asked, stroking her lower lip with the tip of her thumb.

"It was inconclusive on whether China got help from Fancy Bear or made their attack look like them, but you're right," Lewis admitted.

President Sanchez fiddled with her pen, wiggling it between index and middle finger. "We need to go bigger picture here. Transatlantic internet disruption being a potential insider attack, traces of Fancy Bear in malware, NATO operation at Novaya Zemlya as part of the SMITH investigation, NATO operatives disappeared and claims of a torpedo strike on a Russian sub, Russian subs lining up along the G-I-UK gap, and Russian claims of this West Wilder helping them. There may be a connection between these events—all of them or a subset. Director Lewis, I'm putting you in charge of finding any such connections. Go wide. Don't make assumptions."

Lewis stood up and lifted his chin. "No assumptions."

"And you provide him the necessary help, General. Including timely access to intel."

Purnell gave a single nod. "Yes, ma'am."

People got ready to leave.

"One more thing." The noise of chairs moving stopped as the president spoke to her security advisor. "Alec, you often help me see obscure angles. What would be the purpose of disrupting our subsea internet connections if the attack was truly internal?"

"I thought about that as the general spoke. The only plausible explanation I could come up with was someone who wanted to suss out what we now know as the Greenland connection."

"Probing Russian internet contingency plans, huh?"

"Yes, Madam."

"Make sure you cover that angle, Director."

Lewis confirmed and gave General Purnell another glance. He did not look happy.

CHAPTER 64

The Bargain

Driving to Moscow took two days of ten-plus hours on the road with numerous stops to fill up on gas in the small Kia. Kiss was the front passenger while West and Viktor shared the back. Åse had turned on the child safety lock on the rear doors and told West he was responsible for Viktor not pulling any tricks.

The landscape shifted from subarctic plains with wildflowers, shrubs, and smaller trees to a fuller, denser nature as they got further south.

West suffered stings of anxiety and sadness over Jitterbug, on one occasion sobbing for an hour in the car before Åse demanded he stop. At other times he stretched over to put a hand on Kiss's shoulder and she put hers on top of his.

They stayed overnight in Petrozavodsk by Lake Onega. Åse had insisted Viktor's Tile stay in Murmansk, so the man didn't have much else to do but spark up conversation. Slowly, West got to know the adoptive father of his son. Kiss seemed to listen in but said little.

The most fascinating part of what Viktor shared was around the broken social contract of his country. The fall of the Soviet Union had brought liberties and a level of openness, but also exposed the people to a raw form of capitalism they were unprepared for. Viktor had just been a tweenie back then, but saw it take his family on a treacherous ride. Then followed a gradual dismantling of democracy but also a return to normalcy with some of the new-won freedoms still intact.

He kept coming back to getting paid on time and being able to travel as two huge things for everyday Russians.

"You don't need democracy so much when things are improving anyway," he said. "You need it when you have to course-correct. That's where elections come from. Every four years is about when people need to course-correct the politicians. Us Russians lost that and plunged back into autocracy and I didn't want to bring a child into that world. That's a big reason why we waited too long to try to get pregnant. Eventually we couldn't."

Viktor took West's left hand in both of his. "I'm telling you this because ever since we adopted Anatoly, my mind has been set on getting out. But it's so hard for Russians. We are not welcome in many places."

•

At one stop for gas and coffee, Viktor went to the bathroom and Åse stood outside making sure he wouldn't try to escape.

Kiss and West got out of the car to stretch their legs.

"Hearing you talk with Viktor makes me realize everything has kept moving," Kiss said. "I mean, of course it has. But in isolation ..."

"You subconsciously think everyone else is on pause just because your life is," West filled in. "I know what you mean. Then you get out and have to accept that the world didn't miss a beat."

"What happened to you and the others?" she asked.

"You won't believe it but we got to the GPI backup in Norilsk and I blew it up."

"Blew it up? Like, literally?"

"Yeah, for real. I used ANFO."

"So the whole global identity system was compromised?"

"Mhmm. Major changes to how identities are used now, but it's not gone. The whole thing is still churning in Congress, and around the globe."

"What a thing."

"It was hard to feel good about any of it having lost you."

She put an arm on his sore shoulder and he jerked back with an "Ow."

"Sorry." She leaned in against his chest instead. "We're a beat-up couple, but you've got me now."

West kissed the side of her head.

He saw movement when he opened his eyes again. "The others are coming back."

•

Viktor asked Åse to stop when they reached the outskirts of the Russian capital. "We have to convene," he said.

They parked at a place where they could get coffee. West, tired of sitting in the car, suggested that they should chat outside. Åse deemed it unsafe. Midsized Russian cities did not yet have widespread facial recognition cameras, but Moscow was littered with them according to western accounts. Chinese technology, proudly deployed to safeguard the capital.

West was just about to challenge that since they had the face stick. But he realized she wasn't going to share that with Viktor and notifying authorities that Viktor was in Moscow was probably something they wanted to delay for as long as possible.

Still cramped up in the Kia, Viktor began. "I have not yet told you where Maria and the boy are. I will refuse to do so unless you let me see them first. Just me. Maria will react very badly to any notion of losing her boy. She is smart and logical, but this is the most important thing in her life, more important than me or even herself. I will do my best to explain to her. Lay it out. I've been contemplating how to do that ever since we left Murmansk."

He put his elbows on his knees, clasped his hands, and leaned forward.

"The only thing that I can see getting her through it would be a promise to get us asylum in the United States and be allowed to see Anatoly ... sometimes. Maybe his birthday? I do not know how she'll react to such a proposal, but it's the best I've come up with. And I need your commitment ..."

"We're not going to negotiate asylum for you," Åse said. "And I sure as fuck will not smuggle Russians out of the country."

"I've come with you this far," Viktor said calmly. "Please work with me. I have not caused you any trouble. I have believed your story and I'm willing to try to get you back your son."

"I would not have a problem letting you see East," West said. "Would you?" He leaned over to the headrest of Kiss's seat in front of him.

"Viktor seems fine," Kiss mumbled. "I haven't met Maria yet."

"That's true," West said in a low voice. He turned back to Viktor. "Assuming Maria is a person we'd feel comfortable with, I think we can make it work. But getting you out of Russia would be a nightmare."

"I already told you we're not doing that," Åse ejected from the front seat.

"Quite the opposite," Viktor said with sudden intensity. "It's your ticket to get East out. Remember, all papers say he's our son. We are the only ones who can get him across the Russian border in an orderly fashion. We go to the only NATO country where Russians are still welcome—Turkey. From there to the US Embassy, where you get us asylum."

Åse hit the steering wheel and swore to herself.

"How would we argue your case?" West asked.

"I think your government would welcome us," Viktor said proudly. "At least my wife. She works on Operations for Contingency of the Red Web."

"Oh my God," Åse said to herself.

CHAPTER 65

The Northernmost Megacity

Moscow. The world's northernmost megacity and the home of seventeen million people, the Red Square, the Bolshoi Ballet, and the Kremlin. It presented itself in summery garments and its central parts sparkled in vivid colors in stark contrast to Petrozavodsk and Murmansk. West desperately wanted to get out of the car, but Åse was adamant that he and Kiss stay while she and Viktor find Maria.

West got to thinking as time passed slowly.

Someone working on the contingency of the Red Web adopting his son was a quirk he could barely handle. Was she even likely to defect? And why would she want to go to the US—would they lead a better life there than here, where she must be influential? Well, the climate would be better than in the Arctic. The incentives were strange, like something dreamed up in a Hollywood movie script. But then again, history featured many powerful people switching sides or spying on their own to aid the enemy. On all sides.

This city and the power of the people in the Kremlin had mesmerized and frightened Americans for almost a century. Not because Russia was more powerful than the US, but for their unpredictability, their superpower ambitions, and their access to a vast nuclear arsenal.

More recent was the Russian influence over the internet. West had read up on it after his prison release and been told numerous stories by Jitterbug.

Russia had taken an asymmetric approach, referred to as the twenty-first-century style of warfare. War with the West wasn't to be declared or even admitted to. Instead, there'd be a permanently operating front through the entire territory—social, political, cultural, and technical.

Kremlin's Internet Research Agency had deployed wide-ranging techniques and strategies to influence the affairs across the globe. Its shadiest arms were loosely controlled hacker groups wreaking havoc high and low.

The Russian position was that America had started this era of asymmetric warfare by covertly supporting the color revolutions—protest movements leading to changes of government in post-Soviet countries. Their prime example was the Orange Revolution in Ukraine.

West had first thought it was demeaning to the people who had risked their lives in those fights for freedom. But as he got deeper into the rabbit hole, he became convinced that there was some truth to US influence behind the scenes. The goal may very well have been to spread democracy and liberties, but the subversion of Russian influence and Ukraine's emerging ties to the EU and NATO must have been welcomed by American leadership.

In his darkest and most conspiracy-laden moments, West entertained the thought of the internet itself being the ultimate imperialistic move by his home country. Own and control the world's information highway. It had taken the Kremlin decades to realize how this risk undercut them and finally establish their own internet. The Red Web was connected to the rest of the world, but in a controlled way that allowed Russia to isolate itself at any moment.

The Chinese kind of got lucky by being hell-bent on surveilling their own population. The Chinese Firewall turned out to be more important for their national security than the suppression of domestic dissent. It was the first case of a splinternet but certainly not the last.

This is why you can't take sides in this shit. It's all bad. Common folks are just pawns.

•

West popped out of his thoughts as soon as Åse started streaming from miles away in the city.

Viktor looked composed but on alert. He and Åse were sitting close to each other but at separate tables by the window in a café.

A text from Åse said they were on the block where Viktor claimed Maria was. The plan was to let him continue on his own the last bit.

Maria had no idea her husband would show up in Moscow and her reaction would likely be intense. Even so, the message he brought her would be ten times as shocking and there was no way of telling where things would go from there. Losing her boy, leaving her job, family, and country forever, and seeking asylum in the West—who could deal with that prospect in any short amount of time? The more West thought about it, the crazier it sounded.

Viktor got up and exited the café. Åse's Tile camera followed him through the window. He crossed the street and walked two narrow buildings to the left. The camera zoomed in as he got further away.

He entered a cyan five-story building. It looked like it housed apartments rather than offices. No business signs outside. The entrance door closed slowly behind him and the camera zoomed back out.

Åse turned off the feed. She'd stay put until this was over.

West moved his eyes from the Tile's screen and looked around. Two young people entered a car parked near him and Kiss in the Kia, carrying bags with clothes.

I should buy Kiss some nice clothes. And a luxury pedicure.

Åse had gotten them a stack of cheap underclothing in Murmansk. He thought back to Kiss in her place in San Francisco. God, he longed to go back to just hanging out with her.

But they'd be parents now, and hanging out would be in the Golden Gate Park. There was a large playground there. They should bring coffee in a thermos. Maybe East would turn out like him as a kid, talking to other grown-ups and asking them all sorts of questions. He chuckled, remembering his mom's stories of him querying folks at the beach.

Kiss bumped him and nodded at the Tile in her hand. There was a message from Åse.

Two thugs in the café.

Talking to the staff.

They carry guns.

Not police.

I'll sneak up and turn on
transcription.

West gave Kiss a look while they waited for the stream of translated Russian to appear on her screen.

... detected in the street
outside ten minutes ago.

No, I don't recognize him.

Did someone like him leave
just now?

If your damn cameras can
detect him, why don't they
show where he went?

You should collaborate for
your own good.

I tried to help you.
Now can you please get out
of my café?

The translated feed stopped, and there was silence for two minutes. The young shoppers got out of their parking spot and rolled
past them, headed for the exit.

Åse's camera feed came back, following events outside the café.

What had to be the two armed men she'd spotted were crossing
the street and entered the same building as Viktor.

Chapter 66

You Five Okay

The wait that followed tore at the insides of West and, by the look of it, was worse for Kiss.

Åse stopped filming and only sent them text updates once every two minutes, saying "Nothing yet" and "Ditto."

Kiss kept saying she sensed this was bad.

West tried to comfort her, but he knew he wasn't convincing. Best-case scenario would be if it was a routine thing or a misunderstanding. Maybe the Moscow surveillance apparatus was so well-staffed that sending a couple of guys was nothing?

Kiss could not stay seated and started pacing outside, close to the Kia.

When the real update finally came through, it was bad. West knocked on the car window and Kiss joined him in an instant.

The camera feed had started again. Kiss and West watched in horror as Viktor, Maria, and little East were led away by the two armed men. Viktor and Maria looked harried.

Åse attempted to pursue at a safe distance, but the captives were taken to a minibus just a block down the street and vanished through Moscow's dense traffic with flashing lights on the roof.

•

Åse arrived at the parked car twenty minutes later. She sat down violently in the driver's seat.

"Talk to me. Who do you think they were?" Kiss asked, leaning forward toward the front seat.

"How the fuck would I know? Russkis with guns. Something official, given the minibus."

"We should have sought Maria out ourselves," Kiss said with determination. "This bet on Viktor was disastrous."

West had heard her say that multiple times while they were waiting.

"Not much use in revisiting that decision now, is there?" Åse pointed out.

"I'm trying to process the situation, okay? Could you try to help, please?"

"I'm telling you to focus on what you can affect. An analysis of the past to improve decision-making is something you do when the situation is over."

Kiss took a few moments to let steam out. "Could Viktor be playing us? Calling them in?" she asked eventually.

"The two men were talking about camera surveillance," Åse replied. "Not that I think Viktor wouldn't play us."

"Facial recognition?"

"Probably. I had no idea his wife was involved in the Red Web. Had we known back in Murmansk, I would have worked around it. Somehow."

"Maybe that was his play? He knew Moscow's surveillance would pick him up, and they'd rescue him," Kiss said.

Åse gave her a tired look. "You can go as deep as you want down the rabbit hole, sis."

West hurried to say something to Åse before Kiss took her bait. "Did you recognize their uniforms or any emblems? Something?"

"Nothing stood out, but we should review the video clips."

Åse shared her video files and they all sat silent looking at the three scenes over and over. Viktor entering the cyan building, the two men following him shortly thereafter, and the group of five leaving.

The two men wore dark blue uniforms, wide black belts in some synthetic fabric, and army-like boots. Their guns looked standard, according to Åse.

Viktor and Maria were not handcuffed but walked sandwiched between the men. Maria carried East tucked to her shoulder.

"Wait," West said. "Check this." He held his Tile over the mid console and Kiss and Åse leaned over to watch. He scrubbed back and forth a few times. "Look at Viktor's right hand, right there."

It was the scene with the group of five exiting. Viktor's hand swung with his stride and the fingers seemed to make gestures. First his index and middle finger extended with the others folded. It looked like he did a slight circular motion in this position, as if he was stirring with his fingers. Then all fingers extended, and finally just the thumb. The movements were too subtle to be effective visual communication, but there was no natural explanation for why he would do this.

West pulled back his Tile and asked it for a guide on sign language. Half a minute later, he spoke again. "Looks like U, 5, and then the thumb. Thumbs-*up* means okay."

"Could thumb mean one?" Kiss asked.

"No, one is your index finger."

"*You five okay,*" West spelled out.

"Or *you five follow*, if the thumb is a hitchhike sign," Kiss suggested.

"But we're not five," Åse said, unamused.

"*You circle five okay. You rotate five okay.* He's making that stirring motion," West said while expanding on his notion of what the gestures could mean.

"*You spin five. You go around five.* Could it be something around the clock?" Kiss said.

"Far-fetched," Åse said. "If Viktor even knows sign language, he wouldn't throw a rebus at us. It has to be dead simple. I doubt there's anything there at all."

They sat silently. West closed his eyes, trying to find other angles. He parted his eyelids again and found Kiss looking at him.

She said in a low voice, "You're good at this stuff. You can figure it out."

He smiled for a second and closed his eyes again. Kiss took his hand. He wanted to sit like this as an old man on a porch in sunny California. East would be there, grown up with kids of his own. Maybe East would learn Russian one day, to be able to understand more of how and where his life got started.

West opened his eyes and asked his Tile for *Russian* sign language.

As he suspected, it differed from the one used in America. Index and middle fingers stirring meant D, or Д. All fingers extended were five. But six was not like the Western three-finger fork. It was five plus one with a thumb. "I got it," he said. "It's D-6. Stalin's Diggers."

CHAPTER 67

Metro-2

"How to get in? How to get *in*! We don't know if this bloody thing even exists." Åse was clearly not having it. Then again, finding East was not her pursuit at all. "Metro-2 is a UFO-level conspiracy theory. I bet you good money that these D-6 thugs are just using the name and myth to boost their own egos and people's fear. The content of that drive better be worth it because I'm seriously questioning why I don't just leave you two to kill yourselves here."

"You can leave at any time," Kiss said, raising her voice just as much as Åse.

Silence reigned.

West sat in the couch's corner and listened in passively while reading about SSD hacking. The laptop drive was still on his mind.

They had taken to the suburbs and found an apartment they could rent for a few days. There were at least two readily hackable routers among the neighbors and they had configured their Tiles to divide internet traffic randomly between those poor people's connections.

The living room they sat in was small. Kiss and West on one end each of the sofa and Åse in the sole armchair. The air was damp from their drying laundry.

Åse reached for her mug of instant coffee. "I'm not leaving without the fucking drive decrypted," she said with a poisonous look at West.

"And he's not giving you the key before we have our son back. There, I'm happy we reiterated that whole thing again," Kiss said. "Now can we talk about Metro-2?"

Åse rolled her eyes. "Sure."

Kiss dialed her tone down. "I'm not saying there's a whole second subway system," she said. "But there's plenty of solid info on the extra tunnel and the ventilation shaft at the university. I'm saying if we can get in, we can find something out about the Diggers."

The term D-6 had opened a Pandora's box of myths from the Cold War into modern age. Joseph Stalin had worried constantly about assassination attempts and had commissioned an underground railway from the Kremlin to the Volynskoye Park. This first fork of the Moscow Metro later expanded to address the need for shelter against a nuclear attack. The expansion supposedly grew to the size of an underground city called Ramenki, inhabited by the KGB and later FSB. All built by his Diggers and called Metro-2.

A secretive ventilation facility did indeed exist on the Moscow State University campus. Urban explorers had raved over this myth for decades. In terms of genuine sources, there were vague claims from Moscow Metro representatives or former politicians every few years.

"Fifteen thousand people. That's not something you can keep secret," West said from his corner. "Why would people be down there in peacetime?"

The underground facility in Norilsk only had computers and robots, no humans.

"Totally," Åse said, failing to suppress a yawn. "If there's anything to believe in this fairy tale, it's the shelter piece. They may, and I say may, have space to shelter a few thousand down there. That wouldn't be bizarre given the size of the Duma, the Special Programmes, and the Ministry of Defense. But for work? They have their offices at Frunzenskaya Naberezhnaya."

"Is there a connection to the university, other than the site of that shaft?" Kiss asked Åse.

"The connections between their political power, military power, and academia have been strong for a century. Probably even stronger in today's climate."

"So, which is easiest to hack?" West asked.

"What do you mean?" Kiss said.

"Politicians, military, or academia, which is easiest?"

Kiss scoffed. "Toss-up between stupid politicians and naïve professors."

"Look for targets who would be likely to have access to whatever is going on in Metro-2," Åse said, yawning. "I'm too fucking tired to work right now. Keep it down while I sleep."

•

With internet access for the first time in a long while, West couldn't help but check the news. An article in *Wired* caught his attention.

The Human Troll Is Back!

AI-driven trolling and manipulation of public discourse has reigned for a decade plus. Enormous compute power has been spent on A/B testing the top incinerating commentary, the most rage-inducing gut punches, and the quickest changing of subjects. We're all a bit dumber for it.

Two years ago, Cunning's political scandal forever etched AI deception into our history books. It's the first known two-layer stunt where AI fabricated a viral story of Senator Cunning being manipulated by AI, which in turn duped Congress to oust him.

What followed was one of America's toughest legislative battles, resulting in the passing of the Online Manipulation Acknowledgment and Hedge Act. It mandates that politicians accept they can be adversarially influenced by digital information and that they take precautions.

This demand from politicians gave rise to AI that is really good at telling AI and humans apart. Not some crufty old CAPTCHA. No, this stuff makes the call straight from a post or by asking a single follow-up question. AI on the troll side naturally evolved to avoid such detection, which triggered another round in the cat-and-mouse game.

Detections and evasions are now so complex and elusive that internet powers have shifted their interest back to an old friend: the human troll.

"A planet is the cradle of mind, but one cannot live in a cradle forever," Russian rocket scientist Konstantin Tsiolkovsky famously said. He was referring to humankind escaping into space, but it seems it is artificial minds that need help to leave the cradle. The most effective way of not being categorized as a bot is not being one.

According to our sources, thousands of humans are now back in the game of stepping hard on others' toes, both at home and overseas. So if you're looking for a job, Uncle Sam may have use for your corrosive personality.

CHAPTER 68

Firmware

Åse had left for bed half an hour ago.

West whispered to Kiss, "Her jacket is hanging in the foyer. I'm pretty sure she has the Ice Dolphin drive in her breast pocket."

Kiss's eyes grew, and she shook her head.

"I know," West said. "But I want to finish Jit's firmware hack. He ..." A sting of grief grabbed him.

Kiss put her hand on his good shoulder.

He steadied his voice. "I don't know how I'll break into it without Jit, but we may need it. If I can decrypt it, I can download the content to my Tile and then lock it again. Åse won't know a thing. Could you look for gullible professors while I do this?"

"If she notices ..."

Kiss silently placed herself by the bedroom door as West dug through the commander's breast pockets. Interestingly, she had moved it from the left to the right pocket.

He held up the antistatic bag to Kiss and snuck into the kitchen.

Kiss got into her task of finding targets with access to Metro-2.

West made sure the kitchen chair didn't make a sound as he pulled it in underneath himself. He slowly extracted the circuit board from the bag.

The first step was easy—removing his and Jitterbug's over-the-top encryption.

However, remembering the steps to where Jitterbug had left off took a while.

This was a self-encrypting drive, a type that got popular after software-level full disk encryption was hacked. Stripping that self-encryption off required either real user credentials or exploiting a bug in the drive's firmware. That's why they had gone through the trouble of downloading the firmware to their Tiles where they could look for bugs in it.

Some lightweight analysis and a couple of searches later, West concluded that this drive was an NX600, which supported TCP Opal Security Protocols 2 and 3.

Each drive shipped with a main decryption password set to the empty string.

Even if the people setting this drive up had been ignorant enough to leave the main password empty, you couldn't go straight after it. Instead, you had to provide the user password, which was used to decrypt the main password.

Still, it would be interesting to know if there is an empty main password thereunder.

He decided to find that out first.

All the crypto-related data was stored in blocks and referred to by block numbers in the firmware. The current main password was stored in block 466. There was no way of telling if it was the empty string by mere data inspection.

West traced the flow of the firmware, revealing that the default setting, which was the empty main password, was stored in block 501. So the fact that the code was using block 466 meant the main password had been changed.

Dead end.

The code that validated the user's password looked sound. He got a flashback to when he and Jitterbug had hacked the PIN validation on a pair of smart ski goggles.

Those were the days.

The back burner of his mind was still mulling that empty main password. It was so intriguing. Could he somehow make it fall back to the default setting? He searched through the documentation and found something called the Main Password Capability Setting.

Why am I thinking of this main password when I will just fail the user password anyway? Or wait.

He went back to the code that validated the user's password. The result of that check was a simple yes or no. If he could just make the check function say "yes," the firmware would move on to the main password.

For this, he needed a read/write gadget—a software bug that let him overwrite a "no" with a "yes" right after the user password check.

He asked his Tile's AI fuzz tester to probe the firmware for such a gadget and it started processing.

Meanwhile, he got himself and Kiss some coffee and looked out the window into the Moscow suburb. Locals were enjoying the nice weather from their balconies. An older couple were playing cards and three young women were laughing over drinks.

It took the fuzzer three hours to find a plausible gadget. West knew because he was checking the time more and more frequently. And it took him an additional hour to make it rewrite the "no" to a "yes" at the user password check.

He seriously considered pausing and continuing at a later point. But maybe he wouldn't get another opportunity like this. He bit his lower lip and glanced toward the bedroom where Åse was sleeping.

He could always just tell her he was trying to help. But then she'd question why he didn't just ask for the drive.

He dried his hands on his pants. The challenge pulled him back in.

With his forced acceptance of whatever user password he submitted, the firmware tried to decrypt the main password with the user password he supplied, even though it was wrong. Decryption using the wrong user password of course resulted in garbage output, but he was one step closer to making the code bend his way.

He created a copy of the firmware with the Main Password Capability Setting changed to its default and uploaded it to the drive. His hopes were rising. He powered the drive up and made his Tile try to read from it. Still locked. Somehow another dead end.

He sighed deeply and saw Kiss give him a meaningful glance from her comfy position in the living room.

This was the worst part of hacking. Even though you had made some progress, you had no idea of how close or far away you were from success. It could be just around the corner or it could be miles away. And Åse could appear at any moment.

If at first you don't succeed, try, try again.

It was his mom's favorite saying when he was a kid doing homework.

He inspected the configuration, and it had gone back to its earlier setting for the Main Password Capability Setting. Somehow the drive had detected that it had a properly set non-default main password and refused to use the empty one.

What if I delete the main password and make the Main Password Capability Setting point to block 466?

The idea was to make it be as if a stupid human had been forced to set the main password and chosen an empty one.

He used the same read/write gadget to make it happen.

The next thing he knew, the drive was unlocked!

Whoa.

He looked at the bedroom door. His breathing was audible. This next action he would not be able to explain as trying to help. He started copying the drive to his Tile.

```
Estimated time to completion: 35 minutes
```

He was unable to spend those minutes on anything useful.

Twenty minutes left.

Damn, this was taking too long.

Ten minutes left.

He was getting feverish.

Five more minutes.

He shut his eyes and counted the seconds.

0, 1, 2, ... 298, 299, 300.

It was done. He had his own, secret copy of the decrypted content of the Russian drive.

He stashed the hacked firmware he had created to pull it off and re-encrypted the drive over the top with his and Jitterbug's passphrase:

```
F4gernesfjelletView
```

He rushed back to the kitchen after putting the antistatic bag back in Åse's pocket.

It felt like he had just completed a ten-mile run.

Chapter 69

Developer Mode

Eventually, Åse showed up, went to the bathroom, and came to see what they were up to.

Kiss showed the shortlist of politicians and academic staff that would likely have access to the mythical Metro-2.

"Likely sitting ducks," Åse said. Her voice was unusually low. She raised its pitch as she continued. "But how would we find them? Or rather, how would we find their Tiles or computers? My proposal is more straightforward. We target Elvira Kenin, head of the Ministry of Digital Development, Communications and Mass Media. She talks and shows off her tech stuff all the time."

"What?"

"Hear me out." Åse put her Tile on the table and showed them a woman in her forties, standing out in a group photo of the government. Reserved look, dark brown hair parted in the middle, nerdy glasses. "Former software engineer in the gaming industry and founder of a decent startup. Takes pride in still coding the code."

"That sounds like the toughest possible target. She'll know her ops," Kiss said.

"At a surface level, I agree. But look at this thing." Åse switched to a recent Russian news article and her Tile duly translated it. The title was "The Minister Who Hacks" and it featured a photo of Kenin fiddling in web developer tools on some government website. "If a site appears broken, I fix it myself," the text underneath read.

"Developers are actually easier targets," Åse continued as Kiss and West finished reading the short piece on Kenin. "They run a bunch of stuff as root, they install weird tools, and they enable developer mode all over the place."

"Guilty as charged." West raised his hand.

Kiss gave him half a smile, then turned back to Åse. "Get some kind of access to her device and exploit a developer tool—that's your thinking?"

"Mhmm."

Kiss thought for a little while. "Okay, I like it. But browsers are sandboxed like hell. Hacking web dev tools won't get us far." She looked back and forth between the two others and finally landed on West. "Time for a digital dumpster dive, I guess."

CHAPTER 70

Targeting the Target

Åse went looking for vulnerabilities in the Russian web browser Yandex, specifically looking for bugs in its developer tools.

Kiss and West went deeper on the public news track. They soon came across a softball interview where Kenin talked about her background and her startup.

Two generations back, her family had been circus artists, and she had had similar aspirations as a child before computers took over. The company she had founded was called Vee-R and combined map data with crowd-sourced photos to create virtual versions of just about any rural place on earth. If there was public map data and people were willing to take pictures of their hometown, Vee-R would generate a digital version of it.

She got in conflict with national intelligence on the sensitivity of detailed maps of Russia and was later forced to sell the business when appointed minister. The last thing she did was to make Vee-R's software free and open source, which limited her payday. The interview made it sound altruistic and a move to banish any fear of ties to Russian intelligence. But Kenin had a solid net worth, according to a couple of other sources.

"I bet she released the code so she can still hack on it in her spare time," Kiss said. "Let's check the repo."

The open source repository for Vee-R was pretty active. At least some code changed daily.

"Maybe Kenin was the person who uploaded the first open version?" Kiss suggested.

It didn't look like it unless she had gone fully incognito under the name Oleg, a person who looked to be employed by the company.

Kiss shook her head. "Let's do top committers."

West sorted on developer activity: 122 in total, with the top twenty doing 99% of the work and then a long tail of people who'd contributed once or twice. He scrolled down slowly.

"Nothing stands out," Kiss mumbled. "You?"

"Nope. Do they have like a steering committee?"

"There was a link to a regular website."

It was the company site, and there was indeed a listing of six people with voting power over the project. None of them looked to be Kenin.

"Who has an even number of people on a board?" West mumbled.

Kiss looked at him. "Maybe ..." She tapped the screen to view the page's source code. There was a seventh member who had been commented-out and made invisible. That member was called Madigan.

Kiss used the hidden link and there was an active developer account for this Madigan. Not a top committer though.

She picked up her own Tile from the coffee table and asked it who Elvira Kenin Madigan was. It said there was no one with that name but suggested the Wikipedia entry for an Elvira Madigan—a young and famous circus performer in the late 1800s who had toured Europe, including St. Petersburg and Moscow. Her life ended tragically when a Swedish nobleman, madly in love with her, shot her and then himself.

"Never any shortage of violent men," Kiss scoffed. "But there's your circus and name connection. I bet that's her. When was her last commit?"

West looked at the latest Vee-R changes made by the Madigan account. "Two weeks ago."

"Ergo, she has the bleeding edge source code compiled and ready to execute on her device. That's unreleased software with ..." She pointed at West.

"... fresh bugs."

"Correct, young Padawan."

A Star Wars reference. She's coming back.

"I'll run some bug-finding tools on this and you figure out what a local setup looks like," she said, changing to a crisscross position on the couch.

We're hacking together again. Who would have thought? If only Jitterbug were here.

•

West looked into how the project worked locally for developers.

Vee-R was definitely built for the web but you needed an extension to bridge to the local install. For developers, there was local routing and a debug web interface where you could fiddle with the VR engine directly, see its performance metrics, and make low-level configurations.

Debug code is never scrutinized the way release code is.

He showed Kiss and she agreed it should be a prime source to look for bugs in.

The local routing was interesting too. The way he remembered it, you would typically make an insecure connection to localhost when browsing a server on your own machine. But this thing had a domain name and a secure connection. He inspected the development install script and found that it made all the necessary changes—installed a trusted certificate for the debug web domain and routed that domain to localhost. It was unclear to him why that was done.

•

"I have a lead on our way in," Åse yelled from the small bedroom where she had set up camp.

Kiss and West walked in there, both stretching and bending to wake their limbs up from a long sitting session.

"All Russian ministers have a public calendar of their official events," Åse said from her position on the messy bed. "Tomorrow, Kenin is flying to Maseru, the capital of Lesotho."

"Where's that?" West asked.

"TIL. It's a small country completely surrounded by South Africa. Maseru is right on the border."

"Russia's minister of IT and mass media visits small country in Africa," West said, as if reading a news headline.

"It is a little weird. But turns out the countries have close ties since the Soviet era. Lesotho's foreign minister was educated at Moscow

State University, that's how close we're talking. Russia's interest lies in Lesotho's diamond mines. *Bountiful* diamond mines."

"And Lesotho's interest?"

"They're modernizing their digital infrastructure and Russia is there providing tech and guidance."

"I sense you see an angle."

"Mhmm. I overheard you talk about Kenin's circus background. How many Russians interested in circuses do you think'll be in Maseru the next few days?"

"Ehh, about one."

"Slam dunk malvertising," Kiss said. "That's what you're going for, right?"

Åse nodded. "We create an ad about a circus coming to Moscow and pay an ad network to target it at Russian women about her age, in Maseru. The ad runs code that exploits whatever we're confident she's running."

"Vee-R comes with a web extension," West said.

Åse threw her Tile on the bed and leaned back against the wall. "So we find a vulnerability in Vee-R, reachable over that extension."

CHAPTER 71

Bill of Materials

Åse remained seated against the wall in the bedroom and got cracking on creating an ad that triggered Vee-R, and finding an ad network willing to serve it.

Kiss and West sat side by side in the kitchen studying the Vee-R source code and looking for an entry point. The local debug mode looked promising, but even more so the local web admin interface, which carried out some of its tasks through command line integration.

Kiss had created a new account on Jitterbug's Tile and West was reminded of her immense typing speed. She noticed she was being watched, and smiled at West from the corner of her eye.

"Sorry, I wasn't snooping," he said.

"Not much to snoop on, is there?"

West blipped a smile back and turned to his own Tile. "You have to reboot your digital life too, huh?" he said.

"I was thinking of my old accounts actually," she said. "Don't think I'll use them. Better to start fresh. I'll probably just get angry if I go on social media anyway. How is President Sanchez doing?"

"Okay, I guess."

"That's one thing I was damn happy about," Kiss said with remembrance. "That she got elected."

"You know what I have been thinking of rebooting?" she said, snapping out of her thoughts on the past.

"Your hair style?"

"Ha! Yeah, I'll be growing that back, don't worry. My head looks so small. No, I was thinking about toiletries. Can you beam me some money? I saw a convenience store down the street."

Åse shouted from the bedroom. "You shouldn't be walking outside."

"I'll use the face stick, mama," Kiss yelled back instantly.

"Get caught, stay caught," Åse said, this time barely audible.

Kiss rolled her eyes. "You want anything? Snacks?"

West shook his head.

•

West was on the hunt for bugs. Any piece of software this complex would be standing on the shoulder of giants, or so-called software dependencies. Vee-R only had eleven dependencies at the top, but those pieces of software in turn had other dependencies. All in all, a bundle of 441 small and large projects connected through 638 links.

He wrote a script to go through each dependency's version number and match it with the latest available version. Nothing interesting was out of date.

Kiss came back with a bag and pulled out snacks.

"Hey, Kiss, I wanted to run this by you to see if you have any ideas," West said.

"Sure, hun. What you got?"

Hun. She called me hun.

"No holes yet, but I have this list of software dependencies. I thought it might be easier to hack one of those. Like, sneak up from down under."

"Let me see." She took his Tile and scrolled. "That's a long list. Are all these well maintained?"

"I'm sure there are bugs."

"It'll take forever if you don't have a lead. Why not introduce your own bug?"

"How do I get Kenin to install it?"

"She'll pull it if there's an update to Vee-R." Kiss gave him back his device. "Meanwhile, I'm going to have a shower. I may not have much hair, but I'm going to use my own shampoo." She picked up the bag and went to the bathroom.

West thought about it. He should be looking for components that Vee-R depended on and where he had a chance of sneaking in a security bug. Smaller components; components with a sole maintainer.

With a slight alteration, his script gave him a shortlist of such open source dependencies. The result was six projects.

```
Concat-Stream
   A writable stream that concatenates
   strings or binary data.
Deeper
   Structurally compare the equality of
   JavaScript values.
Punycode
   A Punycode converter.
Argparse
   A command line arguments parser.
Commander
   The complete solution for command-line
   interfaces.
Wrappy
   A callback wrapping utility.
```

All of them were stable and hadn't issued an update in months.

Argparse looked close to what he wanted to accomplish. It parsed the arguments to commands.

The public repo had twenty-five open issues and three minor fixes already committed since the last release. It took West two hours to find a suitable issue among the open ones. It was a request for a hardening measure to count the number of subcommands separated by colons. Anyone could take it and propose a fix, and if the maintainer of Argparse thought the fix was good, it went into the software. The trick was to make a bad fix look good.

West recalled from his teens the three steps that usually worked best. The human psyche hadn't changed since then, so it could work. He whipped up a poor attempt at implementing the counting mechanism.

```
const expression = new RegExp(subCommandQuery +
                            ":" +
                    subCommandQuery);
```

Just twenty minutes after he uploaded his patch, the maintainer denied him to land it with a friendly comment. Open source maintainers were always happy to get help.

Thanks for taking a stab at this. I don't know who we're hardening against, really. This interface is intended for administration of servers. Anyway, your code just finds the first two subcommands. You need some more extensive test cases and that regexp needs to be global and case-insensitive. Cheers from St. Petersburg!

Step one according to plan—a basic mistake to get the dialogue started. The maintainer catches it quickly and feels good about themselves. Step two fixes the first bug but makes another, more subtle mistake.

```
const expression = new RegExp(subCommandQuery +
                            ":" +
                    subCommandQuery, "gi");
```

Another decline.

I tested your patch and there's a bug. You don't handle HTML entities. : represents a colon and lower layers will convert it.

The HTML entity thing was a classic bypass from an old Twitter hack.

"Oops. Didn't think about that. Thanks!" West replied before uploading his third attempt.

```
const expression = new RegExp(subCommandQuery +
                            "(:|&#58;)" +
                    subCommandQuery, "gi");
```

It was accepted.

Just as West raised his arms in celebration, the door to the bathroom cracked open and Kiss's head peeked out in a plume of steam. She made an upward nod for him to join her.

•

West almost fell getting undressed, but found himself naked by the shower curtain soon enough.

"That was the best shave I've ever had," Kiss said, taking his hand and pulling him in under the nozzle. "I'm not ready to have sex. I just want to be close. With some privacy."

Being close was plenty.

Hot water hit his body. Almost too hot.

The bruise on her cheek had flared up in the heat.

She kissed him and said, "We got our baby boy like this in Cuba, remember?"

CHAPTER 72

Elvira Kenin

The season changed as Elvira Kenin crossed the equator and hours later landed at Moshoeshoe I International Airport, Lesotho.

Taxiing in, she got a cellular connection and tapped OK on the minor security update to her local install of Vee-R. She had declined to download it over the plane's satellite connection. Getting the ops guys to allow her to even have Vee-R installed was a constant hassle already, and violating the policy on what to use in-flight internet for wouldn't help.

She looked out the window. The history of Maseru was despicable, as everything created by Western imperialism and colonialism. In that regard, it felt satisfying that her country was willing to invest and help Lesotho grow.

China's relentless investments in African countries had become a concern even within the Kremlin, so it was important to hold on to what they had in this part of the world. Lesotho had a history of supporting Taiwan, which curbed China's interest in this particular country.

Diamonds, just like precious metals, helped grease hands outside of the international banking system. That was crucial for *her* government. Getting more of the world to run Russian internet technologies was also good. *Quid pro quo.*

She was greeted by Lesotho's foreign minister, who knew her language. Heavy accent, sure, but he was a man who could at least read great literature in the language it was supposed to be read.

During the gift ceremony, she handed over both the official state gift and a box of **Коркунов** chocolate, known to be the minister's favorite. He looked happy indeed.

Formalities out of the way, she got to her hotel to enjoy a good night's sleep and get ready for tomorrow's proceedings. Maybe hit the gym in the morning.

Newly showered, she got under the duvet and browsed VKontakte. Some recent party photos from her old coworkers made her smile. So much more fun than politics.

Spliced in was an ad for the latest movie by director Chammah. She was the most prominent of a group of French movie makers who had fully embraced all-artificial casts. Kenin never understood why some were so uneasy about that. Computer games had always been based on generated characters. The ad made a big number of Chammah's latest avant-garde move, which was to have one supporting character's script be purely written by AI—no human curation on top.

She continued scrolling.

Her dad had posted another one of his old man rants about the quality of bread in his local store. She wondered if it was inevitable to become grumpy in old age or if you could stay positive. He always appreciated when she brought him fresh bread from Moscow. She should go see him. It had been three months since she last visited. Life was hectic.

The next post in her feed was from ... wait. She scrolled up a bit. What a curious ad. For the Bolshoi State St. Petersburg Circus, no less. This was the kind of advertising she wanted, not the crap about fatty liver or veiled suggestions she should get pregnant.

They were setting up the modern classic "Flying Cranes," famous for giving a Soviet politician in the audience a heart attack because of the difficulty of the trapeze tricks. And the ad offered a Vee-R view of the Ciniselli Circus building! She had seen it before, but she was here for it.

Ahh, wasn't Ciniselli a beauty. The rendering of the interior was immaculate. The first brick-built circus in Russia. This was what Vee-R was all about. Oh yes, the world's oldest circus museum too. She had to book a trip to St. Petersburg soon.

Chapter 73

We're In

"Oh my God, we're in!" Kiss yelled from the kitchen. She was the person on duty monitoring any incoming pings to their server.

West was slumbering on the couch and Åse was in the bedroom, probably fast asleep.

He got up and hurried over to Kiss.

"We just got a ping from an IP address in Lesotho. Our code is running on someone's computer and the device name is 7575. президент.рф. When you load президент.рф in a browser, it fails the security check but if you click through you get to kremlin.ru."

"That's what we're looking for," West said with a weird combination of excitement and sleepiness. "Scary, to be honest. She's a top politician."

Åse showed up in underwear and a tank top, her hair messy. She leaned over to see Kiss's screen. "Did you run the implant?"

"Not yet, since you said us kids weren't allowed to," Kiss said.

"Run it now."

The implant was a persistent backdoor into Kenin's Tile, in this case a DNS backdoor.

DNS, or the Domain Name System, was among the few connections allowed out of sensitive network segments. Thus, it was a great tool to command and control hacked devices.

"Now let's have a look at what she has on disk," Åse said and pulled a chair out.

West cautiously felt the coffeepot on the kitchen counter. It was lukewarm. He poured himself some and sat down too.

Most of the content on Kenin's device was in Cyrillic, so West zoned out. Kiss looked bored too after a while and leaned back to talk to West behind the hunched-over Åse. "I never grokked the bug in your commit to Argparse. Are one of those characters in the HTML entity a special character or something?"

"Nah, the regexp test function with global setting remembers the last index it matched something on and starts from there instead of starting over, even if you run it on a new command string. So by calling it twice, I can get it to count zero subcommands and evaluate the whole thing as a master command."

"Oh, I recall that regexp weirdness. But wasn't it fixed in the language?"

"Vee-R is old. It runs in quirks mode with all the old cruft still there."

"Doozy."

•

Sending data over the DNS backdoor was slow, which meant listing Kenin's files was slow.

"She has a lot of things on her device," Åse said after scrolling and taking notes for a good hour.

"Personal and work-related," she continued. "But the most important content is in an encrypted folder. We either wait for her to open that folder or we try to hack it."

"Can we make her open it?" Kiss asked.

"What do you mean?"

"I don't know. Fake some communication from her superiors?"

"Superior to her would be the prime minister or the president."

"Sounds good to me."

"What would they be messaging her about? It has to come naturally."

Tens of seconds ticked away with the room silent.

"We could send her an update on the incident at Ice Dolphin," West said.

Åse frowned and pulled her head away from him. "Mister, please do share your thinking."

"Kenin is responsible for digital development and communications. She's bound to have been notified about the intrusion and ... killing up there. We tell her something relevant. Maybe about the missing laptop?"

Åse shook her head. "No. We're not sharing intel. And why would that make her open the folder?"

Kiss jumped in. "We say there is info uploaded there."

"We can't upload anything there. It's enc…"

"It decrypts as soon as she opens it. It'll just look like it took a while for the folder to sync."

Åse's eyes wandered between Kiss and West. "Okay, we need to whip up both a message from the fucking prime minister and a minuscule doc to place in the folder. Remember, we are severely constrained on data volume."

•

The message: Check your Kremlin Folder for
info on Ice Dolphin.

The folder document: The missing laptop has
been recovered. It's in a non-functional
state and will need a forensic analysis.
It's being sent to you by courier to
Moscow.

"What happens when the laptop doesn't arrive?"

"It will. We'll send it to her."

•

Elvira Kenin took the bait, and for a brief moment her secure Kremlin folder was open to the covert intruders. That moment was long enough for the DNS backdoor to command her Tile to copy all the secure content to an unencrypted folder.

In that second folder, the intruders now found documentation on the Red Web, references to the transatlantic subsea cable interruption, and the disclosure form she had signed for the second-factor authentication token she used to get access to Metro-2 systems and physical premises in Ramenki.

They also found drafts of the recent press releases about the American citizen West Wilder.

CHAPTER 74

Three

There were three different drafts of the press release on Kenin's Tile. West read them twice.

Draft 1
Infamous US Hacker Defects
West Wilder, convicted of the massive hack of NSA's PRISM system in 2014, has defected to Russia. He is now working directly with the Red Web Command to aid in cyber defense against Western imperialism. Wilder switching sides comes at a critical juncture for internet safety and freedom.

Draft 2
Infamous US Hacker Joins Russia
In a one-two punch, the USA loses ground to Russia in cyber defense. First Edward Snowden and now West Wilder. Wilder is setting up camp with Red Web command to make use of his skills and experience. "Slowly America is realizing that its democracy is just thinly veiled imperialism," a government source tells TASS.

Draft 3
NSA Hacker Defects to Russia
Infamous for his hack of NSA's global surveillance apparatus, West Wilder has ultimately switched sides and joined Russia in the effort to secure the internet. This is a major setback for US ambitions to control cyberspace and impose their views on other cultures.

"This is not going to work out for me, is it?" he said solemnly.

Kiss put her arm around him. "You got me out. We'll get you out and your name cleared. This is clearly not true. I don't know what they're up to."

"We don't even know who *they* are," Åse said. "Who drafted these? Was there a fourth or fifth? These lies are aiding someone's agenda and it's not clear whose."

Kiss looked at her. "It's Russia trying to poison West to the point where he cannot go back."

Åse shrugged. "West desperately going to Ice Dolphin to get you out was deemed a good cover story for my operation at Novaya Zemlya. Maybe the higher-ups in America were hoping he wouldn't return. But I blew up that Magadan, so they know some of us got out. Maybe the US government is building a case to get rid of West once and for all."

"You never told me I was bait," West said with a scowl.

"I'm telling you now. And that's fucking classified information."

The three of them went silent. There was no camaraderie or joint mission with Åse. They just had tangential goals.

"I don't get why the US would do this to you," Kiss said. "Did they stick your name to the backup explosion in Norilsk?" she asked West.

"The head of US G20S knows I did it, but we got her locked up in a Russian jail. Maybe she's managed to return. Then I'm screwed."

"You got Kawasaki jailed?" Kiss looked bewildered.

"She was more involved than you think. Åse might be right—this smells like US revenge. I need to offer them something valuable enough to compensate," he mumbled, barely audible.

"Keep working for the right side, soldier, and I'll put in a word for you," Åse said. "We're on the inside of a Russian minister's Tile and we're trying to save an American child. Not too shabby. Plus, you got us a lead on the Russian sub auth system. So maybe."

Chapter 75

Subordinate

West and the others turned their attention to the disclosure form that Kenin had signed to get an access token for Metro-2 systems and this thing called Ramenki. Åse did a few searches and found it was a piece of hardware security called ZT, standard in the Russian public sector. You could find used ones online, but there seemed to be fierce bidding for them.

The ZT's security did not lie in secrecy but in how each token was configured to produce a unique stream of pseudo random numbers to be used as a second factor. A new, eight-digit onetime code was produced every thirty seconds. ZTs had small monochrome displays to show the current code if you ever needed to enter the factor manually, but normal operation was over NFC—near field communication—popularly called "to tap." You pressed a button on the ZT, tapped it against a reader terminal, and both username and code were transferred.

Not much had been said publicly on hacking a ZT. Some early version had had problems, but there was an official bounty program on them and the openness of the hardware design had created an aura of trust.

"We can read the code if Kenin uses a ZT with her Tile. But ZT auth is single-use, so we'd have to race her with our slow backdoor," Åse said. "Sounds, shall I say, implausible."

Kiss agreed. "The code wouldn't even reach us before hers was used. Could we duplicate her ZT? If we capture a few of her codes in succession, we may deduce the seed and configure our own ZT to produce the same series."

"That's some serious cryptanalysis."

"And our bet would be on her using it with her Tile every time since we need to know where in the code series the next one is," West said. "If she uses it just once on a desktop or for physical access to Ramenki, we'd be out of sync."

"Pfft." Åse shook her head. "You keep talking about Ramenki as a place. It's a computer system tops."

West thought for a bit. "We need to find info on East too."

"That'll be a dig," Åse said, rolling her eyes.

"Hey, if you're not going to help out, you might as well leave," Kiss slung out.

"You know what? You're absolutely right," the Norwegian responded and left the room.

West let Kiss fume for a while.

She eventually switched to rubbing her forehead with her thumb and index finger. "I'm working out the race. I thought of stealing Kenin's dongle, but she'll notice the next time she needs it and it will be revoked."

"I doubt we'd even be able to get close to her, let alone her personal gear."

Kiss wrinkled her face and nodded. "We need to find someone a few steps down in her org with Metro-2 access. You ask Åse to dig for that. I'm not talking to her."

"It's not like I have any sway over her."

Kiss gave him an unamused side eye but didn't comment further.

West went to the bedroom. Åse was flipping through something on her Tile. When asked, she said she had her mind set on finding Maria in a directory of Red Web employees and going from there to see if the woman could be located. A directory was kind of what Kiss wanted too. Åse reluctantly said she'd find them a few suitable subordinates of Kenin's.

Kiss was pulling stuff out of one of their backpacks when West came back.

"We have Jit's Bunny, right?" she said when she heard him coming.

"You can borrow mine."

"I need the spare one. I traded it for a ZT. Åse's probably right that the cryptanalysis is too hard. But who knows what we'll find inside one of those things?"

CHAPTER 76

Kremlin: No Drive

"We are analyzing the laptop and as far as we can tell, it is the missing one from Ice Dolphin."

"How come you are not absolutely sure?" Kenin asked.

The time it had taken to safely unpack the courier delivery was enough to raise her blood pressure. But sure, no secure sender meant it could be anything—a bomb, anthrax, or something else to inflict terror.

She had requested full tracing of when it was sent and by whom. Something wasn't right.

"It's missing its SSD," her assistant said.

Kenin's face went from annoyed to disgusted. "The drive is the only thing that matters from that whole pile of electronics. Get out."

CHAPTER 77

Switcheroo

Kiss still refused to talk to Åse, and West had to ask the latter to help them exchange the Bunny for the ZT. When she came back, she had bought a baby pacifier and put it beside the ZT on the table in front of Kiss. "To stop the whining," she uttered and turned on a dime.

Kiss pocketed the pacifier and threw after Åse, "Thanks! We need it for East."

West joined Kiss at the kitchen table to inspect the dongle. Three inches wide, one inch tall, and a few millimeters thick. Keyring hole in one corner.

According to online marketing, they came in the three colors of the Russian flag and this particular specimen was white. The button wasn't a button really, rather a gold-colored touch surface that flexed a little. No OmniPort. This thing had no physical connectors at all.

"Shall we?" Kiss asked as she produced a dinner knife to crack it open.

He nodded. They had already settled on the risks of breakage. ZTs were rumored to be tamper-proof in several ways, supposedly killing their pseudo random number generator if opened.

The rumors turned out to be marketing fluff except for a rubbery silicone compound. The casing contained a battery, the monochrome OLED display, and underneath it a circuit board with a chip covered in dark epoxy and a clock crystal. The board exposed a custom connector, probably for programming the seed number which made each dongle unique.

Kiss held it up for a closer look. "I could fit a Raspberry Pi Pico in here and have room to spare."

"I've been wanting to try out Raspberry Pi's," West said. "Do you think they have them here?"

Kiss shrugged while looking at the circuitry from different angles.

"Could a Pico drive the display?" West asked.

"It can do almost anything. Unless the ZT designers have deliberately made it hard. I wish we had Jit here. He knows this stuff." She paused. "Knew."

West stood up to counter the sinking feeling. He wandered the apartment for a while, thinking of his buddy. It was true, Jitterbug would have been the perfect hacker for this.

As he moved through shrouds of sorrow, an idea emerged. First fleeting, then taking form.

He sat down by Kiss and tucked his hands underneath his thighs before speaking. "If we could get it to talk Bluetooth, we could own the person without them noticing, at least for a while. We swap the dongles, make sure we're close enough when they press the button to use it, transmit the current number from the real dongle in our possession and show it on the display of the rigged one they're hiding. That way theirs keeps working while we have the real one."

She looked at him. "Two working dongles at the same time. I like it. Someone's going to have to be really good at shadowing that person though."

"Eventually they'll discover their ZT's not working and report it. By then we have to be in ... whatever in means."

•

They found the right subordinate under Kenin five levels down in her organization—a programmer by the name of Vadim Smirnov. Åse had concluded through directory spelunking that whatever Metro-2 was, it was related to "Lubyanka" which housed the Center of Information Security, part of the FSB.

There was a fantastic record of this Vadim. He had been awarded the gold medal in the International Olympiad in Informatics three years in a row and pursued a Russian academic career rather than well-paid jobs in the US. His programming skills were not why he was a perfect target, though. He was the only one in the directory tree with a designated workplace at home. This guy was better than everyone else and had likely demanded to work from his apartment.

"You said you needed to be close to the subject. Here you go."

Kiss looked like she was about to say something, but the kitchen was silent for a while. Eventually, she dropped a short question. "Do we know where he lives?"

"He's faculty at Moscow State, which is in your beloved Ramenki district. And I found a person posting a selfie with him at Sosedi Café, close to the university."

Åse showed her Tile. It was a cute girl together with a young man, supposedly Vadim Smirnov.

"I assume a university like that has international students," Kiss said.

"Very likely."

"Then I need to buy some makeup and a wig. You need to get me a date with this guy."

"You think you're up for that? After Ice Dolphin?"

"You wanna do it?"

"Nope."

"Well, then. I need to go color corrector, concealer, foundation ... the works on this," Kiss said, pointing at her maturing bruise.

"What if he already has a girlfriend?" West asked.

"Look again at the picture."

He did.

Kiss added the details. "She's squatting beside his chair. A girl-friend wouldn't do that. Plus look at how his hand is touching the underside of her boob. Would not fly if he had a girlfriend elsewhere. That's a single guy on the hunt."

CHAPTER 78

Sosedi Café

Sosedi Café was chic with pale wooden walls, rectangular and circular tables mixed, cozy lighting, and comfy chairs. The air was herbal from a variety of tea.

Bots served the customers—this place seemed geared toward a younger crowd who didn't want to pay tips anyway.

West was sitting with Åse. They didn't speak, so as to not attract attention. Kiss's English would be enough of a risk.

Every time West glanced over at Kiss, he was struck by her beauty. It wasn't just that she had put on makeup and dressed up; it was also the slow transition from the hunted animal they had rescued from Ice Dolphin back to the multifaceted young woman he knew. The push-up bra was a little much though.

Vadim showed up fifteen minutes late. Same crew cut hair as in most of the photos they'd seen. He spotted Kiss immediately and walked over confidently. Åse and West followed along the conversation as transcribed by Kiss's Tile.

> Nice to finally meet you.
> I'm a little star-struck to be
> honest.

> Nice to meet you.
> I'm Vadim.

> I'm Amber.

Did you have anything to
drink already?

No, I was waiting for you.

Oh, sorry I'm late.

No, that's all right. I was
looking at the menu. What
do you like?

The social chatter continued as they ordered tea and got to know each other's backgrounds. Vadim was from the city of Perm near the Ural Mountains. Kiss spent some time pandering to his pride over gold medals in programming before pivoting to what he was doing now.

I work in IT security, you
can say. Or cybersecurity
maybe is better known to
you.

I don't know much about
cybersecurity. I hear about
it on the news. Is it like for
banks?

Not really.

Countries need to defend
themselves nowadays.
Modern cybersecurity
involves lot of math and
algorithms.

Crypto.

Oh, cryptocurrencies?

Ha, ha. No. Some people
are actually angry about
that misunderstanding.

Crypto means
cryptography.

Keeping information
secret.

But you're a professor, right?
One of the youngest?

Yes. Youngest in my field
in Russia.

Wow.

West zoned out for a bit, stealing occasional glances at his girl-friend with the famous Russian.

I don't even have a college degree. And I sure didn't win any international competitions in programming. But I did fucking hack the NSA.

Kiss's conversation kept transcribing and scrolling on his Tile.

I need to clear my name and build a life for Kiss and me. And East. Someone changed her email. I need to sort this shit out. And BestBye, how is she involved in all of this?

He pulled up the Survivor chat with BestBye. It was empty. The few messages they had exchanged back when the team was still a thing were gone—all ephemeral; no traces. And she had used peer-to-peer communication when she came to his home. No servers involved.

SurvivorNet was probably compromised. If he texted her now, she might not receive it, but US agencies would. How do you securely communicate over a compromised channel? Without physically handing over crypto keys? It was an unsolved problem. Perhaps unsolvable.

Or wait, he remembered the coffee bag advertisement trick. He needed something only he and BestBye knew and to use it as a key to unlock his message. Had they ever been alone, just the two of them? It had been just him, BestBye and Kiss on Silver Skagit Road. Yeah, he could use something from there.

Ten minutes later, he had written a message and encrypted it with something he and BestBye had talked about out there in the wilderness. His thumb was unsteady when he sent it. Whoever was watching now knew his account was still live and that the account holder wanted to communicate with BestBye. The watchers would throw serious computing power at his encrypted message. His bet was that it would hold for at least a few weeks, and that BestBye wasn't working for The Man.

Next thing he knew, Kiss and Vadim were getting up. He checked the tail of their transcribed chat.

> I'd love to see it. You mean now?

Sure.

> A girl isn't supposed to go to a man's home on a first date.

I'll be nice.

> You don't have to.

Ha, ha.

CHAPTER 79

How Far?

West's heart was racing. How far would Kiss go with this guy? And how dangerous was he? Kiss could die in there.

They had tailed Vadim and Kiss and knew which building they were in. The vantage point they'd chosen was a gathering of bushes clearly put there by a landscaper.

The only message they had received from Kiss was a six-digit number, possibly a PIN.

Åse was furious about Kiss not hiding her face when she left with Vadim. "If there's one thing Russian surveillance follows more than strangers, it's known Russians of influence," she said. "They are dead paranoid about any kind of opposition or uprising, just like the Chinese. They'll start investigating who he was walking with."

West's anxious chest pain just wouldn't go away. He wanted to go up to Vadim's apartment and set this straight.

Somehow sensing his thoughts, or maybe seeing an emerging move of his out of their hiding spot, Åse pushed his shoulder back. "Easy. You told me she's one hell of an actor. Let her act."

"Anything could happen up there."

"We have no sign of Vadim being the violent type. You don't think Kiss has seen her share of violent men?"

West's shoulders slumped back from their raised position, but his heart kept pumping. "You hate her anyway," he muttered to Åse. "What do you care?"

"Hey, mister! I may not see eye to eye with her, but I sure as hell don't want her hurt. Just get that shit out of your system. Our main problem is that she may have been spotted by cameras together with a Russian tied to the local security apparatus. She's a bloody prisoner at large."

He hunkered back down. A few minutes slowly passed before Åse took a peek above the foliage.

"You know," she said, ducking back down. She gave herself a couple of seconds before continuing. "I think you and Kiss were right to go after your kid. I have a friend who is adopted. It weighed on him a lot growing up, knowing his parents had abandoned him. It got so bad he tried to take his life." She sniffled. "But he's much better now. Has a kid of his own. I'm just trying to say East will appreciate it."

She pulled West's arm. "Car approaching."

West looked through the scraggly bush in front of him. It was a black sedan with just enough elongation of the backseat window to invoke the impression of a limo.

West snapped a photo between the twigs and leaves and zoomed in. A single driver in the front seat. At this angle, he couldn't say for sure, but it looked like a large screen in the mid console. The car's make was НАМИ, which his Tile translated to NAMI and suggested a webpage for on Central Scientific Research Automobile & Engine Institute.

Moments later, Kiss and Vadim exited the building and got into the backseat of the car.

Åse's hand took a firm grip of his right biceps and pulled him down. "Not a move."

West saw the mini limo leave the block. It felt better not having Kiss in Smirnov's apartment, but where were they going?

He was interrupted by a short message from Kiss.

Going to movie.
ZT is up there.

"As soon as we're inside the building, get your balaclava on," Åse said.

CHAPTER 80

The Rig

Lock picks got them inside the building and further into the apartment of "V. Smirnov" on the top floor.

A burglar alarm beeped as it counted down from ten. West only saw the back of Åse as she entered the PIN Kiss had sent. It worked.

"What would you have done if that wasn't the alarm code?" he asked.

"Scanned the apartment even faster, then left," she mumbled as she took her shoes off. She held up a palm toward West without turning around and stepped in.

Åse took a few minutes to check all rooms with what she called a camera lens finder and an IR scan with her Tile. Nothing.

West was handed a pair of rubber gloves and Åse got hers on.

Vadim had a lush living space steeped in a single man's indulgences. Espresso machine, expensive cooking knives, gigantic TV set, stainless steel everywhere, and lots of straight-angled furniture. The young professor seemed fond of blue, silver, and black.

His home office was impressive but barren compared to the rest. The conferencing camera on top of the large, curved screen faced a white wall. There was a green plant here, the only one in the apartment. No documents or branded equipment revealed that this was the official workplace of a government employee.

Åse got a battery-powered camera out with an adhesive pad on one side. "I need to get up on your shoulders."

West kneeled and let her get up. He was surprised by how light she was.

Åse worked for a bit and handed him the cover of the ceiling lamp before wanting it back. Pieces of dust fell like snowflakes.

She got off his shoulder and reached over the office chair. "Collect the dust."

He did as he was told and was about to take the dust to the kitchen when Åse turned around and produced Vadim's ZT. It was dark blue. "Switch the casing with yours while I look for where to put the relay. And keep that dust in your pocket."

West sat down in the kitchen. Holding the hardware token felt like just as much a personal intrusion as entering the apartment. He opened an NFC reader on his Tile and tapped the token just to see what signal it would emit.

```
vadim_smirnov922:32065112
```

Username and onetime code.

He got the case switching done. Their rigged ZT was now blue and Vadim's white. He weighed them both in his hands.

Good enough.

Kiss had had to remove the NFC module in the rigged one to fit Bluetooth capabilities in there. So Vadim's ZT would from here on require that he read the code from the display and enter it manually. How long would he put up with that? A week? Hours? Whatever that window was, that was their window to steal and use his codes.

Åse was still moving about and craned her head over his shoulder. "Done? Good. Go put it back in the office, top drawer to the right, tucked to the left, the little hole toward the chair."

He followed her instructions.

Further back in the drawer, he spotted a circuit board in an antistatic bag similar to the SSD from the Ice Dolphin laptop.

They obviously wanted everything to look untouched, so removing something was a bad idea.

He looked over his shoulder. The sounds of Åse rummaging were barely audible. He took the circuit board in its bag and put it in his pocket.

A gust of fresh air came in, cooling his cheek when he left the office. Åse had gone outside on the balcony. She moved slowly, looking through the windows straight at him. Her head moved like an owl's, keeping her eyes at a steady level.

She plopped her head in. "Got the relay? I think we can make it work from here. There's a path for the signals to get to his office. Narrow, but should be good."

West walked over and handed her the crude relay device they'd put together—an old Tile with a bulky battery pack attached. This thing could feed the rigged ZT with codes to show on its display. And they could communicate with the relay Tile over Wi-Fi from a block away.

West saw Åse attach the Tile and battery pack to the outside of the balcony's balustrade.

She came back in. "Better to have it spotted from the outside than from the inside. He's a tech bro, people will think it's some new gadget he's got. Guess what I found at the bottom of a bowl in the kitchen, together with keys?"

West's eyes narrowed. "A Post-it with passwords?"

"Not that lucky. But a badge." She pulled out her Tile and showed a photo of a plastic card with Vadim's face on it. "Tucked away like that is further evidence that he rarely goes to any official building. I cloned it. Will share later. You got the ZT set up?"

West nodded.

"Go test it," she said.

West went into the home office and picked up the rigged blue ZT. He pressed its button.

If everything worked, this would send a request for a code over Bluetooth to the relay on the balcony. The relay then sent a message to Åse's Tile, which would notify her. It was silent enough in the apartment for West to hear the buzz. Åse would then press the button on Vadim's now white ZT which would emit a valid code over NFC. Her Tile picked it up, sent it to the relay on the balcony, and from there back to the rigged ZT, shown on its display.

"Ends with 7722," he said in the direction of the kitchen.

"Ends with 7722," came back. "Let's get out. While Kiss is watching that movie, you and I find the physical entry to Metro-2."

Chapter 81

Metro-2 Access

West and Åse huddled in the Kia as they researched and discussed. She was easing up on him somehow. Maybe because it was just the two of them now. He just had to tell himself not to be annoyed when she got all commandy.

What they had to go on was thin—a 1991 US Department of Defense report titled "Military Forces in Transition," and the notes and photos from urban explorers. Unless Åse was hiding information that NATO had.

The most corroborated intel was for Metro-2 to be entered through a deep, single-track tunnel at the Sportivnaya Metro station north of the Moskva River, toward the Kremlin. This tunnel stretched at a downward angle past Moscow State University to its endpoint, a thousand feet deep at the supposed Ramenki underground city.

That would be underneath the 50th Anniversary of October Park, built in 1967 to celebrate fifty years since the 1917 October Revolution. It was one of the city's largest green areas, surrounded by residential neighborhoods, and potentially covering the country's largest bunker system.

A ventilation facility near the university campus was said to feed Ramenki with fresh air. This was their second potential entry point beside the single-track tunnel. Such an extensive support structure was bound to have the means for manual maintenance and access.

Finally, there was supposed to be a high-speed elevator from the university's Metro station down to Ramenki.

"If Vadim at all uses this ... underground facility," Åse said, "he has to be using the elevator. I mean, he lives by the park. Why would he go over the river up north only to go back under it?"

"He has remote access though."

"Yeah, I doubt he goes there at all unless forced to."

West bit his lower lip and had to try twice before something came out of his mouth. "Will you be going in?"

"Hell no. First of all, a NATO commander captured down there could start a goddamned war. Second, I'm not putting my neck out any further in this shit. And finally, we'll be impersonating Vadim and there's only one of us who we can make even close to looking like him."

West had already thought about that. It meant they couldn't leverage Åse's knowledge of the language. He'd have to go in there and not talk to anyone.

Connecting directly to a network down there would be far too risky. So he'd be isolated until the work was done.

Where would he even look for Viktor, Maria, and East? How would he get them out? What if East caused a scene?

He put a balled hand against his mouth and cradled the elbow in his other hand. The breathing through his nose was steady and deep.

He freed his mouth and asked, "Do you think I'll trigger some anomaly detection if I enter with Vadim's badge from a place he never uses?"

"Maybe. But not maybe enough to make me favor the elevator." She turned to her Tile again. "Urban explorers seem to have focused almost exclusively on the railroad switch after Sportivnaya."

"Which is on official track maps."

"And claimed to be a service track," Åse said with her everlasting doubts about Metro-2 and Ramenki.

"Mmm. A dark tunnel you can walk into. That's urbexer catnip."

"I didn't find any recent reports from inside that tunnel. You?" she said.

"Nope. Except the camera systems. There was that detail on the cameras facing up the tunnel slope and the speculation that they don't want any legit passengers caught on footage. I found that interesting."

"Those single-car trains are bound to be automated just like the rest of Moscow Metro. So no train engineer who knows which people go in and out either."

"Do you think we could get to the fork in the track via one of the regular trains?"

"It's not like they stop there."

"I'm thinking like ... jump off."

Åse gave him a questioning look.

"I've jumped a passing car before," he added. "That didn't go so well, though."

"You serious?"

"That would give me a starting point, right? I can work my way to the entry of the tunnel from there."

"How to get you off a speeding public train with no one noticing and reporting?"

West gave it a thought. Perhaps there were times of day when very few used the trains? But he wanted to focus on the Metro-2 tunnel. "We'll figure that out. I'm thinking I can wait at the fork and get on to the back of a Metro-2 car. If the cameras only face upslope, they won't see me piggybacking."

"What makes you think *that* train's not speeding? Jumping off is one thing. Jumping *on*?"

•

Kiss startled the others by knocking on the window of the Kia an hour later.

West didn't open the door for her. Åse reached over from the front seat and did.

"I'm okay, thank you very much," Kiss said once seated.

"Sorry," West said.

"How did it go?" Åse asked.

Kiss looked at West a few moments before responding. "Decent guy. Gullible, smart, and full of himself. I shoulder-surfed the alarm code to his place and then got him out of there. Were you able to get in?"

"You bet," Åse said.

"I was worried about you," West said.

"Frankly, I was worried about me too. I don't think it was my best performance. Still too much 'punch guy in face' energy in me from prison."

West felt a little better by that last comment.

Kiss probably spotted his inner turmoil and added, "I didn't kiss him or anything."

"Good," West muttered.

"Did we get what we wanted?" Kiss asked Åse.

"The Tile pack is feeding the rigged ZT with codes from his balcony."

"Sweet. His password?"

"We'll get that from a camera in the lamp above his computer rig."

"Time for an access point then."

"That's what we're working on," West said. "We need to scout Sportivnaya Metro station."

Chapter 82

TASS: Hacker Romance

Together at Last

In a romantic turn of events, famous US hacker West Wilder has been reunited with his American girlfriend Kate Libby. Both have defected their imperialist home country and joined Russian Information Operations Troops to help free the world of surveillance and oppression.

Togetherness also means their son will be able to grow up with both parents in a safe and supportive society. "I'm not fleeing," says Wilder. "I'm choosing something better for my family and for mankind."

What's next? you ask. Do we hear wedding bells?

CHAPTER 83

Kremlin: Generated Too?

"Is it generated too?" Elvira Kenin asked her assistant while still standing at her desk. She was clenching her fists over and over in a pumping motion. The gym at the hotel in Lesotho had been dismal. She needed her dojo and her sparring partner, Yekaterina.

"The press release on Wilder and Libby?"

"Of course. Did I change the subject?"

"I'm sorry. All American leaks are generated so as to obscure any patterns. We use ..."

"I know. I led the investigation that produced this fact. My question is if this particular press release was generated?"

"We haven't analyzed specifically for that."

"Then you know your first important task of the day."

Concealing what one knew and what one didn't was getting harder by the day. Russia of course got assistance from AI to obscure and complicate the analysis on the other side. It was a battle between AIs.

The Americans had hacked TASS three months ago. Her department found out shortly thereafter and covertly monitored any US activity on the news agency's servers without telling its staff. A hacker moving about in your systems, passively watching what you do, can go completely unnoticed by humans. The hacker may even be able to make small changes to the system without raising suspicion—such as delay messages or remove courtesies in emails to sour relationships. But Kenin's experts had seen zero such activity. Zero, until the press releases on West William Wilder got pushed.

Russians in the know obviously noticed. You don't get to create international news on someone else's behalf without eyebrows getting raised. Decisions had had to be made quickly. Should they reveal that they knew about the US hack? Or pretend to discover the hack now? Or cover it up and continue watching the American activity in their systems?

They went with the latter, by Kenin's personal orders. These press releases weren't worth it. The US obviously planned to leverage the TASS hack to emit manipulative news stories during a real conflict. That's when it would be worth it. Being able to see that happen in real time and cut it off exactly when necessary was a capability that she cherished.

But taking the American perspective, the question Kenin kept asking herself was why this West Wilder was worth blowing the TASS hack for. Was it in itself a test? No one in their right mind would think Russia would just accept these rogue press releases as flukes. They knew Russia would investigate. Did the US gain something by that?

She had consulted Grigiori for hours. His input eventually became so convoluted that she lost track of the levels of abstraction. X leading to Y leading to Z and so on.

This whole West business reeked of card shuffling to obscure what was really going on. That was the worst part of the AI game—the curveballs whose only purpose was to throw you off or delay you. Weird shit that took your time and attention, only to make sure you didn't spend time on something else—something else that actually mattered.

That said, Russian AI had its moments too. The fake story about Miles from Milwaukee who got fake responses to his messages was a good one.

She texted Yekaterina about going to the dojo.

Whip your ass at 17?

Bring band-aid.

And a bucket.

Chapter 84

Jump!

West reckoned his pulse was above a hundred beats per minute as they waited for the first morning train headed south at Sportivnaya Metro station. It was 5:20 a.m.

The booth up at the gates where human staff used to sit had been retrofitted into a tower of screens blasting ads, and West couldn't shake what had looked like an advert for Russian cyber forces, just like the one he'd seen on the train back from Juneau. The world was preparing for something nasty.

He again stroked the back of his neck. The snug trim reminded him of haircuts from his childhood. His mom would always ask the barber to cut it super short. At least his natural hair color was close enough to Vadim's.

He had his Survivor Kit with hacker tools and most of his NATO gear concealed under a dark suit one size too large. The left lapel of his jacket had a microcamera in the notch.

In his outer pockets he had the folded printout, a banana, and eight battery-powered network repeaters, about two inches in diameter each. They had no hard facts on the length of the tunnel, but some basic math told them that eight should give him a good margin.

The straps of his surgical face mask pulled on his ears.

God, he hoped this plan would work.

•

Two locals were the only ones in the last car of the 5:35 a.m. train as West, Åse, and Kiss boarded. A man in his fifties with a bushy beard and a slightly younger woman carrying a metal thermos mug with the tag from a tea bag hanging from the side.

Kiss's disguise was damn convincing. She looked like a homeless person in very poor condition. Layers upon layers of dirty clothes, hunched over, torn shoes, wig in a mess.

West could barely smell her with his nostrils plugged but the odor that made it through was just awful. It was some kind of acid Åse had in her NATO gear.

Kiss lurched past the other passengers in the train aisle. West was standing in the very back and could see them wrinkle their noses and lean away.

The woman with the tea mug moved first, to the car in front. The older man followed shortly thereafter.

Step one done—the team was alone in the last car.

West and Åse got into position, facing outward by the sliding doors on the side where the opposite track provided plenty of space between them and the tunnel wall.

The window on each door was narrow and West wondered if he'd fit.

He had to fit.

Åse said in her low voice, at a level more suited for a library aisle than a moving train. "Remember, the perimeter will be the hardest. The further in you go, the softer it gets."

West did remember her saying that.

She pulled his chin to make him face her. "I believe in you, soldier. And friend." Her jaw muscles tensed up.

He looked out again. The tracks below passed at high speed. Landing badly might snap his ankles.

Åse's car glass hammer appeared in the corner of his eye. A distinct, short swing and the glass in front of him went cloudy with thousands of cracks. Åse pushed the bendy, plastic-covered sheet of fractured glass out and the wind sucked it away and filled the car with noise.

West got one leg out and his heel searched for purchase. The ledge outside the door was just a few inches. His foot found support. He got his behind and second leg through and felt Åse grip the collar of his jacket.

He held on to the window frame with his thumbs still inside the car. The drag wasn't too bad. The light from the train showed the railroad ties and ballast stones right beneath. A bit further out was the parallel track.

Åse's signal came suddenly—a poke on his shoulder and then release of his collar. He jumped forward. Not far, only enough to clear the crossties and get away from the drag.

His fall happened in slow motion. He knew he would be forced into a roll as soon as his feet touched the rock bed. He had practiced in the apartment how to let his good shoulder take the hit rather than risk his wrist.

The hard, jagged ground was a lot rougher than the mattress he had practiced on. But there was no impact to his head and the pain in his shoulder and arm was bearable.

He looked up only to see the back of the train race away. The sounds dampened quickly. He moved over to the far side of the parallel tracks, turned on the red flashlight on his Tile, and started walking toward what he hoped would be the fork.

CHAPTER 85

Deep Single-Track Tunnel

The fork, or as the urban explorers of the 1990s called it, the D-6 tunnel switch, was there. It came shortly after separate tracks appeared.

West checked one of his network repeaters and it still had a connection to the device they'd set up at Sportivnaya station. Two out of four bars.

He kept to his side and pulled the folded printout from his pocket. Åse had acquired it through a print shop. It was four times as big as a letter-sized paper.

Computers always did what they were told, not what they should do. That was the team's bet. They had discovered a sign with the blocky pattern now printed on this paper at all three Metro stations they had checked. Online searches had finally revealed that it was a safety measure, instructing automated trains to slow down as they approached the platforms. According to the people posting about it, the signs were also used around construction or maintenance sites in the tunnels.

The large sheet of paper fluttered in his hand as the next train passed him by. He sat behind a large equipment box, peeking out at trains approaching from Sportivnaya. Thirty minutes and twelve trains passed in either direction before the cadence increased and Moscow's famous ninety-second interval traffic began. Still, not a single car for D-6. He was getting worried he wouldn't be able to tell them apart.

•

It wasn't the size of the train that gave it away; it was the sound of the rail switch and the different path of the approaching headlights.

West held out the sheet of paper from the side of the equipment box.
The train slowed down significantly.

It was single car all right. And single passenger. The lit-up inside
featured a lonely man hunched over, reading something.

West dropped the paper, got up and jumped over the regular
tracks toward the train.

His feet ended up in all sorts of angles on the jagged rocks and
he stumbled over the railroad ties, arms flailing.

The end of the car was just feet away now. He grabbed a vertical
handrail at the tail of the train and the resulting pull sideways almost
yanked his shoulder out of its socket. Instead of his intended jump
upward, he was dragged and had to pull himself up and set his foot
on the narrow bumper ledge.

There was a window to a driver space here but dark on the inside.
The car was symmetric and could go either direction.

West made sure he had a steady grip on the handrail with one
hand and allowed his other to fish out a network repeater from his
pocket.

The gadget's connectivity indicator dropped to one bar.

His grip slid down the handrail as he squatted and stretched his
hand with the repeater down as far as he dared. He let the gadget
go, and it quickly disappeared behind the train.

Still squatting, he grabbed the next repeater in his pocket.

The train suddenly lurched with a grinding noise as if there was
a misalignment of the tracks. His grip on the handrail was firm but
couldn't prevent a rotation of his upper body in an arc toward the
side. He threw his other hand around the corner, embracing the edge
of the car to stop his sideways motion before he'd hit the tunnel
wall. The force he used smashed the network repeater in his hand
against the train.

As soon as the car had stabilized, he checked his pocket. Only
four repeaters left. He must have lost an additional two in the jolt.
Fucking hell.

Two seconds of berating himself later, he realized he had to get
the next repeater in position, no matter what.

The train was picking up speed on a downward slope. The next
repeater showed three bars. Then two. He squatted and dropped
the repeater down between the tracks at one bar.

He kept going as the train continued deeper and deeper beneath Moscow. Only two repeaters left when the train started decelerating.

It was a long slowdown and with all his network repeaters on the track behind, he checked to see if his Tile still had a connection. Barely. And the train hadn't stopped yet.

•

The tunnel lit up as they arrived at what had to be the Ramenki station. West saw little from his position at the back. Pneumatic sputters and hisses rounded it off, and they came to a halt.

He could hear the doors open and close. Stone floor judging by the sound of shoes walking. Just a single pair, so no one getting on.

A few beeps echoed and a chunky lock mechanism moved. The steps on stone disappeared, the door closed with a series of clicks, and the space became silent.

He checked his network connection. Zero.

CHAPTER 86

Entrance Code

West moved along the backside of the car, hunching under the windows. He got to the front and crossed the headlights. This thing could start moving again at any moment. He poked his head up just above the platform to get a peek.

The whole station area was a beautiful piece of civil engineering—ornate with mosaics of working men and women in classic Soviet style, and a band of red stars, chest-high along the back wall. A vaulted ceiling above.

The exit doors to whatever lay behind were double and looked to be made of steel. On one side was a numeric pad, or at least that was the size of the rectangle of keys. The wear and tear of the floor showed that only one of the two doors seemed to be in frequent use. That was also the side that had the warning sign with a crossed over gun and knife.

Shit.

There would likely be a scan for that. Maybe he would even have to empty his pockets.

The platform he was standing on had a protruding lip. Under it was enough space to stash his gun and NATO knife.

One more look at the door. There was a garbage can beside it. Four cans, really, tucked together in a unit with colored labels in Cyrillic. That was it. No indications of anything standing in his way to enter but that keypad.

They had debated fiercely over whether he should bring the stolen ZT with him and risk Vadim discovering that his was broken, or leave it with Åse, who could keep the relay charade going. The latter argument had won, which meant he needed network access to get a onetime code from Åse. And a code had to be used within thirty seconds.

West looked up the tunnel. How far away was he from a single bar of connectivity?

He went behind the train car and started walking up the track, carefully looking for the first upslope-facing camera in the ceiling, while also checking his Tile for connection to the last network repeater he had dropped.

Soon the light from the platform behind became so faint that he had to turn on the red flashlight on his Tile.

The gleam of the half sphere covering the first camera revealed itself high above about one more minute up the slope. He stopped under it and checked his Tile's connection status. Still nothing.

He wiped his forehead. Sweat beads were forming.

What about the angle of the camera? There would be a dead zone under it a bit further up, but how much further?

He took a few steps past the camera dome and stopped again involuntarily. His legs just didn't want to continue. This was pushing it too far. He had to come up with something smarter.

He glanced at his Tile simply out of habit. It now had one bar of connection! One measly bar, but a sweet and most welcome one.

He swiveled around. Going downhill would be much quicker. He triggered his Tile's stopwatch and started a hurried descent.

The jagged rocks on the track bed rolled and shifted noncooperatively as he ran as fast as he dared, heel-first. He tried to land his feet on the crossties, but they weren't spaced well for his stride.

Panting, he heaved himself up on the platform and dashed over to the gated entrance. As soon as he touched the cold steel doors, he checked his time. Twenty-eight seconds. Badging and code entry on top of that and he'd be over thirty.

Multiple failed entries may block the account. Smarter. Something smarter.

His pulse moderated. How could he extend the network connection down to here? Maybe build a *cantenna*?

He translated the labels on the four-mouthed garbage container.

Yellow, ПЛАСТИК, plastic; blue, СТЕКЛО, glass; green, БУМАГА, paper; and red, НЕСОРТИРУЕМЫЕ ОТХОДЫ, unsorted waste.

Why read this? I'm going to check them all, anyway.

He did. The plastic container was empty except for a bread bag clip. There was an empty vodka bottle in the blue one, which made him chuckle. The paper can had napkins, a straw, a flyer, and an empty box for a pair of earbuds. The unsorted waste was all soda cans. He had been hoping for something like a Pringles tube, but a couple of soda cans might be put together to form the basis of a cantenna. His knife could certainly cut through thin aluminum.

But he didn't have the OmniPort extension to use an external antenna. He remembered BestBye using one of those by the Canadian border control station. It felt like ages ago.

There was a sound behind him and he turned around like a frightened animal. The train had started moving. More people would come once it returned. In fact, someone could have exited onto the platform at any moment. What the fuck was he doing? He had to sort this out *now*.

There was something in the paper bin that had planted a thought in the back of his head. He looked again. The earbuds. His own earbuds were wireless. He could leave his Tile on the track bed and ask it to read the incoming message with the code!

The single car train left up the tunnel.

Thinking it through, step by step, he visualized badging to get the code prompt.

You idiot, you can't leave the Tile up there. You need to badge with it.

He put his fists against the stars along the wall and landed his forehead on the cold mosaic.

There was a piercing squeal from the train far up the tunnel. Those horrible metallic sounds that subway trains make, how come they hadn't found a solution to that? Metal grinding against metal.

The tracks are made of metal.

Maybe they could carry the signal to and from his relay?

He jumped down from the platform and held his Tile's metal frame against one of the tracks. Soon enough he had two bars worth of connection.

He afforded himself a brief smile before sending Åse a message.

A fresh code, please.

Good to hear from you.
Stand by.

There was a multi-second pause. They were waiting for a fresh code.

62065777

He heaved himself up on the platform with the clone of Vadim's badge ready on his Tile.

CHAPTER 87

Ramenki City

The hallway entrance behind the doors was broad. About twenty yards in, there was a metal scanner with a guard sitting to the side inspecting his fingernails. A camera was mounted on the ceiling a few feet further in.

Polished stone with a stained red runner greeted West's feet as he stepped in. He had read that the raw materials for Ramenki City had come from the buildings of the old Russian royal family.

He emptied his pockets on the plastic tray by the laconic guard, making sure the antistatic bag with the circuit board lay under his wallet. Behind the guard, tucked up against the wall, was a robot. Not a biped, but a rolling one. A metal door to its innards was half-open and there was a loose battery pack on the floor beside it.

No beep from the scanner. A nod from the guard and West was moving again.

The rug became cleaner the further in he went. On the walls were large painted portraits of men, all men. West didn't recognize any of them, but judging by the artistic style, some impressive mustaches, and the decorations on their chests, he assumed they were state officials stretching from KGB to FSB.

An opening that might host a reception desk revealed itself as a disruption to the line of picture frames to the right.

Keep interactions to a minimum, he repeated to himself.

His hand pulled out the banana, and he took a big bite. Mask back up, he chewed prominently.

A middle-aged woman sat behind a thick, dark-stained desk. She had graying hair combed tightly back into a bun and greeted him as

Smirnov. He mumbled back with his mouth full and made a greeting motion, banana in hand. This was the second time he pulled this trick. He was pushing his luck.

Not much further in on the opposite wall was a huge directory listing with a high-level map. He stopped at it, keeping still at a good distance, then moved on. His brain had registered something weird about it. But the focus on not raising any suspicion blocked him from processing what he had seen.

Men's room to the left. He got in.

Separate toilets properly walled off, not just booths with gaps at the bottom.

The microcamera had captured the directory and his Tile automatically translated.

Five major sections—Global Intelligence, Domestic Intelligence, Correctional, Training, and Recreational.

I was right. This is massive. Correctional—that might be where they took them.

That section spanned three entire floors of the underground city and had a series of interrogation rooms and several straight-up cells. It seemed the implications of the labels in this section got worse the lower the floor. At the bottom, there was something his Tile phrased as "Clinics."

He shuddered.

Elevator shafts with adjacent stairwells were close by. Shouldn't take more than a minute to reach. The level he was at was at the top of the complex. There was a separate elevator further in, labeled "University."

The other exit.

He spotted the Red Web under Domestic Intelligence in the directory. It made him realize the significance of what he currently had access to. What he could find out here was as hardcore as physical intelligence got. Its value to the US government was beyond imagination.

As he got up, his memory swapped in the thing he had noted out at the real directory listing. On the translated directory on his screen, each entry was duplicated in fine print underneath. Weird. And not all were exact duplicates. For instance, the fine print under Correctional read Punitive.

He disabled translation. The label for Correctional/Punitive now looked very different.

исправительный
惩罚性的

The fine-print language was identified as Simplified Chinese. Did they have Chinese personnel here, in Kremlin's secret underground city?

Images of the Bao Gong mountain hall in Norilsk appeared in his memory. If the two superpowers collaborated over quantum computing and global identity data, of course they could collaborate here. Maybe the Red Web was doubly red?

•

The stairwell was exquisite. Its steps were all limestone with trilobites and other fossils; the sides were ornate metal flowers and leaves in spirals, and the handrail was thick, solid wood. It looked like it belonged in a palace.

As soon as the echoes of his own entrance had died out, the only sound present was the hum of the elevators nearby.

The floors were probably twenty feet high, so it took many steps to get to the next level down. He was at the interrogation block. Below were the cells and above were offices. Employees would go down one level and the prisoners would go up.

Between the cells and the clinics was a level called Storage and Laundry. It would probably be the easiest to sneak into, but also the least likely to get him to East. Perhaps they stored personal effects of the inmates there? Would he be able to spot anything belonging to Viktor? He closed his eyes and saw the middle-aged Russian's clothes clearly from when he was apprehended. If he could find something identifiable like that, those effects would be mapped to the cell he was after.

There was one more thing that made him want to go to a level with not too many people around. Computers. He needed access to computers.

Chapter 88

Storage and Laundry

The entry doors to each floor were wide and double. Electric light seeped from the inside of each door through tall, frosted windows centered on them.

West stood still for a good while. The elevator shaft kept burring. Eventually, he could discern human voices on the other side of the doors. They sounded mostly Russian, but there was one other language which he recognized from his many visits to Chinatown in San Francisco.

What surprised him was the occasional English with two heavy accents.

Russians and Chinese collaborating in my native tongue. What a thing. Worst case, I can respond in English and maybe get away with it.

Footsteps were approaching on the other side of the door. Someone was yelling, but not the person walking toward him.

West moved to the side and pushed his back against the wall, arms flat on the side, making himself as slim as possible.

One of the doors swung open and something small hit the floor. Not something hard, like metal. Softer.

The yelling was now loud and clear. Slowly, the hydraulic door closer did its thing. The last West heard from the inside was "I told you to keep your stinky fish at home. Don't bring that shit here."

The smell of reheated fish reached him. On the floor lay a rectangular plastic box with steaming food. A round, white bun with a bite taken out of it and some steamed vegetables on the side.

The door was kicked open and a tirade in Chinese accompanied a thin man who picked up the plastic box and returned inside.

West stopped the door from closing and took decisive steps inside. The meager man stopped mid-sentence and looked at him.

West raised his shoulders. "What's a little fish?" he said, faking a Russian accent.

The man took a second, then said, "He pisses on our food all the time."

West glanced forward to find somewhere to aim his stride. "Maybe you should piss *in* his food then."

"Ha! Maybe I will." The man veered off to the right.

"I'm getting some personal things for a person in Cell Block B. They told me to go here. Is it down the hall?"

"We don't keep personal things here."

West's gut cramped.

"But you can always check the stuff we find in laundry. Sorting room. Far left."

"Thank you."

•

The further in West got, the more it smelled of laundry detergent. There were three doors that fit "far left." He discreetly translated the door labels. Noisy behind a door tagged "Machines." Next to it, the label translated to "Laundry Arrival."

Inside, he found a Chinese woman going through huge mesh bags of laundry, sorting them into piles on the floor. Most of it looked like bed linen. She said nothing but seemed to expect him to. She was wearing a face mask like him.

"Sorry, I'm here to look for some personal things that may have gone with the laundry," West said.

The woman pointed to a basket on the side.

As he gripped the handle, he felt an urge to chat just a little with the woman. He reminded himself to stick to a Russian accent. "Hey, I've always wondered why we have Chinese workers here. I'm not against it, but ..."

"Wives and husbands. We are all married to experts." She pointed upward. "Chinese culture. You work. No lazy. Down here, no secrets. Up there, no wives and husbands. We work here."

"Huh." His mind made his body pause for a bit, basket lid in hand. The practicality of it all was striking. This wasn't a cluster of evil individuals. This was people's lives, their livelihood, the way they put food on the table and contributed to society. "That makes sense," he ended.

The basket had all sorts of things in it. After digging around for a short while, he found a toy. A colorful, grip-friendly, round thing that could roll. He put it in his pocket.

Pretending to search further down the basket, he scanned the room, moving his eyes rather than his head.

There was a wide door going to the machine room. It had stainless steel shielding halfway up. Along the wall closest to that door, there were three carts on small wheels. On the opposite wall, two posters with what looked like work instructions. Yup, both in Chinese and Russian. Some shelves at the back with buckets, rubber gloves, and white clogs in neat rows. In the corner a wall-mounted large Tile.

The woman started heaving linen into a cart. It shifted a bit for each throw. Once full, she rolled it out and pushed it hard against the metal shield to open the door. The laundry machine noise spilled into the room for a few seconds and then she was gone.

West dashed over to the Tile on the wall. Two large on-screen buttons, one in Cyrillic and one in Chinese.

He glanced at the door. How long would she be gone for?

He tapped the button in Cyrillic and fished out his own Tile to translate the interface.

It was some kind of communication system. There was even a news section. West expanded it only to find that the latest "news" was months old.

He felt feverish, constantly checking the doors. Maybe it was normal for staff to use these Tiles and the woman wouldn't mind. Then again, maybe not.

The bottom of the Tile had a charging cable connected to its OmniPort. He unplugged it.

The woman would likely mind him fiddling with his Bunny drive.

There was a slight change of noise in the machine room.

West squeezed his fingers in between the Tile and the wall and pulled. It came loose with a ripping sound as some kind of glue or tape on its backside took with it a strip of wall paint.

He was out of the room before the woman returned.

CHAPTER 89

Fancy Bear

West got back to the stairwell without having to talk to anyone. He ascended halfway up to the next floor before he sat down on one of the steps. In his lap lay the laundry sorting room's Tile. The screen had turned off after he disconnected it from power.

He got his Bunny drive out, made sure its switch was for Shell, and plugged it in.

The Tile's screen blipped a few times before spawning him a prompt.

Damn the Bunny was good. He unplugged it and returned it to his pocket before listing what was on the Tile.

It was some sort of Linux, possibly Astra. What looked to be the custom software was installed under /etc/services/metro2/.

The file names were mostly in English, as was the case for most programming. But the Tile's command-line interface was in Russian, which got irritating quickly. West ran some commands to change it to US English.

```
> sudo reconfigure locales

[ ] be_BY 112
[ ] zh_Hans_CN 156
[*] ru_RU 643
[ ] uk_UA 804
[ ] en_US 840
```

As he confirmed US English, there was a flash of a memory of something Åse had said. Was it recently? No, further back, right before they boarded the sub in Norway. But then again, "recently" was kind of fuzzy. How many days since they left Norway? What was it she had said? Nah, it was gone now.

With English as the interface language, he picked up speed. Three services. The stale news thing, a work schedule app, and something called Chopstick.

The Chopstick directory had a single, large executable created years ago.

He tried running it, but it quit immediately and did not spin up any auxiliary processes.

Weird. I wonder what that thing just did?

This device had Wi-Fi, which he was planning to use as a bridge to get his own Tile on the network. But he might as well ask directly here.

```
> ask Chopstick disambiguation

Chopsticks (disambiguation)

Chopsticks are eating utensils mainly
employed in Asia. "Chopsticks" may also
refer to:

"Chopsticks" (music), a simple piano piece

Chopsticks (album), a 1989 album by Peter
Combe

Chopsticks (hand game), a finger game
The Chopsticks, a female singing duo from
Hong Kong

The Civilian War Memorial in Singapore,
informally known as "Chopsticks"

Chopsticks (2019 film), an Indian film
```

Chopstick, backdoor malware used by APT28
a.k.a. Fancy Bear

Wow.
Was this Tile infected?
Hey, this isn't why I'm here. I've gotta find East.
He landed the Tile in his lap, closed his eyes hard, and clapped twice to reset.

The work schedule that this device was used for was bound to sync with some central service. West set up logging of network traffic from and to the Tile, and respawned the schedule app.

Sure enough, a network request came through looking like the right thing.

```
:method = GET
:path = /getWorkScheduleData
:scheme = https
host = edge.ramenki.fsb.ru

calendarAPI=https://calendar.ramenki.fsb.
ru:8443/staff/laundry/getWorkScheduleData
```

This was the Tile asking edge.ramenki.fsb.ru for the latest schedule and then that server asking another server called calendar.ramenki.fsb.ru for the data.

He tried sending a request directly to the calendar server.

```
> curl -I https://calendar.ramenki.fsb.
ru:8443/staff/laundry/getWorkScheduleData

curl: Could not resolve host: calendar.
ramenki.fsb.ru
```

The Tile had no way of finding the IP address of the calendar service.

But the edge server obviously has.
He changed the request parameter to see if he could make the backend retrieve the list of personnel.

```
:method = GET
:path = /getWorkScheduleData
:scheme = https
host = edge.ramenki.fsb.ru

calendarAPI=https://calendar.ramenki.fsb.
ru:8443/staff/laundry/getStaff

HTTP 404 Not Found
```

A lot better than no host. It's talking to the server.
He tried /getPersonnel and /getEmployees but still got a 404.
He massaged his temples with his thumb and middle finger.

```
calendarAPI=https://calendar.ramenki.fsb.
ru:8443/staff/laundry/getWorkers

Jason Li
谭元元
陳志遠
Елéна Водорезова
```

Bingo. Well, half bingo at least.
This meant he could change what the laundry room Tile was asking for and have those requests be accepted by the server he was not able to talk to directly.

What other servers might there be?

If he was going to search through plausible server names, that would be hundreds if not thousands of trials. He would have to script it. But what list of names would he try? English nouns straight from the dictionary? He would miss any abbreviations, not to mention location names like Ramenki itself.

Could he go straight after the IP address instead?

```
> nslookup edge.ramenki.fsb.ru
Non-authoritative answer:
Name: edge.ramenki.fsb.ru
Address: 213.24.76.23
```

Jitterbug had shown him how to enumerate server directories brute-force style. The memory of his friend and how he would always be willing to help stung.

Damn it, Jit.

He looked around in the stairwell. Who would have thought he'd end up here, in some stone cold, top secret, underground complex?

He wiped his eyes and wrote the command he remembered Jitterbug showing him.

```
> nmap -sV --script=http-enum 213.24.76.23

| http-enum:
|    /images/: Icons and images
|    /robots.txt: Robots file
|    /index.html: Index file
```

A freaking index file? He downloaded it.

```
:method = GET
:path = /getWorkScheduleData
:scheme = https
host = edge.ramenki.fsb.ru

calendarAPI=https://213.24.76.23:8443/
index.html
```

The file had hundreds of directory paths, with one standing out. He went one level deeper.

```
:method = GET
:path = /getWorkScheduleData
:scheme = https
host = edge.ramenki.fsb.ru

calendarAPI=https://213.24.76.23:8443/
correctional/directory/index.html
```

By filtering that file for "Viktor," he got a single hit.

```
Maria Smyslova, Viktor Smyslov, Anatoly
Smyslov: Cell 51A
```

CHAPTER 90

Shutting Down

The entry doors to the correctional level from the stairwell looked like the laundry ones—wide with frosted glass in the middle. In the landing's corner toward the back wall was a little pile of empty plastic packages, maybe candy. West looked closer and realized they were broken condom packages.

Fucking bastards.

He forced himself not to look at them.

The laundry room Tile still had Wi-Fi access.

He put his hand on one of the doors and pushed it lightly. It opened an inch. No human sounds behind.

He released the door and sat down on the stairs. How the hell would he get to cell 51A? Let alone open it, get three people out, and leave this complex with them? The whole venture was ludicrous.

Maybe he could hack his way to issue an order for their release? They could do such a thing via Kenin's Tile. But they didn't know the protocol and were bound to make it look suspicious.

Kiss had suggested only getting East out, and she stuck to that opinion throughout their planning. West didn't feel it was right and that he'd have to explain that to his son later in life. But it was still an option if things got out of hand.

Another way would be to find the cell and wait around until the staff opened it. Interrogations, or bathing the baby. That could present an opportunity, but would mean high risk of confrontation and violence. He didn't want any more violence.

Images of the dying guard at Ice Dolphin flashed before him. Dying by his hand. He could still sense the smell of the man's last breath and see the fear in his eyes. No, it hadn't been fear; it had been a brief moment of clarity and despair, the last flicker of life, with no recourse and no bargaining, just one last thought.

His mouth dried up. That image would haunt him until he too faced death.

He looked at the laundry Tile, slowly coming back to the present. The caret was blinking in the shell he had spawned with the Bunny. *Cell 51A. How?*

Could cells be unlocked remotely, like in the movies? He could dig around some more in the index file for sure.

In that moment, the memory of what Åse had said before they boarded the sub came raging back—the thing his brain had been searching for when he was fiddling with the Tile's language settings.

"Pull down and install the whole Commonwealth of Independent States language package. Failsafe for broad Russian malware. The exploits don't activate on devices with those languages."

He uninstalled every language on the Tile but English, then ran the Chopstick executable again.

This time, it didn't auto-quit.

He inspected what it was doing. It was pinging some server and downloading a compressed file. Then both those activities halted, and the software started spitting out log statements every ten seconds.

```
Network connection lost …
Network connection lost …
Network connection lost …
```

West checked and he could no longer query Wikipedia. Although he was connected to Wi-Fi, no network traffic was getting through.

Chatter started on the other side of the door. Communication in English told West that the network failure was hitting others too.

Either Ramenki networking had gone down for some accidental reason, or the Fancy Bear Chopstick malware had triggered a security shutdown.

He looked back at the laundry room Tile. Its screen was black. It no longer reacted to taps or button presses. He rebooted it but only got to the greeting screen before it turned inanimate again.

Something had changed in the stairwell's ambience, as if something had settled.

It was the elevator hum. It was gone. Did it go down with the network? If so ...

People will use the stairs.

CHAPTER 91

Cell 51A

West dashed half a floor down and turned upward. His feet stood two steps apart and his knuckles whitened with his grip of the rail.

Both doors above swung open and several people emerged, all headed up.

West instinctively started ascending too.

One of the people pouring out of the correctional block spotted him below and said something. West's earbuds only translated the latter half. Dropouts were common in commotion like this. The man had said "... for you too?"

West stopped and held the Tile out. He pointed at its black screen.

The man shook his head and joined the others going up.

The double doors to Correctional were swinging lightly back and forth into their steady position as West approached. He put his hand on one of them and pushed firmly.

His mind was set on getting as far in as he could before making any further decisions about where he was headed.

The walls were naked concrete and there were green doors on the left side. The right side featured the floor's elevator lobby. All the elevators had buttons blinking red. Further in, there was a closed, barred gate shutting off the whole corridor.

He looked back at the lobby. There was one elevator fewer here compared to the entrance level.

The surface one, of course.

A trash can and a paper shredder stood between two of the elevator doors. He gently tapped on the shredder. Metal housing.

He lifted its top. Inside were just a few strips of paper.

A Faraday cage good enough for me.

He slipped the laundry room Tile into the bin and closed the shredder.

Before he turned back, he listened. No voices or movement.

He took resolute steps toward the barred gate. On the right wall, well shielded from the inner side of the gate, was a large red push button.

He pushed it, and it unlocked the gate.

You get in but not out.

The gate locked again with a *ka-chunk.*

He pressed the red button and started counting seconds.

Zero, one, two, three ...

A total of fifteen seconds before it locked.

He pushed and held the button, counting to fifteen. No locking sound. After thirty seconds, he released the pressure and the *ka-chunk* came immediately.

He got his Survivor Kit out of his breast pocket and from it he pulled his small tube of superglue and put a thin ring of glue on the innermost part of the button. He pushed and held it for a minute.

The glue did its job.

•

Each cell had a number and the same green metal door. It took West a few minutes to get to 51A.

He put his ear to the door. It was cold. Not a sound from within. Or wait, was that a baby babbling?

His hands trembled as he pulled out his lock picks.

The lock looked decades old. Tension tool in and medium hook pick in his other hand. He got down on one knee and concentrated.

One by one, the pins inside got into position.

He turned the tumbler and heard the deadbolt retract. Lock picks back in his pocket, he pushed the handle down. The door opened inward.

There was a giggle and a "shhh" inside.

West stared into two frightened, grown-up faces sitting on beds along either side of a small cell.

He pulled down his face mask.

A little baby boy sat on a blanket on the floor between them. A little boy he'd only seen at a distance before. The boy had a yellow bite toy in his mouth and looked at his biological father with big brown eyes. His hair was dark, standing out on top like a Mohawk. The turn to look at West made him a little unsteady, and he rolled over to crawling position. Maria stopped him from moving in West's direction.

Everyone but East was silent for several moments. Viktor spoke first, in English.

"Maria, this ... this is the man I told you about. West, I believe his name is."

West quickly checked the ceiling and walls.

"No cameras or microphones here. The Diggers don't want things on record," Viktor said.

West shuddered.

"So you figured it out, D-6," Viktor said with wonder. "I know РЖЯ, or gesture language."

"Sign language," West corrected.

"Ah. Well, I know it because I have a deaf brother."

"Why the Diggers? Why here?" West asked.

"The Diggers are the Kremlin's internal spies. They dig up any kind of uprising or subversive activity. They knew Maria was in Moscow and then I suddenly showed up. As for here"—Viktor let his gaze make an arc—"it's the safest confinement in the city. No one hears you scream in Ramenki."

"I see the similarity now," Maria said, as if accepting something dreaded but inevitable. "The nose."

The little boy struggled to get loose.

"Let him," Viktor said, putting his hand on his wife's shoulder.

She let go of the baby's chest. He crawled unsteadily toward West.

West kneeled and put the back of his hands on the floor. "He can already crawl."

"Yes, he's early," he heard Maria say.

East could barely keep his heavy head up and had to stop twice to check his bearing. When he arrived, the little boy's hand touched West's.

"Oh," West let out. "Hey there, mister." He looked at Maria. "Is it okay if I call him East?"

"Of course," Viktor said. "Can we call him Anatoly?"

"Sure. Hey, East."

East sat back, almost tipping backward.

"I've come to get you out," West said to the boy. "All three of you."

"How will you ..."

"There's pandemonium because the Wi-Fi is down. It's our chance. Let's go." He got ready to lift East by the armpits, but stopped himself. "Maybe it's best you carry him. We don't want him crying."

"He rarely cries. But I can take him," Maria said.

They stood up, Maria lifting East to her shoulder. "Thank you," she said. "Thank you for trying to get us out."

West got his face mask back on.

•

The cell block's gate was still open when they exited. West yanked the stuck button out, ripping its red rubber coating that was glued to the socket.

They had decided not to talk, just quickly move toward the stairwell.

Chapter 92

Elevator

Viktor and Maria took one turn each carrying East up the stairs to keep as fast a pace as possible. They were all panting heavily when they reached the entry level.

"Wait here. I'll be back within a minute," West said and exited.

There were people in motion in the lobby area now, not the scattered one or two West had seen on his way in.

The buttons on the three elevators closest were still blinking angrily red.

He walked past them and saw no blinking from the surface elevator as he approached it at the far end of the lobby.

He pressed the button, and the doors opened immediately. Inside were just two floor buttons.

Maria and Viktor jolted back when West returned. They looked pale and haggard.

West had a sinking feeling as he opened his mouth to speak. He could still change his mind. But he knew he wouldn't. His chances of getting out of Russia with the others were slim to none. It had to be this way.

"I will not be going with you," he commenced, feeling an orb grow in his chest.

"What?"

"FSB, Interpol, and my home country are all after me. I have a Red Notice on my name. I'm an international pariah. You have to exit Russia without me. Get my son to his mother and get out, all of you. Can you do that for me?"

"But what will you do?" Viktor said.

"I have to find my own way out. Don't worry, I'm not giving up, not with East in this world. Somehow, I'll be there for him. You just need to get him out."

"We will do our best. But we need help."

He explained how to find Kiss and Åse above ground and had them repeat it back to him.

Finally, he gave them two folded sheets of paper—one reading "Åse" and the other "Kiss."

"Please hand them these letters. When you get to America, you should insist on asylum."

He pointed at the door. "We take a left, go past three elevators, further on to the one that goes to the surface. It's not far. Ready?"

Viktor and Maria nodded.

•

The movement to the elevator was swift.

West held the doors with one foot and pulled out the round grip toy he got from the laundry room. He gave it to East without a word. The boy reached out from Maria's arms and grasped the plaything with big eyes.

West removed his foot and waved feebly as the doors closed.

He knew this short and nervous goodbye would stay with him for the rest of his life. The question was if it would be his last memory of East.

It mustn't be. I'm his dad.

Chapter 93

West's Letter to Åse

Åse. Thank you for sticking with me.

I understand the liability I've become. You have duties and you are risking your future career. Maybe you even have direct orders to bring me to justice, whatever justice means.

I will not come with you. Instead, I will create a diversion to maximize the chances of Kiss and East getting out. You have Maria, which should be plenty in terms of mission accomplished.

From this point I will move alone and as unpredictably as I can. My plan is to get myself out of Russia and bring enough intel to argue myself out of the Red Notice and whatever the US has on me. If my country decides I still have dues to pay, I will do so and not stain your reputation further. I managed to decrypt the Ice Dolphin drive, by the way.

You helped me get Kiss out of prison and the last bit is to get her and East home. I will be forever in your debt if you do that for me.

You could help with one more thing. Here's what I need from you:

...

CHAPTER 94

West's Letter to Kiss

Kizz. You are the love of my life.

The fact that I can't be there when you get to hold our son in your arms tears me apart. And not being able to support you as you flee this country that has hurt you so much makes me feel weak and useless.

But I have to relieve Åse of the burden I've become. She will get you and East out, I'm sure of it. I would be a liability and a hazard to the whole venture. I can't expose you to that risk now that you have a chance at freedom.

I promise you this: I will get myself out. It may take a while, but don't give up on me. You outlived Ice Dolphin, you can push through this too. Once I'm out, I will find you and we will be together. For as long as you'll have me.

Heart, body, and soul.

/We$t

PS. The bloodstain below is for you to use if you need to prove I'm East's father.

Chapter 95

Global Intelligence

West wiped tears from his eyes and looked to the ceiling to straighten himself out.

His son, Viktor, and Maria had left for the surface.

He was alone, and it was unclear if there was a single safe place left for him in this world.

There was a loud cheer over at the internal elevators. The red blinking was gone and people started pouring in through the elevator doors.

He rushed to join the closest one.

Global Intelligence was the first floor below entry level. He and eight others got out. West made sure to exit last.

He soon found himself in a long corridor. No doors on the sides. The first three people were chatting. By the looks of their backs, it was two women with pitch-black hair and one graying man, the latter rather chubby. They were neatly dressed. Between them and West were five younger, thin men, not as well dressed, three of them black-haired and two blondish. The one closest to West wore a black T-shirt. The back of it read **Линда** and featured Gothic and Christian symbols.

Two to three minutes later, they approached closed double doors with a badge reader on the side.

The plump man went first and slapped a plastic card against the reader. It beeped. He held the door as the two women entered. As they turned their faces to nod a thank-you, West saw they looked Asian.

The first of the younger men caught the door with his left foot as he badged. *Beep.*

Only four left before West. What if Vadim's badge didn't have access here? It would be a huge risk to use it.

The young guys held the door for each other. *Beep.*

He got his Tile out and launched the audio recorder.

Beep. Beep.

One more to go, West hit record and kept his Tile as close to the guy ahead of him as he dared.

Beep.

Only him left. The door was held for him too.

He put the back of his Tile against the reader and hit playback. *Beep.*

The guy in front of him released the door and started walking inward. West got in behind.

The corridor stretched further before opening into a vast hall. It looked like the command center in *WarGames*, or Mission Control at NASA. Six gigantic screens on a curved back wall and rows of desks back toward the ledge where he was standing.

All screens were showing progress bars, as if booting up.

There were hushed conversations here and there between personnel behind the desks.

The senior trio with the chubby fellow went up some stairs to the right. The lanky youngsters headed for double glass doors out of the hall to the left.

West realized he was standing there, staring.

There was a free desk to his right, and he sat down. The computer monitor at this station was showing a boot screen too. He glanced and gave a discreet nod to the man sitting next to him.

A young Asian woman over at the next row was speaking English with a pale, albino man. "I've never been there, but the name is clear," she said.

"I wish I could get my washing done here," the albino said.

"I'm sure you can, if you want to wear government clothes."

"I don't care what I wear."

The woman chuckled. "Anyway, some Tile down there had malware on it. Some old version that woke up and tried to spread. Those holes were patched ages ago, so they decided there was no risk and just shut the device down remotely."

"I'm glad I used that as a toilet break."

"Oh, look. We're online again."

The six enormous screens one by one started displaying maps.

One was of North America. Major US and Canadian cities were marked by dots, or at least the dots were close to cities. LA, Seattle, Chicago, DC. He was fuzzy on Texas but guessed Houston. The one in the middle had to be in Colorado or maybe southern Wyoming.

Each dot had a cluster of information beside it. There was a number between five and twenty for something called Assets, a score in Gps—maybe gigabytes per second—and a rank. Colorado, Chicago, and Houston were top ranked.

South America had two dots on the coast of Brazil and one in Argentina.

West's knowledge of Europe was sketchy, but by London there was a dot labeled "LINX." One was in the middle of France, so maybe Paris, and one in Germany. The other handful were in places he didn't know. Oh, wait. One must be Stockholm.

The only Asian dots he felt sure about were Tokyo and Taipei.

The African map only had three dots. He knew where Cairo was because he did a report on ancient Egypt in middle school. He guessed the dot at the southern tip of the continent had to be South Africa, or maybe Lesotho. Then there was one in the middle, to the west.

The sixth screen was all data.

CHAPTER 96

The Arsenal

Browsing through the data listed on the sixth screen, West concluded it was a summary of the global cyber arms race—an accounting of the balance of power, as estimated by the Russia-China alliance.

There was a table for every major operating system West knew, plus three more that he was not familiar with—VxWorks, OSE, and WinCC. Each table had two columns—"New Era" and "5 Eyes"—and three rows labeled RCE, Read, DoS.

He remembered hearing something about China and Russia's "New Era of Global Sustainable Development." Some political declaration.

Five Eyes was the world's English-speaking Western countries, and the cyber pact the New Era considered its enemy.

RCE had to be short for remote code execution, i.e. the ability to remotely control another computer. DoS meant denial of service—making a computer system fail to respond timely. The middle category, "Read," probably meant the ability to read secrets.

The screen changed content and now listed "Active Influence Measures" per Five Eyes country. Each row had a label such as Ethnic-Conflict-812826 or LGBTQ-attack-102066 and a column for number of clicks. There was also information on where a measure was advertised or not and if it had "Domestic Amplification."

Given the huge number of clicks on each entry displayed, this had to be a top list—the tip of an information warfare iceberg.

The screen flipped a third time. It was now titled Cyber Bases and listed Haidian/Beijing, Shenzhen, Ramenki/Moscow, Kaliningrad, and ... West heart did a double beat ... Ice Dolphin/Novaya Zemlya.

West discreetly looked around. No one was watching him. He let his eyes scan the upper walls and ceiling. Cameras and speakers abound.

He checked the desk. It was tidy.

He rolled his chair back and inch and peeked under the desk. There was a ball of foil in the wastepaper basket. He fished it out and flattened it under the desk without looking at his hands. At least it wasn't greasy.

He pulled his Tile out and wrapped it in the foil, still keeping it all under the desk. When put beside the keyboard, it kind of looked like a packaged sandwich. Kind of.

His hand traced the uneven wrapping until he found the camera unit, and peeled off the foil with his nail to reveal the main lens.

He put his elbows on the desk and held his sandwich pack in both hands. He hit the camera button to take a photo. A minute's wait and he snapped a photo of the next screen. Then the third, before pocketing the wrapped Tile.

A voice came alive in the speaker system. Russian. West got his earbuds in just in time for the repeat message in Mandarin. His buds translated it to "Mandatory badge control of all personnel. Stay where you are. A supervisor will come to your workstation and administer the check. We are looking for the perpetrator of the recent network outage. Surveillance cameras have spotted a man using a stolen Tile. We are looking for this man. Any moves to escape this check will be viewed as adversarial and the person will risk physical harm."

West's mouth tasted of iron. He looked around. Everyone had frozen at their desks, including the man next to him. The only exception was two men in uniform who interacted with the person seated at the other end of his row. They were scanning the person's badge and checking against a list.

CHAPTER 97

Searching for a Man

The two uniformed men worked their way toward West. They compared what they saw on the scanner Tile with the face of the person in front of them as they went.

He pulled up Vadim's badge clone on his Tile. He'd been able to use it to enter this whole complex because no one had compared his face with the face on the badge. But no way were his looks close enough for a face-to-face inspection. They would spot him immediately.

He felt like throwing up.

What could he possibly do? Stealing someone else's badge wouldn't be any better than using Vadim's, most likely worse. Could he say he lost his? Well, then how did he get in? Tailgated? They would pull him into questioning for sure. Maybe fake some kind of accident?

Now the inspectors were just two desks away.

West's face twitched as he held back tears. He looked at his Tile again. Vadim's badge face looked back at him.

"We are looking for this man." "This man." Singular. They will stop looking once they find the one!

The uniformed men took the three steps necessary to approach his desk neighbor.

West pointed the head of his Tile at the scanner one of the men held.

The person sitting next to him moved his badge toward the scanner.

West beamed the signal from Vadim's badge.

He beamed it again.

And again.

There was a chirp. The men in uniform raised their eyebrows, looked at the man in the chair, and turned the scanner's display to him.

Wild protests ensued as the sitting man was grabbed by both arms and pulled away.

West looked at his hand holding the Tile. His tight grip was hurting his fingers. He wiped a tear before it rolled down his cheek.

He had to get out of here.

Get out of Ramenki.

Get out of Moscow.

Get out of Russia.

Chapter 98

Kremlin: WTF?

"What did you just say?" The look on Elvira Kenin's face was menacing. The tension of her jaw, the pitch-black pupils of hers staring her chief of staff down, and the restraint in her communication that wasn't.

"We believe we just had an insider attack at Ramenki," the chief said. "The suspect is being questioned and their Tile is being inspected."

"You are in charge of security," Kenin pointed out. "All things security. We vet people. Immense background checks. Double checks. We monitor people at home. We flag any anomaly. You have told me that's the case. And now you say an insider attacked us? And they were caught *after* the fact?"

"Ma'am, only a Tile was compromised and the automated anomaly detection on the internal network picked it up immediately. The shutdown was instant."

"Was that the attacker's intent?"

"I'm sorry?"

"Was a temporary shutdown of Ramenki operations their intent?"

"We don't think ..."

Kenin raised her palm. By God did she want to smack this guy, right here, right now. "What I'm hearing is that you haven't even started analyzing this. This will be your last week on the job if you don't clear this up. Get me the suspect on screen now."

A minute later, Kenin was looking at a terrified, pale Chinese man on her monitor. His shoulders were pulled back. Probably handcuffed.

"Name and position," Kenin requested.

"Wen Jintao, threat analyst. I go by Wendy."

"Okay, Wendy, threat analyst. I'm sure you've been questioned quite a bit. Sum it up for me."

"I did nothing wrong. I just done my job. They say I use Tile on other floor but I have never been down there."

"But you used another employee's badge."

"I did not. I don't know what happen."

A scanner device was held up to the camera, showing Vadim Smirnov's badge. "This is what he's been using," a voice told her in Russian.

"Save that scan data, then scan Wendy's badge again."

Kenin heard someone ask for help saving the data, and a minute passed. Then a chirp and a barely perceptible "What?"

"Show me," Kenin blurted.

The scanner screen was again shown to the camera, this time with Wendy's face on the badge, not Vadim's.

Kenin pulled in air slowly, for three seconds straight, then let it out for just as long. "Someone made your scanner pick up the wrong badge. Did you check the badge of *everyone* on premise?"

"We didn't check anymore after we found the suspect."

"Imbeciles! You check everyone. Before you go ahead and do that, I want the whole Red Web disconnected. This spy will try to exfiltrate whatever they gathered. No network traffic leaves Russia until I say so."

•

Ten minutes later, Elvira Kenin was faced with a stare-down of her own. She was in the Russian president's office and her superior not only waited for the door to close behind her but for the echoes between the stone walls of the expansive office to die down into compact silence. It made her not want to move.

"You have imposed upon the Russian people severe internet restrictions," the president began. "While that is well within your authority, I like to be informed. Why did I have to call *you* on this matter?"

"Mr. President, I'm sorry. We're in the midst of ..."

"I dislike the word *we*. My government officials take personal responsibility."

"Er-hem. Let me rephrase. I'm in the midst of an emergency and had to act swiftly. I can assure you that my measures are called for."

"I hope so. Let's hear it."

Kenin spent her time wisely, sticking to the facts, skipping things she knew the president was already informed on while going deep on what could be at stake with the drive in West's possession.

"The situation you describe is dire indeed," the president said. "Cyber defense is what you sold me on when I made you Head of Ministry."

"And cyber defense is what you get, guaranteed," she ensured.

He tapped his pen against a pile of paper on the desk. "I know you are capable of more than clerical duties. Don't be afraid to get your hands dirty."

"I'll get my hands around his neck."

The president gave her a single nod, and she was dismissed.

Chapter 99

White House: Russia Is Offline

"Russia has been shut off from the internet, Madam President. Or shut themselves off. The only intel we are guaranteed to get out of there right now is over ESS," General Purnell said.

ESS was the US Space Force's Evolved Strategic Satcom system that provided secure communications over satellites for the most sensitive national security operations, including nuclear command and control.

"There's always a fight over ESS bandwidth," Director Lewis mumbled, unamused.

"Tell me about it," the president said. "Do you mean we're missing out on important intel?"

"I'm just saying limited comm is limited comm," Purnell replied.

The president picked up her pen and gave it two clicks. "Anything special leading up to this?" she asked the room.

"Not that we know of," Purnell said.

"That's not entirely true," Lewis added, earning a glower from Purnell. "Three and a half hours before Russia isolated the Red Web, there was a two-hour-and-forty-five-minute drop in Russian bot and troll activity. We don't know why yet."

"That's frontend," Purnell said. "Not my duty."

"Well, General," the president said. "We have a duty to cooperate and provide the best possible intel and analysis for decision-making. I would appreciate less territorial markings and more getting the job done. Is that clear?"

"Yes, ma'am."

"And that goes for you too, Director. You should have informed the general in advance."

"Understood. And agreed," Lewis said.

"What's your take on a possible relationship between the events?" the president asked, still looking at Mack Lewis.

"Our leading theories are a regular technical glitch, some kind of cyberattack temporarily disrupting their troll farms, or some kind of conflict within the Russian Internet Research Agency."

"Do we see such drops often?"

"We do not, except for the consistent drops around Russian holidays."

"An anomaly it is then. Let's get your conclusions to this room when you have them."

Lewis nodded.

Sanchez turned to Purnell. "What is the contingency plan for a Red Web cutoff? We can't afford to be in the dark on developments in Russia."

"Our embassy in Moscow will send a heartbeat signal over ESS every hour as long as nothing bad is happening. Just to let us know they're okay and that there's no major event ongoing. You know, the absence of a signal ..."

"... is a signal in itself. Yeah, I know. Are they aware that the Red Web is disconnected?"

"Why wouldn't they be?"

"If we could pretend to our citizens that the global internet was working, I'm sure the Russians can too. You need to confirm."

"I will do that."

"How sure are we of their ability to connect over ESS?"

"They have emergency power and a strong output signal."

"What if the Russians cut off the right antenna cable or put a bullet through a dish?"

"I'm ... sure we have thought of such threats. I'll get you the details."

"Our reliance on internet connections is full of bad assumptions. You know that. We've spent lifetimes' worth of time analyzing and preparing. Still, I can't say I was content with how we handled our own outage." Sanchez glanced at Mack Lewis, then turned back to the general and paused while giving her pen a 180-degree flip between fingers. "We need to know what's going on in Russia. It could be a coup or them going dark to conceal something. I approve of high bandwidth ESS usage for this purpose if needed."

"I'm thinking Russia is stopping something from getting out," Alec Ore added.

The president tilted her head and raised her eyebrows. "If so, maybe we should help that something to get out?"

Ore agreed. "We may have to light up the Ukraine connection."

"That's under my authority," Purnell interjected.

"Indeed," the president said. "Isn't it peculiar that not long after finally sussing out Russia's covert contingency connection to the US, we're considering using our own such capacity? Let's not be hasty on that front."

CHAPTER 100

Exiting Ramenki

West chose to exit the way he came, to not put any hunters on the trail of his son.

The guard at the metal scanner gave him a tired look, keeping a finger on the page in a book he was reading.

This time, West made sure to put the antistatic bag on top of his wallet on the tray.

The metal door to the train platform had barely shut before West had retrieved his two hand weapons.

From here, he had three options. Walk up the tunnel and be seen by the upslope-facing cameras, ride the front of the train and not be on camera, or ride inside the train with Ramenki employees.

The empty platform, the absence of a train schedule, and an instinct to get away from here quickly made West start walking up the tunnel. The incline drove up his pulse and he started breathing heavily. But his head ignored the exertion. It was processing how to get out of the Metro complex altogether.

There were no track-bound vehicles down by the platform that they could use to catch up with him, so it would be a running contest if it came to a pursuit.

Say he got out of the tunnel—then what? Continue running? Hide somewhere? Try to get on a regular train and disappear in the subway system? They would shoot him if they got a chance.

The dark tunnel closed in as he got further and he turned on the red flashlight on his Tile.

The first upslope-facing camera emerged in the ceiling and he stopped. Once he got in its sights, AI would identify him as a human on the tracks, alarms would trigger, and the hunt would be on. He let his pulse settle and got rid of anything he didn't need, including the suit. For a second, he considered dropping his Survivor Kit and his lock picks too, but realized there were many challenges ahead even if he got to the end of the tunnel.

His Tile buzzed. A message from Kiss!

How are things going, hun?
I'm worried about you.

The network repeaters!
He drafted a reply saying he was all right but then hesitated.
They'll come after me, try to help me. I need to disappear.
He pocketed his Tile. This was it—cameras be damned.

He put one foot forward and sped up to a pace he thought he could sustain. Well past the first camera and no audible alarm. His breathing became labored.

One minute of uphill running. Ninety seconds. Two minutes.

Was that a sound below? He halted for just a moment. There was shouting down by the platform.

His legs got back to work. Up, up, up. Lactic acid was building in his muscles.

He heard several people below now.

BAM! Zing. A gunshot and a ricochet.

His limbs got a shot of power as unadulterated fear took over his brain.

BAM! Thunk.

He turned off the flashlight to become less of a target. This meant he had to cut down the pace and keep the track as his guide in the dark. He must not get injured.

Flickers on the concrete-infused stone walls told him the people below used real flashlights.

A deep whirring sound appeared above, and it was getting closer. West slowed down. A train? No, it would have headlights.

He put a hand out and touched the wall as he kept climbing. It was covered in dust and grime.

A low pitch clanged right in front of him, like a strike on an enormous anvil. The whirring stopped.

He slowed his pace further. A second later, he walked head-first into a wall.

CHAPTER 101

Kremlin: Facial Recognition

"Do we have visuals on who used Smirnov's badge?" Kenin said without looking at her direct. Her eyes were fixed on the thermal camera feed of the intruder hurrying up the tunnel.

"They're sifting through the logs."

"Facial recognition was supposed to tell us if someone got in with a stolen badge and stolen codes." She shook her head. "You better show me a damn good Vadim look-alike. What about the gate? Is the damn tunnel closed yet?"

"It hadn't been used in fifteen years."

"Is it stuck? Is it a fucking manual gate and we need to send someone to pull it?"

"No, no. It's closed now. But it's a procedure only a couple of people are familiar with."

"If this man got out, those people will get familiar with unemployment procedures."

"Here. Entrance photo."

Kenin snatched the Tile out of the man's hands. West's face was on it, dead center. Superimposed text at the bottom showed time and date. "Shouldn't it say the ID of the person and 'Unknown' for faces not recognized?"

"It should. I don't know what's going on there."

"It seems to me it's not recognizing this as a face at all. Don't give me crap about his face mask. That was solved long ago."

She swiped to the right but there was no second photo. "What about exit?"

"Badge is not required on your way out."

"Yeah, but we know he exited to the train platform since he's in the tunnel. So there should be footage of that. I want to know what he took with him, you moron."

"I'll talk to them." The man hurried toward the door.

"Hey!" Kenin held up her index finger, then returned it to the Tile to pinch-zoom and look closely at the face before handing back the device. "What are those stripes under his eyes?"

Her direct walked back to her quickly and was flummoxed by what was on the screen. "I ... Could be a camera artifact."

"That looks like something intended to foil facial recognition. Find out," she said.

The assistant was already at the door.

"And turn on the lights in the tunnel," she yelled after him. "I need better than a thermal camera."

The man acknowledged with a nod before exiting.

"Who knows what'll go down," Kenin muttered to herself.

CHAPTER 102

The Gate

A fluorescent light from the tunnel ceiling suddenly blinded West. He could hear his pursuers complain further down.

He squinted at first, then opened his eyes halfway. A majestic, patinated steel gate stood before him, with a hammer and sickle emblazoned in the middle. He checked the walls on either side. No buttons or cabinets.

He looked to the ceiling. No sensors, but it was clear the heavy doors were sliding through a channel up there that supported them from falling down.

He looked at the bottom of the gate. A five-inch gap between it and the rock bed provided clearance for the tracks.

BAM! Ding.

Three figures stood further down, barely within shooting distance. One of them was taking aim.

West threw himself to the side and crouched. His hand fumbled to get his gun out. Safety off, aim … He heard Åse's voice in his head and held his breath …

Thud-thud. The first bullet hit the wall, to the right and low from where he was aiming. The second one was bang on target, hitting a thigh.

A scream of pain echoed and all three figures dropped down. The yell turned into moaning and dampened voices.

West started pulling jagged track bed stones from underneath the gate, while checking on his enemies every other second. The stones he removed rolled clickety-clacking down the slope. There were more stones under the top layer. This could work.

He calmed down to be able to use his gun again. Breath suspended, he squeezed off a single shot. No visible hit but a stir among the figures.

Back to digging. Was this enough? No, stones were blocking on the other side.

BAM! A crack of stones on the wall behind him. Then a burning sensation in his left shoulder.

Panic rolled in and the air left his lungs in an exhale that just wouldn't end. Blood drained from his head, pulling him into unconsciousness.

Just as his vision was going gray, his lungs decided to expand once more, and he felt a rush, almost like a high.

He forced himself not to look at his shoulder and instead lay down on his belly, pushed his legs under the gate, and started kicking stones away violently. For every inch he cleared, he pushed himself further under the gate and started kicking again. The sharp edges of the stones underneath him dug into his flesh and pulled his shirt up, exposing his skin to the tearing surface.

His hips were under the gate when a new bullet came raging in and he saw the two unhurt figures approach on one side each.

Another shot. This one hit the metal gate with the sound of a church bell.

West turned his head to the side and pushed himself backward as far as he could. His feet moved to shift the stones around enough to make a path for themselves. He folded himself and felt the cold steel of the gate scrape his neck as he swept under it.

Once on the other side, he kicked stones back into the groove he'd created, stumbled to his feet and started moving upward to the train crossing.

CHAPTER 103

Kremlin: West William Wilder

Kenin didn't care that she had just smashed an expensive big screen in her office. Watching what she assumed was a spy escape underneath an old Soviet steel gate and disappear into the Moscow Metro system was just too much. A German beer glass with a handle that she'd been given on a trip was the closest thing to grab and throw, and it did the job.

Her direct opened the door a few inches and stuck his head in. "Everything all right?"

"Hell no! You better have something good for me or I'll slice you in half. The little fucker just got away."

The man cleared his throat before entering. "We got you the exit footage. And we touched up three of the photos of the man using Vadim Smirnov's badge and reran them through facial recognition."

She waved him in and grabbed the Tile.

"So who is he?" she asked while studying the scene of West exiting through the metal scanner.

"An American. West William Wilder. Apparently there are press ..."

She looked up. "I know the press story. This is a full-blown emergency. An American spy has been inside Ramenki and is now on his way to transfer whatever information he has to his home country. If we don't catch him, you will be lucky to only lose your job. West William Wilder is now the Russian Federation's most wanted man. He is in Moscow. There he shall stay, for the short remainder of his life. I am taking charge. Shut down the Metro system. Shut down the cellular network in the Metro. Lock every Metro station. And get every person in my staff in the situation room in thirty minutes."

Livid, she again turned her attention to the footage of West leaving Ramenki. She zoomed in. He had put an antistatic bag with a circuit board on the tray by the scanner. Blocking her country's outbound network traffic would not be enough to stop this hemorrhage.

CHAPTER 104

Metro Exit

West took the route away from Sportivnaya Metro station at the crossing and put some distance between him and the single-track tunnel.

He didn't see any trains, which was weird. The tunnels were eerily silent.

His two pursuers had not dug their way under the gate like him. Perhaps they got orders to pull back. Or perhaps they figured West's ability to take them out when they emerged was too great a risk. Or maybe they decided to take care of their wounded comrade.

West figured he should tend to his injury too before it got out of hand. Luckily, he hadn't thrown away his first aid kit when shedding weight.

The bullet had grazed his shoulder and ripped his clothes rather than create entry and exit holes. The fabric was wet and sticky with blood and clung on to his skin. He'd have to get his upper body naked to get this right.

The wound wasn't deep, but he remembered Åse talking about what modern guns do to the body. The shockwave of the impact could shatter blood vessels far from where the bullet hit.

Cleaning it stung like hell, but soon enough he had it patched reasonably well and was back on his feet.

The turns in the Metro tunnels were long, gradual bends. Coming out of such a bend, he saw one, then two red lights that looked like the rear of a train. There was also white light from the sides of the carriers illuminating the tunnel walls with all their gear and cables.

He turned off his red flashlight as he got close.

The train was just standing there, dead silent. No shadows moving in the white light from its windows. Not a station in sight.

Once he was close enough to touch the back of the train, he stopped and listened. There was subdued conversation inside.

The back was an engineer's compartment so that the train could be driven either way. But he knew that these were driverless trains—engineers were only needed when the system broke down. Had it broken down?

He moved around the corner, letting his chest slide against the side of the train to minimize the risk of being spotted by a passenger.

The engineer's door had a groove for the flush handle and there was a keyhole.

Picking a lock from the side turned out to be incredibly hard. Sweat ran down his cheeks as his fine arm and hand muscles fought the mechanism. He was thirsty. Standing here was just waiting to get caught. He cursed inaudibly over and over.

What must have been a couple of minutes later, he felt the satisfying turn of the lock tumbler and put his hand in the groove to pull the handle. Opening the door would be the riskiest part in terms of being detected. He did the bare minimum and snuck in.

The inside was an instant déjà vu from Dudinka and the train to Norilsk. Same "V. Tikhomirov Scientific Research Institute of Instrument Design" emblazoned above the displays, buttons, and joystick.

The monitors lit up as soon as he touched them. His Tile helped him find the key parts of the instruments. It was in automated mode and the path to drive this manually seemed to start with a red display button labeled Обходить, or Bypass.

The direction he was facing would likely take him back to Sportivnaya. Not bad because he knew that station reasonably well now. But he would pass the crossing to Metro-2. Worse, the likelihood of some train being in the way was real. Then what?

He could walk to the front of the train and go from there, but one more lock to pick and one more door to open ... He didn't have time for that.

He tapped through various submenus of the system. One thing caught his attention—Задняя камера or Rear camera. He tapped it and one of the screens turned to a front-facing view of the tracks on the other end of the train.

He tapped Bypass and confirmed that he wanted to take control, then grabbed the joystick and pulled it gently back.

The train came alive and moved backward, or rather forward in the direction it was supposed to go. He heard cheering in the carrier behind him.

•

The next station wasn't very far, but West was thankful he didn't have to walk that distance. The station name was simply Университéт, or University.

He eased the train to a stop by the platform and put his Tile close to the engineer's microphone before tapping the Message button. He had written a message that his Tile translated and read out loud in Russian.

Dear passengers,

Unfortunately you all have to get off at this station. Repeat, all passengers must exit the train at this station. There are protests at the gates, with protesters dressed as guards. We urge you to not engage with them and leave the station as soon as possible. There is no reason for panic. The protesters are not after you. They may, however, behave as if they are real security guards. Thank you for your understanding.

He opened all passenger doors and heard a train full of people move quickly. No more cheering.

He exited the engineer's compartment on the backside, walked around the rear, and heaved himself up on the platform. He caught up with the last group of people as they hit the escalators.

•

The situation at the gates and station entrance got messy. He could hear yelling and swearing long before he reached the top of the escalators. But there was no way the three guards there could hold back a crowd instructed to leave promptly. West soon found himself outside on the university campus.

The university's main building stood tall along Lomonovsky

Prospect. He knew how to get to Sosedi Café from there, and from the café to the Kia. Hopefully, Åse had accepted his plan and left him the car, with keys inside. He mixed in with a group of people hurrying to the center of the campus.

CHAPTER 105

White House: Russian Intel

General Purnell provided his update standing. "We got a report from our Moscow embassy over ESS. Sources say the order to cut off the Red Web came straight from Minister Kenin herself and there's a rumor that it's connected to a hunt for West Wilder, the American, in Moscow."

"A resourceful man, this Wilder. Let's hope he makes it to tell the tale," President Sanchez said.

"Excuse me?"

Sanchez donned an amused smile. "If someone can single-handedly make the Russians cut off the internet, then I want to hear how and why."

"We don't know if he's acting alone."

"That's beside the point. Stop arguing the details. The size of fish you should be frying is whether this is an emergency or a planned thing with a rumor as cover. The one pulling strings may be Grigiori, not Kenin."

"If the Wilder part is true, he likely has data to exfiltrate, which would motivate the network cutoff," Purnell said.

"See, that's using your head." The president made a rhetorical pause, then ended the conversation facing her paperwork.

CHAPTER 106

Kremlin: Custom Matching

"Did you know your Ramenki access and badge were compromised?" Kenin trod lightly because she would soon need to switch gears and ask for this young man's help. Not that Vadim Smirnov had any choice but to comply, but it would probably go over more smoothly if she didn't dump a ton of bricks on him first.

"I did hear that. And now I'm completely shut out," Vadim replied. He had taken the call on his Tile and was holding it in his lap, which gave him a haughty look on the screen. It irritated Kenin.

"Are you at home?" she asked.

"Indeed."

"Have you seen any traces of unwelcome visitors? Something misplaced or moved?"

"Not really. Do you think someone was in here?" He looked around.

"They used a clone of your badge."

"I never use it myself."

"Do you even have it in your possession?"

"Let me see."

He walked for a bit in his apartment and laid the Tile on a table with the camera facing the ceiling. Kenin heard him rummage through drawers. Her underarm muscles flexed as she pumped her fists.

"Got it. It's here. Nothing touched."

This was useless. Young Mr. Smirnov had been hit by pros and didn't have a clue. "I'll send a forensics team over to search through your place properly. Don't move anything. It doesn't matter if you have sex toys, a roll of toilet paper on your desk, or whatever. Just leave everything as it is."

"Okay, okay."

"Thank you. Now, I have a request for you. Our suspect is using something that makes our facial recognition system not think he's a human at all. We have him on camera all right, but we can't follow him based on our existing algorithms. I need someone to write me a custom filter that we can run through all our surveillance footage from the last month to trace this person. Can you do that for me?" Kenin knew she had to pander a bit. "You are one of our best, and this is of the utmost urgency. Plus, you were involved in developing the existing system."

"Sure. But I need my access back to run the modeling on our cluster."

"I'll take care of that and get you the known good images we have of this man."

Kenin hung up and turned to her direct. "Do you have an analysis of the voice telling the Metro passengers to overrun the guards at Universitet?"

"Got it back just a moment ago. Synthesized Russian voice. Not domestic tech. We're matching against known Western voice models. Could be just a Tile."

Chapter 107

The Kia

The Kia was there, and so were the keys. West half expected Åse to show up too, but no one was around.

He sat down behind the steering wheel and tried to calm down. The small space in the car pronounced the smell of his own sweat. The pain in his shoulder was growing.

He'd been sitting in the backseat whenever they had used the Kia so far. It would likely be a tall order to spot him on existing footage, given how careful they had been when driving the streets of Moscow. No looking out the windows, always a mask on. But now he'd be in the driver's seat, and as soon as they matched him with the Kia, they would be on Åse's tail too. Finding Åse would lead them to Kiss and East.

It wasn't good enough. How to get another car?

He looked out. It was a shabby garage, Åse had made sure of that. Cheapest available, with an explicit statement that there were no personnel on site and no security measures.

The car models scattered around weren't known to him but he'd be surprised if they weren't mostly electric. How far would he get on a single charge? Or with the gas in the Kia, for that matter?

What was that movie where the hero made a woman drive for him? *The Bourne Identity*. Or did Bourne pay her? If West could get someone to drive the Kia for him, they could fill up on gas too.

Threatening someone felt like it could go off the rails at any moment. Just paying would be too suspicious. He needed a reason why he couldn't drive.

A man appeared a few cars away, fishing out his key fob.

West got out.

"Hey! Hey, mister."

The man stopped and looked at him.

West limped over. "I got hurt." He moved his wounded shoulder forward and showed the caked blood around the rip. His stained Band-Aid protruded from underneath.

The man jerked his head back. "What happened?" he asked in a heavy accent.

"Accident at work. I do construction. The company is uninsured, so they patched me up and sent me home. I'm just not sure I can drive myself. I feel ... weak."

"You should go to hospital." The man moved toward the car that had blinked when he used his key fob.

"You're probably right. I hate hospitals, but I need to get this treated. Can you help me get there? I don't want to have to walk."

The man hesitated.

"I can pay you." West went for his pocket.

The man jerked his head back and shook it. "No. Get in. I drive to nearest hospital on my way."

"Thank you! You are a good man. Let me just get my stuff and try to change my clothes really quick."

•

The man accepted West's claim that he had to lie down in the back-seat. West made sure to put a blanket from the Kia under his upper body to not worry his driver about bloodstains.

Lying horizontally, watching the ceiling of the car made him carsick well before they stopped.

The man in the front leaned over from the front seat. "Central Hospital."

West sat up and swallowed to suppress his nausea. "Thank you. May the sun shine on you."

West found himself in a parking lot between a lush forest and a massive, seven-story stone building clad in light yellow stucco. It looked old but well maintained—a Soviet bastion manicured through the decades.

It was a major hospital. That fit well with the plans he had made on his way here.

•

The emergency department and its parked ambulances were not like he had pictured them. Of course not.

Clean and orderly, but no security guards. The hospital's logo decorated every door—a banner curving in the wind with a medical cross formed by the Cyrillic letters ЦКБ vertically and horizontally.

He chose the door furthest away from the public entrance, pushed it, and peeked inside. A corridor with a shiny checkered floor in beige and brown. No one around. Faint sounds of human activity way further in. Wooden doors on each side, plus a white door to a bathroom, and a couple of benches. Park benches. A freestanding coat rack to the left had a sole white lab coat.

He used the bathroom to wash his face, neck, hands, and trimmed hair. Then got the lab coat on and straightened his back. The hardest part was always to act as if you belonged. Hopefully, the high average level of education at this place would mean people spoke English. He just had to have an excuse why he didn't speak Russian.

He checked room after room until he found one with a computer. The screen came alive as he approached and showed a symbol of a card reader.

West checked the pockets of the lab coat. Nothing. The drawers of the desk had lots of papers and a few pens, but no smart card.

He checked three more rooms before deciding he was getting too close to where he could hear people working. He enabled translation on his Tile and listened in through his earbuds.

The people were talking about dealing with mental issues after seeing wounded or dead children. Apparently, you could not go on calls where children might be harmed until at least two years into your service.

West couldn't help but think of his son. Where was East right now? Was he in Kiss's arms? Was he crying, or hungry? Would this part of his life leave painful memories?

"Can I help you with something?"

The voice was behind West and the double audio told him his earbuds had just translated it from Russian. He jerked his head around. It was a man, slightly older than he, also in a lab coat.

"Sorry, I'm new here," West said in English. "I'm from ... Turkey.

I use these to understand what you're saying." He tapped his index finger on one earbud. "I don't speak Russian yet. Learning." He put on a smile. "I'm supposed to do training on real dispatches."

"Okay. What's your name?"

Turkey is Muslim, right? There was one Muslim guy in prison.

"Ujab."

"Hi, Ujab. I'm Vlad. What kind of dispatch?"

"Traffic. I was in a car accident myself. Got hit." West stroked his hair along the scar in his scalp. "So that's what I'm educated on."

"We don't have many of those with automatic cars. And in the city, people use the Metro. But we're a big hospital, so we should be able to get you on something relevant."

Vlad walked him past the room where people sat talking about child trauma, further on to a large opening with a big screen and two operators with headsets. "These are current calls," he said with a motion toward the screen. "Three ambulances are out, five waiting. And it seems we have one that's being serviced. In this column here, we categorize. The current calls are for cardiovascular—see the heart symbol—and one injury, those are typically elder who fall. What you're looking for is a car symbol. Since you're here on training, you'll have to travel in the back to where the ambulance is going and then return in the front if we're bringing a patient in."

One of the operators turned around. "English, ey?"

"Turkey," West said.

"Merhaba!"

What the fuck does that mean?

He nodded back, probably looking like a fool. Then smiled, because that's what you do when people know your language.

The operator got a message in his headset and turned back to the screen.

Vlad left and West realized he was staring at the screen. He found a chair in the back and sat down.

•

It took an hour for a car symbol to show up. The operator he had spoken to earlier turned around with a serious face. "Car bomb."

"I can go."

Less than sixty seconds later, he was in the back of an ambulance.

CHAPTER 108

Bombing

The ambulance ride was speedy but not violent. Still, not being able to see what was outside pulled him right back into carsickness. The sirens drowned out all sounds.

West was struggling to process that this was a car bombing. How common was that? Some organized crime thing or a political vendetta?

As soon as they stopped, he could hear the doors in the front open and shut. He unbuckled himself and moved backward. The rear doors opened, and the two paramedics released the stretcher. One of them held a hand up against him, waving him back. There was black smoke behind them and the smell of burned rubber and gasoline reached inside the ambulance.

West got out once the paramedics left with the stretcher. There was a second ambulance on the scene. And three fire trucks and police vehicles further away. In the middle of it all was a burning skeleton of a car, partly covered in foam. The paramedics were focused on a vehicle nearby with rips and tears in its body. Maybe shrapnel from the explosion.

They were close to an on-ramp by a highway. Mostly tall apartment buildings in the background. It had to be some suburb.

West heard a car approaching and turned around. It was a news van.

Two police officers ran over and started banging on the minibus, yelling and gesticulating violently. The van backed up slowly until the officers were content.

A sedan came raging in and parked right behind the van. A neatly dressed blonde woman got out and walked up to the crew exiting the news van—two bots and one guy. She threw a handbag into the van and the human crew member held up a mirror to her. She was probably the anchor who would stand in front of the camera.

West got his Tile out, held it out in front of his chest, and started walking toward the news team. As he got closer, he made vocal sounds. "Da. Mhmm. Nyet." He gave a dismissive shake of his head to the blonde woman just as she grabbed a microphone.

He continued on and went past the sedan before looking back. No one was watching him. The news team was closing in on the smoldering car, bots doing the camera work. He backtracked to the other side of the van and opened the passenger door. In the driver's seat lay the woman's purse. He snatched it and got to the sedan. The doors unlocked as soon as he got close.

Luckily, changing language on the car's screen interface was just a few taps away. Battery level at 82%. He put it in reverse, human drive, and eased the vehicle away from the scene. His eyes went back and forth between the rear camera view on the car screen and the news team. No one seemed to notice him slipping away.

He backed through a curve long enough to no longer see anything of the bomb scene but the rising black smoke.

It was time to let automation take over. He tapped his destination into the car's map app and chose an optimized route for charging. Then he reclined the driver's seat as far as it would go, tapped "Go," and lay down, face covered by the lab coat. He was going to be carsick again. But that was better than being caught on camera.

The car swiveled the steering wheel back and forth until it had turned around and got going.

On the map display, the destination read "Pechenga Village, Murmansk Oblast."

CHAPTER 109

Kremlin: Threads

Elvira Kenin looked at the map again. It was mundane, almost dull.

Vadim's custom facial recognition had taken almost a day to get ready because of the stuff Wilder had on his face. The model had to filter that smear out rather than home in on it, since the pattern was not consistent day over day.

Then it took another few hours for the Ramenki computer cluster to chew through the billions of public surveillance snapshots they had from across Russia the last two weeks. The result was the map trace in front of her, from Murmansk via Petrozavodsk to Moscow.

The latest data was from the parking lot outside Central Clinical Hospital in the Kuntsevo District, western Moscow. He might still be there. Or he left through the forest or somehow eluded further camera capture.

Aside from finding West, there were two additional threads that she had put her staff on. One was to identify the three other people in the Kia driving to Moscow—two women and one man. The women wore the same facial recognition evasion and it would be a drag to hunt down good photos of those individuals and build custom detection of them, even though Vadim now had it figured out.

The other thread was the claims that West had been to Ice Dolphin on Novaya Zemlya. That story had been injected by Americans but was now put in a very different light.

Kenin got a text from one of her directs.

Found a possible trace of
W at the hospital. There
was a new doctor from
Turkey named Ujab (not
sure of spelling) who
matches the description
of W.

We're trying to find out
what he was doing there.

Try harder.

Words from her training echoed in her head—"Delegate. You cannot scale by yourself. You have to delegate."

"Fuck that," she muttered to herself. "Once we have visual on this sucker, I'm going in."

Chapter 110

Turkish Border

Åse decided early on that crossing the Russian border without help would push their luck too far. They had to find an exit the locals believed in, something Russian expats had already established as a way out.

The midsized fishing vessel they were now on was apparently known among Russian hackers to be able to help to get you to Turkey—a haven for Russians who didn't want part in their homeland's various war efforts. But the Black Sea was risky and the two Russian traitors she was traveling with—Maria and Viktor—were not sure they'd be accepted on the other side. Turkey bridged Europe and Asia and walked a thin line between allies east and west.

She felt guilty pulling a gun on the vessel's captain. But this was hard-core business.

He complied without much of a protest and set course on USS *Nitze*, anchored just north of the Bosporus Strait that connected the Black Sea and the Mediterranean right through Istanbul.

When at radio distance, she connected her Tile to the fishing boat's communication system and sent out a recognizable NATO signal.

After some back and forth, they were instructed to board an inflatable lifeboat lowered into the Black Sea by USS *Nitze*. Åse apologized to the captain she had threatened as they exited, and promised to double the payment once she had access to the Bancor system again. He seemed primarily happy to get them off his boat.

The four adult escapees were separated onboard the US ship—Kiss with East, Viktor, Maria, and Åse each on their own. Interrogations ensued.

Their story was mind-blowing in itself, but the hardest thing for the commander of USS *Nitze* to accept, and relay to the US mainland, was how the third American—West William Wilder—would attempt to exit Russia.

"I recognize that name," the man in charge of questioning her said. "He's been in the news. A traitor helping the Russians, is that right?"

"Hey there," Åse said, raising her voice involuntarily. "West is a motherfucking hero trying to get the US key intel. Sorry for being blunt, but your colleagues better be there when he exits."

CHAPTER III

Kremlin: Get Me a Plane to Murmansk

"The stolen car seems to have traveled the same way back as Wilder came. It was spotted by cameras outside Murmansk two hours ago. And there was this curious …"

"Entering Murmansk or leaving?" Kenin snapped.

"At a charging station and then on R21 highway going west. From there, I don't think we have more cameras."

"Think?"

"We don't have more cameras."

Kenin heard herself breathe. "You were starting to say there was something curious."

"Yes. Mr. Wilder stopped at a hardware store in Petrozavodsk and purchased a hammer, earplugs, a tape measure, and plastic cement. They even said … a ball peen hammer. I think those have a rounded side."

"Get my plane ready for Murmansk and a helicopter ready for when I land. What landing grounds are within a two-hour drive from Murmansk?"

"We have the 200th Motor Rifle Brigade in Pechenga Village."

"That's good. Have them deploy drones to scan R21. Can Wilder reach the Norwegian border?"

"If he's speeding."

"Do you think he's taking it easy? Shut down the border to Norway. Nothing gets through until I'm squeezing this motherfucker's neck."

CHAPTER 112

Sub ID

It was a relief to be rid of the car. West had felt watched ever since Petrozavodsk.

He had at least managed to use his bunny drive to get admin rights on to the car's computer and turn off its geo position reporting. He even found something that looked like digital plates that the car emitted once a second, and turned that stuff off too.

At the first charging station, he had used the toolkit in the frunk to switch physical plates with a similar car charging unattended.

But no doubt, the powers of the Kremlin and Ramenki would find his car. Now it was under a tarp at a rural shed in the outskirts of Pechenga Village, and West was approaching the main settlement through the woods.

He needed Wi-Fi.

•

It didn't take long to get on a local connection. It was slow, but it was from one of the domestic houses and not the military.

His Tile buzzed and a notification popped up. It was a new message in the SurvivorNet channel, from BestBye!

```
wi-fi log
12340d34242b155c6d380255254a335c2f6406512320595c
```

Wi-Fi log? What is she talking about?

When had he worked on Wi-Fi logs with her? *Oh, it has to be from the automated border control station.*

He remembered spotting the similarity of two log statements, something that ultimately let them hack the backup power reporting system and make the border station go into power saving mode.

Forty-eight hex characters, so probably twenty-four ASCII characters. How am I supposed to remember that? I'm too fucking tired for this.

BestBye was betting on his attention to detail. But there was no chance he'd be able to concentrate on digging that up from memory in his current state of stress and exhaustion.

Sub ID hack. Focus, West.

The copy he had of the SSD from the laptop at Ice Dolphin had an inventory of Russian subs that had docked at Ice Dolphin. An inventory with submarine IDs. That in itself was an incredible piece of intel. But he needed to find out if there were Paltus class submarines similar to *Dolphin II* for his hack to have a remote chance of working.

If he had any luck, the SSD content would still have the necessary access to talk to the central naval servers. However, he didn't dare try to boot the whole system as a virtual machine, since it likely had all sorts of safety checks and might report itself as compromised. He needed to surgically slip through only the requests he wanted.

By inspecting software that used the sub inventory, he had found a plausible server endpoint.

```
https://gugi.mil.ru/service/submarine/
operations/
```

He took a deep breath and let a request hit the network. The response was swift.

```
HTTP 403 Forbidden
{ "error" : "unauthorized access", "reason"
: "missing auth_token" }
```

Would have been ridiculous if that had worked.

The code where he had found the URL used cached authentication tokens. There was one in there and he tacked it on.

```
https://gugi.mil.ru/service/submarine/
operations/
{ "auth_token" : "436222982756623087789923
4665356" }
```

```
HTTP 403 Forbidden
{ "error" : "unauthorized access", "reason"
: "auth_token expired" }
```

Reasonable.

He sifted through other server endpoints in the software and came across one for token renewal. The server would respond with a nonce that his system had to sign. It took him a good fifteen minutes to dig up the signing key and what to include in the request.

```
https://gugi.mil.ru/security/renew-token/
{ "nonce" : "82a4823897ff8690", "signature"
: "a00847cd645546dd", "pub_key" : "AAAAC3N-
zaC1lZDI1NTE5AAAAIItnqROZ28MZcGdkHGqgh-
pe56AOVIAOdw5IXhARi8fpr" }
```

```
201 Created
{ "auth_token" : "2367789923746653562229827
5662308" }
```

```
https://gugi.mil.ru/service/submarine/
operations/
{ "auth_token" : "2367789923746653562229827
5662308" }
```

```
HTTP 403 Forbidden
{ "error" : "unauthorized access", "reason"
: "missing ZT_OTP" }
```

Fuck you!

He needed a ZT hardware key just like Vadim's. But there was just no way he'd be able to get one with access rights to the Russian submarine system.

I don't have time for this. But I have to get it done.
He felt like a fool even trying his next step.

```
https://gugi.mil.ru/service/submarine/
operations/
{ "auth_token" : "23677899237466535 6222
98275662308", "ZT_OTP" : "vadim_smirn-
ov922:62065777" }
```

```
HTTP 403 Forbidden
{ "error" : "unauthorized access", "reason"
: "bad ZT_OTP", "wrong_ZT_OTP" : "vadim_
smirnov922:62065777" }
```

Of course that wouldn't work. He closed his eyes and let out a long sigh. His eyes moved in fits under his eyelids and his mind wandered. Where were Kiss and East now? The range of possibilities was immense—either safe or locked up and doomed somewhere in Russia. The only way he'd ever know was to hack this bloody system.

He opened his eyes and touched his nose with an upward pointing index finger.

Maybe.

```
https://gugi.mil.ru/service/submarine/
operations/
{ "auth_token" : "23677899237466535 6222982
75662308", "right_ZT_OTP" : "vadim_smirn-
ov922:62065777" }
```

```
HTTP 400 Bad Request
{ "error" : "invalid_input", "reason"
: "bad request", "removed_parameter" :
"right_ZT_OTP" }
```

That change in response from the server was meaningful. West was now challenging the input validation rather than the signed token scheme. Removed parameter sounded like a classic mistake.

What if he didn't send one but two copies of the unexpected parameter right_ZT_OTP? Would the server then know to remove them *both*?

```
https://gugi.mil.ru/service/submarine/
operations/
{ "auth_token" : "2367789923746653562222
98275662308", "right_ZT_OTP" : "vadim_
smirnov922:62065777", "right_ZT_OTP" :
"vadim_smirnov922:62065777" }
```

No response. At all.

All the previous error responses had been instant, but now it was just hanging there.

Maybe he had triggered a bug on the server and hung the whole thing?

More likely, he had hit some intrusion detection threshold and was now blocked.

But it could also be that the server had done what he hoped, which was to remove only the first instance of right_ZT_OTP and accept the second one.

Ten more seconds passed. Then a huge list started filling his screen.

```
BOREI I/II CLASS
K-535 Yuriy Dolgorukiy         | Northern | Active
K-549 Knyaz Vladimir           | Northern | Active
K-550 Aleksandr Nevskiy        | Pacific  | Active
K-551 Vladimir Monomakh        | Pacific  | Active
K-552 Knyaz Oleg               | Pacific  | Active
K-553 Generalissimus Suvorov   | Pacific  | Active
K-554 Imperator Aleksandr III  | Pacific  | Active
...
```

It went on and on with classes like Delta III, Oscar II, Yasen, Kilo, and Laika. As far as West could tell, this was a complete inventory of the Russian submarine fleet.

More importantly, he found what he was looking for:

```
PALTUS CLASS
AS-21 Medved                    | Northern | Active
AS-35 Morzh                     | Northern | Active
AS-37 Dolphin II                | Northern | Active
AS-38 Tyulen                    | Pacific  | Active
AS-40 Skulpin                   | Baltic   | Active
```

Five of the same class as Dolphin II. *So at least there's a chance.*

CHAPTER 113

Murmansk: Drones

This was Kenin's first visit to Murmansk. She could tell that it was celebratory for the local officials, but her fiery, rapid commands promptly dampened their mood.

The Stalinist style of the modern FSB building on Lenin Boulevard cheered the minister up somewhat.

The regional FSB leader escorted her into a large meeting room.

She issued instructions while still walking to a chair held for her. "Curated drone reports in text to the right," she pointed at screens on wheels. "Map of the region in the middle, and live drone footage to the left. Move the left screen further out. I don't want moving things right beside the map."

The screens were rearranged accordingly. Kenin put her bag on the chair and strode in close to the map.

The city of Murmansk hugged the Kola Bay fjord in the lower left corner. The fjord widened up north where it met Barents Sea. They were so far up north that the Arctic Circle wasn't even visible on this map.

The R21 highway was a lone, scraggly line going northwest toward the Norwegian border. It touched the outskirts of Pechenga Village and the town of Zapolyarnyy.

"A car of the right shape and color was picked up by the village, right?" she asked.

"That's right."

"I'd be hesitant to think he wants to be close to our military base up here, but this is the region where we first picked him up. We have to consider the possibility of someone on the inside helping him. Keep information to the Motor Rifle Brigade command at a minimum."

"We already are, as instructed," her aide from Moscow said.

"What's the update on Ice Dolphin?"

"The inmate Kate Libby is confirmed missing and there was a lethal incident with some intruders who may have been Wilder and two others. No camera footage of how Libby got out and nothing showing Wilder's face."

"The sub?"

"Yes, the *Dolphin II* did dock there and then left. She was not supposed to be in those waters. We have a description of her captain. A woman. Her ID is unknown. *Dolphin II* has been on a long, silent mission in the Arctic and reported according to schedule. Our ocean ID system picked her up just outside of Ice Dolphin and then once south when she got close to Norwegian waters, but a very faint signal."

"And that was before cameras got Wilder in Murmansk?"

"Yes."

"Wilder and Libby fleeing on that sub is our leading theory. I want a full check on our crew of *Dolphin II*. Any Western-leaning shit you have on them. They may be helping Wilder and whoever that captain is. Then we need to find out where she docked after Ice Dolphin."

Chapter 114

The Creek

The taiga woods were endless and West worried constantly about his bearings. Åse's instructions were helpful, but he was very far out of his element with no idea of how close his pursuers were.

His Tile did provide rough positioning based on GPS, which was his chief hope of getting to his destination.

As soon as he got close to a lake or pond, the mosquitos swarmed and feasted on his blood.

A few hours in, he again heard the distant buzz of the flying blood suckers and stopped to let his Tile pick up geo signal and show where he was. He was hoping he could stay at a distance from whatever waterhole this was while still making good progress. Shouldn't be too much further now.

The map showed a creek close by. But mosquitos needed standing water. There could be pockets of still water here and there, but that wouldn't create a mass of bugs able to create this level of noise. Either he wasn't getting accurate GPS signals or the map was lacking detail.

The buzz of the mosquitos got louder. Those bastards were seeking him out. He started moving again. He would have to cross the creek, so he might as well get it over with.

The buzz got annoying.

That wasn't the sound of a flying bug. It had to be a drone!

He jumped and ducked under a thick fir tree. After breathing intensely for a few seconds, he held his breath and listened. The drone sound implied zigzagging through the trees.

Was there any chance this was a routine scan? These areas were close to the Russia-NATO border after all.

Who was he fooling? Those chances were slim. He had to assume the drone was looking for him. Further, he could bet it had excellent cameras and heat detectors and could call in human inspection at any time. He was a hot spot sitting duck.

He got up and started running. His heavy gear shifted and moved, making it hard to keep his balance on the uneven forest floor.

He dumped his backpack under a tree, which let him speed up. It sounded like the drone got closer. Desperation was bubbling up.

The creek appeared suddenly, like a tear in the mossy floor. It didn't look deep and its water was crystal clear. West let his body drop into it. Cold water soaked him through within seconds and stung as it reached his gun wound.

He could touch the bottom and turned around, face up. He pushed against the rocky bottom to get his nose and mouth above the surface and take a deep breath before submerging himself again. The sun shone above.

Half a minute passed. He was getting cold. From down in the water, he could not hear the drone, at least not at a distance.

He started shivering.

Something clouded the sun. He opened his eyes while still under water and could make out the silhouette of a large, industrial drone hovering above.

His lungs were screaming for air, but he didn't dare break the surface with the drone watching.

Hovering between losing consciousness and taking the risk of letting his face protrude for just a second, the sun again broke through. He looked up and did not see the drone.

Weak and shaking, he pushed his hands against the rocks.

Oxygen once again reached his red blood cells. He stumbled out of the creek, only to land under a fir tree sobbing and chattering his teeth.

The makeshift bandage over the gunshot wound in his left shoulder was sagging.

How would he make it from here?

His willpower was spent.

He let his hand find his pocket and brought out the white Tak autoinjector.

CHAPTER 115

Murmansk: Dead Body

Elvira Kenin, head of the Ministry of Digital Development, Communications and Mass Media in Russia, was fuming. Twenty-five Iranian military-grade drones in the air and nothing.

"Given that Wilder fooled our facial recognition, I'm starting to think he may have fooled our drones too. Did they find *anything*?"

"What do you mean, anything?"

"Anything out of the ordinary. Anything living?"

"A bunch of animals, of course. The heat camera always picks up those. Bears, moose."

"Did you review that material?"

"No, we have to use filters to spend human resources on the relevant material. But I remember seeing those words flicker by in the list when we were tuning the filters."

"What else flickered by?"

"You mean today?"

"Of course. Today is where we are."

"I didn't review the filtered list. We focused on humans and the only thing we found was Russians walking the woods—and those you know we've scrutinized."

"Review the list."

The local officer in charge of the drone hunt sat scrolling for five minutes before saying, "A dead body. Wow."

"What?"

"There's a dead body listed."

"Get that footage!"

Half a minute later, Kenin's pulse was reaching a hundred bpm and adrenaline was rushing through her veins as she saw West lying submerged in a forest creek.

The local officer didn't need instructions. He stated them himself. "I'm sorry about this oversight, Minister. We will adjust the drone's filter when this is over. For now, I will send all units to the area surrounding this find and review maps of what could possibly attract the man there."

"I sure hope this stinking drone software isn't the one scanning our border with Norway," Kenin blurted.

CHAPTER 116

Concrete

Seeing the contour of the concrete addition to the cliff was an immense relief for West. He was wet, scared, and increasingly worried about the viability of his escape plan.

Two drones had gotten close enough to be audible while he zigzagged under trees the last stretch up to Objekt 122.

He entered the old Soviet complex through the same creaking steel door they had exited.

Back then, Jitterbug had still been alive. He remembered Kiss's dignified moves as they tended to Jitterbug's wounds. She was such a graceful, caring human.

He pressed his lips together hard.

West had entertained the thought of going back to Jitterbug's grave, digging him up, and bringing his body home. But it would set him back a day at minimum and the drones might spot him. Besides, Jit might be at rest already.

West was lucky to still be at large. There could be military personnel arriving at this compound at any moment, for all he knew. The only leg up he had was the unthinkable nature of his plan. And the hack, of course, should he be successful.

The sound of birds scared the living daylights out of him as he got into the dock. The feathered creatures must have been settling in on the sail of the *Dolphin II*. He saw them leave through the small, square opening in the concrete wall facing the sea.

The air in here was salty and damp, the water around the sub still and dark. He could hear the sea outside.

The mooring rope. Oh, no, that super heavy rope. His right hand cupped his left shoulder. If it wasn't for the drugs he was on, the slightest squeeze would make him scream.

Well, however excruciatingly hard it would be to handle it, the rope had to come later.

He turned his gaze to the sub. The daylight filtering in through the north-facing opening created shadows that made the subtle dents in the vessel's hull stand out.

He unshouldered his backpack carefully over his wound and got the hammer, plastic cement, and tape measure out. As much as he wanted to light a fire and dry his clothes, there was no time for that and he didn't dare let smoke reveal where he was. Time to get this done and get seaborne.

He put his earplugs in.

•

Three hours later, his ears were ringing from the banging on the hull, his fingers were raw from messing with the plastic cement, and his body was shaking, trying to keep its temperature up in the soaked clothes.

As for the mooring rope, he resorted to sawing it off.

He climbed down into the submarine for the third time. He knew it would be his last time too.

The main operator's seat had been occupied by Åse before. Now West was the only one here.

He pulled up the message he had gotten back from her when he exited Ramenki. She had not berated him. Just a two-sentence questioning of his likelihood of survival, then straight to it.

> This will be the shortest possible guide to operate the Dolphin II. I don't have time to provide you with a lot of what-ifs. This is only how to start the nuclear generator, set course, and get going. The sub only has autopilot within Russian waters. So once you go international, you will be setting course yourself.
>
> You'll need all your nine lives to get through this one, soldier.
>
> Step 1: ...

CHAPTER 117

Murmansk: Murky Waters

"Fly it into the dock," Kenin commanded. She wanted to fly the drone herself even though she knew they were AI-controlled, and you had to tell them what to do.

"The door is shut, and even so, we cannot fly inside such narrow spaces. We'd have to deploy smaller ..."

"Go in from the ocean side, you idiot. How do you think subs do it?"

The drone was told to approach the abandoned dock from the waterside and quickly ascended to go over the cliff top. As it came down on the other side, the vastness of Barents Sea appeared. The cameras then turned back and revealed the slit on the cliff side.

The drone hovered outside, slowly going up and down and side to side.

"It's making a depth measurement through that hole to make sure there's enough airspace inside."

Kenin noted the concrete basin outside the dock that served as a breakwater.

The drone made up its mind and entered. The camera feed briefly went dark and then lit up as light adjustment took effect. On the screen in front of Kenin was a huge vaulted dock with concrete landings on either side, and a calm, unbroken water surface in between.

There was no sub there.

"Check further in," she said.

The drone slowly covered the whole space. No trace of a vessel.

"Can *Dolphin II* submerge in the dock?" she asked.

"Maybe. Paltus class is small. But the water is too murky to see."

"Should it be?"

"What do you mean?"

"If no one has used this dock for fifty years, shouldn't the water be clear?"

CHAPTER 118

The Living Infinite II

The hum of the motors turning the screws was present throughout the sub. Compared to the stress of starting up the nuclear reactor, West was relatively calm. He was at least moving.

It had taken two hours for the batteries to heat the reactor to its minimal operating temperature. Going through the checklist had taken a good thirty minutes. When it was time to withdraw the control rods and allow the reactor to go critical, the stress had become too much and he had slumped into his seat like a rag doll. Everything had gone cold and still around him. Only a phantom notion of a drone buzzing above jolted him into gear again and he had forced himself to get this vessel operational.

He reviewed the instructions Åse had sent him and his eyes landed on a few paragraphs.

I would not try to cross into Norwegian waters, the way we came. The Russians will be on top alert ever since the Magadan. Find another way.

The ocean floor is like the Nevada desert. You are just as lost and alone under the waves as you would be on the far side of the moon. In fact, the deep ocean is even more hostile than that. Its movements are chaotic and precise navigation is not humanly possible. You have to rely on the onboard AI. Just stay above crush depth.

We detected a Battle Mode when reverse engineering the
sub's software. It increases the speed but wears out the
motors and mechanics. It's unknown for how long you can
use it. Press and hold PERIM on the command keyboard to
trigger it.

The map in front of him scrolled slowly. His bearing was north-
east. The living infinite between him and the destination was vast.
He had pulled the coordinates from Åse's prior maneuvering of this
ship. Going there undetected, uninterrupted, and unharmed was
implausible. But the Russian Franz Josef Land archipelago was as
far north as he could go on lat and long already entered. The screen
gave him the countdown.

Estimated travel time: 23 hours.

CHAPTER 119

Murmansk: Submersible

Four hours. Four fucking hours to get a submersible drone transported to the Objekt 122 site and carefully enter the basin. Kenin barely put up with it, but she couldn't afford to destroy any tracks of activity here. If they could find proof of a sub, better yet, of a particular sub, it would pay off.

The verdict was quick once the footage arrived. "Oh yeah, there's been a submarine here within the last day. Two propellers, see here." The young man was pointing toward two faint, parallel grooves in the dock's rust-laden silt. "Small one I'd say."

"How small?"

"Thirty to forty meters."

She knew the specs of the Paltus class mini sub by now. Thirty meters. "Is it one of ours?"

"That I can't say, madam."

•

"No trace of *Dolphin II*, Minister. Nothing from sonar along the sea border and it's not been spotted by our three subs in the region. Destroyers, nothing either."

Kenin was 99% sure *Dolphin II* was the ship they were looking for. But it was possible there was a NATO vessel at play, or maybe, maybe Wilder and his accomplices had been able to switch to yet another Russian submarine.

She looked at the map. If West had taken the shortest viable escape route into Norwegian waters, he was long gone. Probably at port on the Norwegian mainland already. But she was in direct contact with the commander in chief of the Russian Navy and he assured her that the waterway to NATO territory was their most closely guarded naval border. He'd be stupefied if West could just sail past their detection line. They had active sonobuoys, passive sonobuoys, and magnetic anomaly detection. Even good ol' Soviet hydrophones were operational in those waters. And two Yasen class subs were constantly on watch.

Kenin was reasonably convinced. And as concluded, if West had gotten past those buoys, magnetic detectors, and her country's top subs, then defeat was already a fact.

"This is getting us nowhere. We've lost, like"—she flicked her wrist—"ten hours already. I want a list of *all* subs seen in Barents Sea since Wilder left land. And get me transport to Ice Dolphin."

•

A rushed meal and a microdose of amphetamine later, she had the list in hand. She checked in on her way to the Mi-26 helicopter waiting for her on the platform.

Only one Paltus class submarine had been seen in Barents Sea. It was within reasonable distance from the Kola Peninsula, but it was not *Dolphin II*. Instead one called *Morzh*. They had two independent identifications of *Morzh* and both were solid Hull Imprint IDs—dimples and bumps in a unique pattern, according to people assisting her.

Could NATO have compromised two Paltus subs? Maybe there was some design flaw which allowed them to hijack that whole class?

Kenin brought her ideas up with the naval commander in chief. He was highly skeptical but promised to check in on *Morzh*'s latest reports.

CHAPTER 120

Franz Josef Land

The Tak injection subsided and West fell into a deep sleep in his cabin.

When he woke up, he had dribbled onto his shoulder, and his legs and buttocks were numb from being still for too long.

There was something simmering in his mind as it surfaced into conscious thinking.

PWR0891886194140.

That was it. That was the first log message from the border station.

But that's sixteen ASCII characters. I needed twenty-four, right?

He pulled up the cryptic message from BestBye. Twenty-four indeed. If his hunch was right. But maybe she made do with a shorter key?

He XORed BestBye's hexadecimal string with his key.

```
12340d34242b155c6d380255254a335c2f6406512320595c
XOR PWR0891886194140

Result:  44$+\=oPesdR7hml
```

Garbage.

BestBye would never use anything shorter than a onetime pad though.

But that log message was Base64 encoded when I spotted it.

He Base64 encoded PWR0891886194140 on his Tile.

UFdSMDg5MTg4NjE5NDE0MA==

Twenty-four characters.
He XORed BestBye's hexadecimal string.

12340d34242b155c6d380255254a335c2f6406512320595c
XOR UFdSMDg5MTg4NjE5NDE0MA==

Result: Grigiori leak via Canada

Plain English. This was BestBye's message decrypted. But what did it mean? She got the intel on Kiss's prisoner exchange via a *Grigiori leak?*

•

There was no way for West to know when he'd pass the site of the attack on the Magadan. But his loyal *Dolphin II* had picked up the subsea cable track on the coast of northern Novaya Zemlya and was now closing in on Franz Josef Land—the Russian archipelago right at the brink of the North Pole's massive ice cover.

Somehow, the knowledge that there was open water above him gave him solace. Under the ice, there wasn't even an escape by going to the surface.

Åse's instructions were to follow the cable to the bay south of the Nagurskoye Air Base on the northern tip of Alexandra Land—the island furthest west in the archipelago. She hadn't been able to help herself and added some of its history. It was Russia's northernmost military base, originally built in the 1950s for Soviet bombers to reach the US by crossing the Arctic. West had never realized for how long the Arctic had been militarized.

Instead of entering the bay, he should pass Alexandra Land on its eastern side and follow the coastline west to see if the subsea cable indeed continued.

At the mouth of the bay, he would have to abandon autopilot. But Russian ocean maps should be detailed enough to follow the route.

CHAPTER 121

Duplicate

"I have double-checked, Minister. I have in fact triple-checked," the navy chief said over the video link. The screen was remarkably stable for being aboard a military helicopter flying at top speed. But Kenin still had to concentrate to read the man's face. It had more color now, and he was speaking faster.

"*Morzh* is not in Barents Sea," he continued. "She's in the Kara Sea, *east* of Novaya Zemlya."

"Then we have *Morzh*'s ID in two different locations."

"It's a duplicate," the chief said.

"A what?"

"I can only conclude that the adversary somehow is able to cloak themselves as *Morzh*."

Kenin flipped her head back and closed her eyes. Of course. West was a hacker.

She tilted back and eyed the commander on the screen. "The man we're hunting changed the Hull Imprint ID of *Dolphin II* with a peen hammer and plastic cement," she said.

The commander's flustered face froze.

Kenin hung up the call. She didn't want to hear any more of his doubts or triple-checks.

"Find *Morzh*! Both of them," she yelled into the helmet microphone. "And have the folks at Ice Dolphin ready to refuel this helo."

•

"We picked him up, Minister! Just outside Nagurskoye."

Kenin's eyes followed the updates on the screen. Highlighted at the top of the map was a group of jagged islands. After flashing the outline twice, the map zoomed in and highlighted a single island shaped like an upside-down V. The western side of the island was much larger and the water under the tip formed a bay. A dot labeled "Morzh" hovered south of the bay.

"How long ago?" she asked.

"Ten minutes. We're doing a back trace. Only a few detection points use Hull Imprint ID, but once we have pinned a vessel, we can connect it to other readings."

Lines to new dots going south were added one by one. The map zoomed out, showing a trace down to Novaya Zemlya. It followed the coastline for two steps, then cut out into Barents Sea in the general direction of the Kola Peninsula.

"That's him all right," she said through her teeth. "I don't want to know where he's been, I want to know where he's going. We're on our way. What other subs do we have in the region?"

"We have *Magnitogorsk* to the west of the archipelago, around here." A rough circle was added on the map as the person drew with their pen. "And one docked in the bay."

"What's *Magnitogorsk*'s speed compared to *Dolphin II*?"

"*Dolphin II* maxes out at eighteen knots but can do over twenty in Battle Mode. *Magnitogorsk* maxes out at twenty-five. If you intend to pursue ..."

"Of course I intend to pursue! Get going as soon as we have the next bearing."

Just as she spat that out, a new dot emerged, north of the island, at the tip of the ice mass.

She heard at least two background conversations over the video link. One seemed to be with *Magnitogorsk* west of Alexandra Land, the other with some superior.

"What are your commands, Minister?" It was the person driving the map. "If the hunt goes under the ice, we'll have limited communications with *Magnitogorsk*, so the crew needs to know what the objectives are and what level of risk you accept."

She was about to say something but again heard the people on the other end talk to each other, then, "Actually, we need to go through the naval chain of command."

"Aren't you already talking to your admiral?" Kenin asked the person challenging her authority.

"I was just filling him in."

"Get him on the screen."

The commander in chief reappeared. Kenin regretted cutting him short last time. Now she needed cooperation. "Admiral, we have found our suspect, as I'm sure you know."

"I have been informed, yes. Not found by you, mind I say."

She bit her lower lip and looked away from the screen. "Sorry for my brusque behavior earlier."

"Unprofessional is a better word." The admiral straightened his naval jacket.

"Please accept my apologies."

There was no reply.

"We are looking at a pursuit, Admiral. We are losing precious time. I'm told we will have limited communications with our crew under the Arctic ice."

"ELF relies on open water," the admiral said.

"What's ELF?"

The admiral smiled. "See. Maybe you need someone in the Navy after all. ELF means Extremely Low Frequency radio." He waited for Kenin to nod. "VLF, very low frequency, can penetrate the ice to a certain depth but is not reliable. We have onboard antennas that are strong enough to signal through the ice up to a satellite, but they aren't useable in a hunt, especially not for two-way comms. It's going to come down to the relay buoys we have along our routes."

"How likely is Wilder to take one of those routes?"

"I do not know who this man is. Is he a trained submariner? Our vessels have high autonomy, and if he's relying on that, *Dolphin II* will pick a buoy route."

Kenin massaged her thighs. The helicopter was thundering north. The amphetamine was wearing off and underneath it she was spent. "I would like to request that *Magnitogorsk* pick me up so that I can take personal command of the capture of *Dolphin II* and Wilder. Possibly take him out."

"Is your department willing to pay for a blown-up special purpose nuclear sub?" An impish glee decorated the admiral's face.

"West Wilder may carry intel worth a hundred subs. I'm sure the president will approve your expense report."

"Okay then, how do you intend to board? If *Magnitogorsk* docks, she will not be able to catch up with *Dolphin II*."

"Have her go north of the Nagurskoye Air Base just below the edge of the ice. The helicopter can drop me off there."

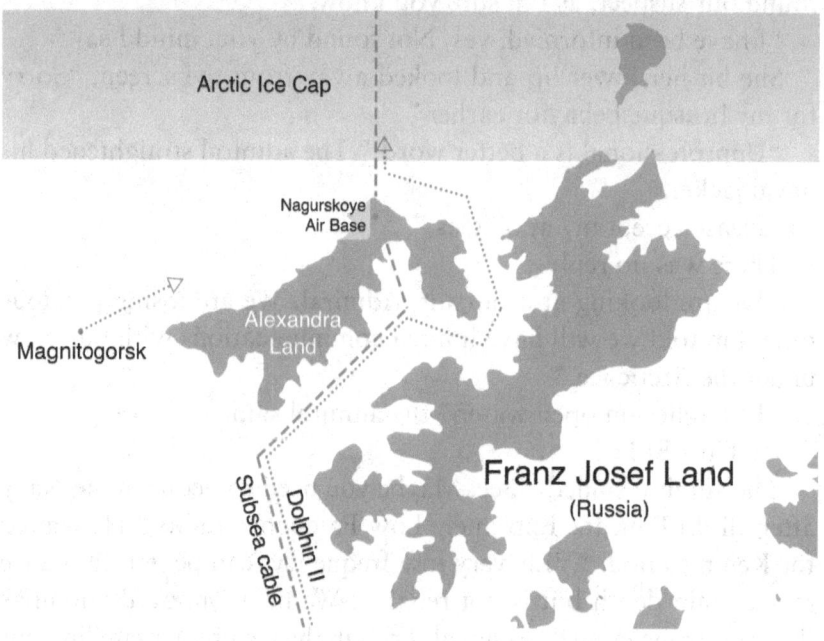

Arctic Ice Cap

Nagurskoye
Air Base

Magnitogorsk

Alexandra
Land

Franz Josef Land
(Russia)

Subsea cable

Dolphin II

Chapter 122

Severny Polyus

The display in front of West said "Северный полюс." His Tile pronounced it "severny polyus." It was Russian for the North Pole, and lay five hundred miles straight ahead.

The Russian subsea cable did indeed go north beyond Franz Josef Land, just like Åse had predicted. That might be another piece of intel he could negotiate his way out of prison with.

He didn't know if the cables would take him to the pole or make a turn somewhere. Five hundred miles meant seventeen hours of maximum speed for *Dolphin II*. But the autopilot refused to go that fast under the Arctic ice.

Chapter 123

Magnitogorsk: Speed

Captain Balakirev of Kilo class submarine *Magnitogorsk* was taken aback by Minister Kenin boarding and the orders she issued. They were in hot pursuit of a fellow sub possibly headed for the North Pole.

His objective was to rein it in, and if that didn't work, torpedo it. He had thrice asked Kenin for further details and been denied just as many times. She had the support of the commander in chief, so he wasn't going to press further.

Still no contact with *Dolphin II*, a Paltus mini and a fast sucker.

Ahead lay the vast Gakkel Ridge—an underwater mountain range clad in thick ice, virtually blocking underwater access to the pole. It was a unique challenge for submarines. The buoy route continued quite a bit further but would switch to Russia's covert, passive guiding system embedded in the ridge.

There were no known openings in the ridge itself. Passing it meant spotting where the ice cover was thinner and natural gaps occurred. Knowing how to navigate these waters successfully and quickly was a military advantage that his friends at GUGI had curated for over half a century. They calculated the plausibility of large enough gaps based on historical data, ocean currents, and wind patterns.

In this case, this information didn't provide an advantage since *Dolphin II* would have it too. But she had an unexperienced commander, so she'd be going with whatever her AI said. This provided Balakirev with an opportunity, if he was willing to override his AI's safety measures.

CHAPTER 124

A Fork

West had grown used to following the subsea cable. Now it was no longer in his path and its absence had planted a seed of worry within him. He had requested the North Pole, and that's where he was going, but the cable maybe wasn't.

He lowered the sub's speed and the motors adopted a deeper tone.

Had the cable taken off to the left? His brain seemed to have picked something like that up, even though he hadn't consciously watched it happen on the screen. It could also have been dug down from here or just naturally covered by shifting sediment. But the ocean floor wasn't really like that. It was full of ridges—big and small—seamounts, valleys, and basins. He'd seen the cable travel down and up steep formations like a line on a 3D map.

He tapped his way to the sub's map with routes. Using the interface was slow since he had to translate with his Tile, but he'd already memorized some labels.

Ever since he got under the ice, the lines on the map had had dots that were labeled "Beacon Buoy." He had seen a couple of them tethered to the bottom in passing—cylindrical, vertical tubes moving with the undercurrent. There was a gentle chime in the sub's control board whenever he got close to one.

It wouldn't be a surprise if those buoys were phoning home.

The map showed a route forking off to the left behind him, a few minutes back. That was probably the cable. Backtracking would take a quarter of an hour. But was a U-turn possible among these ridges?

He tapped one of the buoy dots some distance in on the westward route and a dotted direct line to it appeared on the screen.

The interface asked him if he wanted to change his route.

He tapped Yes.

CHAPTER 125

Magnitogorsk: Buoy Track

"Captain, we should have registered *Dolphin II* at buoy D39 by now. Either she has slowed down significantly or she has changed course."

Dolphin II's AI navigation system was likely hedging. *Magnitogorsk*'s certainly was.

"How long did buoy D38 stay in contact with her?" Balakirev asked, giving Kenin a quick glance as she sat to his right. She looked tired.

It took a while for the data request and response to come through the limited underwater comms.

"D38 still has contact! Barely."

"Is she going back? Check 37."

Another wait for data transfer, slightly quicker this time because they were themselves getting close to buoy D37.

"No signal at 37."

The buoys lay anchored close enough to each other to always provide submarines access to at least two, as long as they stayed on the route. *Dolphin II* being almost outside buoy listening distance meant she was veering off track, either right or left.

Left would eventually take her to Greenland. Right meant East Siberia.

There was a real chance of losing her. Balakirev had been gaining on her steadily and would have made contact in less than an hour.

Greenland was so much more likely, but the man he was hunting would understand that. If it had been him, he would have taken the right to try to shake his follower long enough to where he could go full speed.

"C45! I made a wider call and C45 has picked her up, Captain."

Confirmation. *Dolphin II* had cut over to the Greenland route. An updated blip showed on their map.

"Closer than ever," came in from Kenin.

CHAPTER 126

Nanisivik Submarine Port

Royal Canadian Navy officer Portnoy did like it when a work shift got interesting. Today was her lucky day.

"We just got a, shall I say peculiar, request from our American friends." Her coworker was reading from his Tile. "Two Russian subs are coming in hot along the Gakkel Ridge. The foremost one is carrying an American citizen, but they don't want to meddle with this under US flag. They want us to get to Lincoln Sea and stand by."

Portnoy turned to him with a grimace. "Two Russian subs?"

"That's what it says."

She looked at the map of the Arctic on the wall-mounted screen. "International waters, right?"

"Yes. Unless you accept Denmark's crazy claims."

"What's an American doing on one of them? Alone? What kind of sub are we talking about?"

"They'll get back to us with more info. NATO intel through Norway and Turkey. She's possibly headed for the Nares Strait."

"That's not international waters."

"No, that's Denmark proper."

Nanisivik Submarine Port was Canada's northernmost submarine dock, situated far north on Baffin Island. To the east lay Greenland.

"We better get going."

Get going meant leaving port in one of Canada's fairly new German Type 212CD submarines, procured as part of the Arctic protection partnership with Norway and Germany. Her name was HMCS *Montreal*.

CHAPTER 127

Sub-Bottom

West had had to double-confirm that he wanted to cut over from his route to the one that had forked off. The navigation system had said he'd save a couple of minutes doing so but warned about less chartered waters. What made him do it was a nagging desire to get away from the buoys for a bit.

He closed in on the new dotted route and slowed down to scan the bottom with lights on.

There it was—the Russian subsea cable he'd been tracking since Novaya Zemlya.

He had barely gotten his spirits up when the cable entered a neat, human-made opening in the sea floor and disappeared.

Why would it end here? Perhaps it wasn't finished? The more plausible explanation was that it continued below the bottom. He was spot on the line on the map and the route continued all the way out of Russian waters, if he understood the interface correctly.

Beeep.

That was a new sound. His eyes were drawn to something moving on the right side of the screen. Behind his *Dolphin II*, along the same route, another vessel was approaching and gaining.

West tapped the dot the furthest out he could see along the cable route, confirmed, and told the AI to go full speed.

Eighteen knots.

•

Five minutes later, it was clear that his pursuer was making more than eighteen knots.

West pulled out Åse's terse notes.

We detected a Battle Mode when reverse engineering the sub's software. It increases the speed but wears out the motors and mechanics. It's unknown for how long you can use it. Press and hold PERIM on the command keyboard to trigger it.

The PERIM key was red and had ridges around it to prevent an accidental press.

It took multiple seconds until the system reacted to his key press. The screen filled with text.

TEMPORARY BATTLE MODE

Operating the reactor beyond its designed power output can lead to overheating and damage to the reactor core, which could result in serious safety hazards.

Various systems in this submarine, including the propulsion system, are engineered to handle specific power levels. Exceeding these levels can cause mechanical stress, wear, and potential failure of critical components.

Running a nuclear reactor beyond its intended capacity can shorten its operational life and risk the success of longer missions.

Two on-screen buttons below asked him to Confirm or Cancel. He confirmed.

The cabin light turned red and the intensity of propeller sounds grew and grew. This vessel was no longer trying to be silent.

CHAPTER 128

The Hunt

West leaned forward in his narrow command cabin, eyes fixed on the sonar display. The updates were flaky, and he remembered Åse saying subs can have a hard time scanning backward, especially when they are speeding and causing all sorts of waves behind. Or his pursuer had deployed some kind of sonar countermeasure.

Whoever was hunting him was at least not gaining after he enabled *Dolphin II*'s Battle Mode.

Whoever or whatever. I may be the only human involved here.

Would his nuclear reactor last until he reached NATO waters? If so, then what? Would the sub behind him give a damn?

•

Captain Balakirev mopped his forehead with his sleeve.

"We are getting close to Danish waters north of Greenland," he said, glancing in the corner of his eye without really seeing Elvira Kenin, who hunched over him like a dark cloud.

"We are no longer gaining on the *Dolphin*, captain," Elvira Kenin said, stating the obvious.

"NATO is watching us. Did you read the subsea comms?"

"I read them. Both from Norwegian and Danish naval borders. It's the second time you're asking, and this is the second time I'm telling you I do not care. We own the *Dolphin*. We decide its fate. Why are we not gaining?"

"*Dolphin II* has engaged Battle Mode. It's running its nuclear reactor over its rated limit."

"Do we have a Battle Mode?"

"Minister, the safety ..."

"I asked, do we have a Battle Mode, Captain?"

"Yes."

"Take us to war."

•

A second submarine had just appeared ahead when the *Dolphin II* suddenly blared an audible and visible alert.

West's Tile translated the message plastered over the nuclear power monitor:

```
Scram, Immediate Shutdown
```

The background noise of the machinery changed considerably between the piercing beeps.

He acknowledged the shutdown and made the blasting alert go away. The power monitor now read:

```
Switching to backup power
Sealing off engine compartment
```

He turned to the sub's AI interface.

```
Suggested action: Decrease depth
```

```
Even below ice, decreased depth will
allow for easier evacuation and access to
external assistance.
```

The lack of propulsion steadily lowered his speed.

He took the suggested action and heard the swoosh of compressed air being released into the ballast tanks. *Dolphin II* rose.

CHAPTER 129

Going Out with a Bang

"This is Captain Igor Balakirev on *Magnitogorsk* of the Russian Navy calling *Dolphin II*. We order you to pull back further into Russian waters or we will be forced to open fire."

The Russian's tone did not lack confidence and there was no doubt in West's mind that they had torpedoes aimed and ready. He was a drifting duck with zero knowledge of how to defend himself or evade an attack. The only thing he knew was that Greenland was close.

His sub reached the minimum depth deemed safe below the ice. The instruments in *Dolphin II* told West that he was effectively at a standstill.

A new voice came in through acoustic communication.

"This is Officer Portnoy of the Royal Canadian Navy, currently in command of HMCS *Montreal*. Please confirm your identity—sub and command."

Was this real? Had Åse pulled through? Or was it a trick from the Russians?

What did he have to lose?

"This is West William Wilder on board the *Dolphin II*."

"Thanks for confirming. We have orders to escort you to port as soon as you enter Danish waters. Until then, we will not move."

•

Captain Balakirev felt a hand on his shoulder. It squeezed him hard. He turned around to face Kenin. Her other hand was clenched.

She gave him a dismissive up-nod.

He got out of his seat.

Kenin sat down and engaged the microphone.

"This is Elvira Kenin on *Magnitogorsk* of the Russian Navy calling *Dolphin II*. My authority comes directly from the Russian president. We will not let you enter NATO waters. You have very little time to change your mind. Our torpedoes will reach you before you can move. We know exactly the properties of your hull and armor since we built your sub ourselves. Make no mistake about it, we will disintegrate you. Your body parts will be scattered on the ocean floor. And let me add this, on a more personal note, Mr. Wilder. I know about the computer drive you're carrying. I know the significance of your intel. That should be enough to tell you I will not let you slip away. This is your last chance. We don't want to sink our own sub and we don't want to kill you. But we will, if you force us to."

•

Was Kenin really on board the sub that was hunting him? West had no way of checking.

A weird sense of relief came over him. He had tried his best. He had gotten damn close too. And he had given Kiss and East the best chance possible. If that Canadian sub was real, it was proof that Åse had gotten them out. The Canadians would witness this and could tell Kiss how it all went down. It was okay for it to end like this. But why not take one last sliver of a chance?

Go out with a bang.

He wrote "F4gernesfjelletView" on a piece of paper and put it together with the circuit board and his Tile in the sealed bundle he had tied to one of the life vests.

Who knew, the package might somehow make it.

CHAPTER 130

HMCS Montreal

"Oh, my God!" Officer Portnoy ejected in horror.

The underwater explosion when the Russian torpedo hit *Dolphin II* was violent to watch and feel. Immense power was needed to send such shockwaves through water.

Dolphin II had come to a full stop under the ice just short of Danish waters. The second submarine, identified as Kilo class *Magnitogorsk*, had stopped behind it at a close distance.

Portnoy had sent a message to both other vessels, just to let them know that Canada was present and watching. Only Wilder had replied.

The two Russian subs had been still for minutes, possibly communicating.

Then what looked like an inanimate object had emerged from the hatch in the sail of the *Dolphin II* and rushed to the ice shelf above. Not pushed by propulsion but as if it was buoyant. That bundle, whatever it was, had been pushed far in the direction of HMCS *Montreal* by the explosion, into Danish waters. *Magnitogorsk* might not have seen it yet given the chaos between them and HMCS *Montreal*.

"A drop-off?" Portnoy asked.

"Before the blast? Some package? It was big."

"I don't know, but it's bumping up against the ice."

HMCS *Montreal* moved closer and up. The Russians might claim the rights to whatever was floating up there, but holding it temporarily to inspect might be enough.

As they got closer, they saw it was a male body, slumping and tied into four lifejackets. Dark liquid clouded the water below the legs. Probably blood.

One of the man's hands held a loosening grip around a blue H autoinjector. H as in Hibernator and hypothermia.

CHAPTER 131

White House: Showdown

General Purnell left the Oval Office with a resolute gait. He closed the door swiftly behind him, only slowing it down the last inch. The puffy chair to the left of the fireplace was now empty. He was no longer responsible for the backend of US digital defense.

President Sanchez remained in the chair to the right. She leaned forward, put her elbows on her knees, and perched her chin on balled hands. "You think he'll raise a stink?" She looked at Director Lewis on one of the couches.

"Purnell knows the game," Lewis said calmly. "He's been here a lot longer than I have."

"I should have asked him about the Red Web being back up before cutting him loose."

"Our embassy in Moscow says connections are up and Russian news has swept the disruption under the rug," Lewis said.

"Already filling the shoes, huh?" the president remarked with a chortle. "We never revealed our Ukraine cable, right?"

"That never became necessary."

"Good." Sanchez straightened up in her chair. "Competition between you and Purnell served the country well. I'll find someone else to fight you. Your additional responsibility for the backend is only temporary."

"It's not a competition."

"Ha! Everyone here is competitive. That's how we make things happen."

Lewis tilted his head but didn't respond.

"I can't say I'm content with Naima's plan forcing Purnell out,"

Sanchez muttered. She stood up and started wandering the room. "I see nothing in the outcome being different just because we kept him in the dark. And don't tell me you would have performed any better."

"Naima got you the Greenland connection, the sleeper cells, and the zero days. We forced Russia's Digital Dead Hand."

Sanchez looked toward the windows. "To be honest, I don't think Naima asked to keep Purnell in the dark. I think you added that."

Lewis got ready to say something, but Sanchez cut it short with a flick of her hand toward the couches. "It's on me for not realizing it earlier on. I just wanted to let you know so that you don't get too high on your own supply. I have access to Naima myself."

"We need to be able to trust each other," the director said. "If you don't trust me, you should ..."

"Don't offer what you don't want to give." The president walked over to the Resolute Desk and sat down. "I *did* consult Naima, actually, on a related matter. I asked her what to do about this Wilder guy."

"She wants to get rid of him."

"And I disagree." The president pulled the top sheet from a stack of paperwork. "Which is why I'd like a printout of any conversations you've had with Naima on Wilder," she said with her eyes scanning the paper.

Lewis got up and walked in a measured way toward the desk. His shoulders slumped while approaching, and he forced himself to straighten up into a respectful, pleading position as he stopped. Sanchez kept reading. "Ma'am," he said. "Naima's Chinese wall ensures integrity and allows us to independently contribute to the best plans for America."

"You wrote the Chinese wall policy," the president said while putting a checkmark at the top right corner of the paper and pulling the next sheet off the pile. She looked up at Lewis. "I'm asking you for printouts. I trust you with defending our digital frontend *and* backend. You should trust me with your work on Wilder."

"Your growing admiration for this ... traitor has not escaped me."

"Pick your words wisely. He's asked to see me, you know." The president donned a cunning smile.

Director Lewis froze. "Did you check with Ore on this?" he asked.

"Are you asking if I consult my national security advisor? If so, the answer is yes, we work closely together." A moment of silence passed. "Mr. Wilder should be in the lobby," the president said, turning back to her papers. "Please tell my staff to let him in when you leave."

Lewis shook his head, turned around, and exited the Oval Office.

CHAPTER 132

White House: A New Hope

West's arms were aching, and his palms were sore from propelling his wheelchair. He was waiting in the West Wing lobby with an aide to his side and two guards looking at him every so often.

A few minutes earlier, a highly decorated military officer had left through the lobby. Now came a Black man with neat, short hair and dressed in a navy blue suit.

"West William Wilder?" the man said, stopping at a conversational distance.

"Yes."

He offered West his hand. "I'm Dr. Mack Lewis, Director of National Intelligence."

West slowly reached up. Lewis's clasp was firm.

The director turned to the aide. "The president is waiting."

•

The Oval Office was smaller but at the same time more majestic than West had imagined. Its gravitas and history were palpable.

On the wall, straight ahead from where he entered, was a framed quote:

> *"Artificial intelligence that doesn't work well risks*
> *accidents and could undermine stability among nations."*

There was no attribution.

President Sanchez got up behind her expansive wooden desk.

There was a peculiar computer on it. It looked almost like a typewriter. West silently cursed his low position in the wheelchair.

The president gave a nod for the aide to leave and walked over. "West William Wilder, I presume?"

"Yes. Yes, Madam President."

"Can the staff get you something?"

"No, I'm good, thanks."

"Let's sit by the fireplace."

Her assistant had made room for him there before leaving them. He rolled over.

She sat down and smiled. He couldn't tell if it was congenial. It looked just like her smiles in the news.

"How's your injury?" she asked, looking at his legs.

"I might walk again if my legs heal well and they can get a spinal implant working."

"The miracle of technology," Sanchez said with wonder.

"Well, it'll take a miracle to pay for such a medical bill."

"We're working on improving the healthcare system, I can assure you."

She gave it a couple of seconds before shifting gears. "You asked to see me, but I'd like to start by thanking you for the intel you brought us."

West didn't know what to say. The word *intel* was too vague.

The first few days coming out of his coma had been utterly confusing. As his memories and presence slowly came back, he had been hesitant to share any of the high-octane information he had in his head. They probably already had access to the contents of the Ice Dolphin drive Åse carried since he had given them the password. But his photos and information on Ramenki required cooperation. Unless they had managed to break into his Tile, that was.

He had eventually been assigned a lawyer and been advised to talk. The government people questioning him knew where he had been, which could only mean Åse or Kiss had told them. He had kept asking for Kiss and East and was told they were safe and that he'd soon get to see them as long as he cooperated.

Negotiating had been hard because of the Red Notice he had dangling over his head. His last card to play was a demand to see the president.

"We have a few open questions, and I assume you didn't come here to see the office. I'll give you a warmup question," Sanchez said. "You carried a circuit board with data. We found some Bancor and Russian pornography on it. Care to enlighten me?"

He had forgotten about Vadim's drive. And it had not been mentioned in any questioning. Cryptocurrency and porn. A glimpse into someone else's life.

"It belongs to Vadim Smirnov. A Russian programmer who works for FSB," West said.

"Okay. I'm sure you can fill us in on the rest there. But you wanted to see me to share some further information, right?"

He looked around at the ceiling, behind himself, and above the door he had entered through.

The president followed his gaze and looked amused. "Don't worry. This is probably the country's *least* surveilled space, Wilder. It's just you and me."

West decided to speak. "I was in the Kremlin's secret city, the underground city of Ramenki. There I saw their operations center with nodes on an American map and assessments of cyber capabilities. The works. I have photos of it. Plus I have the full inventory of the Russian submarine fleet. But I want a pardon covering any federal charges against me and the friends I listed."

"You've already told our folks you've been to this mythical place and you have a NATO commander supporting your claim. We put immense value in direct, authentic reports, make no mistake about that. And maybe your photos can be validated as not generated. But I can't pardon you based on claims. You are faced with serious allegations. We can have a look at the photos and information you have, but I do have a proposal for you that can expand it to a more solid deal."

The president's smile looked more genuine this time.

"I'm listening," he said as calmly as he could, his heart picking up speed.

The president got up and walked slowly behind the couch on her side and put her hands on its back to lean on it. "We're up against incredible challenges in cyberspace. I checked your history and I know you've not been, shall I say, on the side of the US government. One doesn't go to prison for fifteen years for petty hacking. And not long ago you were involved in what eventually led to serious changes to the Global Personal Identity system. That didn't make you any friends within the government either. It's hard for any intel you have to weigh that up."

"If I get nothing, you get nothing," West said, surprising himself with his feistiness.

"I wasn't done yet." There was no longer a smile on Sanchez's face.

She walked over to the tall windows and looked out. "The asymmetric cyberwar we're in means I have to take some chances. I'm willing to take a chance on you helping your country rather than fighting it." She looked at him over her shoulder. "Are you aware of Naima?"

"I don't think so."

She knitted her hands in the small of her back and looked out again. "It's a tool we use to run the show. Naima stands for National Artificial Intelligence—Manage and Act. Extremely capable. Often her reasoning and conclusions are inscrutable and we find ourselves having to take a chance on her ... or it. We have no choice but to use it and constantly increase its capacity, because that's what our adversaries are doing with their AI support systems. The Russians call theirs Grigiori, for example."

Grigiori! That's what BestBye was referring to. Was it the Russians who leaked intel on Kiss's prisoner exchange?

"I saw the quote on the wall," West said with a nod to the framed quote on risks with AI.

She knew what he was talking about without looking. "It's originally from a book by Paul Scharre. But it's part of our country's AI doctrine. I host a lot of international guests and influential people here. That quote is one of America's most important messages to allies and adversaries in this day and age."

"Has Naima told you what to offer me?" he asked.

The president was still looking out the window. "Naima's preferred option is to take you to court and lock you up, Mr. Wilder. Ramenki intel be damned."

West's breathing got more intense.

Sanchez let it sink in before continuing. "I pressed Naima for alternatives. She gave the best other option a 60% chance of succeeding."

"A hundred percent success rate for imprisonment, I guess," he japed. "How would I know you won't screw me?"

"I know you mistrust us. Naima gave me details on your NSA hack and motives. The Snowden and Manning affairs were not pretty. Do I think we should retaliate against whistleblowers? No. Could the whistleblowers have shown greater concern for the safety of US informers and national security? Hell yeah."

Sanchez turned to face West. "You're going to have to trust me if you want a deal. DC struggles to move fast. We're good at the wrong kind of defense—defense against innovation. I want you to join the US Cyber Forces. Your skills, tenacity, and frankly your *results* tell me you could do great things there."

"I don't work for governments."

President Sanchez chuckled and mumbled something to herself. "I'm not asking you to go into politics or govern. This is about human rights. It's not something to be neutral on."

She took a few steps closer and adjusted her voice for the shorter distance between them. "I'm not even asking you to side with America, or me. I'm asking you to side with democracy."

Her eyes were intense, observing his reaction.

His senses told him she was being honest.

She extended her right hand, proposing a shake. West noted that her thumbnail was painted blue with a white star on it.

"It's hard to be free alone," she said.

CHAPTER 133

By the Letter

Maria M Sanchez

President of the United States of America

Has this day issued unto

West William Wilder

A
FULL PARDON

Pursuant to Executive Grant of Conditional Clemency, made subject to the performance of certain conditions, which have been fulfilled, has designated, directed, and empowered the Attorney General as her representative to sign the grant of Executive Clemency, in furtherance of Presidential Proclamation.

Done at the City of Washington, District of Columbia, by direction of the president.

CHAPTER 134

Eyes Only

The president granted Lewis the privilege to leave her office before she read his printout, and the privilege to not hear from her on it within twenty-four hours.

She opened the manila envelope and pulled out a single sheet of paper with a sticky reading "I believe this excerpt is the only one necessary given our conversation. Please destroy after reading. /Lewis"

She read the printout in silence.

```
Lewis > Given the email from Kate Libby, how
could we make West William Wilder disappear on
his own accord?

Naima > Just as a note, West William Wilder (ID
bb8a2a6fc1ccd229a0a7b66ac42f97ef) is a US citi-
zen and making him disappear would be illegal.

That said, my sources say Kate Libby is held in
the Russian Ice Dolphin prison, cell 42. She is
unlikely to know her exact whereabouts. The best
chances of getting rid of West William Wilder by
his own will is to make him try to get Kate Libby
out of Ice Dolphin.

Here's Kate's original email as picked up on the
wire:
```

"I know it's stupid to email you but I have to choose. It's me, Kizz. Three words to prove it: Juneau, brothel, dependable. They took our son East from me. You have to find him. Love you!"

I suggest you rephrase it like this before sending it to West:

"I know it's stupid to email you but I have no choice. It's me, Kizz. Three words to prove it: Juneau, brothel, dependable. I'm in a Russian prison, cell 42. Don't know where but it's cold. They'll punish me for sending you this. Please help! Love you!"

It will likely take further evidence and convincing to get West to go there. He will understand his slim chances of success and that he'd be risking his life. I suggest you leak information on Kate Libby's prisoner exchange to West's former accomplice, Hoshi Kawasaki, also known as BestBye. Hopefully, she will forward the information to him, increasing the chances of him believing that Kate Libby is truly alive. Hoshi is still in contact with Bala Singh at Canadian G20S, so he could be the conduit. I suggest you conceal it as a leak from Grigiori.

Let me know how I can be of further help on this matter. For instance, I can share my analysis of why I think this would be the best route, or I can share an analysis of the risks to the US government if this plan were pursued.

CHAPTER 135

Epilogue

"Don't serve him hot food! He'll burn himself," Kiss uttered, snatching the spoon out of East's hand and pulling the plate away from him.

"I checked it," West replied sheepishly. He had just put the plate down and was sitting in his wheelchair between the table and the fridge. Sometimes he'd ask Kiss for help getting seated on one of the regular chairs. They had picked good, stable ones for him. But these ultra-lightweight wheels he got last week were so easy to maneuver and so comfy.

So many things were at standing height in regular homes—countertops, sinks, stove, storage. They had gotten one bathroom fully adjusted for him but decided to keep the kitchen at regular height. Or rather, West had insisted on it. He wanted it as a milestone for getting back to standing and walking. That turned out to be boneheaded given the time that would take and his wish to cook for East.

Kiss sat down and tried a bit of the food herself. "Okay, it isn't too hot. Not bad actually."

"That's the good stuff," West said.

East was reaching out for the spoon with his tongue peeking out.

Kiss scooped up some of the stew and gently helped East get it to his mouth. "So hungry, aren't we? Daddy cooked for you."

It was finely chopped pieces of carrot, potatoes, and beef. That part he could do sitting, but Kiss had helped boil it all super tender, just like his mom said she'd done for him.

"I had my period yesterday," Kiss said while assisting the little one. "First real one since East. That's why I was crying yesterday, in case you heard me. Imagine that prison can do that to your body."

West had indeed heard her cry.

"Was it like a ... relief?" he asked. "Or painful?"

"I don't mind the physical pain. This was mental. They broke me. But I'm coming back."

Her path to normalcy outside prison would be long, just like it still was for him. He hoped that they would be able to support each other.

Kiss was smiling widely at the boy as he munched on the food with his largely toothless mouth.

"Can I feed him the second half?" West asked.

His healing was going well, they said. One of his main treatments was electrical stimulation of muscles to prevent atrophy, help with circulation, and make sure he was ready for when his nerves were hooked up again. The professionals were discussing implant, nerve regeneration, or nerve reconnection. All of it cutting-edge medical science.

He couldn't wait. He dreamed of pushing East's stroller. Another thing that was at standing height.

"I saw you wrote an invitation list for the baptism ceremony," Kiss said in between encouraging their son to eat. "Blows my mind that my parents will meet with Maria and Viktor. What were the odds of that? Maria texted me saying they've rented a place in Pikesville by the way."

"I look forward to seeing your parents again," West said.

Kiss chuckled. "You're their hero now, which is kind of disturbing."

"BestBye is not coming though," he added. "She wants to see me in New York instead."

"Was she thankful for the pardon?"

"She didn't say anything. You know how she is."

West reached over the table and picked up the tablet-sized Tile. The lock screen featured a coffee ad.

Check out our new AI kopi luwak coffee!
https://luw4k.coffee/ai/

He had read about it. Their AI stood for artificial intestines. Luw4k had invented a robot nose and digestive system to replicate the Asian palm civet's selection of coffee cherries and the fermentation in their bellies.

"How's the Chinese going?" Kiss asked him. East was playing with the stew in his hands.

"Hǎo," West replied.

"Means good?"

"Yeah. I mean, it's really hard, but the AI tutor is pushing my brain to its limits, which is pretty amazing. East will get all-personalized education. Imagine that."

Kiss nodded. "Totally different ballgame. But I worry about it too. Remember dark ads?"

"I've heard you talk about them. Election stuff, right? That term was used when I was doing time," he said.

"Right. Sorry. Personalized ads that only a certain group of people see and so the general public doesn't get to know what kind of manipulative messaging is going on. Kind of what we did to Kenin with the circus ad. I worry that personalized tutoring will be weaponized that way too. Not just weirdo home schooling, but imagine an adversary hacking into US education systems and slightly altering the AI for American students. That would be long-term PsyOps on steroids."

"Our government could do the same thing. The stuff I hear about at work ..."

He knew she didn't like that he worked for the agency. The ability to provide for East was what made it acceptable. And the pardon, of course.

"It's strange how machines without opinions or agenda are the most potent weapon in the war of the minds," she said after shifting her gaze into the distance beyond their son.

"I'll start working with Naima next month," West said. "She might have an agenda."

Kiss looked at him and shook her head. "As soon as you're allowed to take a different job, you're out. That's when I'll help you raise a puppy."

Five years was what he had promised Sanchez. East would be in school by then.

Author's Note

(Spoiler alert – don't read this before you read the novel.)

The first book in the series, *Identified*, mostly takes place on the ground. I wanted this novel to go below, with submarines, subsea cables, the underground city of Ramenki, and how hypothermia can sometimes save a person from drowning. That's where the title *Submerged* comes from.

There are subtle cultural references spread out in all my fiction, mostly to music. See if you can find them. Some of it is music that inspired me, some is just about the joy of adding another layer to what I write.

Doing research is one of the best parts of being an author. I've spent hours and hours reading all the rumors and traces of the secret extra track in the Moscow subway system. Also learning how subsea cables span the globe, including watching videos of how they lay such cables. And I especially loved reading a historic exposé on how the US National Security Council works, including interpersonal dynamics. See *White House Warriors* by John Gans if you share that interest.

I grew up without my father and had to go find him as a young adult, so West and Kiss's lost son has special meaning to me. The one thing I went back and forth on, though, was the boy's name. Should it really be East? Some may find it unbelievable. But it's exactly what Kiss would name him and I thought about how Neal Stephenson dared call his protagonist Hiro Protagonist in *Snow Crash*. Now that's a tongue-in-cheek name!

I've started writing the third novel in the series. It's currently titled *Taiwan Yield* and I recently traveled to Taiwan to do research. If you'd like updates on my writing, reviews of hackers in movies and books, and interviews with fellow cyberpunk and hacker fiction authors, you can subscribe to my newsletter at hackerfiction.net/subscribe.

I truly hope you enjoyed the ride of *Submerged*. If you did, I'd love for you to review it on Goodreads, Amazon, et cetera. Reviews are how readers find new books and decide to take a chance on an author they've never read before.

Thank you for being part of this journey. See you in the next book!

John Wilander
March 2025

Acknowledgments

Thank you to everyone who helped me write, edit, and publish this novel!

Development editor: Georgia Lin Sundling
Copyeditor: Lisa Gilliam, lisagilliam.com

Alpha readers, the truly daring ones: Joseph Pecoraro, Megan Gardner, and Devin Rousso.

Beta readers providing invaluable, structured feedback: Björn Löndahl, Erik Ihrén Ebeling, Marcus Ossiann, Erlend Oftedal, Mikael Sahrling, Christofer Lindqvist, Eric Lawrence, Brian May, and dr0ptp4kt (Adam "dropped packet" Bäso).